Emma E. E. Minto

A Memoir of the Right Honourable Hugh Elliot

Emma E. E. Minto

A Memoir of the Right Honourable Hugh Elliot

ISBN/EAN: 9783337195250

Printed in Europe, USA, Canada, Australia, Japan

Cover: Foto ©Raphael Reischuk / pixelio.de

More available books at **www.hansebooks.com**

A MEMOIR

OF THE

RIGHT HON. HUGH ELLIOT

A MEMOIR

OF

THE RIGHT HONOURABLE

HUGH ELLIOT

BY

THE COUNTESS OF MINTO

EDINBURGH
EDMONSTON AND DOUGLAS
1868

NOTICE.

THE greater part of the volume now published was privately printed some years ago. The interest which many have expressed in the career of Hugh Elliot has induced his descendants to give it to a larger circle, the desire to make him better known to his countrymen having outweighed the considerations which have hitherto prevented the publication of so slight and imperfect a sketch of his life.

To the contents of the original volume as privately printed, which terminated with the correspondence of 1785, have been added a few chapters containing a narrative of his various diplomatic missions subsequent to that period; his own papers, whether public or private, having been invariably the source whence the information given about him has been drawn.

As the concluding chapters, which deal with public affairs, may be said to have somewhat of a historic character, it has been thought desirable to give translations of the original letters addressed by sovereigns to Mr. Elliot, or by him to sovereigns.

MINTO, *Sept.* 1, 1868.

PREFACE

(TO THE VOL. PRINTED PRIVATELY IN 1862.)

———◆———

THE correspondence of Hugh Elliot may be divided into two portions: the first collected from the Minto MSS., containing letters addressed to his family, by himself or by others, on matters affecting him; of these none are earlier in date than 1762, none later than 1776: the second portion composed of several volumes of letters, private and official, written to him by various persons between 1772 and 1785. These were all in his own keeping at the time of his death, and were sent to Minto a few years ago by my mother,[1] along with some other MSS. of a later date, which had also belonged to him.

The letters bound in volumes have been generally

---

[1] Emma, daughter of the Right Honourable Hugh Elliot, married General Sir Thomas Hislop, Bart., G.C.B.

collected under three heads : Family Letters ; Foreign Miscellaneous Letters ; English Miscellaneous Letters. There are, however, two or three volumes entirely occupied by the correspondence of particular friends, as Mr. Liston, Sir James and Lady Harris, and others ; and there are volumes of official correspondence with the Office and with his colleagues at foreign Courts ; among whom were Lord Stormont,[1] Sir R. Keith,[2] and Messrs. De Vismes,[3] Wroughton,[4] Morton Eden, and Osborn.

All these papers, and many others which have undergone no such process of classification, were left with other property of Mr. Elliot's at Dresden in 1802, when he was transferred from that mission to Naples ; and he appears to have taken no steps for their removal before the French occupation of Dresden in 1806, which rendered their recovery impossible. Mr. Elliot had long since given them up for lost, when, some time after the peace, he, being then governor of Madras, received a letter from Dresden, which informed him that his property had been safely preserved by some friends there, who, having saved it from falling into the hands of the French, now only waited his

[1] Minister at Vienna and Paris.
[2] Vienna.
[3] Stockholm.
[4] Warsaw.

directions to restore it to him. As it comprised plate, pictures, china, and other things far more valuable as plunder than manuscripts, he was as much surprised as pleased by the communication; nevertheless, with his habitual carelessness, he took no steps to recover his losses for some years, and it was not till 1826 that he was prevailed on to let his youngest son Frederick, who was then a mere lad, proceed to Dresden in quest of the long-lost property. There, accordingly, in a cellar, perfectly intact and uninjured, were found some of the most valuable contents of the *ci-devant Hôtel du Ministre Britannique*, which, in the moment of flight, had been abandoned to their fate.

The only paper which my grandfather had been anxious to recover was a private memorandum in Mr. Pitt's handwriting, containing instructions for his guidance, and this, on regaining it, he sent to the Foreign Office.

The mixture of order and disorder in the arrangement of these papers is extraordinary. It might be supposed that some one, acting on a suggestion that all the letters should be classified under specified heads, had thrown the contents of desks and drawers into so many several heaps, and had then, without further selection, proceeded to bind them together. Along

with letters from royal personages, generals, and statesmen, are found the most trivial notes. Letters of
introduction to insignificant persons are preserved as
carefully as those from Mirabeau, Romanzow, and
Nelson. More than a third of these bulky volumes
might be burnt without loss, and yet enough would
remain to give a finished picture of the society in which
my grandfather spent his youth.

The letters of 1775 and 1776 are so numerous, and
so abundant in personal details, that one feels on intimate terms with the writers and the correspondents.

Strange that it should be so! that, after so long a
silence, the dead should speak again,—should be restored to our knowledge in all the freshness of their
youth, introducing us to sorrows which they themselves
long outlived, and to sentiments forgotten sooner still.
But if these thoughts be startling to us, what would
their feelings have been could they have foreseen that
the follies of the moment were to be handed down to
generations unborn? What would the flirting *dame de
cour* have said could she have guessed that the indolent
Englishman, who rarely troubled himself to answer her
notes, would preserve them for the amusement of his
descendants? And what would have been felt by the
mother and sisters, who believed themselves to possess

all his confidence, had they been told that to us would
be given the clue they never found, to the thoughts and
affections of one of those dearest to them?   That Minto
—that generation—has long since passed away, and we,
now sojourning here, wonder whether they in their day
knew as much of each other as we know of them.
Truly, even in this world, all hearts are laid open, all
secrets made known; even here, a day of judgment is
for ever going on.   E. M.

MINTO, *July* 1862.

CONTENTS.

CHAPTER I.

1762 to 1776.

CHAPTER II.

1772 to 1777.

CHAPTER III.

1777.

CHAPTER IV.

1777 to 1778.

CHAPTER V.

1777 to 1778.

CHAPTER XIII.

CHAPTER XIV.

—◆—

APPENDIX.

CHAPTER THE FIRST.

1762 to 1776.

HUGH'S EDUCATION—EXPEDITION TO POLAND AND THE
DANUBIAN PROVINCES—MISSION TO MUNICH—RECALL
TO ENGLAND.

IT has been impossible to me to read my grandfather's
papers without conceiving a strong desire to make others
of his family better acquainted with a man who played
no unimportant part in the public affairs of his day, and
whose name was never mentioned but with the tenderest
affection in the home of my childhood. Since, however,
no one but myself has leisure or inclination to attack
masses of manuscript in depths of trunks, I see nothing
for it but to attempt a slight sketch of his early career,
founded on facts which I have gathered from his correspondence.

With the laudable desire to begin at the beginning,
I should gladly trace the manner in which my grandfather's earliest years were spent, but unfortunately I
have no means of doing so; the oldest letter in my
possession is of the date of 1762, when he was ten years
old, and was living with his family at Twickenham; and
in none of the subsequent letters have I found any internal evidence as to the locality which they looked

B

upon as home.   In none is there any allusion to favourite
haunts, to gardens or games, to dependants or pets ;
nothing to show affection for home as a place.   Strong
family affection has been ever a characteristic of the
race, and to be together was at all times an object of
tenderest longing, but where the meeting should take
place seems to have been a matter of indifference.

I therefore suppose that during the youth of the
family their parents led an unsettled life, probably dividing their time between Parliamentary duties in London
and visits to relations in Edinburgh, occasionally living at
Lochgelly and occasionally at Minto.   It is possible, too,
that the home life may not have been of the kind to make
itself remembered with unmixed pleasure.   Sir Gilbert[1]
was a grave, highly cultivated man, immersed in politics,
and, like all fathers of his time, he seems to have inspired
his family with as much awe as admiration.

Lady Elliot,[2] clever, high-spirited, and imaginative,
was not, like one who filled her place in after years,

> "Blessed with a temper, whose unclouded ray,
> Can make to-morrow cheerful as to-day."

Her preference for those of her children[3] who most re-
sembled herself was openly avowed, and in Isabella and
Hugh, she cultivated rather than repressed the uncon-

---

[1] Sir Gilbert Elliot of Minto, third Baronet, M.P., a Lord of the
Admiralty, distinguished by his literary tastes as well as his political
abilities.

[2] Agnes Murray Kynynmound, heiress of Melgund in Forfar, and
of Lochgelly and Kynynmound, in Fifeshire.   She was habitually addressed as Lady Elliot Murray.

[3] Isabella ; Gilbert (1st Earl of Minto) ; Hugh, 6th April 1752 ;
Alexander ; Robert ; Eleanor.

trolled sensibility, the romantic impulsiveness of character, and "high imaginings," which, in the case of the
sister, probably increased constitutional tendencies to
the extent of rendering them morbid, and which in that
of the brother diminished the successfulness of his career
and the happiness of his life.   Her eldest son Gilbert [1]
and her youngest daughter Eleanor, were not supposed
by her to be of the porcelain clay of which the rest were
made, and her allusions, soon after Hugh left her, to
Gilbert's coldness of manner, as compared with Hugh's
more demonstrative nature, is not less striking, when we
find that she lived to give her entire confidence to her
eldest son, and to be on terms approaching to estrangement with the younger.

To a want therefore of home sunshine, it is possible
that we may in part ascribe the fact that the letters
written from home deal chiefly with news, with politics,
or with advice, while those addressed there by the
absent sons, are confined to matters affecting their
studies and pursuits.

From their earliest years the boys were training for
the world.

"Life," says Byron, "has no Present," but childhood
is a time of life which should form an exception to the
rule, a time when stores of mental as of bodily health
may be laid up in days of careless enjoyment.

At twelve years old Hugh was with his elder brother
in Paris, learning French and *l'usage du monde* under
the auspices of David Hume.

---

[1] The absence of Alick in India, and the youth of Bob, prevented
them from playing an equal part with the others in the family drama.

The circumstances of the family probably had much to do with the eagerness with which the boys were prepared to enter on the arena where honours were to be won. Poor, and proud of the position to which character and abilities had raised them, the parents strove to fit the sons to keep what themselves had gained. Gilbert, writing to his mother from Edinburgh, in reply to a letter of congratulation on a successful display in the Rhetorical Society, deprecates her being too much elated by his success; though, he says, he well knows the importance of obtaining the power of public speaking.

I am, however, anticipating events; so, to proceed with my story in order. In 1762, Mr. Liston[1] was engaged to be their tutor, and during that and the following year his pupils appear to have lived at Twickenham, and to have prosecuted the ordinary studies of their age under his superintendence. Towards the end of 1764 they went to Paris, where they spent two years in a military school, directed by the Abbé Choquart. While there they made the acquaintance of Mirabeau, a boy of their own age, for whom the school of l'Abbé Choquart had been specially selected as being more like a prison than a school. "Je l'ai mis chez l'Abbé Choquart," wrote the old Marquis de Mirabeau, "l'ami des hommes," but certainly not the friend of his son, "cet homme est roide, et force les punitions dans le besoin."

No complaints of harsh treatment have, however, been recorded in the letters of the Elliots. In a style

---

[1] Robert Liston, Esq., of New Liston, near Edinburgh, afterwards Sir R. Liston, minister at Madrid, ambassador to Constantinople, etc.; his salary as tutor was £25 a-year, bed, board, and washing.

of which the idiom soon became more French than
English, they describe the little events of their school
life : their studies in ancient and modern languages ;
their lessons in dancing, swimming, fencing, tennis ;
their military drill on Sundays ; their parties in fine
weather to Argenteuil, " a village on the Seine not to be
compared to Richmond," and in winter to the theatre to
see Zaïre, "a tragedy by Monsieur de Voltaire ;" the
changes in their uniforms from blue and gold in winter
to blue and silver, with a blue silk waistcoat, in summer.
These and similar topics form the staple commodity of
the boys' letters.   The two great field-days of the school
year—the king's fête-day, and "le jour des prix"—deserve
fuller notice.

"Gilbert told you in his last letter," wrote Hugh to
his mother on the 12th of September 1765, "that I
would give you an account of the fête of St. Louis.   I
therefore begin in the following terms :—

"Our first appearance was in arms after having performed military operations till dark.   The place where
we exhibited, which was in the middle of a small planta-
tion at the end of our garden, which was excessively
pretty when illuminated with garlands and lustres, was
at once changed from a field of battle to a dancing-
school.   For having laid aside our arms we danced stage
dances till ten o'clock, opera-singers warbling cantatas
to the king's praises between every dance ; then the
whole was shut by a firework."

Nothing could well be less like the amusements of a
holiday at an English school than this mixture of mimic

war and the opera. The day of public examination, at
which Mr. Liston wrote that his pupils had gained some
credit, is described by Gilbert:—"The Abbé had
thought to make a great coup by making the examination open with a new exercise, which none of the troops
in France will do till May; but, alas! it was throwing
pearls before swine, for there was little else than ladies
and clergymen to see it, who did not know the new from
the old one. Our friend Mirabeau then repeated a long
discourse in praise of mathematics, composed by the
Abbé; and after a general clap, was examined on that
part of his studies. I was examined after him on the
same subject. We were yesterday with the Countess of
Boufflers, and dine with her on Sunday. We were with
Madame de Forcalquier yesterday. "Ces dames," adds
Hugh, in French, "nous reçoivent on ne peut pas mieux,
et nous avons un fond de babil assez honnête."

Mr. Hume, to whom they had been specially com-
mended, showed them great kindness, and often visited
them and superintended their studies. Nothing surprised Mr. Liston more than the absolute neglect by
their friends of the French boys at the Abbé's school;
from year's end to year's end no one inquired for them.

In 1766 they returned to their own country, and
were sent to continue their studies in Edinburgh, under
the superintendence of Professor George Stuart. In
those days, as at present, the education given in Edinburgh was of a multiform description. Both brothers
studied mathematics, classics, and rhetoric; attended
lectures on natural and moral philosophy and chem-

istry; learned drawing, fencing, and dancing; and when
to all these subjects Gilbert was made to add civil law,
and Hugh bookkeeping and writing, no wonder Gilbert
informed his father that their studies were " much too
crowded. What I mean is not that we have too many
hours employed, but that we cannot give sufficient time
to each subject. The scene shifts too quickly from one
to the other." Their week-day time being thus fully
employed, Sundays found them glad to enjoy the recrea-
tion of a quiet dinner party with their grandmamma [1]
and aunts,[2] who lived in Edinburgh.

After a slight illness of Hugh's in 1766, Mr. Stuart
writes as follows to Sir Gilbert :—" Hugh's popularity
is such that since he has been allowed to see any one
his *levée* has been crowded." In the same letter he
says, " Gilbert is pleased with himself; he does nothing
for show."

About this time Hugh wrote to his mother an account of a visit which he paid to Mr. Liston's farm for
change of air. "We are just returned from a jaunt to
Mr. Liston's farm, where I have in a good measure
made up all the beef I lost in my last illness. We
arrived there at eight o'clock on Saturday night, and
were most agreeably surprised by the sound of a fiddle.
I immediately conjectured that it was a penny wedding,
and directly ran into the barn from whence the sound

---

[1] Helen Stuart (Dowager Lady Elliot), daughter of Sir Robert
Stuart of Allanbank, Bart., Berwickshire, and widow of Lord Minto,
Justice-Clerk.

[2] One of these, Miss Jane Elliot, was the authoress of the much-
admired ballad, " The Flowers of the Forest."

proceeded; but was greatly disappointed when I saw some young ladies of six feet high, with immense fly-caps and silk negligées, dancing with some farmers very near as tall as themselves. Quite vext at my own insignificance, and frightened that I should be crushed to pieces every moment, I could scarcely be prevailed on to dance; however, the first tremour being over, and seeing the tallest and most terrible strain his ankle, so that he could not return to the dance, I ventured to take out his partner, whose apron-strings I scarcely came up to, and danced down a country dance."

In the spring of the following year, after describing the order of their studies, Mr. Stuart writes :—" In everything where Hugh's age admits, he is really wonderful." Two months later, he says, " Your two young men are going on well in their studies, and are superior to most of their companions. I never had occasion to see two brothers so contrasted, and indeed I should find it a more difficult task to manage Hugh, were it not for the example of his brother. He is lively, agreeable, and popular. No wonder if his viva-city is now and then above his reason. As it is, he needs a very sharp eye ;" and then follows an amusing account of some excesses into which poor Hugh had been led by the injudicious hospitalities of some of his friends. " Hugh has great honesty and candour," he writes on another occasion; " if his quickness and vivacity hurry him away, it will not be for want of taste and penetration."

Dr. Somerville, writing to Lady Elliot in January

1768, mentions a circumstance which confirms the above account of Hugh's readiness :—" I attended them one evening to their Society (the Rhetorical); few of the young orators happened to be prepared upon the question of the night, and the debate was like to have come soon to a stand, when Mr. Hugh stood up with great spirit, and, to good purpose, spoke for some minutes in reply to what had been thrown out before. It gave surprise to every person present, and I never before had reason to think so highly of his abilities. If his appearance had not been superior to what might have been expected from many who are justly enough esteemed promising young men, I should not have said one word about it."[1]

At this period of their lives Hugh got into scrapes by " mixing too much salt with his repartees;" while Gilbert ran some danger of finding that sweets have their " soure " too. It was surmised at home that he neglected his law-books for the society of a young lady of his acquaintance; but his defence seems to have been complete when he wrote to his mother that, " after all, it had only made him take up Thomson's Seasons once or twice instead of his Roman History;" and he proceeds, perhaps in self-justification—" this town is proving idler every day. It is already much thinned. There are at present in Edinburgh above a thousand people perfectly idle. The journeymen tailors have for some time given up their work, insisting on higher wages.

---

[1] For a further account of Hugh Elliot at this period, see Dr. Somerville's " Life and Times," p. 125.

The masons and carpenters have all followed their example," etc. etc.

In 1768 the brothers went to Oxford. Soon after Hugh's arrival he wrote a letter to his father, from which the following extract will suffice to show the manners and customs of Oxford nearly a century ago :—

"My dear Father—We are now beginning to be a little settled to our business and situation, and I hope we may go on very well. As yet I have seen nothing which may interrupt us, for although most of the young people here are much idler than I could have conceived, yet as there are so many of them in the same way, and they have always enough to join in any idle scheme, they never trouble their heads about anybody else but those who are present.

"This, I think, is the ordinary way the noblemen and gentlemen commoners spend their day : get up at eight and go to prayers ; breakfast at nine, and some hour in the forenoon read some Greek or Latin with their tutor ; the rest of the forenoon is given up either to tennis, riding, shooting, but for the most part to lounging ; dine at one ; after dinner, they invite one another to each other's rooms, and sit there mostly till between three and four ; then they go home and read another hour or two, and spend the evening between the coffee-house, cards, and the billiard-table, till supper-time, when they sup at each other's rooms, where they stay, mostly, till twelve or one o'clock. . . . I dare-say some spend the day to much better purpose.

"The tutor we met with seems to be a very good

kind of man, and a good classical scholar, but I cannot
find out that he has any other knowledge, at least not
to any degree of perfection (I include history in the
classics). We have just been dining with Dr. Markham,
and I do not know anybody that he has had twice in
his house in so short a time. He asked us what part of
learning we were most deficient in. My brother told
him that we knew little Greek, but that we found ourselves equal to most young men of our age in Latin,
and that we had applied ourselves particularly to *mathématiques*, and had got the rudiments of most of the
sciences. He answered that, to be sure, *mathématiques*,
and those kind of things, were very necessary for a
gentleman, but that it was only classical and historical
knowledge that make able statesmen, and then he went
on to recommend the study of Greek. As, however,
you intend me for the army,[1] I should think it very
improper in me to give my time to it, as long as I have
any of what he calls those 'kind of things' to learn.

---

[1] General Scott of Scotstarbet, who was an intimate friend of
Sir Gilbert's, presented his son, Mr. Hugh Elliot, in 1762, with a
lieutenant's commission in a new levied regiment of which General
Scott had got the colonelcy.—(Letter of Sir Gilbert to Justice-Clerk,
1762.) Hugh was born in April 1752, and was at this time just
ten years old. The favour was unsolicited, and, though an abuse, was
considered as a privilege of the colonel, and had been often exercised
without attracting public notice or animadversion. According to
the custom which had prevailed in other instances of commissions
given to youths too young for actual service, Mr. Elliot's time should
have counted from the date of his first commission, and should thus
have entitled him to the same rank with those who had been in the
regiment during that period.

He also recommended the natural philosophy, as some of its branches were very necessary for an officer to learn, especially hydrostatics. In short, I think he endeavoured to recommend everything which is taught here, and dis-recommend everything which is not taught here. As for myself, this is the plan which I have laid down:—If I am to read law, six to eight, law; eight, prayers, which we all attend; sup and breakfast, nine to ten; we go to our tutors, ten to eleven; law again; eleven to one, history; one to two, dine; two to three, when I can get the dancing-master, who is very good, and who I shall soon have; draw, three to four; natural philosophy, four to five; after five, *conique* sections; the astronomy, by all accounts, is nothing; at half-past five I will go to the coffee-house—everybody goes there.

" We are told we must take great care never to speak upon politics, or prefer any other University to this.

" Frederick Stewart had given himself the airs of despising everything that was English, and speaking of everything that was Scotch, and had offended my uncle by speaking in the coffee-house of his father's intrigue with the Princess of Wales. . . .

" Pray, papa, if anybody asks you how we like Oxford, don't tell them that we find fault with anything, for I never saw people so bigoted to any place in my life, and they are jealous of the least thing that can be construed against it."

In 1770 we again find both brothers at Paris. An

amusing letter from Hugh describes some of the first
visits they paid on their arrival :—" As soon as we were
equipped we waited on Mr. Walpole, who seems to be
as dry and cold a kind of gentleman as ever I saw. He
cleared up a little when he heard that we had some
French acquaintance, and did not depend entirely upon
him for introductions. His behaviour was not particular
to us in this respect, but is the same to all the young
English ; and, indeed, I think he is so far in the right,
as it would be impossible to take any charge of such a
parcel of raw ignorant boys as most of them seem to
be." In the same letter he describes a visit to Madame
de Boufflers,[1] " who was at her studies in her bed-
chamber. She received us very kindly, and spoke about
all our Scotch and English authors ; if she had time,
she would set about translating Mr. Smith's Moral
Sentiments—' Il a des idées si justes de la sympathie.'
This book is now in great vogue here ; this doctrine of
sympathy bids fair for cutting out David Hume's Imma-
terialism, especially with the ladies, ever since they heard
of his marriage.

"Madame du Deffand has told us to come to her
petits soupers whenever we please. We are both a little
awkward yet in company, and not so much at our ease ;
that, however, is wearing off every day, and by the time
we shall see you again, we hope to be quite masters at
least of our bodies. As to our studies—the police did
not give us back our books till yesterday, and we have

---

[1] Comtesse de Boufflers, frequently mentioned in Walpole's *Correspondence* as *l'Idole du Temple.*

met with a great check in the poor old Abbé Choquart,
who, by all accounts, is one of the best men of France
for composition, being in the Temple, the French Fleet
prison. I would go to him there, if it was not such an
immense way off, and that there is no standing the
stench of his room when once you are in it. He is to
give us a list of military books. I am now reading
Blond's Artillery. We are lodging at the Hôtel de
Londres, Rue Dauphine, and are to pay 5 louis per
month; we could not find anything under which would
do."

Gilbert, writing in French, describes, with some
particularity, the society of Madame Geoffrin,[1] and
dwells on the trouble it gave her to " gouverner ses
savans." The coterie of Madame Geoffrin was divided
into two sets, which met alternately at her house on
Mondays and Wednesdays, and disastrous would have
been the fate of him who, by intention or mischance,
should have presented himself before her on the wrong
day. " Si les deux venaient par hasard à se rencontrer,
elle dit que sa maison serait jetée par les fenêtres ! "
Gilbert gave the preference to the Wednesday meetings,
on account of the presence of Mademoiselle l'Espinasse.[2]
Madame du Deffand's society they described as " plus

---

[1] Madame Geoffrin was celebrated in her day as a *bel-esprit*, and
the patroness of literary men, the most eminent among whom met
frequently at her house. Montesquieu, the *Encyclopédistes*, l'Abbé
Delille, and La Harpe, were among her most intimate friends.—*See*
article on Madame Geoffrin, *Bibliothèque Portative.*

[2] The *ci-devant* companion of Madame du Deffand, the friend of
D'Alembert, and authoress of some celebrated letters.

élevé que le Parnasse de Madame Geoffrin," and it was, as we know from Walpole, composed of all that was eminent in France, either by intellect or position.[1]

Gilbert writes at this time with some brotherly pride of Hugh's popularity with men and women, but a more impartial testimony to the merits of both brothers will be found in Madame du Deffand's published correspondence with Horace Walpole :[2]—"Nous avons ici les enfants de M. Elliot. Ils sont infiniment aimables. Ils savent parfaitement le français, ils sont gais, doux, et polis, et plaisent à tout le monde. Je les vois souvent, j'ai pour eux toutes les attentions possibles, mais ils n'ont besoin de personne pour les faire valoir, on leur trouve une fort jolie figure."

In the autumn of 1770 Gilbert returned to Christ Church, and Hugh[3] proceeded to Metz, where he proposed to study military science, and especially fortification, a camp being at that time held there for the instruction of the Duke de Chartres ; and Madame de Boufflers and others gave him introductions to the officers in command. He seems to have been struck by the absence of courtesy on the part of the French officers to their English guests : "The Swiss and Ger-

[1] From Madame Riccoboni, another celebrated literary lady, and the authoress of several novels, there are two or three letters in this collection written to my grandfather at Munich.

[2] Vol. ii. p. 81.

[3] It appears from the letters that Sir Gilbert, believing that his son's claim to regimental rank would be in nowise affected by deferring the moment at which he should join, was anxious that his previous military education should be as complete as possible.

man are, however, all the more civil to us on that
account, for they are on ill terms with the French."
From Metz, Hugh went to Strasburgh, and thence
returned to England.   What became of him during the
following year I do not discover; but it was in the
course of 1771, and when he had barely attained his
nineteenth year, that he met with a disappointment which
rankled in his mind through life.   Having received, as
has already been said, when still in his early childhood,
a commission in the army, an honour which procured
him the notoriety of an allusion in No. 45 of the *North
Briton*, he now learnt that Lord Barrington refused to
ratify the appointment, on the ground that such commissions, passing over inferior grades of rank, could only
be given to princes of the blood-royal.   The *rank* of
captain, however, appears to have been granted him for
the purpose, as we learn from one of his father's letters,
of enabling him to enter a foreign army with certain
advantages.[1]

The blow to Hugh must have been severe.   All
the military ardour which had been fostered by his
supposed destination in life was blighted, and at that
time his love for the profession of arms is described
as a "passion."   He did not, however, at once forego
his hope of gratifying it; but, with the consent of his
family, he set out for Vienna, in the spring of 1772,
with letters of introduction to Lord Stormont, General
Prince Poniatowski, and to General Langlais.

---

[1] At that time no officer of the Austrian army holding a rank
inferior to that of captain was received in Viennese society.

It is impossible to read this episode in my grand-father's life, given with all the details of unreserved family correspondence, without remarking the change— it must be admitted for the better—which has taken place since those days, both in the manner of granting and of receiving appointments in the public service. Publicity has depressed patronage, and has made it necessary that young men should have such claims to preferment as will bear the investigation of the envious or the less fortunate; and the disappointed candidate hardly wonders while he grumbles at the discovery that, for every vacant appointment there are found "five hundred good as he." In 1772, the refusal to ratify such an appointment as that claimed by Hugh Elliot was looked on as the most cutting insult, the cruellest injury: foes were supposed to triumph over so great a disgrace; friends could not do enough to wipe out so crying an injustice.

A short stay at Vienna sufficed to show there was little or no chance of obtaining the desired admission *with rank* into the Austrian army, but the time spent there was not without results, as it gained for Hugh the cordial friendship of Lord Stormont, the British Minister at Vienna, who remained his fast and useful friend.[1] From that period, too, dates his correspondence with Countess Thun, one of the most agreeable and cultivated women in Viennese society, of whom Wraxall[2] in his *Memoirs*

[1] Hugh was presented to the Emperor Joseph while at Vienna, and his father, in one of his letters, congratulates him on an opportunity of seeing that "remarkable young sovereign."

[2] Wraxall's *Memoirs*, vol. ii.

of the Court of Berlin, etc., thus writes : " No capital
in Europe can produce persons more distinguished by
natural and acquired endowments, or of minds more
liberal and enlarged than the Countess Thun and
Countess Pergen; the houses of both are the rendez-
vous of everything that pretends to refinement in this
capital." Years afterwards, Madame de Thun, in speaking of Hugh Elliot's appearance at this time at Vienna,
said to Mr. Brydone, " Such as he was at eighteen years,
so would I wish my son to be."[1]

Nothing can more strongly prove the engaging and
attractive character of his manners at this time, than the
interest he inspired in persons so well acquainted with
the world as Lord Stormont and Countess Thun, and I
cannot resist giving one more extract in his praise from
a letter of Lord Stormont's, which, though shown to his
family, had not been written for their eyes.

" Vienna, Aug. 5, 1772.

" I must leave off, as I have several letters on hand,
and give a little farewell dinner for Elliot, who sets out
to-morrow. I really see him go with much concern. The
sweetness of his disposition, the manner in which the
' *elements are blended* ' in him, the variety of his accomplishments and pursuits, make him a young man so
much after my heart, that I often lament in secret I am

---

[1] Mr. Brydone, writing from Vienna to Hugh in 1776, says,
"Madame de Thun has everything but beauty. I have never seen a
more agreeable or sensible woman. Her only wish, she says, is that
her son should be like you."—*MS. Letters*, 1776.

Mr. Brydone, the Sicilian traveller, had been, like many other English travellers, introduced by my grandfather to Madame de Thun.

not the father of such a son, though, God knows, I never was less disposed than at present to try my chance."

In writing to Sir Gilbert, Lord Stormont expresses a hope that, though Hugh had failed in the object of his journey to Vienna, " he would have no reason to repent it; it is an advantage to an Englishman to examine the detail, and contemplate all the consequences of severe discipline, though he may not expect, and perhaps should not attempt, to introduce it at home."

Spurred on by a thirst for military adventure, Hugh proceeded from Vienna to Warsaw, taking advantage of the escort of the Pope's nuncio; " who," wrote one of Sir Gilbert's correspondents from Vienna, " is the most sacred character under whose wing your son can be sheltered against confederates fighting for their religion; and the most abandoned of them will fall down and worship him."

From Warsaw Hugh wrote to his father on the 30th September 1772 : " I have met with a very favourable reception here. The King's[1] person and manner are strikingly engaging and manly. I never was so moved with any scene as with the first aspect of this court. Remorse or despair get the better of the forced cheerfulness with which they endeavour to veil the approach of ruin, slavery, and oppression.[2] But these only prompt them to complaints; not one man is bold enough to draw his sword in the common cause. All the blood that has been shed in the numberless con-

---

[1] Stanislas Augustus Poniatowski.

[2] The partition of Poland was determined in 1772.

federations was only the consequence of private piques
and jealousies, fomented by the intrigues of France.

"I could not help expressing my surprise to the
King (the last time I was with him) that he did not
raise his standard in some part of the kingdom, as I
was sure, from my own feelings, that he would soon have
an army of volunteers, able at least to defend his person
from danger. He took me by the hand, and said :—
'Ah ! mon cher Elliot, nous ne sommes pas des
Anglais.' He is now reduced to the greatest distress,
as his revenues are entirely in the hands of his enemies ;
he has hardly wherewithal to pay his household servants, much less an army."

In spite of the deplorable condition of the country,
overrun by the armies of the three great powers, and of
a monarchy tottering to its fall, Warsaw was at that
time the most brilliant and dissipated Court in existence; and though the haughty minister[1] of Catherine
did not think it worth while to rise from his chair when
the King approached,[2] yet Stanislas Augustus, gifted
himself with every grace, ruled over a nobility un-
equalled in Europe for beauty of person, for polish of
manners, and for every accomplishment which lends a
charm to society. No wonder then that the young
Englishman should have found attractions enough to
delay him there. From the correspondence which he

---

[1] Staekelberg.

[2] Everybody knew Stackelberg to be the real King. If Stanislas
entered the room when the Ambassador was at cards, the haughty
Russian, without leaving his seat, motioned to the King to take
another.—Wraxall's *Memoirs*.

subsequently carried on with the British Minister at
Warsaw, Mr. Wroughton,[1] it appears that Princesses
had conspired to detain him, and that the great Ambassador, Count Stackelberg himself, had been glad to see
him go.

The "red planet Mars" was, however, still in the
ascendant, and under its influence he again set forth to
join the Russian army, then employed in Moldavia
against the Turks. Finding on his arrival at Bucharest
that nothing in a military way was passing there, owing
to the "unexpected prolongation of the armistice and
the meeting of the congress there," he joined an English
officer on a further expedition to Constantinople, from
whence he wrote to his father, December 17, 1772, that
having received from the Turkish Ambassador at Bucharest a permission to see the Turkish army, he and his
companion, Colonel Ainslie, had visited Schumlat, their
headquarters, and had passed some time with the Great
Vizier and other principal officers of the Porte. The
Vizier had shown them much civility, presenting each of
them with a horse. "We have had in this jaunt the
advantage of seeing an army of which Europeans in
general have little acquaintance, and form very false
conjectures : the people, the manners, the government,
seem to be as little understood."

From Constantinople he returned to Bucharest,
where he appears to have been laid up for nearly two

---

[1] Mr. Wroughton, afterwards Sir Thomas, and minister at Stockholm. It was said that in his youth he had been a favoured admirer
of Catherine II., and that he was removed from St. Petersburg by the
Grand Duke's desire.

months with a severe attack of fever; from which he had barely recovered when he joined the headquarters of Marshal Romanzow at Jassy.

The expedition to Constantinople, when known in England, seems to have been viewed with some displeasure by Sir Gilbert, who wrote his son several letters in a somewhat severe tone, on the instability of purpose and want of self-control displayed by him, in converting a journey to Vienna in search of military employment into a pleasure-trip for the gratification of curiosity.

To these letters, which also enjoined his immediate return to England, Hugh replied from Jassy that, with every desire to obey his father at once and implicitly, he owed it to his name and his uniform not to quit an army on the eve of its commencing hostilities; that to do so after a *séjour* of five months would be a disgrace which he, the only English officer with the Russian troops, could not incur; and in consequence he announced his intention to join the division of Colonel Soltikoff, which was about to attack Russig, a fortress and town on the other side of the Danube; and to return to England as soon as it shall "be clear to all that the desire of obeying his father's orders, and not the desire of avoiding danger, alone makes him quit the field." He added that the hope which had guided him through all his wanderings was that of obtaining such military distinction as would induce the authorities at home " to realise" the military rank which he nominally held in the British army.

Most unfortunately I can find no details of this

episode in his life, though allusions to some brilliant exploits of his, in an action before Silistria, are frequent in the correspondence.[1] The fullest account of Hugh's movements while with the Russian army is given in the following letter from Marshal Romanzow to Sir R. Gunning, British Minister at St. Petersburg :—

"Monsieur—Votre Excellence voudra bien permettre qu' encouragé par les Bontés que Messieurs ses Prédécesseurs ont eues pour moi, j'ose lui addresser la présente. Saisissant avec bien de l'empressement l'occasion de lier un commerce avec elle, je l'entretiendrai un peu amplement au sujet d'un de ses compatriotes, M. Elliot.

"Cet officier, ayant appris l'automne passée, à Varsovie, que les Plénipotentiaires pour le Congrès de Fockiany se sont séparés, dans la persuasion que les hostilités recommenceraient, se rendit à notre armée, en vue d'y servir comme volontaire. La négociation

---

[1] Since writing this, I have seen a fourth edition of Tooke's *Life of Catherine the Second*, in which, after an account of a surprise of the Russian army at Giurgevo by the Turks in the campaign of 1773, the following passage occurs. "An Englishman named Elliot, in the service of Russia distinguished himself in an extraordinary manner at Giurgevo. He sprang with no less agility than boldness over the heads and sabres of the Spahis, and fell into the river, which he crossed by swimming." A family tradition exists of his having accomplished part of the distance by holding on to the tail of a Cossack's horse. Another story is alluded to in the family letters, which must have happened about this time, of a wonderfully rapid journey made by him (probably from the camp to Warsaw), all the authorities on the route vying with each other in expediting the traveller, who represented himself to be the husband of a Moldavian princess, flying back to her after a triumphant campaign.

renouée, il profita de cet intervalle pour faire une course à Constantinople. Il vient à mon Quartier-Général au moment que la dernière négociation tirait vers sa fin. Il apprend que la guerre va recommencer, et me demande d'être employé. En attendant, il lui arrive, à ce que j'apprends à présent, des ordres de Monsieur son père, qui lui enjoignent de revenir en Angleterre. N'étant point de la trempe de cet officier, à qui un Maréchal répondit (lorsqu'il lui demanda à l'ouverture d'une campagne la permission de pouvoir se retirer de l'armée, prétextant des ordres de ses parents pour cet effet): 'Honore père et mère, et tu vivras long-temps :' —il me conjure de l'expédier pour un corps où je croyais qu'il y aurait le plutôt affaire. Je l'envois en Vallachie. Là on lui dit que les Turcs passent près de Silistria. Il se rend en poste au corps du Général Potemkin. On y vient aux mains ; et dans le rapport que ce général me fait de cette affaire, il me dit merveille de Monsieur Elliot, de façon que je n'ai pu me dispenser d'en faire mention à ma souveraine. Je me crois encore obligé à lui rendre justice auprès de votre Excellence. Ses aimables qualités ainsi que sa conduite à cette occasion lui ont acquis mon estime, et je ne nie point à votre Excellence que je m'intéresse beaucoup à lui. J'ose donc la prier très humblement de calmer Monsieur son père, et de faire connaitre à sa cour, l'ardeur militaire de ce jeune officier. Il mérite d'être encouragé. J'aurai les plus grandes obligations à votre Excellence de cette condescendance pour moi. Je finis cette lettre, peut être déja

trop longue, par lui présenter les assurances de la
considération avec laquelle j'ai l'honneur d'être, Monsieur, de votre Excellence le très humble et très
obéissant serviteur,
                                        CTE. ROMANZOW.

            " Jassi,
    " Ce $\frac{13}{24}$ Avril 1773."

Writing on the same day to Hugh himself,[1] Marshal
Romanzow congratulates him on the distinction he had
achieved, and goes on thus :—

"Permettez que je vous parle à cette heure en ami.
Vous avez parfaitement soutenu l'idée que j'ai conçue de
vous, que j'ai généralement de votre nation. Vous vous
êtes exposé une fois, ne le faites plus. Conservez vos
jours pour des exploits dignes d'un bon citoyen qui se
doit à sa patrie. Peut-être aurais-je un jour la satisfaction d'admirer, à la tête de vos braves compatriotes,
les talens que vous venez de déployer chez nous; et de
me rappeller avec bien du contentement qu'en suivant
votre penchant, vous vous êtes préparé à l'armée que j'ai
l'honneur de commander, les voyes, qui vous conduiront
par la suite dans le chemin de la gloire, dont vous avez,
j'en suis convaincu, les plus justes notions."

In spite of this friendly advice, Hugh apparently
could not tear himself away from the army ; for we find

---

[1] From this letter it appears that Hugh had been serving with the
division under Potemkin.

Potemkin, who was disliked and distrusted by Romanzow, was
shortly afterwards sent to St. Petersburg with despatches, and was almost
immediately installed in the post of favourite, from which time his power
was scarcely less than that of the Empress herself.—*Life of Potemkin.*

him writing to his father from the camp at Jalamutz on the $\frac{26th\ July}{17th\ Aug.}$ 1773.

"My dear Father—Since my last I left Count Solti-koff's army, and hurried night and day to be present with the Feld-Marechal at his enterprise upon Silistria. I, however, found him already across the Danube, and a short march from the place. All the officers of note, who have seen other armies and other wars, agree that never were troops in a more desperate situation, or with-drawn with more skill. The present existence of every individual in this army is merely owing to the conduct and capacity of the Marechal, joined to the bravery of General Weisman, who made our retreat good, though at the expense of his life. I shall not endeavour to give a detail of the several operations which distinguished the attack of the town, and our retreat of thirty miles in a country where a regular army would scarce attempt to pass in the most profound peace. I hope that you will not think me advantageous[1] if I mention that the Mar-shal was so good as to give me equal marks of approba-tion for my conduct during this expedition as in the former rencontres, when he was pleased to treat me with a most flattering distinction.

"I am most uneasy to know how you will take my disobedience."

Sir Gilbert was naturally much mollified by the dis-tinction gained by his son during his short period of

---

[1] A Gallicism, owing, no doubt, to his constant use at this time of French, in which language *avantageux* sometimes means vain or boastful.

service with the Russian army, and by the praises of his
spirit and conduct which flowed in from all quarters.
M. Pouschkin, Russian ambassador in London, was
desired to report to the English Government the very
strong expressions of approbation with which Marshal
Romanzow had mentioned the young Englishman in his
despatches to his own government; and Mr. Wroughton,
in a letter to the Earl of Suffolk (Secretary of State for
the Northern Department), dated Warsaw, 29th July
1773, thus writes: "Field-Marshal Romanzow, in his
relation" (to Count Stackelberg of a victory over the
Grand Vizier) "speaks of Captain Elliot with uncommon
praise, who, by all accounts from the army, has distinguished himself with a truly British courage; he is indeed a young man of extraordinary merit."

In a letter which Hugh addressed to the Marshal
after his return to England, he ascribes his appointment
as Minister to the Court of Munich to the favourable
impression which had been produced on the King by the
praises which Romanzow had bestowed upon him during
his stay with the army, and he characteristically adds—
"Pardonnez si j'ose regretter leurs effets, puisque le
Roi a jugé qu'elles me rendaient dignes d'un avancement
fort peu ordinaire dans ce pays à mon age : quoique je
me sens fort flatté de cette distinction, c'est avec bien
de la peine que je me vois forcé de laisser partir seuls
deux de mes compatriotes qui vont vous chercher aux
bords du Danube."

The first intimation of Lord Suffolk's intention to
admit him into the "foreign minister line" was given to

his father in the spring of 1773, and is mentioned in a letter addressed to Hugh at Warsaw. From this time Sir Gilbert naturally became most impatient for his son's return to England, which, however, did not take place till the autumn of the year. On the 27th September 1773, Sir Gilbert wrote to Hugh that he was appointed plenipotentiary at Munich in Bavaria, with a salary of £5 per diem,[1] though his immediate predecessor had been reduced to £3, a sum manifestly inadequate to the expenses of a foreign minister, however economical he might be.

Though he was aware of his destination so early as September 1773, it appears that his appointment was not officially made until the spring of the following year. It bears the date of 29th April 1774.

From the allusions which are made to this period in the subsequent correspondence with his family, I imagine the winter to have been spent by them all in London, and that Hugh took his full share of the amusements of the day. His *maccaronism* seems to have been a subject of jest among his friends, and his fun and his "flames," his adventures and masquerades, and his attendance at Ranelagh, are frequently referred to in his sister's letters.

The feelings with which Hugh set out on his new career may be guessed at by his letter to Marshal Ro-

---

[1] This was a mistake. Lord Suffolk, when making the appointment, expressed his intention of raising the salary from £3 to £5 per diem, and did not apprehend there would be any difficulty in so doing ; but from subsequent letters I find that no such alteration was made, and the salary remained as it had been in M. de Vismes' time. Mr. Harris at Berlin had £1500 a-year, and spent, it was said, £3000.

manzow. In announcing his appointment to a friend,
he goes on :—"The only thing that consoles me is,"
etc., and he probably shared fully in the sentiments of
disapprobation which were excited among his quondam
comrades by the announcement of his new profession.
"Comment," writes to him Lieutenant-Colonel Petersohn,[1] from Koutschouk Cainardgi, 25th July 1774,
"vous désertez les drapeaux de Mars et vous rentrez
sous le joug de la politique? Mais ce sont des contes !
Eh quoi ! cet Elliot aimable, sociable, léger, étourdi,
galant, petit maître, consent à s'enfermer dans le fond
des cabinets ! mais c'est un larcin fait à la société ! Cela
me confond dans mes idées. Quoi le vif et léger Elliot,
va donc prendre sur soi l'air sombre et flegmatique d'un
ministre, après ce phénomène je ne désespère pas un jour
de voir le Pape habillé en hussard."

On his way to Munich, Hugh made some stay in
Paris, where the political changes which followed on the
accession of Louis XVI. gave him matter for some interesting communications to his Government.

His first despatch from Munich is dated 23d June
1774.

There was at that time little or no business of any
interest depending between the Courts of Munich and
of London.[2] The questions which occupy the chief

[1] Colonel Petersohn, *chargé-d'affaires* of the Russian Court.

[2] Since the conclusion of the Seven Years' War (1763) Austria and
Prussia had continued to be rivals for power, within the Germanic
Empire, while France was suspected of a design to check the ambitious
views of both, by instigating an alliance of the secondary German powers.
The duty of an English minister consisted in watching the progress of
their various intrigues.

portions of my grandfather's official correspondence relate to matters which affected the German Empire and
the King of Great Britain in his electoral capacity; perhaps for that very reason they were all the more interesting to the King, whose cordial approval of the young
Minister's despatches was frequently signified through
Lord Suffolk in public and private letters.

It appears to me, as far as I am able to judge, that
though no important events occurred to call forth the
manifestation of superior abilities in him during his residence at Munich, he displayed, nevertheless, from his first
entrance into public life, considerable tact and unusual
decision of character. A rapid penetration into men's
motives, and a readiness in availing himself of the knowledge he had gained, were evidently characteristics of
his mind; and on one occasion they were conspicuously
shown, when, in conducting a delicate negotiation with
the Electoral Court, having reason to suspect that the
Bavarian ministry were influenced by Austrian intrigues,[1]
he spiritedly refused to transact the business through
them, and in a personal interview with the Elector, took
on himself the responsibility of urging a policy on that
Prince which, as being adverse to the interests of the
House of Austria, was viewed with ill-will by the minister,
Count Seinsheim, whose sympathies were known to be
Austrian.

His conduct on this occasion received much approval
both abroad and at home.

---

[1] Relating to the succession to the Duchy of Saxe-Lunenburg, in
which the Hanoverian and Bavarian interests were opposed.

If the political correspondence of the British legation at Munich is deficient in interest, the same cannot
be said of the mass of private letters which flowed from
and to, and *through*, as will be seen, the hands of the
minister. The only difficulty in dealing with these is
where to stop in our selections. In turning them over,
the eye is caught by names of such celebrity or notoriety as would rejoice the heart of a collector of
autographs; but experience obliges us to confess that
less imposing personages might often have written better
letters.

Madame du Deffand gives us nothing so amusing as
an account, by a young English traveller, of an evening
at her house, when a Salade à la Génoise was concocted,
with much fun and laughter, by some of the most brilliant
members of her society. Prince Potemkin's interest in
Bavaria seems to have been limited to the concerns of a
few pretty women. The first of a long series of letters
from Dr. Mesmer opens with a *trait* which is more entertaining than anything that follows :—" Un remède contre
les nerfs doit fort intéresser *votre nation !*"

The great majority of the miscellaneous letters are
occupied with gossip, and were written to Hugh Elliot
from Munich when he was at Ratisbon, or *vice versâ*.
The contents are often purposely disguised under an
involved style—initial letters standing for names. Thus,
a correspondent, writing from Ratisbon, tells us that
" les nouvelles particulières d'ici se réduisent à peu
de choses, les amours de M. de B. et de la Comtesse
C. sont finis quant à l'extérieur, ils s'aiment encore,

mais n'osent se le dire.   Le Directeur de Madlle. C. la
porte à renoncer à son inclination pour M. qui la
demande en mariage.   Elle déclare qu'elle renonce á
lui, la bouche le dit, le cœur ne le pense pas; ils s'aiment
toujours, et n'en sont que plus malheureux.   Les
amours du gros L. et de Madame d'Y. sont finis et
assez mal, car ils n'ont pu venir à l'amitié après leur
rupture ; ceux de N. avec R. sont plus tranquils," etc.
etc.

The only impression left on the uninitiated reader
by such a composition as this, is that the letters of
the alphabet have taken to disorderly courses.   But
after a careful examination of many such documents,
order rises out of chaos, and something like a vision
of the social life of the Bavarian capital dawns upon the
mind.

At the period of Hugh Elliot's arrival in Bavaria,
nothing could exceed the poverty and misery of the
people, or the extravagance and gaiety of the Court.

In an official letter to Mr. Eden, 10th September
1774, he writes :—" To draw any picture of the state of
this country would be to go back two ages in the progress of society.   They are in nothing on a par with the
rest of Europe, except in music and debauchery. . . .
That you may judge of the universal ignorance that
overspreads this country, I shall only give you two
anecdotes which have fallen under my own observation.
The trial by torture is the ordinary method, in this
Electorate, of convicting criminals.   Some time since,
three poor fellows, after having been by this means

forced to a confession, suffered capital punishment. A
few days afterwards, their innocence was proved by the
capture of the really guilty parties. An Englishman
who happened to be here at the time, expressed his
surprise that so cruel a catastrophe should have occurred
under the generally mild government of the Elector;
this remark had like to have provoked a discussion, to
avoid which the Englishman said that this point was
much better treated of in a chapter in *L'Esprit des
Lois*, than by anything he could say on the subject.
Our Premier, with whom he was speaking, repeated
several times the word *esprit*, on which the Englishman
asked him if he had not read it. He said he believed
it was among the number of books which the Pope had,
considering his situation, given him a dispensation to
read, but that, for his part, il n'aimait pas les *esprits
forts*.

"Speaking lately with the President of Finances of
the calamities occasioned by the late famine, and of the
various plans proposed for avoiding the recurrence of
such misfortunes, he said that in other countries pre-
cautions might be necessary, but in this, in case of a
want of grain, they had an easy resource in the course
of the Danube, by which they could always send off
numbers of people on a short warning, and that they
had already experienced the advantage of this method
of getting rid of the superfluous mouths in the last
famine, when many thousands went to live in the
Austrian dominions. To this ingenious plan is owing
the present unpopulousness of this once peopled country.

I am told the Austrians have now in their service enough of Bavarian subjects to conquer the whole Electorate."

Mr Liston,[1] writing to Lady Elliot a few months after their arrival at Munich, tells her, " that several of our people of fashion and men of letters are still employed in search of the philosopher's stone,[2] and Mr. Elliot has almost drawn a challenge on himself, by venturing to doubt that burning the hand with St. Hubert's key was an infallible cure for the bite of a mad dog."

Miracles, too, were rife in Bavaria, and the young *protégé* of Hume and of Madame du Deffand must have had some difficulty in listening with patience to the feats of a certain Gassner, who, under the protection of the Bishop of Ratisbon, undertook to exorcise devils for the benefit of the Electorate.[3] He was said to have expelled legions of evil spirits from the poorer orders; and, to judge by the descriptions of Munich society, it is much to be feared that the fiends must have taken refuge with the higher.

The Court at that time consisted of the Elector and Electress, who were childless (the question of the Bavarian succession loomed already in the distance); of the Electress of Saxony, sister of the Elector of Bavaria and daughter of the Emperor Charles the Seventh; of the Elector Palatine and his wife, who, like the

---

[1] Mr. Liston had accompanied my grandfather to Munich in the capacity of private secretary.

[2] Wraxall in 1779, found the Viennese nobility engaged in the same search.—See his *Memoirs of the Court of Berlin*, etc., vol. ii.

[3] See account in Wraxall's *Memoirs of the Court of Berlin*, etc.

Electress of Saxony, were only occasional though frequent visitors to Munich ; and of the Prince of Deux-
ponts,[1] who claimed to be in the Bavarian succession
after the death of the Elector Palatine, the immediate
heir of the Elector of Bavaria, but who, like him, was
childless. An old Margravine of Baden completed the
circle of royal personages, and her death followed the
arrival of my grandfather within the year, and was thus
notified to him by a fair maid of honour whose letters
are among his correspondence :—"La pauvre Margravine
se meurt d'une hydropisie, et cela pour une pudeur mal
placée, ne voulant montrer ses jambes qui étaient
enflées. Grands Dieux ! où la pudeur va-t-elle se
placer."

The Elector, an agreeable and accomplished, though
weak man, seems at once to have been propitiated by
Mr. Elliot's pleasing appearance and manners, and to
have made him his frequent companion in his hunting
and shooting expeditions. "The Elector," wrote Mr.
Liston, " is extremely fond of hunting, and Mr. Elliot
has added considerably to the favour in which he
already stood, by attending him every day he has taken
that exercise, not to mention his having made almost
the whole Electoral family drunk with punch, once or
twice, after their return from the chase in the evening."
The Electress, of whom we hear little, except that she

---

[1] Prince Maximilian of Deux-Ponts, afterwards King of Bavaria by
the name of Maximilian I., became an intimate friend and a frequent
correspondent of Mr. Elliot's. He was godfather to my uncle of the
same name, born at Dresden 1796.

had the unfortunate habit of winking her eyes in
moments of unusual emotion, was surrounded by a bevy
of fair ladies, among whom Madame Daun,[1] the correspondent, already alluded to, and the "black-eyed
Salerne," were the most admired.[2]

The other chief personages, whose names or letters
are of frequent occurrence in the correspondence, are
the Prime Minister, Count Seinsheim; the Austrian
Minister, Count Hartig, "a little decrepit man," who is
described as constantly pushing forward to attract the
Elector's attention, while the latter coolly talked over
his head to my grandfather, to the great amusement of
the Court; M. de Folard, the French Minister; Baron
Sarny, the confidential counsellor of the Elector; and to
these we may add the Preisings, Torrings, Bercheims,
and others, all leading members of the Bavarian nobility.

[1] This lady, though unmarried, had brevet rank in virtue of her
appointment at Court. Her letters are signed *Delta*.

[2] A testimony to the attractions of Madlle. de Salerne may be read
in Mozart's letters, where the following passages occur:—

"Munich, Sep. 29, 1777.

"This afternoon I went to Count Salerne's. His daughter is a maid
of honour, and was one of the hunting party (at Court). Young
Countess Salerne recognised me at once, and waved her hand to me
repeatedly (as she passed in a procession from the royal chapel).

"Oct. 2, 1777.—Yesterday I was again at Count Salerne's. Papa
must not, however, imagine that I like to be at Count Salerne's on
account of the young lady; by no means, for she is unhappily in
waiting, and therefore never at home; but I am to see her at Court
to-morrow.

"Countess Salerne is a Frenchwoman. The daughter plays nicely,
but fails in time. I thought this arose from want of ear on her part,
but I find I can blame no one but her teacher."

Madame de Torring-Seefeld enjoyed the unquestionable
dishonour of representing Madame de Montespan at a
court which boasted to be a Versailles in miniature;
and to prove that French sentiments on such subjects
were in the ascendant, I need only quote a curious
phrase in a note of *Delta's* to my grandfather:—"Notre
pauvre Adelaïde" (Madame de Torring-Seefeld) "continue toujours malade, et l'on parle même en ville de
choses qui me percent le cœur et qui me rendent triste.
On dit qu'elle devrait se retirer; elle n'est ma foi, pas
encore d'âge à cela." The scene of the chief pleasures
of the Court was Nymphenburg, a country palace of the
Elector's which Pöllnitz describes in his letters as a *lieu
enchanté;* gardens, waters, woods, hunting-grounds,
diversified its delights. Three times a-week during the
summer the Electress held a court there, when tables
for play were prepared in the galleries, while, for those
who preferred them, gilded gondolas floated on the lake,
and pony phaetons driven by a "cavalier" were at the
orders of the ladies who chose a moonlight drive through
the woods. A supper, to which all foreigners were
admitted, closed the entertainment. In Munich itself,
the amusements were not fewer:—"La Cour de Bavière
est, sans contredit," says Pöllnitz, "la plus galante et la
plus polie de l'Allemagne. Nous y avons Comédie
Française,[1] bal, et jeu tous les jours. Il y a trois fois

---

[1] In 1774 they had an opera too, for on the 17th January of that
year my grandfather writes that he is just "come home from hearing
an Opera Buffa composed by the famous Mozart, whom you may
remember when only eight years old in England. He is now *maître
de chapelle* to the Bishop of Salzburg, and receives about three guineas

par semaine concert, tout le monde y assiste masqué ;
après le concert on joue et l'on danse. Ces assemblées
publiques, où l'Electeur et toute sa cour assistent, sont
d'un grand revenu pour les valets-de-chambre de l'Electeur ; car outre que chacun paye à l'entrée, ils ont aussi
l'argent des cartes, et ils sont intéressés dans presque
toutes les banques. De sorte que ces domestiques ont
presque tout l'argent de la noblesse."[1] Mr. Liston, too,
speaks of similar expenses at Nymphenburg as being
very heavy.

Such were the scenes, and such the *dramatis personæ*
to which the young diplomatist was introduced in the
summer of 1774, at the early age of twenty-two. The
accounts of his presentation at Court are amusingly contrasted in his own and Mr. Liston's letters. " Le bon
Liston," as he is frequently called by Hugh's foreign
correspondents, gives a somewhat pompous description
of the ceremony ; of the dignity and grace of the
Minister, which put the Princes themselves out of countenance, while the poor Electress took to opening and
shutting one of her eyes " with the quick involuntary
motion" which " invariably betrays her embarrassment :"
—of the extravagant praises of the ladies of the Court,
and the open envy of the Austrian envoy ; and last, not
least, of the " bare-faced advances" and " masculine
attacks" made on him by the fair sex in general, winding
up thus :—" What I admire the most is, that he has cou-

a-month salary. I never felt the power of music before, but am now a
convert, and have already begun to play upon the flute."

[1] *Lettres du Baron Pöllnitz*, tom. i. p. 328.

trived not to make enemies of those he has refused, a
point which is surely not to be managed without difficulty." There certainly does not appear to have been
much scope for romance at the Court of Munich, and
perhaps it was lucky for my grandfather that, as he himself says, " there is not one good-looking woman in this
town, by good fortune, for I should be in great danger
of learning to talk *en Pastor Fido,* such is the style of
this country."

His letter to his mother, written (July) after his presentation to the Electoral family, is full of boyish fun :—
" I made my speech and bows with becoming gravity,
and did not once lose command of my upper lip, which
I find sometimes apt to betray the mournful composure
to which I can now at command bring the rest of my
face." On leaving the presence of the Electress a terrible
dilemma presented itself—how to retreat without turning
his back on the courtly circle ; happily the terpsichorean
instructions of M. Gallini rushed on his mind, and a
neatly-executed *pirouette* extracted him from the difficulty " in a manner which could not have wounded
the susceptibilities of the most sensitive *Frau* in the
empire."

His letters to his father are formal and constrained,
recalling old Fuller's remark that, " Some, for fear their
orations should giggle, will not even let them smile."
To his mother went all the fun, the folly, the sentiment,
and speculation, which found themselves at the tip of
his pen :—" I wish you was as thoroughly convinced as
I am of the maxim that to enjoy is to obey. I really

believe that one would better deserve canonisation for
having established societies for the reception *de l'allegro,*
than for having founded the most mortified, starved com-
munity of monks that ever wearied Heaven and themselves with their gloomy penances and prayers. As for
me, I believe I have spirits enough to enliven a whole
German court. I am now settled at Munich. The town and
society are both very agreeable ; and my future prospects
promise nothing that is tinged with a sable dye."

And so he began his new life—"youth at the prow,
and pleasure at the helm ;" but by the spring of 1775
clouds were appearing on the horizon ; dissatisfaction
with the tedious frivolity of the society, disgust with the
" venal creatures" who preyed upon the Court, and daily-
increasing money difficulties, contributed to give a tone
of gloom to his mind. The most cheerful feature of
the time consisted in the occasional presence of young
English travellers, who, amid much folly and vice, were
not wholly unmindful of better things. Among these
the most conspicuous were Mr. Pitt,[1] one of my grandfather's constant correspondents ; Mr. Stanley,[2] a son of
Lord Derby's ; Mr. Bagnall, of whose romantic passion
for a fair Bavarian Delta writes as follows :—" Il est
devant une jolie femme comme en présence d'une laide
Impératrice,—c'est bien Anglais ;" and Lord Lindsay,[3]
who was travelling with Mr. Brydone. Mr. Brydone,
Mr. Pitt, and my grandfather, in their subsequent corre-

[1] William Morton Pitt, afterwards M.P. for Dorsetshire.

[2] Mr. Stanley died in 1779.

[3] Only son of the Duke of Ancaster, succeeded his father, and died
in 1779.

spondence, frequently allude to a scheme which appears
to have originated with my grandfather, and of which
the object was the formation of a society of patriotic
men. " I mean," writes Mr. Pitt, " of true patriotic men
—not such as the word now means—who should unite
to carry on good schemes during their whole lives."[1]
" How many hours we have spent in discussing the
plan," he writes on another occasion, and how infinitely
superior to the society in which they lived did such discussions make them! All glory to English influences,
which, in the midst of idle dissipation, can still suffice
to raise ennobling aspirations. To borrow a phrase of
South's, " leaning on hope's anchor, they did not stick
it in the mud," but looked on from present follies and
failures to future years of useful life at home.

Dreaming patriots, and black-eyed maids of honour,
what fate was yours? Did the beguiling phantoms of
your youth become the haunting ghosts of after years?
I know not; but to one of you life was checkered
henceforth with joy and sorrow, with failure and success,
in a greater degree than common, and time floated him
rapidly away from the sheltered scenes of youth.

It seems to have been the misfortune of my
grandfather's temperament, and one which was strength-

---

[1] One of those schemes appears to have been the emancipation of
the Roman Catholics. A great impression had been produced in these
young Englishmen by the sight of the numbers of their countrymen
who, with English hearts, were serving in foreign armies. Mr. Pitt
mentions that four hundred English officers belonging to the Austrian
army had been presented in one day to the Duke of Gloucester, then
travelling abroad. Many of those brave men were affected to tears.

cned by circumstances, that fits of energy and of high
aspiration were rapidly succeeded by depression and
ennui. With romantic notions of honour, he combined
habits of carelessness and irregularity, and a facility of
disposition which could not fail to bring his affairs into
disorder; with a peculiarly sensitive and imaginative
mind, he was placed by circumstances in a society
which ignored every species of delicacy; with intellectual tastes, his life led him among singularly unculti-
vated minds. And these contradictions of temperament
and of conditions were not overruled, as they might
have been, by a determined will. There was in him a
certain indolence and instability of character which
made performance ever lag behind promise; liking
display but hating restraints; doing as others did with
a dissatisfied consciousness that he should have done
better; loving keenly his absent friends, but alienating
them by unpunctuality or neglect in his correspondence;
morbidly brooding over disappointments, while forgetful
of the singular good fortune of his career—his letters at
this period give one the feeling of a character that was
out of joint.

To an application, early in 1775, which he made for
leave, for the purpose of setting his affairs in order,
Lord Suffolk returned a most kind and friendly refusal.
Nevertheless, on the score of ill-health, he did shortly
after absent himself from his post, and placed himself
under the treatment of a celebrated quack doctor at
Berne, M. Shuppach.[1]

---

[1] Shuppach was a Swiss peasant of small learning, but "with fifty

That the reasons for this journey were chiefly
connected with money matters is proved by the fact
of his assuming a false name —that of Mr. Thomas
Bellamy.

From his boyish days Hugh seems to have been
careless and extravagant in his habits. From Warsaw,
when setting out for Constantinople, he wrote to his
father thus :—" As I am living on my patrimony now,
I must live on nothing hereafter;" a communication to
which his father might have replied, like the man in a
French play, " L'air, monsieur, est un fort sot aliment."
But no previous difficulties had approached in gravity
to those which he was now obliged to confess to his
family, and Sir Gilbert's letters to his son are both
severe and affecting. In one of them he expatiates on
the mortification he had experienced in abandoning
some intended improvements at Minto—a step which
the demands made upon him by his sons had obliged
him to take. In another letter he says, with admirable
good sense, " We may certainly live happy in great
poverty, but in modern Europe one cannot act in any
public situation without great fortune or unrelenting
economy."

It does not appear from the correspondence that the
embarrassments my grandfather had to contend with
were attributable to any other cause than carelessness
in his general habits. At a period when the leading
young men of his country were confirmed gamblers, he

years' experience of the practice of medicine," during which he had
discovered the effect of many herbs, and was supposed to have been
successful in the treatment of various diseases.

seems to have had no taste for play, though living at a place where it formed the staple amusement. He no doubt did play, and may have lost more than he could afford, but of serious debts incurred on this account there are no traces. The unfavourable reports of his manner of life which seem to have reached his friends in England at this time, are by them referred to two heads : 1st, Expensive habits and a taste for show; 2d, An undisguised contempt for the society in which he lived. To these accusations Mr. Liston replied in detail.[1] The first charge he dismissed at once, by the statement that from the moment my grandfather had perceived the inadequacy of his means to support the ministerial dignity, according to the notions he conceived of it, he had manfully entered on a system of economy and retrenchment. The second charge was not to be so lightly disposed of. "I wish the dislike were more owing to *maccaronism* than it really is. That affectation would soon wear off, while the uncommon delicacy he feels with regard to characters and manners is likely to attend him through life. He has indeed too much good sense, and is much too well bred to discover the least symptoms of disapprobation to the persons concerned; but it is difficult to reject the addresses of almost every woman in the place, without giving offence

---

[1] Some of the unavoidable expenses of a foreign minister are described as very large. At Munich he was expected to fee every officer of the Elector's household on his introduction at Court ; to be driven in a coach-and-four when accompanying the Elector to his country seats ; and to pay largely when mounted on the Elector's horses.

to some, and his dislike to the society in general is betrayed by a constant preference of English men, English ideas, and English things. He has, however, really much regard for the Elector, the French Minister, and some others." Mr. Liston's letters[1] at this time not only throw much light on my grandfather's life, but prove the writer of them to have been a wise and kind friend, and a judicious adviser.

It appears in those days the *personnel* of a mission at one of the minor Courts was confined to the minister himself. Mr. Liston, who acted as Mr. Elliot's secretary, went out with him in an unofficial capacity,[2] and during this very year, 1775, he had to consider the eligibility of accepting a professorship at Edinburgh, which, however, he rejected for the sake of remaining near my grandfather. During the latter's frequent absences from his post, Mr. Liston was from time to time called on to correspond with the Foreign Office, and he was at last regularly admitted into the diplomatic body as *chargé d'affaires*.

Mr. de Vismes, Mr. Elliot's predecessor at the Court of Munich, had no secretary, " contenting himself with a boy, who understood no language but his own, merely to copy for him."

To return from this digression to my grandfather's

[1] In these letters, Hugh Elliot is named under the disguise of the Prince of Monaco.

[2] Among my grandfather's papers is a letter introducing a gentleman who had officiated as a tutor to the sons of "Mr. Penn, the proprietor of Pennsylvania," and who was now anxious to be employed as secretary, or in some similar capacity.

concerns.—Having spoken of the weaknesses to which
his money difficulties were in part attributable, it must
not be overlooked that his virtues also led him into acts
of prodigality which prudence condemned.   " Have
you," says Mr. de Vismes, writing from Stockholm,
" discovered a gold deposit, that you think yourself justified in giving a hundred louis to Madame Sarny ?"

Madame Sarny was the widow of the Elector's most
confidential and favourite adviser, Baron Sarny, who in
his lifetime had been of signal use to my grandfather,
both by showing him personal kindness, and by further-
ing English views of policy in opposition to those of
Austria.   He had died suddenly, leaving his widow in
circumstances of great distress, from which no one but
my grandfather showed any readiness to relieve her.   In
a grateful letter, which she addressed to him at this time,
she wrote : " The Elector has been with me, and is very
kind, but he did not say anything of assisting me."

Shortly " after Mr. Elliot's arrival at Munich, a circumstance occurred which attracted general attention to
him.   During a violent thunderstorm, the lightning set
fire to a village in sight of the Palace of Nymphenburg,
where the Court then was.   While the courtiers were
crossing themselves, and praying that the next bolt might
not strike the palace, Mr. Elliot hurried out of the
drawing-room, and ran through the storm to the village.
Arrived there, he found the people panic-stricken, and
instantly set them an example of courage and activity,
by going to the assistance of those belonging to the
burning house, at the same time putting his purse, in

which there were from ten to fifteen guineas, in the hands of one of the sufferers."[1]

To his servants my grandfather was indulgent to a fault; and the *fourberies* of a certain valet, La Coste, who had his prototypes in the Scapins of French comedy, are frequently alluded to in the correspondence.

The early part of 1775 found the young diplomatist rusticating in Switzerland.[2] How he passed his time there is not told us; but from a letter of Madame de Thun's, it seems that he had written to her in higher praise of the scenery of the country than of its *passion-less* and apathetic inhabitants, for she writes thus in reply:— . . .   " Je n'aime pas à me persuader ' *que l'homme dégénère quand il n'est que laborieux, frugal, et*

---

[1] Letter from Mr. Liston to Lady Elliot.

[2] During Mr. Elliot's absence from his post, Sir R. Keith passed through Munich, and visited many of its *lions* in company with Mr. Liston. "On Friday," writes Mr. Liston, 16th April 1775, " we saw the ordinary procession of the day, which is sufficiently ridiculous. Sir R. was much amused with the idea of Seefield's acting *le bon Dieu* on this occasion, which he did as usual. We spent that afternoon in the gardens of Nymphenburg. On our return to town we went and saw the procession of the Slaves of Virtue. It consists of the Electresses, the Dames des Clefs and Dames de Cour, and some of the nobility (of these last were Madame Max Preising, the Bercheim, and half-a-dozen more), followed by a dozen of poor girls, who are educated at the Electress's expense. They visited all the churches and chapels in town, and some on foot from three o'clock till near eight. The dress gives them the look of nuns, but it is white and handsome, and serves rather to set them off than otherwise. I observed that your good friend the Daun, not to mention others, had thought a little rouge would give relief to her charms; the Daun especially was plastered up to the eyes. '

sans passions,' il me parait si difficile de bien diriger ces
dernières que je n'aime pas à me convaincre qu'elles sont
absolument nécessaires pour élever l'âme. . . . Je
ne saurais m'empêcher de croire que le peuple sans
passions sera le plus heureux et contribuera davantage à
la tranquillité générale." And then she adds with some
malice, " Si vos provinciaux en Amérique, par exemple,
étaient comme les Suisses des montagnes, ils vous don-
neraient bien moins de besogne aujourd'hui. . . .
Vous conviendrez avec moi que s'ils n'étaient que frugal,
laborieux, et sans passions, ils se seraient laissé imposer
les lois par l'Angleterre, qui n'étant point onéreuses ne
peuvent choquer que leur passion de l'indépendance.

" Je vous demande mille pardons. J'étais Bostoni-
enne de cœur. Je le suis un peu moins à présent;
cependant j'ai toutes les peines du monde à me rendre
bonne Anglaise dans cette occasion."—(Luxembourg, 24
Août 1775.)

The Austrian fine ladies were, like their sisters of
Paris, " *Bostoniennes* de cœur ;" but a few more years
of the reign of the reforming Emperor Joseph, and a few
more steps taken in the direction of revolution in France,
sufficed to change the current of their sympathies.

In Munich itself, the dread word Reform was heard
in the current year, and was received by the courtiers
much as the blast of the last trumpet may hereafter
be.

A visit from an Austrian Archduke led to expensive
fêtes at court, and to still more expensive presents.
Though the visitor was grave, taciturn, and shy, " in-

sensible comme un Anglais" to the advances of the
dames de cour, still etiquette required that he should
be made to feast and to dance; not a pearl or a diamond
was left at home when the court assembled to do him
honour, and when he went away, parting gifts of extraordinary splendour were bestowed upon him. Delta's
next letters hint of a day of reckoning. " On fait des
projets d'économie ; M. de Bercheim les conduit tant bien
que mal à leur fin, et tout le monde se borne à le maudire
et à désirer le voir pendre ; nous, femmes de la cour sommes de ce nombre." Again, " Ou veut toujours faire des
Réformes. Oh ! mon Dieu ! que fera t-on de nous ? "

A play (I fail to decipher its name) came out which
attacked the prodigality and corruption of the government and the nobility. Certain well-known anecdotes
were introduced in the dialogue, the house applauded ;
more delicate allusions were loudly interpreted by the
audience. Voices called out " C'est pire que cela, telle
et telle chose a été oubliée, j'ai donné pour ce service là
une bague de 1000 f. ;" and the epigrams of the stage
received their point from the pit. Delta ends this
curious account of a first night by the remark, " On
croit qu'on ne donnera plus cette pièce."

The Court betook itself to prayer :—" À ce point
nous sommes à la devotion, surtout à la cour; bon gré
mal gré il faut prier ! " Was it in an economical mood
that the maids of honour sent to the tailor for an old coat
of the young minister's, with the professed intention of
dividing the velvet and embroidery among themselves—
" Habit de velours, Nacarath—broderie en or ? "

My grandfather returned to Bavaria in the course of June or July, his affairs having been arranged and his health re-established ; and, except during short intervals, he remained there until he finally left the country in the autumn of the following year.

For economical reasons, and perhaps partly too in indulgence of a morbid dislike to society, the life which he now entered upon at Ratisbon[1] [December 1775] was one of such extreme seclusion as to cause much remark and censure among his friends.[2] The economical views which justified it were probably those which he was most anxious to conceal from the public, and, with his usual heedlessness of the opinion of the society in which he lived, he did not, by disguising that he despised it, seek to avoid giving offence. Several of his correspondents at this time condemn his universal

---

[1] He was accredited to the Diet at Ratisbon as representative of the Elector of Hanover.

[2] "I am here," he wrote to his father, "in an inferior position, which requires neither show nor expense. I am master of every minute in the day. . . . That I might be still less liable to interruption, I have taken a small house upon an island in the Danube, where I am fed by the woman it belongs to, without trouble to myself, and at a moderate price. I have already begun the course which I intend to follow as long as I remain here. I rise early about six ; till breakfast I do any business that is necessary. The whole morning till two I am employed in reading, chiefly a plan of study as an introduction to this line, which Lord Stormont gave me at Paris. . . . From two to three I make a solitary dinner. From three to five I have German and fencing masters, and then I walk, ride, or drive about the hills and woods that surround us till dusk, when I go into the Danube ; and after that I walk about my island, and am often with you and my family."—13th August 1775.

scepticism. "You are too hard on the fair sex," says one. "I had rather not be so clear-sighted as to men's motives," says another. It was a phase of feeling which most men pass through. Self-deceived even more than deceived by others, they have still to learn that life will reflect their own image—"as in water face answereth to face, so the heart of man to man."

While a young man does not pay his debts, all men are rogues to him; while he makes love to twenty women, the faithlessness of the sex will be his favourite theme.

It must have been in a sanguine mood that Hugh Elliot, from his retirement at Ratisbon, wrote to various friends at Munich, in the hope of firing them with the charms of philosophy. To Delta especially he seems to have urged the great superiority of friendship over love. "Distinguons" is easily said, but under certain circumstances it requires a strong head and a subtle wit to do it.

She replied: "Vous êtes vraiment singulier! bien éloignée de vous taxer d'impolitesse, votre lettre et la belle franchise qui y règne m'a fait beaucoup de plaisir; du reste, j'oubliais de vous faire des remerciments des conseils que vous me donnez. Je les trouve grands et beaux, et vous avez raison; mais on s'ennuie parfois avec toutes ces combinaisons. Excusez si je vous dis que vos réflexions sont une suite de votre départ." At all events, if she was to take up philosophy, she wished to hear him philosophise. "Que je voudrais vous entendre discourir; quelles réflexions!

quelle variété! et tout cela avec Liston, votre chien et les champs pour les seuls auditeurs."

His retirement at Ratisbon provoked two excellent letters from Countess Thun.

"Je suis résolue de vous gronder, et cela tout de bon. Allons, justifiez vous. Vivez-vous comme un ours ? pourquoi fuyez-vous le monde ? pourquoi vivez-vous comme une taupe dans un trou ? Pourquoi maltraitez-vous les femmes ? que vous ont elles donc fait ces pauvres femmes ? vous ne les haïssiez pas trop autrefois ! Pourquoi cachez-vous les talens que le ciel vous a donnés ; et enfin, pourquoi n'êtes-vous plus cet aimable garçon d'autrefois? Si c'est humeur, il ne faut pas se la passer ; si c'est mélancolie, il faut faire un effort pour s'en tirer ; si c'est chagrin, il faut se dissiper ; si c'est une passion tendre, c'est trop : fi ! je ne veux pas seulement le croire, il faut une raison plus essentielle et plus sérieuse pour un changement comme celui-là."

Mr. Elliot must have replied to this letter by a statement of the pecuniary difficulties which had made it incumbent on him to withdraw from the expenses of society, for, in a letter dated December 14, 1775, after congratulating herself on having drawn from him a confidence so honourable to him, she proceeds to give him some excellent advice on the necessity of making his system of economy compatible with the other requirements of his daily life, since "le moyen d'une retraite absolue" is not always within one's power, though no doubt more agreeable to a young man's humour than a constant carefulness in the management of his expenses.

To his misanthropical objections to society, she also replies with no less good sense (Vienua, 1775) :—

" Je ne prétends pas que vous voyïez le monde avec les mêmes yeux dont vous l'avez vu avant de le connaître,—il est impossible d'être longtemps la dupe de son néant. . . . Mais que diriez-vous d'un acteur qui se trouvant sur la scène s'occuperait de l'illusion au lieu de remplir son esprit et son cœur de son rôle ? Chacun se doit à soi-même et aux autres de jouer son rôle de son mieux tant qu'il est sur la scène, . . . Rien n'est plus dangereux pour un jeune homme avec votre esprit, votre cœur et vos talens, que ce système d'indifférence. Il l'est d'autant plus, que vous sentant par l'élévation de vos sentimens, et par le mépris de ce qui fait l'objet des désirs du commun des hommes, au-dessus du reste de l'humanité, vous ne vous en défiez pas !

" Quand on ne trouve rien dans ce globe digne de la peine de l'étreindre, quand on raisonne lorsqu'on devrait agir, quand on laisse éteindre ses passions plutôt que de les diriger, et qu'alors on manque de l'aiguillon que la Nature nous a donné pour nous faire agir, on reste dans une inaction qui finit par nous rendre coupable. Et c'est là où vos raisonnements vous conduiront insensiblement. Je suis de votre avis qu'un homme qui se sacrifie au désir de se faire une réputation est bien la dupe ; mais je crois aussi qu'il y a une sorte d'ambition qu'il ne faut jamais laisser éteindre en soi,—celle d'être utile à ses semblables. Ce but là est grand par soi-même, et mérite bien la peine de s'en occuper. Quand aux femmes, vous pensez bien que je ne vous en parlerai pas sérieusement. J'en demande pardon à mon sexe, mais j'aime bien mieux qu'on ne parle à aucune que de s'occuper uniquement de toutes. Je ne connais rien dans la nature plus méprisable qu'un homme qui en fait son unique affaire."

Of an indifference to fame, or an unreadiness to seek it in active exertion, Hugh Elliot could not be accused; his mistake lay in supposing that he could only usefully serve his country in one way, and that way one which was not open to him. Either while in Switzerland, or soon after his return to Germany, he had communicated privately to Lord Suffolk his ardent desire to join the army in America as a volunteer.

Believing that his knowledge of foreign languages and of foreign armies might make him useful in acting with the foreign contingent, he begged that if his services could be made available, he might on any terms rejoin his old profession.

Lord Suffolk's answer is most kind. (Private, August 1775.)

" The personal activity with which you are eager to support the cause of Great Britain does you the greatest honour, and I must request you not to think me insensible to the spirit which animates you on this occasion, if I attempt to check the zeal of it at present, and advise you to defer, at least, the execution of the ideas it has suggested. I don't say that the time may not come when such an example as you propose may be of essential service; if it should, I will join with you in laying aside all other considerations, and recommend it to you to set it. But at this moment I should not act with the regard I feel for you if I did not dissuade you from quitting the walk you are in, in which you do so well, and are so likely to be advanced."

In the following spring Hugh again repeated his desire to join the army, and was again with equal kindness dissuaded from doing so by Lord Suffolk. By this time, however, his intentions and wishes had reached his family, and had naturally excited their warm opposition, and apparently the matter soon afterwards dropped.

Sir Gilbert's letters on the subject show more impatience of his son's Quixotism than of sympathy with his feelings. His mother warns him that the cause of his country would not be much advanced by his losing an arm or a leg; while Mr. Eden,[1] already a friend and soon to become a relation, writes as follows :—

"I fully feel with you that the period is come when the noble enthusiasm of individuals in the Old World is the only weapon that can be brandished with success against the mad multitude of the New, but your father sees and thinks that there are spirited Britons enough still left to answer the national purposes, without his hazarding a son who has too fair a prospect in his present line of life to turn from it without some more pressing exigency than yet exists."

The mania of volunteering for the army appears to have seized at the same moment upon all the young

---

[1] William Eden, Esq., Private Secretary to Lord Suffolk. He married, in the autumn of 1776, Eleanor Elliot, Hugh's youngest sister, and in 1789 was created Lord Auckland.

Englishmen who had spent the winter of 1774 or 1775 at Munich together. One of them, Mr. Stanley,[1] did accompany his uncle, General Burgoyne, to America; the rest were obliged by their families to content themselves with vain aspirations after "distinctions to be earned on Bunker's Hill."

Lord Lindsay, the only son of the Duke of Ancaster, was one of those most bent on volunteering for the army. He was prevented from doing so by the commands of his father and the tears of his mother; while Hugh Elliot, who was supposed to have inoculated him with the obnoxious idea, was reproached bitterly by his own family for having countenanced so wild and senseless a plan. The parents of Lord Lindsay might have seen cause to reconsider their determination could they have read the letters written about their son by his mentor and companions at this time. That an active profession was the only chance of saving him from a wasted and disgraceful life was an opinion shared by all.

Madame de Thun, who had become acquainted with Lord Lindsay at Vienna, prays that when her son grows up, she may not be so blind to his real interest as "cette pauvre Duchesse." Mr. Brydone, in one of several letters from Vienna, thanks my grandfather for having inspired Lord Lindsay with some of that "generous and noble patriotic zeal which you alone seem capable of communicating to all who converse with you. . . . Till he had the good fortune to meet with you, I always dreaded that pleasure would have been the

---

[1] General Burgoyne had married Lady Charlotte Stanley.

only pursuit of his life; you have convinced him of the extreme insipidity and contemptibleness of such a character."

Madame de Thun's wise advice had fallen on good ground, and was bringing forth fruit.

The summer of 1776 was probably the most agreeable which my grandfather had passed since his arrival in Germany. At Ratisbon he became intimate with a coterie of pleasant people, of whom the Count[1] and Countess Neipperg formed the centre. Count Neipperg represented Bohemia in the Diet; he was afterwards, for many years, Austrian Minister at Naples, and was well known as a cultivated agreeable man; his wife, young, pretty, and by all accounts of most engaging manners, was supposed by the fair ladies of Ratisbon to have some share in drawing forth " le sauvage Elliot " from his retirement. However that may have been, he became the life and soul of *the set*. Many pleasant meetings took place at the Neippergs' country-house at Stauff; and, when these were over, and my grandfather was recalled to England, "in order," as Lord Suffolk wrote to him privately, " that he might be intrusted with affairs of greater importance, his Majesty having been so well satisfied with his previous conduct," we learn much of the regrets his absence caused, from the letters of Mr. Liston, and of the Marquis Louis d'Yve, a near

---

[1] His sister was the celebrated Princess of Auersperg, who, for many years, was the object of the devotions of the Emperor Francis; the last act of his life had been to give her a draft on the Royal Treasury for 20,000 francs; the first act of Maria Theresa's widowhood was to confirm it.

relation of the Neippergs, and not an unfrequent correspondent of my grandfather in after years.

Mr. Liston, who, from being tutor, secretary, and adviser, had now become the confidant of a sentimental correspondence, writes with most amusing distress to the volatile Minister of the difficulty he had in inventing probable excuses for his chief, when post after post arrived without any letters for a certain lady; while, on the contrary, *hers* were so heavy and frequent, that Mr. Liston was obliged to take them out of their covers— "though, on my honour, I don't read a word"—and even then the postage was ruinous!

Again, the lady *would* learn English, and *ce bon* Liston was made to undertake the part of instructor. "I should not so much mind," said he, "if the husband" (who was a literary character) "were not always present, puzzling me with questions about grammar."

On one occasion an archery *fête* was held at Stauff, and, as a delicate compliment to England, the target was made to represent an American, "revêtu de toutes les marques distinctives dont vos ennemis se sont décorés," and the fair Countess herself had the good fortune to knock down the head—a feat which afforded no small pleasure to her, and some amusement to her guests. The scene was retailed in a letter by Mr. Liston to my grandfather, and he adds, "They overwhelm me with the most flattering distinctions, which, however, lead me into many expenses." Poor Mr. Liston! neither loving nor beloved, his place was no

sinecure. He had to remonstrate, to moderate, to
excuse, to write, to teach, and to pay! Whatever
scrapes his chief got into, *il laissait rédiger les pièces
justificatives* by his secretary. And he did not even
stop there, for he often required his friend to hold out
to others the helping hand so readily extended to himself. The despatches which passed through the British
legation, and reached their final destination under the
protecting seals of England, were by no means confined
to political subjects. " Nineteen in a week from the
Prince to his *chère* Caroline are too much !" wrote the
greatly harassed Liston; but there was worse behind.
It was one thing to receive them, another to find an
opportunity for passing them on to their rightful
owners. And when on one occasion they were greatly
in arrear, the lady, accompanied by a chaperon, came in
person to make inquiries of the minister, who was in
the confidence of both parties. " To my horror," said
Liston, " as you were not there, I had to appear, and to
confess being in the secret ; however, they did not seem
to mind at all, and urged on me the importance of
immediately forwarding all that should pass through
my hands; and if it were not for my age and figure,
I really might think that the old one was inclined to
make up *to me*. I am not so fastidious as you, but *that*
I can't stand !"

The writers of the letters were personages of sufficient importance to make the confidence a doubtful
advantage—the gentleman being the Prince Max de
Deux Ponts (afterwards King of Bavaria), who, by all

accounts, was "frantically in love;" and the lady a beautiful young married woman of a noble Bavarian family.

Various circumstances, and among others the jealousy of her husband, who determined to carry her off to the country, invested this affair with an unusual degree of interest. It is alluded to in all the letters :—" Le Prince Max est fou de la jeune P.; tous les jours nouvelles scènes; toute l'illustre famille électorale s'agite; le mari est jaloux à l'excès, tout le monde est soupçonné de faire des rapports." At last the prince was ordered to rejoin his regiment in garrison at Strasburg, and the parting scene appears to have taken place in public, for an eye-witness says, "He was beside himself, and, but for the assistants, would have fallen on his sword."

The writer, an English traveller, had himself been much struck with the same lady, but, discouraged from all thoughts of further rivalry by the scene at which he had assisted, he quietly withdrew to Vienna, from whence he wrote to his friend that "he felt himself a pitiful ass for having stayed so long."

Towards the end of the summer of 1776 Hugh Elliot's first mission came to an end, and Mr. Morton Eden " reigned in his stead;" the latter made his *début* at Munich with great success; the people pronounced him "*engel-schön*," and the *dames de cour* smiled graciously on one who promised to be less indifferent to their charms than his predecessor had been.

I wish, for the sake of my grandfather's reputation

for politeness, I could have ended this chapter of his
history without mentioning a trait, which is, however,
too characteristic to be omitted.   " How could you,"
says his friend Mr. Pitt, writing to him some time afterwards, " think yourself justified in telling your Munich
friends that the day of your departure was the happiest
of your life ?   Was it not unnecessary to make a round
of visits for that purpose ? "

NOTE.—On his way through Paris my grandfather visited Madame
du Deffand, and thus she writes of him to Horace Walpole :—" Le
petit Elliot est tout-à-fait aimable ; il a beaucoup d'esprit, il sent
encore un peu l'école, mais c'est qu'il est modeste, et qu'il est la
contre partie de Charles Fox ; la sorte de timidité qu'il a encore sied
bien à son âge ; surtout quand elle n'empêche pas qu'on en démêle le
bon sens et l'esprit."—*Corres. de Madame du Deffand.*

CHAPTER THE SECOND.

1772 to 1777.

THE FAMILY.

I HAVE now brought down the narrative of my grandfather's early life to the period of his return to England
and the close of his first mission, in the autumn of 1776,
and in doing so I have confined myself solely to that
portion of his correspondence which bears directly upon
his affairs. It will therefore be desirable, before going
any further, to cast a backward glance over the other
portion of the letters now before me—that which relates
to the circumstances of his correspondents. An additional reason for doing so, before entering on another
year, consists in the changes which occurred in the
family in the early part of 1777, and which amounted to
a break-up of the family home.

When, in 1771, Hugh "tore himself from his mother's
arms," as she expresses it, "to seek honourable employment in a foreign land," the family group had already
lost one of its members by the departure of Alick for
India, which had taken place some time before; but there
still remained under the paternal roof-tree two sons and
two daughters. Gilbert, the eldest, was pursuing his

studies at Oxford. Bob was a Westminster school-boy. Isabella, a young lady going out in the world, was the delight of her mother's life. Eleanor, a wild young girl, called by her brothers by many *aliases*, was studying French, with no great success, under the charge of Madame Dumont, and setting all rules of English grammar and orthography at defiance.

It could not be expected that Sir Gilbert's letters to a son under the age of twenty would contain any confidential communications on political matters. Nor do they. But there are indications in the general correspondence of his political influence having suffered some diminution about this time, or rather before it.

Horace Walpole, in his last Journals, under the date of February 1773, mentions Sir Gilbert Elliot as the man " whom the King most trusted, next to Lord Bute, but who nevertheless had been acting discontent for the last two years." He also frequently alludes to misunderstandings between Sir Gilbert and Lord North, and on one occasion describes a popular vote of Sir Gilbert's, on which he divided the House against Ministers, as a revenge for Lord Barrington's refusal to give a commission in the army to one of his sons.

This theory is not, however, consistent with two others equally put forward by Walpole. *First,* That Sir Gilbert, in opposing Lord North, was acting secretly by the King's instigation. *Second,* That military patronage was entirely at the disposal of the King. For it is obvious that, had Sir Gilbert's influence with the King at this time been so great as Walpole supposed it, he

would not have met with the treatment from Lord
Barrington, by which he thought himself so much
aggrieved.

Certain allusions in the letters rather lead one to
suppose that the King himself may have been somewhat
cool in the matter of Hugh's commission, and that when
the latter left England, his father's position at Court
was not what it had been. At all events, there can be
no doubt that Sir Gilbert saw in the refusal of Lord
Barrington to nominate his son to a captaincy in the
Guards, a studied insult to himself, and a triumph to
his enemies. It was " a party move," as indeed every
question affecting a " Scot" was sure to be considered
in those days. Lady Elliot not only shared in her husband's feelings, but was still more sensitive to the hard-
ship of parting with her promising and brilliant son, at
a moment when she had believed him to be about to
enter an honourable career in the service of his country ;
this distress bore all the harder upon her because she
was at the time suffering from ill health, and smarting
under the disappointment of a hope she had conceived
of seeing her eldest daughter suitably married. Many a
long letter did she write to her absent son on the subject
of her grievances.

" These things give me a disgust to the world that I
can hardly overcome, but yet am chained to the oar, and
called upon to drag still into public a dispirited tor-
mented mind. I can seldom go anywhere without
meeting persons and objects mortifying to me. Lord
Barrington—faugh ! my soul rises at him !—is very

studious to make up to me when we meet, which politeness I return with equal politeness, although I see an
evident sneer on the face of a false heart. What a farce
is this world !"[1]

Again she writes, "One sees one's-self, from faction
and narrow jealousy, an object of universal ill-will, and
no support from any quarter except the talents of a
person however in some degree upon the decline." Lady
Elliot's style, like her feelings, was vehement, and that
her family did not share in the latter to their fullest
extent, is evident from another passage in the same
letter, in which she says, "You know the characters of
your father and brother's philosophic minds so well as
to know that they cannot enter into nor understand
what agitates me; their affections are equal to mine,
but their imaginations are not so sensible, and they often
do not perceive, or do not care for, what agitates me."

This assertion is partly justified by the very concise
manner in which Gilbert informs his brother of the event
that had so wrung his mother's spirit—namely, the marriage of Isabella's faithless adorer to another lady. "Mr.
R.'s marriage gives us all great satisfaction. My sister
is glad he is out of her way;" and in the autumn of the
same year, he rejoices that an alarm of opposition to Sir
Gilbert in the county was to carry them all to Minto,
and would give Lady Elliot an occupation she was better
fitted for than that of match-making. A few months
more sufficed to give her some of her children's philosophy; and, alluding to her once desired son-in-law, she

[1] Lády Elliot to Hugh, 1772.

F

barely admits "that he *might* have made a good husband, though corpulent and a money-worm."

The summer of 1772 was a melancholy one in England and Scotland, owing to the numerous failures of
banks, among which that of Fordyce was the most felt.
Dismal are the scenes described. "Not a workman to
be seen in the Adelphi, the Adams having stopped payment. For some days everybody alarmed and suspicious,
and the run on the banks so great that it was a wonder
any of them stood it." In the midst of these dreary
descriptions it is refreshing to find Isabella writing
cheerily of her London amusements.[1] "The Opera is
still good, though the departure of Madame Heinel half
broke the maccaronis' hearts. The pleasantest thing
we have done was a water-party to Richmond in papa's
barge. We dined there, and walked and drank tea.
We had Banks and Solander,[2] and their music, that, if
they had gone round the world, would have gone with
them. At Richmond we met another party, with your
friend Colonel Harcourt and his music, and we joined
parties and went together to Vauxhall. We stopped at
Kew, and serenaded the Prince of Wales. Solander is
very happy that he is not sure of going his voyage,
though he does not dare say so. They have quarrelled
with Captain Cook, who goes in the ' Resolution.'"

The autumn found the family at Minto, where they
were joined by Gilbert in time for the Kelso races; he

---

[1] Isabella to Hugh, June 23.

[2] Sir Joseph Banks and Dr. Solander, both eminent naturalists,
accompanied Captain Cook on his first voyage round the world (1768).

making his journey from Scarborough in a collier, which
was unable to make the Tyne at Newcastle, and landed
him and a friend on the Durham coast.

While in the north, Lady Elliot and some of the
family went to Edinburgh to see the Dowager Lady
Elliot, who died in the following year; and from thence
Lady Elliot writes thus characteristically of the society
to her son Hugh :—

"The misses are, I am afraid, the most rotten part
of the society. Envy and jealousy of their rivals have,
I fear, a possession in their minds, especially the old part
of the young ladies, who grow perfect beldames in that
small society; but upon the whole there are many worthy,
agreeable, well-principled people, if you get over the language, manner, and address, which are at first striking."

Early in 1773 we find Lady Elliot writing again from
London. As I have already said, Sir Gilbert was taking
an active part in Parliament, and one not always friendly
to Lord North; but the kind letters of Lord Stormont
respecting Hugh, and the active friendship of Lord
Suffolk, were producing kindly civilities on the part of
the King; and before the summer Sir Gilbert wrote to
his son that it was intended to send him Plenipotentiary
to Munich. The letters from Sir R. Gunning and Mr.
Wroughton, which were addressed to the Foreign Office
in London, and made such gratifying mention of Hugh's
military exploits, were read by the family at Minto with
equal pride and rejoicing; and before the winter arrived
they had had the happiness of welcoming him to England,
and of embracing him again in his London home.

At that time Hugh was clearly his mother's favourite
son; "the joy of my life, the friend of my heart," as she
frequently calls him; "planted firmly in the hearts of
all;" and all the dearer to her, perhaps, because not all
her pride in the parts and character of her eldest son
could ever make her overlook his habits of silence and
reserve, which were probably increased in her presence
by her utter absence of self-control. In the course of
1773 he was entered at Lincoln's Inn, and, his mother
tells us, was highly popular there, "where prepossession
in a man's favour is nine points of the game." No
doubt that during the following winter both the brothers
entered fully into the amusements and follies of the
town, for their subsequent correspondence has many a
reference to those "merry days," with no less frequent reflections on the drain they had inflicted on
" *the Rhino.*"

From the correspondence which recommenced on
Hugh's departure for Munich, early in 1774, we gather
that the well-known figure of the young maccaroni riding
a long-tailed pony in the park had been sketched by
Lord Townshend for the benefit of his pretty new wife,
and that she carried it about in her work-bag, though
not deeming it "prudent" to let her young adorer have
a copy of her own portrait. Miss Walter, the great
"fortune," afterwards Lady Grimston,[1] had been much
touched by the sight of Hugh's dejection on bidding her

---

[1] James, third Viscount Grimston, married, 28th July 1774, Harriet,
only daughter and heiress of Edward Walter, Esq., of Stalbridge,
county Dorset.

good-bye, though " she was not so romantic as I should
have been," said Lady Elliot, " and preferred a rich peer
to a young envoy ;" but " Miss" somebody else " would
really have done for you, and made you a rich good
wife, if you had not been determined to say she was
crooked and squinted, before you looked at her."   His
" old flames" the Duchesses of Northumberland and of
Queensberry, " the latter beautiful and coquettish as
ever," are mentioned as frequently inquiring for him,
and so too did the King and Queen.   " No one ever
left so many friends," said his mother.   " We are certainly the happiest family in the world in ourselves," wrote
his sister, " but I think of all I love you and my mother
best ;" and Gilbert in the same strain says,—" I lose in
your absence, my dear Hugh, more than anything you
have left behind can make up—a true friend and almost
the only companion I perfectly love.   We have all lost
a great deal of cheerfulness, and all know it will not
return till it brings you with it."

Yet, in spite of all this love and praise, Lady Elliot's
first letter after her son's departure for Munich shows
that she was not blind to the defects which threatened
to obscure his many remarkable qualities.   Love—true
love—is never blind; quick to see the first germ of
good, it is no less quick to discern the quarter whence
danger may come to the thing beloved.   It is the triumph
of love *not* to love blindly, but knowing all, seeing all,
to love on, through all, and in spite of all.

Writing to Hugh from Minto, July 28, 1774, his
mother tells him she had begun to write letters to him,

which on reflection she had destroyed, but that she was now determined, once for all, to enter fully, to him, into her ideas of his character, and of the dangers his peculiar temperament would expose him to, sparing neither praise nor blame, "for I have never known an ingenuous mind the worse for praise, nor a candid one for blame;" and she then proceeds to draw and to contrast two ideal portraits of a young man who, possessed of certain good qualities and defects, rose, in the one case, by overcoming his faults, to the height of fortune, and, in the other, by want of the same powers of self-control, disappointed all the expectations which had been formed of him.

The letter is too long to transcribe, and has all the peculiar faults of Lady Elliot's style—exaggeration in expression and a redundancy of words—but it is the production of a clever woman and of a tender mother. The picture she gives of Hugh is distinct. Slight and slim of figure, with handsome features and a spirited countenance, his appearance pleased, even before his lively wit and soft and gentle manners confirmed the first impression. Cultivated in mind, and possessing all manly accomplishments, he had made himself "a name in courts and camps before attaining his fifth lustrum," and yet remained the "best of sons and brothers, and the most romantic of lovers."

But now comes *le revers de médaille*, and we are told of the possibility that this uncommon character might "be rendered useless by a want of economy which ruined his affairs; by giving himself up to the indulgence of ridiculing characters that he despised;

by neglecting the common forms of civility and attentions, as visits, letters, etc., and yielding to an
hereditary sauntering, *alias* indolence, which prevented
him from cultivating his talents—led him to lie in bed
in the morning—to lounge undressed till near dinner-
time (as is practised at Horsman's coffee-house, Oxford)
—to dress in a hurry, and be too late for dinner—to
neglect his accounts and bills, by which his family and
affairs went into confusion, his despatches were neglected, and his friends at home disgusted.   Having
formed his taste for characters that are rarely to be met
with, the same want of self-restraint led him to be openly
impatient of others of a different cast, and to show them
a repulsive coldness; thus he contracted an *ennui* that
blasted all the promises of fortune."

It is remarkable that this letter, which was written
in July 1774, a month after Hugh's arrival at Munich,
anticipates every charge which was afterwards brought
against him during his residence there, by relatives at
home or friends on the spot.[1]

Other passages in the same letter show that an idle
winter in London had not been unattended with ill
effects, and that his mother rejoiced over his removal
from "that noxious nest," where frivolity and extravagance were the order of the day, and his brother
maccaronis—"the absurd puppies of the age"—were
given over to gaming and vice.

While Lady Elliot was taking advantage of the

<hr/>

[2] See the letters of Sir Gilbert, of Mr. Liston, Mr. Pitt, Madame de
Thun, 1775-76.

retirement of Minto to give good counsel to her son, Isabella was deploring that he was not with them "to partake of our dancing to a bagpipe, and the charming sweet sounds of backgammon and billiards, and the magic-lantern, which are our devices this summer for passing the evening when we have company, which, after a good ride in the morning, and a good dinner, prepare for a comfortable sleep at night." Kelso races were particularly brilliant that year. In those days the dwellers on the southern Border seem to have frequented them as regularly as the inhabitants of the four counties (Roxburghshire, the Merse, the Forest, and Tweeddale), the Northumberlands and Delavals being as constant attendants as the Buccleuchs, Douglasses, Kerrs, and Elliots.

Parliament was dissolved in October, and, before the new one had assembled, the family left Minto, none of them ever to return, except Gilbert, whose home it was to be, and Isabella, who went there once only, and for a very short period, on a visit to her brother. It does not appear that any of them, except, perhaps, Sir Gilbert himself, entertained any affection for the place, and the ladies certainly considered that going down there "was a great breach in society." The love of Minto, which we now guard like some hereditary spell, came in with a stranger, for Gilbert's wife was the first who is said to have "loved Minto passionately."

But the Minto of those days was not the Minto of these. The sheet of water which now reflects labur-

nums and rhododendrons in sight of the windows, was
then a narrow burn running under banks shaggy with
thorns; where the flower-garden is now, stood a dismal
little church in a corner dark with yews, and dreary
with unkept graves; the manse, surrounded by a few
untidy cottages, overlooked the little glen, and was
near enough to the house for the minister to see the
family as they sat at dinner in the round room on the
ground-floor, known as the "big room" by uncles and
aunts, and as the "*school-room*" by the children of to-
day. The rocks may have been finer then when no
woods hung like drapery on their sides, but from the
old castle one must have looked down on muirs and
heaths where now lie the woods of the Lamblairs, or
the green slopes and corn-fields which smile in pleasant
Teviotdale.

The green hills are possibly the only feature in the
place which remain unchanged, though the village which
clusters at their feet is new.

In those days roads were few, and drains were not,
and the dwellers in a land where high farming triumphs
will sometimes lament the days when fences were odious
and turnips undiscovered. Yet, on the whole, though
sunny days may then have shown bright stretches of
whin or of heather which have disappeared now, we
must admit that we live on a drier soil, and in a more
"innerlie" country, and have a greater variety of cheerful pleasures than fell to the lot of our forefathers; so
peace be to their ashes! even though they did not care
for Minto.

The meeting of Parliament in December 1774 had, as I have said, assembled the family in town. Gilbert, who had taken his first fee at Durham in the preceding summer, was now steadily applying to law, and Isabella is the chief chronicler of the amusements and *on dits* of the town during the ensuing season.[1] "There are forty young Etonians in the new Parliament, and about 170 new faces. Bob, the waiter at White's, is chosen for the same place with Mr. Wedderburn, upon which Lord Suffolk said, he made no doubt they would make a very distinguished figure, being both *bred to the Bar*."

On the 20th February 1775, we find in Walpole's Journal[2] that Lord North astounded the House by a proposal of conceding to the Americans the right of taxing themselves, such taxes to be revised by the Legislature at home; this last clause, however, to be merely formal. Walpole describes the debate very graphically, and his account is confirmed in most particulars by the letters. Lady Elliot says, "Sir Gilbert's part was much applauded. . . . I fancy the measure will be abused in the long-run, according to the present spirit of the nation; and for my own part, I am persuaded, though every means should be taken to prevent the English and Americans from destroying each other, that this is much too crude and hasty a concession not to have the appearance, on the other side of the world, of fear, and therefore will make them ten times more refractory than ever."

"The King does not like this new *piano* opera. He,

like you, has more taste for the bravura songs : but I hate them, and am glad to hear *cantabile,* for I hate hissing and cat-calls. Lord Suffolk sings loud in the chorus of the *piano* piece ; his first secretary, the handsome one (Eden), has been much about Lord North of late."[1]

The Opera occupies a larger space than Parliament in the letters of the sisters.[2] "There is a new opera of Rauzzini's composing, which is the prettiest music I ever heard, upon the story of Pyramus and Thisbe, which is very much admired. He sings and acts admirably, and all the ladies who have any feeling cry at it. I should also have been much affected if I had not unluckily sat behind Beckie Scott,[3] who *sospirid and piangered* so much, and wet her handkerchief so plentifully, that I was like to die with laughing at the time Rauzzini was in the agonies of death. And you must not be angry, but I assure you Lord Stormont turned quite pale, which also diverted my obdurate heart. Fop's Alley was also much moved, so you may with truth assure his friends at Munich, he, like Orpheus, can move oaks and stones with the divine powers of harmony."

Lord Stormont's unreturned passion for Lady Henrietta Stanhope,[4] is alluded to in the published memoirs of the time, and very frequently in this correspondence. "There is no describing," wrote Lady Elliot, "how ridiculous such a passion is in this dispassionate town, where

---

[1] This letter is partly in cipher.   [2] Isabella to Hugh, May 1775.
[3] She afterwards ran away with her music-master. See Walpole's last Journals, vol. i. "A most dismal marriage," wrote Isabella.
[4] Daughter of Lord Harrington, married to Mr. Foley.

genuine serious persevering love never appears;" and then ever keen to feel a slight put upon her friend, and plain-spoken in the expression of it, she pronounces the lady " a sailing peacock, and an insufferable rigid coquette, who made a jest of the poor soul to her feather-headed companions."

In the same letter, intended, as the writer said, to amuse and not to instruct, we learn that " the town was in its usual state as to amusements, gaming, and extravagance this winter. A new married duchess has been the observed of all observers. The newspapers have handled her much too roughly on account of her dress, which is only fantastical; she is giddy and beautiful, and her mother, a woman of unexampled qualities, tries to restrain her, but she has given herself up to the guidance of the club ladies. There was an intention of a play being to be acted when all the fine ladies and gentlemen were to perform. There was to have been a grand ballet in which the Duchess of D., Lady B. Stanley, Lady Jersey, Lady Melbourne, Lady Cranbourne, Mrs. Hubert, etc., were to have showed off, but friends and husbands interposed. The same people, with the two Royal Dukes, are to have a great *fête* on the river the 5th of June. It is to be a race of boats; twelve small boats, just large enough to keep above water and to contain two men, are to sail from Westminster Bridge, and to row against one another, and it is thought they will go sixteen miles an hour. All the city barges are now painting and decorating for it, and the different trades are to have barges with pageants. The whole is to end in a masquerade at Ranelagh. It will cost an immense sum, but nobody knows how it is to be paid; in short, never were people so foolish as in the great world just now; but, thank God! it does not seem to spread below a certain set, who are laughed at by the rest of the world."

When in June the boat-race took place, Isabella wrote —" Alas! for the first time for three weeks, to the utter distress of beaux, belles, and watermen, the evening was blowing and cloudy, and at about seven o'clock, when the boats were to set off, a violent shower of rain came down."

Then, as now, all London talked for weeks of *fêtes*, which, when they came to pass, were voted " the stupidest thing imaginable." Nightly at Ranelagh 4000 people met; 5000 tickets were issued for one night's admission to the Pantheon, to hear a woman sing, whose voice had a greater range than the harpsichord. Masquerades, private balls, and regattas, for the amusement of the two Royal Dukes, occupied the world of fashion, and " we had some very good parties ourselves," at one of which, " a little private party," Franky North personated the young Lady Sutherland, just arrived from the north, and " so well, that your friend Cadogan was quite taken in, and made up to the fortune, till all of a sudden Franky gave a great Westminster halloo, to poor Cadogan's extreme confusion."

While the sisters, and chiefly Isabella, were writing to their brother on such topics as these, his parents found painful matter of correspondence in the condition of Hugh's affairs, which became known to them at this time. Anxiety for his health also disturbed his mother's mind, and when to these causes of disturbance were added the flight of a clerk from Sir Gilbert's office, with a sum of £10,000, for which he became liable, and the grave and threatening aspect of political affairs, which in Sir Gilbert's opinion made the existence of the Ministry very doubtful, it is not to be wondered at that the letters of the parents in no wise partook of the cheerful tone of their children.

" As to the house in general," wrote Sir Gilbert,[1] " I should not be surprised if they were soon obliged to break up altogether. The want of foresight, management, etc., has been terrible. As to your old dog Boatswain,[2] he is as fat and lazy as ever; he does very well to keep the hall, and has a good tongue there, but is not fit for the field.

" Gage returns; Howe gets the command; the ships are in great forwardness. I can't say so much for the army. Your old friend[3] sticks to rules, tape, and packthread. Procrastination is the ruin of business; dispatch in everything is half the battle. Enthusiasm and vigour prevail abroad, and they have certainly officers.

" Our troops have been too few, and their conduct what you see. So we always begin; perhaps things may mend."

Turning to his son's affairs, he says—" The only difficulty you have to struggle with is money, and that is a great one. Your total ignorance of its value, and of what it would do at your first setting out, has been not only a great loss to you, but I am afraid will be felt

---

[1] 31st August 1775.   [2] Lord North.   [3] Lord Barrington.

by you through much of the career you have still to
run.   It is most difficult to recover what might have
been easily saved.   A profuse indulgence to worthless
servants is the most thankless and least creditable of all
expenses—it would ruin a prince.

"Your coming to your present situation so young
wants nothing but a resolute manly forbearance for one
or two years, to render your future progress most prosperous and comfortable.   Foreign situations yield enough
to subsist on, and to act too, but not to represent the
country as they ought; but the country must see to that
—the individual gets no thanks for ruining himself.

"I pray God may bless you, and that many great
and amiable talents may not lose their effect by the want
of a few vulgar and ordinary ones; but of all mistakes
none can be greater than to become poor for fear of being thought so.   Depend upon it, something is always
wrong when a man is ashamed of his real situation, and
seeks to hide it."

The pleasantest feature in the family correspondence
at this date is the delight with which all hail the successful *début* of Gilbert Elliot at the bar.   Every letter
from home dilates upon it, and Hugh's answers are full
of joy and affection.   Lady Elliot tells it very characteristically to Mr. Liston, in a letter which he describes as
filling thirteen pages, " beautifully written."

"I know," she says, " the pleasure it will give you
to learn the success my son has had in his first appearance in his profession.   He has given a rare instance of
resolution in withdrawing himself from the pursuits of

the world to those of the most persevering study.   When
it came to the point, you may believe I had much trepi-
dation, although I had always comforted myself that if
he failed in this, it would be the first thing that ever he
failed in that he attempted in his life; yet, as I had so
seldom heard him speak, I had some degree of doubt of
the rapidity of his tongue and the strength of his voice.
But I was soon relieved with a note from Sir John Dalrymple, saying, ' *Thanks to the Gods ! the boy has done
his duty;*' to which was added, ' *The De'il a fears o'
him;*' to which I answered, ' *Son of Æmilius, and thy
cousin*[1] *Paulus, he must do more, and by the Gods he
will !*'   He is now deemed a counsel learned in the law.
He is greatly encouraged by his success, and firmly
rooted in the ground on which his ancestors on both
sides flourished."

Sir Gilbert's account is not less full; and Isabella writes
that her father's anxiety was greater than her brother's.

The summer of 1775 found the ladies of the family
at Tunbridge Wells.   From thence they wrote long and
characteristic letters to the absent Hugh.

---

[1] In one of Hugh's early letters to his mother, he congratulates
himself on having inherited through her the "Dalrympian gift of
rhetoric !" Sir John Dalrymple and Lady Elliot were cousins. Her
father, Hew Dalrymple, second son of the Honourable Sir David
Dalrymple of Hailes, Lord Advocate, and grandson of the first Viscount
Stair, Lord President, had assumed the names of Murray-Kynnynmound,
on his succession to the estates of his nephew Sir Alexander Murray
Kynnynmound, of Melgund, etc., who died without issue. Lady Elliot-
Murray-Kynnynmound was the only child of Hew Dalrymple by his
marriage with Isabella second daughter of Hugh Somerville, of the house
of Cambusnethan.—See *Douglas's Peerage*, edit. 1813, vol. ii. p. 525.

" I live at home at my ease," says Lady Elliot,[1] " with
good sensible old women with whom this place abounds.
Among them is Mrs. Carter, the translator of Epictetus,
a being full of piety and virtue; and before I finish the
subject of the society here, I must tell you that there is
an old friend of yours who resides about a mile from the
Wells with his mother, who makes the soul of all assemblies or companies he is with,—I mean poor Tom
Erskine, the father of three children, and a fourth about
to come into the world, with the glorious funds of a
lieutenant's pay to support his family ! Ah ! let us
compare and reflect on the contrasts in human life.
Your fate appears to him full of felicity; yet he has
that candour of mind to rejoice in what he thinks your
good fortune, and to wish only he had been as fortunate.
I wish you would write him a few lines to assure him of
your friendship and remembrance; but they must be on
the same companionable footing you were originally
together, for his situation renders him proud and touchy,
the natural consequence of a depressed high spirit. He
has indeed a vivacity, talents, accomplishments, and
knowledge, that I think will at last prevail and raise
him from his obscurity and poverty. Every one who
knows him becomes interested for him with a zeal that
will certainly some time or other make his fortune, in
spite of the cruel embarrassments he has brought himself
into by his mad marriage to a frightful, long-nosed,
awkward woman, who has nevertheless *douceur*, virtue,
and amiableness, to recommend her, and a love of him

---

[1] August 1775.

as strong as it is romantic. His mother has, I believe, about £400 a-year, on which she maintains him and his family, besides an unmarried daughter, . . . and what shows the power of religion, they are cheerful and content, only he is forming schemes of advancement as full of humour as of impracticability."

A great portion of this letter relates to Isabella's lovers. " It has been the decree of Heaven that several have felt her power on their hearts—have writhed under it, struggled, and, by the intervention of some mysterious power, got free," a termination which did not prevent Lady Elliot from describing most amusingly the intricacies of each particular case :—" In one instance," she wrote, " it pleased Providence to raise up an object to supplant her—detestable to the eyes and feelings of all others ! You may say it was an escape. No; he is one of the best of husbands to a most disagreeable and troublesome wife." In another case, probably the one already referred to, Lady Elliot confesses that, to her " shame, the object was not of the value she put upon it." More than once Isabella herself proved deaf to her lovers' prayers and her mother's counsels. " A young man with more character than is usual, with parts, learning, exact principles, and £10,000 a-year, very much made for domestic life, made acquaintance last winter at public places, and seemed very much an admirer. His plan was to walk about the world, both in town, and in the summer at public places, and then to fix for life on the person who, in his rounds, appeared to him the most to his taste. I have little doubt myself, by what I saw,

who this would have been, had not cruel incidents inter-
vened. In short, he came to Tunbridge; and before he
went to pursue his intended tour to foreign places, he
told a person there, who repeated it to me, that he was
so much in love, that if he had stayed any longer he
could not have commanded his desire to unite himself
for ever to the person he adored; and he therefore went
away very abruptly." This prudent gentleman, who was
obviously the original of " Cœlebs in search of a wife,"
having continued his tour, and completed it at Bright-
helmstone, returned to Tunbridge, to throw himself at
Isabella's feet, " for he was sincerely attached ;" but, in
the meanwhile, whatever preference she may at one time
have been disposed to feel for him, had been dissipated
by his own inconsistencies. They both, in short, experienced the truth of the French epigram—

> " L'absence est à l'amour
> Ce qu'est au feu le vent
> Il éteint le petit
> Et augmente le grand."

" He grew morose and jealous, and she, thinking him a
notorious puppy, would have nothing to say to him,
though I could not but believe him to be a good man,
with a wrong head and a strange temper." In the
following spring Lady Elliot wrote that " he" (the dis-
carded lover) " had been shut up with the vapours all the
winter, and I have no doubt he is hypochondriacally
mad. Another escape, you'll say !"

Eleanor, too, makes her first appearance in public
life at this time, and a little romance of hers, which

ended very tragically by the death of the hero, "young Delaval, the only son of the Delavals," caused some diversion to her mother's agitations respecting Isabella; but Eleanor was very young, very gay and pretty, "with the sort of beauty which engages the men without alarming the women," and "a few jaunts" about the country sufficed to restore her spirits. Her own letters on the subject are pleasing and natural.

From Tunbridge the elder members of the family went on a tour of visits, and, among other places, to Luton, Lord Bute's, and to the Norths.

"Luton is the finest and most expensive palace I ever saw," writes Isabella (Nov. 4)—"pictures and every other refinement of taste that can be collected; but it shows plainly that these things are no ways conducive to cheerfulness or happiness, as it is a kind of melancholy grandeur that is inexpressible. He himself struck me very much; he is now the gayest of the family, and amuses himself with his library and *vertù*, and seems to have in a degree forgot past times, but has a sort of horror for all the world, and we are the only visitors, except his own family, that have seen this magnificent fabric. His manners are vastly amiable—a little romantic, which, you know, is to my taste; but a disgust, which the ingratitude of the world has given him, makes him too *sauvage* to mix with it, and his family, when with him in the country, take the colour of their minds from his. I cannot but wonder at the difference, coming from the one to the other of this family, contrasted with the simplicity, jollity, good-humour, and easiness of Lord North's life and conversation; but I should think something between both would be the more happy medium, though never were there better people than the latter." She had written in May of the same year, when the bad news arrived from America, that they had been staying with the Norths. When the minister received it, "he seemed very easy, to our great surprise; but he is the most likeable creature I ever saw, and one must love him and all the family for their good humour and kindness."

October brought the world to town. Parliament re-assembled, and "The House of Peers sat the first day till half-past 11, and the House of Commons till half-past 4 in the morning, and the second day till near 1 o'clock. There was a very great debate and fine speaking. Young Adam, who comes in for Gatton, Sir W. Mayne's borough, attacked Lord North as a friend, but accused him in plain terms of a degree of [illegible] and indolence which made his very great abilities of no use, and blamed him for having allowed these natural dispositions to get so far the better of him, that they were in part cause of the mischief in America. This roused Lord North, who owned his faults, thanked Mr. Adam as a friend, and assured the House that no exertion of his should be wanting at the present crisis, and, in short, made one of the greatest appearances that ever was made. He has gained universal credit. My father spoke after, and they say amazingly well and skilfully. Mr. Fox, on the side of Opposition, made a great appearance, Burke and Barré but indifferent, and

Mr. Fox went away in low spirits, saying there had been much greater power shown on the side of Government than Opposition."[1] The Queen's first drawing-room was unusually full. Prince Orloff, covered with diamonds, was one of the lions of the day, but so many of the great people had only just come to town, and had unpacked nothing finer than "Queen's ware,"[2] that few entertainments were given him. "I hear he is not at all pleased with the reception he has met with in England, as he was immensely fêté at Paris, and the Empress says that no Frenchman shall ever come to her Court without feeling the good effects of it, but here people's heads are taken up with other things."[3] He was, however, happy to stare at the beautiful Lady Mary Somerset, who had lately "come out," and at the equally beautiful Duchess of Devonshire, "the most charming figure in the world." The news from America grew blacker by every mail ; but Eleanor probably spoke the truth, when she wrote in fun, "The trial of the Duchess of Kingston fills the mind of all the inhabitants of this great metropolis ; people seem much more sincerely interested in this cause than in the American war."

The Norths seem at this time to have been the most intimate friends of the younger branches of the Elliot family. "Miss North is still the same charming amiable creature as ever," writes Eleanor. "I was at Bushy for a fortnight, where I saw Mr. Eden several times. He and Lord North took it into their heads to

<hr>

[1] Isabella to Hugh, October 30.   [2] The New Wedgwood pottery.
[3] November 1775.

tell me your illness was cured by a large hump growing upon your back, higher than your head; and they talked so much about it that they frightened me out of my senses. They had a good laugh at me, because I said I would rather have it myself, or that any of my other brothers should have it, for they were not so handsome; besides that Gilbert, besides being an elder son, might put his councillor's wig upon it, Alick might cover it with Indian gold, Bob's gown would hide it, but Hugh and a hump would never do."

No such deformity as that imagined by Lord North could have been more unnatural or grotesque than the edifice which London ladies were then erecting on their heads. "The heads in France are now higher than ever, and England follows apace. Two or three ladies have sported such a quantity of feathers, blonde, flowers, artificial cherries, plums, strawberries, grass, radishes (which is called *coiffures à la légume*), cauliflowers, etc. etc., all at once upon the same head, that it has frightened and surprised the less adventurous part of the sex.'

The year 1776 was prolific of letters, and accordingly it has a whole volume of the correspondence to itself.

Several letters from Sir Gilbert and Lady Elliot relate to Hugh's desire to abandon the diplomatic profession in order to join the army in America as a volunteer. Both write to him in very different styles, but with equal good sense, on the subject.

"You are not a Hercules or a Samson," wrote his father,[1] "with your single arm to perform wonders, and

---

[1] January 24.

as a subaltern officer or volunteer you are undistinguished in the mass, and less serving your country.than
in the more important situation where you now are, and
where a great deal may depend on your own ability and
diligence. . . . . Though to speculate on subjects
of this kind is generally frivolous, yet I cannot help
recollecting what I think Bacon says on the choice of a
profession. One consideration is, not to adhere too
closely to our first destination where circumstances
seem chiefly to obstruct us, or where we are likely to
meet too many rivals possessed of superior advantages.
Thus, says he, Cæsar quitted eloquence at the bar,
finding Caius Hortensius in his way, and took at once to
arms, where Pompey alone was considerable. In what
line are there fewer competitors than in yours ? And in
a state broken into so many distinct departments, and
each department into so many ranks, where can one
hope to go so high, and that, too, by one's own merit and
industry ? To get on in youth is a great consideration,
and that seldom can happen in formed societies.

" To be continually conversant in important national
business, and always corresponding and in confidence
with those at the head of affairs, are circumstances
not without their value, especially when compared to
the minute and obscure drudgery which is inseparable
from most professions, especially on their first outset,
and during many of the best years of our youth."

" If," wrote his mother,[1] " you could succeed in
your object, you might indeed be in your element,

---

[1] February 5, 1776.

and in joy while the war continued, and you were
carrying on great exploits (wherein, however, you might
probably lose your limbs—I don't speak of life, as I
know you would look upon that as nothing); but
when the peace comes, and you are reduced to half-pay
and a dreary, tiresome, inactive, country-quarters life,
without an eye, or a leg, or an arm, with balls lodged
perhaps in your body—faugh! away with your army!
you had better fight the windmills. But seriously, you
would be ten times more miserable, poor Uncle Toby!
than you now are, seeing on your crutches your successor at Berlin coming home to some situation of business
in the state, with a rich wife and all the *douceurs* a
handsome young foreign Minister may aspire to.

"My dear Hugh, cure your chimerical brain; there
is no mortal thinking of America here, except to pity
those that are starving at Boston, and those that are
going to starve. For those that are come home with
wooden legs or a hole in their lungs, they are no more
thought of than an old Chelsea pensioner is. They
obtain a word at the *levées,* and a very, very little
smart-money for their sores, and then their wounds are
supposed to be healed, and they and their wives and
children may shift as they may; an instance of which I
saw this very day.

"I shall say no more on the subject. I find your
father has wrote you a very serious letter upon it; he
is hurt with what he thinks fickleness of mind and
restlessness of temper, and a perfect want of reason."
And then, with a tender desire to mitigate the severity

of her husband's judgment, warring against her consciousness of its justice, she adds—" I see it in a different light;
but still as the highest absurdity."

What followed might have been expected. Hugh
submitted to his father, and turned upon his mother.
Out of the texts she had taught him in his childhood,
from scriptural stories and Watt's hymns, he brought
a battery to bear on her worldly motives and selfish
prudential considerations, to which attack she replied
with perhaps a little momentary forgetfulness. " My
dearest life—Don't think I blamed your idea. I am
not so destitute of spirit as not to have gloried in
it; but I saw your ruin by it, and I was con-
founded and frightened. I confess I am no Roman
matron; and however indifferent you may be about
your limbs, I am not so, and should grieve hugely over
the loss of a leg or an arm. I see you are monstrous
angry that I should suppose such a thing possible. I
don't remember a word that was in my letter, but I
think it was all within bounds. God forbid I should
ever mince matters with you; confidence and freedom
are what I have always used with those nearest to my
heart. You was angry when you wrote me, which I
know by your calling me a Presbyterian, which is a very
[illegible] word for you, though my own opinion is that
it is, not essentially but rationally, the purest mode of
Christian profession. But now I will write no more
sentiments but facts. Your friend Lord Stormont has
taken to himself a wife of the house of Cathcart; her
age eighteen. She is improved in her person since you

saw her; people say she will be very handsome when she comes back from Paris. She is accomplished; that is to say, she sings well. I am disposed to think well of her; and she sets out with an intention to be a good wife. I have no other intelligence to give you. Adieu, my dearest Hugh.—Yours ever and ever."

When Hugh had been persuaded to abandon his military schemes, it was admitted that the chivalry of the idea, though of the De la Mancha school, had not been unappreciated by those to whom it was known. The King had been struck with it, and from this time seems to have been especially gracious in his inquiries for the young minister.

A letter of Lady Elliot's, of the date of February 1776, gives some curious particulars concerning the Ministry of the day:—"The King, always good and well-intentioned, must be much harassed by the embarrassed state of the public[1] and his own servants. As far as I know, he is firm to his servants without favouritism. The Premier is a man of the best nature and humour I ever knew, and with superior talents as a speaker; I believe he is a well-intentioned, honest man, but he has no enlarged views either in men or things. He has been the dupe of little tricking jobbing knaves, the foremost of which is the new baronet, Sir Grey Cooper . . . who has been playing to disunite Lord North and Lord Suf-

[1] In a letter from Mr. Pitt to Hugh Elliot, dated Vienna, February 1776, it is stated that Prince George of Mecklenburg-Strelitz, brother of Queen Charlotte, told the writer that, as far as he could judge (probably from letters of the Queen's), the King had at this time scarcely a hope of succeeding in America.

folk ; but thanks to the good sense, fairness, and abilities
of Mr. Eden, they are, in spite of all schemes to defeat
it, thoroughly united at present. That Lord Sandwich
is omnipotent at the Admiralty, and Lord Barrington
in the Army, is most true ; it is no less true that few
ministers except Lord North would submit to this ; but,
however, I fancy he either must, or quit the helm, as at
least the Army department seems to be one a higher
power will never relinquish.[1] This, however, creates
great embarrassment and confusion in business. . . .

[1] A letter from Mr. Stanley, who had lately returned from America,
where he had been serving on General Burgoyne's staff, corroborates
Lady Elliot on this point. Writing to Hugh from Knowsley, January
16, 1776, he says :—"I shall certainly have a troop by the time I get
back to America. Our *mutual friend* Lord Barrington has opposed me
violently ; he says young Stanhope, Lady Harrington's son, is an older
cornet by a good deal ; but the King told Lord George Germaine and
Mr. Burgoyne, who both interested themselves for me, that Stanhope
had not been in America, and therefore I should have it." In the
same letter occurs a passage which, though *not* to the point, is entertaining enough to justify its introduction here. "We acted the tragedy of *Zara*, two nights before I left Boston, for the benefit of the
widows and children. The prologue was spoken by Lord Rawdon, a
very fine fellow and good soldier. I wish you knew him. We took
above £100 at the door. I hear a great many people blame us for acting, and think we might have found something better to do ; but
General Howe follows the example of the King of Prussia, who, when
Prince Ferdinand wrote him a long letter mentioning all the difficulties
and distresses of the army, sent back the following concise answer—
'De la gaieté, encore de la gaieté, et toujours de la gaieté !' The female
parts were filled by young ladies, though some of the Boston ladies were
so prudish as to say this was improper." A letter from Mr. Stanley,
giving an account of the Battle of Bunker's Hill, will be found in the
Appendix.

From the nature of the man who governs the fleet, and the sub-governor of the army, all [business[1]] is carried on in the most irregular, slovenly, if not mercenary manner, and their creatures employed,—witness Gage and Greaves. Things are, however, becoming too serious for trifling, and they are now obliged to look for men of real abilities."

In the same letter she deprecates Hugh's impatience of the society in which he lived abroad, and points out how little he had to regret in his removal from the temptations of an idle life in London.

" I will say, that if fortune had placed you in a situation to exist among these beings of dissipation and extravagance, you would soon have lost the richer gifts with which she has endowed you. . . . It is true there is now and then a genius and character amongst them that rises in spite of defects and all disadvantages of habit and education, such is Charles Fox, such is Lord Lyttelton ; but what would they have been if they had applied their whole force to embellishing their great talents, and to fulfilling the noble duties of their birth ! What are they now ? ruined profligate gamesters, and obliged to devote themselves to party for subsistence, disregarded and distrusted."

Most of these letters, at the length of which " your father grumbles," contain passages of religious advice and reflections, and among them is a paper drawn up by Lady Elliot for the use of her youngest daughter when preparing for confirmation, which shows a cultivated and liberal mind, as well as deep religious sentiment.

<hr>

[1] Word illegible.

When Lady Elliot was writing to her son, as she constantly did at this time, of the insufficiency of earthly pleasures, and of the transitory and fleeting nature of all earthly things, she little knew that events in her own family were about forcibly to illustrate the truths she inculcated.

In the spring of the year 1776 Alick had returned, somewhat unexpectedly, from India, with the reputation of being the " first young man there for character and abilities." At that time, or soon after, it became known to Sir Gilbert that Lord Suffolk proposed to recall Hugh from Munich in autumn, in order that he might be sent to the far more important post of Berlin. Circumstances of various kinds prevented the family from making their annual visit to Minto at the close of the session, and summer found Lady Elliot preparing to take possession of a house at Twickenham, with the joyful hope in her heart of shortly seeing all her children re-assembled about her again in the scenes familiar to their childhood. They had parted years ago, in their promising youth; they were about to be united, still young, with the promise fulfilled; each of the three elder sons had established for himself a reputation which betokened a distinguished career. Gilbert had just returned from Morpeth, and entered Parliament with every prospect of attaining a position there. Hugh and Alick were both, in spite of their youth, high in the confidence of the governments they served. Eleanor's approaching marriage with Mr. Eden, " whose abilities," Sir Gilbert said, " will carry him high," was a joyful event already loom-

ing at a very near distance.[1]   Isabella, the one whose
future was perhaps the least assured, was idolised at
home and admired abroad, and entered into the successes
of the others with the most cordial and unselfish
affection; and, strange to say, for that one summer
Bob himself showed steadiness and an inclination to
work.   To complete the family picture, we must not
omit the parents, both of whom were scarcely past the
prime of life; Lady Elliot, being not much above forty,
looked, as we are told by her daughter, " ten years
younger, and very handsome;" and both she and Sir
Gilbert might with reason anticipate a long possession
in the future of their prosperous lot, influential in politics, popular in society, and happy at home.   At this
moment of their lives, at all events, they seem to have
been conscious that " the lines were cast to them in
pleasant places."

The family correspondence proves this.   " What joy,"
writes Lady Elliot, " to have your father and *all the six*
with me again! . . . We shall revisit the old places.
Your old school-room still exists."   Alick writes :—" I
have visited the mill, and the rivulet, and the Thames,
the spots where we first learned to love each other, and
now only you are wanting to make us perfectly happy."
And Hugh, writing of the anticipated meeting at Twickenham, says :—" What family can be happier than ours
is now, all meeting again happy and prosperous, and
loving each other as well as of old ?"

The meeting took place in the month of September,

----

[1] She was married in September 1776.

and was followed by a few brief days of happiness; but even during these a speck was in the sky. Sir Gilbert had returned from his son's election, and from a hasty visit to Minto, with a neglected cold and cough. Hectic symptoms rapidly appeared. Soon after the meeting of Parliament, he found himself unable to attend the House of Commons. A change of climate was ordered by the physicians; and early in November he was on his way to Nice, with Lady Elliot and Isabella, and under the especial charge of Hugh.

A letter from Gilbert, dated Lincoln's Inn, 19th November 1776, well describes the sympathy which Sir Gilbert's illness had excited among his friends.

"The warmth, and I really believe the sincerity, with which almost everybody I meet receives the account of your journey and its success, is affecting, particularly in the House of Commons, where he is truly missed by every man who has the least soul, and who knew the part he used to fill there.

"Perhaps his absence, by withdrawing him from all those little competitions which warp vulgar, and I am afraid, even superior minds, may have made the universal concern for his situation more sincere than was expected in that callous scene. But whatever the reason is, it is certainly so; and to me is a subject of the most sensible and touching pleasure I now experience, and yet it makes me melancholy. To find nothing but an affectionate remembrance of one who used to be so principal when present *there*, is a change that makes one feel, and makes one think a little of what all this is that we are busy about."

Hugh accompanied his family as far as Avignon; there he was relieved in his melancholy duties by his brother Alick; and, apparently on account of matters connected with his recent appointment to Berlin, he returned to England, after a parting so sad and painful, that Sir Gilbert is described as frequently recurring to it, saying, with a sigh, "Poor, poor Hugh! how unhappy he was to leave us."

And far bitterer still that parting would have been, could a glance into the future have revealed to him that not only of his father, but of mother and brother[1] he was taking a last farewell; and that when he should see his favourite sister again, his chosen and cheerful companion, there would be " upon her face the tint of grief, the settled shadow of an inward strife," and even he, her best and dearest, would have no power to bring relief to " that which preyed upon her mind, a spectre of the past!"

[1] Alick did not return to England till after his brother's departure for Berlin in the spring of 1777, and early in the summer of the same year he went out to India, where he died in 1778.

H

CHAPTER THE THIRD.

1777.

BERLIN.

THE month of January 1777 was marked by two such events as make epochs in the history of every family— the death of the head of the family, and the marriage of him destined to fill the vacant place; by the one event two generations change places, by the other the foundation of a new family is laid, which may or may not link the past to future hopes.

The nature of the change which had taken place is significantly marked in this correspondence. Hitherto the brothers had written to each other on personal topics chiefly; from the parents came more general information, and sometimes counsel, remonstrance, and reproof; henceforth Lady Elliot's letters will be but few, and those few will relate to matters of a purely domestic character, to her health, her sorrows, and her altered circumstances; while the letters of her eldest son become, and continue, the most valuable portion of the correspondence.

The new Sir Gilbert was well fitted to take the chief place in the family.

Less ambitious and less laborious than his father, less brilliant and enthusiastic than his mother, without his brother's handsome person and lively manners, his were the gifts which need only to be known to gain for their possessor love and honour, and " troops of friends." From his earliest years he seems to have inspired his family with the most entire reliance on his character and conduct, and also on his tenderness and indulgence to those less free than himself from reproach.

When young he accused himself of indolence, and in after years his wife took up the tale; but whatever more he might have done, he did live to fill high situations with honour, and to be distinguished among the band of eminent men who during many years opposed at once the encroachments of the Crown at home, and the influx of Jacobinical principles from abroad.

From his wife[1] there are but few letters among my grandfather's correspondence, these, however, are easily and pleasantly written; and we know that she was a woman of strong character and of warm heart, with looks and manners which betrayed her southern origin, an ancestor of her father, Sir George Amyand, having been a Huguenot refugee.[2]

---

[1] Anna Maria Amyand, eldest daughter of Sir G. Amyand. She and her sister Harriet had been brought up by Lady Northampton, wife of their uncle Mr. Amyand.

[2] The family of Amyand came originally from the south of France. Lady Elliot's eldest brother changed his name to that of Cornewall on his marriage with an heiress, Miss Velters Cornewall, of Moccas Court, Herefordshire. He was the father of Lady Hereford, of Lady Duff Gordon, of Mrs. Frankland Lewis, and of other children.

From various remarks in Lady Elliot's letters while the wooing was in progress, it appears that the marriage was not desired by her, and possibly the young lady's want of personal beauty was no slight demerit in the eyes of one who had a large share of the good gift herself; in her earliest allusions to her son's attachment she talks of it as an "unnatural passion for an ugly woman;" but mobility of expression may do more to make a face attractive than regular beauty of features, when these " have been created without the preamble of ' Let there be light.' " At all events, Sir Gilbert never grew tired of admiring his wife's dark eyes and lively looks.

The marriage, which took place in London on the 3d January 1777, appears not to have been known at Marseilles before Sir Gilbert's death on the 11th. That he had given a cordial assent is clear from some expressions of his quoted by Lady Elliot in her account of his last hours. " He said," she writes, " about five days before the last one, ' By Miss Amyand's letters she is a sensible good woman, and I believe will be a good wife and comfortable relation ;' and then he added with great energy—' What a wise man Gilbert has been to leave the skirts of the fine people and associate with men of sense and character who have led him into a conduct of virtue and wisdom which I hope he is now established in following.' I told him that you suffered cruelly that your affairs had not admitted of your attending him on this journey. He said, ' I know Gilbert feels much that his nature will not permit him to show.' " Of all his

children Sir Gilbert seems to have spoken tenderly and
frequently, while still cheered by the hope of again being
restored to them and to health; but the sufferings
caused by paroxysms of coughing which followed on
any agitation, led him gradually to avoid all affecting
and exciting topics;—" If," writes Lady Elliot from
Marseilles, " I ever gave him any strong expressions
of affection, he said, ' Don't—don't—the least thing
would '—and then he stopped, fixing his eyes with
pity and tenderness on me and on his daughter. As
he lived so he died, a pattern of meekness, patience,
and fortitude."

The return of Lady Elliot to England did not follow
immediately on her husband's death; with a natural
reluctance to leave the scenes where she had last beheld
him, she lingered on in the south of France till the
month of March; arrangements were, however, immediately carried out for the interment of the body at
Minto, where, nevertheless, it did not arrive till the
following August.

In a letter written at this period to Hugh, his mother
quotes some lines composed by her husband on his
father's death, which, she says, are applicable to many of
the circumstances which accompanied his own :—

> " O sacred flame,
> Devotion pure, whose energy divine
> Exalts with humble hope the lowly mind,
> And trust and fortitude bestowest, thou fill'dst
> His pious breast, and resignation taught
> That first great lesson—best preparative
> For life and death—he learnt it and obey'd.

His mind refined and strong, no sense impair'd,
Nor feeling of humanity, nor taste
Of social life, and e'en his latest hour
In sweet domestic cheerfulness was past.
Sublimely calm his ripen'd spirit fled,
His family surrounding, and his friends.
A wife and daughter closed his eyes, on them
Was turned his latest gaze, and o'er his grave—
Their father's grave—his sons the green turf spread.
Such be my fate, indulgent Providence,
When from the tumult of a noisier scene,
The same still grave shall, near a father's side,
Receive the ashes of a son he loved."

" All is accomplished," wrote Lady Elliot in continuation, " but the last part, and I hope that is not far distant. I have also a strong cordial in his having signified to me that my presence with him was his comfort. I have a cordial, indeed, in my dear children's duty and affection, which nothing can surpass, and in their virtues and qualities ; I balance all these things, and I acknowledge the providence of God ; yet nature will weep for what is past, and tremble for what may come."

On the arrival of the sad news in England, steps were immediately taken to ensure the succession of Gilbert Elliot to the representation in Parliament of the county of Roxburgh, vacated by his father's death. The first letter, addressed by Gilbert to his brother Hugh in the spring of 1777, is written from Minto to Hugh in London, and is occupied with the details of his canvass in the county. After describing his prospects of support —the friendship of the Duke of Buccleuch; the almost paternal kindness of Hugh Scott of Harden ; the strong disposition of the county gentlemen in general in his favour—Sir Gilbert winds up thus :—" I cannot shut my letter without giving you all the comfort our misfortunes leave us, and that which I have found a very real and affecting one to myself—I mean the adoration with which my father is, by almost all ranks of men here, remembered."

It appears from the letters relating to county politics at this time, that a political alliance was in process of formation between the Dukes of Buccleuch and Roxburghe, which, unless opposed with infinite spirit and union by the other gentlemen of the county, would, it was feared, place the representation of Roxburghshire entirely at the disposal of the two Dukes. On this occasion the Duke of Roxburghe, at the instance of the Duke of Buccleuch, withdrew his brother, Lord R. Kerr, iu favour of Sir Gilbert Elliot, though Lord Robert's canvass had actually commenced.

So great a sacrifice made by the Duke of Roxburghe as an act of friendship for the Duke of Buccleuch, who, besides being kindly disposed to Sir Gilbert himself, was unwilling to thwart the wishes of the county gentlemen declared pretty unanimously in his favour, sufficiently attested the intimate nature of the connection between the two great peers ; and it was generally believed that a private understanding subsisted between them to the effect that the withdrawal of Lord Robert on the present occasion would ensure for him the Buccleuch interest at another election. Jealousy of this alliance between the two Dukes laid the foundations of

a new party in the county, which, under the name of the
independent interest, frequently and successfully contested in after years the representation of Roxburghshire
with the nominees of the Duke of Buccleuch.   On this
occasion Sir Gilbert was returned without a contest;
and having previously resigned his seat for Morpeth, he
returned to town at the end of February as M.P. for
Roxburghshire.

About the same time Hugh departed for his new
post at Berlin, which he reached on the 1st of April.

The Court to which my grandfather was now
accredited was as unlike as possible that which he had
just left.   In place of the gay and dissipated Munich,
he found a capital of regular and handsome architecture
indeed, but in " the streets of which reigned an air of
dejection at noon-day, scarcely any passengers being
seen except soldiers."[1]   The only court held there was
that of the Queen, the neglected wife of Frederick the
Great;   to her all presentations were made, and her
receptions, at rare and stated intervals, were the only
royal entertainments at which Berliners were called upon
to assist; but so parsimonious were the habits of the
Court, that the occasional glimmer of an old lamp in the
staircase of the palace was sufficient to make a passer-
by exclaim—" Her Majesty doubtless holds high festival
to-day !" and so scanty were the provisions at the royal
table, that those who had the honour of partaking of
them previously fortified themselves with a repast at
home.   Thiébault tells us, that on one occasion a great

' Wraxall's *Memoirs*, vol. i.

lady especially recommended by Her Majesty to the care of the assistants, received for her entire portion one preserved cherry!

The fête-day of the Queen was the grand gala of the year, for then Frederick honoured her with his presence, and taking off his military boots for that day only, appeared for the space of half-an-hour in silk stockings, which, ungartered and ill-fitting, fell in folds around his legs.

No less unlike to the splendours of Nymphenburg was the residence of the Prussian King at Potsdam, "rather a military station than a city. Guards and hussars constituted half its inhabitants;" while the little palace of Sans Souci, a quarter of a mile off, consisted only of one range of apartments on the ground floor.[1] " A sandy barren soil and groves of gloomy fir gave an air of melancholy to the surrounding scenery," says an English traveller whose words I have before quoted; and after expatiating on the evidence of military despotism apparent throughout the land, he adds—" The Prussian monarchy reminds me of a vast prison, in the centre of which appears the great keeper occupied in the care of his captives."[2]

As a parallel to the Englishman's opinion, we may place that of the Marquis Louis d'Yve, a friend of Hugh Elliot's in Ratisbon days, who, on hearing of his appointment to Berlin, wrote to him thus:—" Je crois que le séjour de Berlin vous conviendra à de certains

---

[1] The new palace of Sans Souci was then in process of building.

[2] Wraxall.

égards—on y traite les ministres à la Vénitienne ; la
cour et la ville ont peu de communication avec eux, les
personnes auxquelles ils se lient, et les maisons qu'ils
fréquentent deviennent mêmes suspectes ; ils vivent
beaucoup entre eux, ou seuls, selon leur génie ; leurs
sociétés sont des espèces de *klops* (clubs) anglais, ils
n'ont pas besoin de briller par les équipages, et le seul
train nécessaire est d'être en état de bien donner à
dîner à leurs amis—voilà bien des titres pour Berlin
vis-à-vis de vous ! D'un autre côté, il y a beaucoup
de princes qui ont chacun une manière de petite cour,
il faut les voir et ceci est une gêne un peu multipliée."[1]
The princes alluded to by the Marquis Louis d'Yve
were, besides the King and Queen, the prince[2] and
princess[3] of Prussia—both of whom became subsequently friends and correspondents of my grandfather—
Prince Henry, the King's brother, who lived chiefly at
the castle of Rheinsberg, at about twelve miles from
Berlin, and the princes of Brunswick, nephews of the
Queen,—other princes and princesses there were who
came and went, and some who lived constantly at
Berlin, but in a degree of retirement which prevented
them from being known to the foreigners who at this
date visited Berlin.

Mr. Elliot appears to have formed his earliest social
relations in the country among the members of Prince

---

[1] Ratisbone, 27 7bre /76.

[2] Afterwards King Frederick William, nephew of Frederick the
Great.

[3] A princess of Hesse-Darmstadt.

Henry's court at Rheinsberg. Among these were his
aides-de-camp the two Counts Wrech, designated as le
gros et le petit; "le brillant Kaphengst," of whose
"hot youth" Thiébault tells wild stories: "le beau
Kniphausen, beau comme l'Apollon de Belvedère," and
afterwards too well known in my grandfather's story.
Among the ladies the most prominent were the
Countess de Verelst, widow of a late Dutch minister at
Berlin, and her "fairest daughter"—"sans contredit la
plus belle personne de ce pays." Madame de Verelst,
"née Sophia von Platen" (Thiébault tells us she was a
demoiselle de Bredow),[1] had been one of the band of
high-born and beautiful dames de cour of the Queen
Sophia Dorothea—mother of Frederick the Great.
From those days she had kept up relations of amity
and confidence with various members of the royal
family, especially with Prince Henry, at whose castle of
Rheinsberg she spent every summer. She had been
married en premières noces to M. Von Krauth, a
Prussian officer, by whom she had one daughter, a
beauty and a reputed heiress, whose charms, though
she was barely sixteen, had endangered the peace of
the last English envoy,[2] and were destined to have a
more powerful influence over his successor.

The general society of Berlin was composed of the
native aristocracy, which, from want of means, contributed little to its brilliancy; of foreign diplomatists; of
strangers; and of men of letters—these last were chiefly

---

[1] By Berlin etiquette all *dames de cour* were unmarried.

[2] Mr. Harris, afterwards Sir James, and first Earl of Malmesbury.

Frenchmen who had been induced by Frederick to form an academy at Berlin.

Mr. Harris had described them to his successor as " little above our village schoolmasters ;" but my grandfather,[1] who had both literary and scientific tastes, seems to have frequented their society and to have liked it. There are many letters from various academicians in this correspondence, but the men are best known from the amusing memoirs of Thiébault, one of their number.

To Mr. Harris my grandfather was indebted for a pithy description of the members of the diplomatic body, among whom he was now to take his place.

I insert it here—it will be seen that the names are in the second column, the qualities of the proprietors in the first.

FRENCH MINISTER.— Optimus.	Pons, Marquis de.
PALATINE MINISTER.— Good ; to be consulted about visits.	Schlipp.
SARDINIAN.— Ingenious ; odd ; suits me ; good for an Italian.	Rosignan.
AUSTRIAN.— Clever ; honest ; morgue.	Swieten.[2]

[1] During his idlest days at Munich he had corresponded with Mesmer on the subject of animal magnetism, and with Mr. Brydone on electricity and kindred topics.

[2] He was soon removed, and was succeeded by Count Cobentzel.

SWEDEN.— Enfant avec de la barbe.	
DUTCH MINISTER.— Friend of Harris ; faults, but good.	Heyden.
Nihil.	Pr. Doulgorouky. Sweterheim.
Odd ; avoid familiarity.	Michel.

Avoid generally toutes les femmes.

In addition to this sketch of diplomatic personages, there is a similar table describing the chief persons in society ; but as it can no longer contain any interest, I shall only transcribe one entry.

PRINCE HENRY'S COURT.— Tracassiers, faux, impertinents.	Barons Kniphausen, Kaphengst, Denon, Marechale. Avoid all of the name of Wrech.

Madame Verelst.—Good ; mention Harris's respect and esteem as often as possible.

I find no letters from Mr. Elliot describing his first impressions of Berlin ; but in the letters addressed to him there are passages which throw some light both on the reception he met with, and on his own views of the place and people.

Thus Mr. Brydone, writing on the 2d May 1777, says,—" It gave me great pleasure to know you have met with so agreeable and so gracious a reception ; I was sure, indeed, this would be the case, as you are exactly the character the king likes." And Madame de Thun writes :—" J'ai été bien agréablement surprise de voir par votre lettre que mes alarmes sur les désagré-

mens que je croyais que vous trouveriez dans la société
de Berlin sont inutiles, et que vous êtes si content de
votre séjour; l'éloge que vous en faites, quelque pom-
peux qu'il soit, ne me tente cependant pas, et je vous
avoue que je ne me fais pas l'idée *d'une société* sur
laquelle la subordination s'étend, ni des agrémens d'une
ville qui doit son existence au fer et au feu, encore moins
d'une capitale qui est un camp; où on ne peut faire
campagne gaiement.

"Vraiment si je ne savais pas combien on est
charmé de passer son temps avec vous, je croirais qu'il
doit y avoir à Berlin d'autres agrémens, moins hérissés
de baïonnettes, de tambours, et de manœuvres, puisque
Harvey,[1] que je ne crois pas militaire aussi passionné
que vous, y reste si longtemps."

My grandfather's military tastes had led him to form
an enthusiastic admiration for the great soldier of his
age, and no doubt the military manœuvres which formed
the staple amusement of Berliners were peculiarly interesting to him, but as Madame de Thun shrewdly surmised, Berlin had other attractions too.

Of these, however, he did not think it necessary to
write home, and they find no place in a gay letter to his
sister Eleanor, written in the summer of 1777, in which
he describes his life at Berlin :—

"I very often place myself at your looking-glass
window at Greenwich, and hear you call me mad with
the greatest pleasure, while Eden's never-resting fingers
write notes and politics with that wonderful punctuality

---

[1] William Harvey, Esq.

which none of your indolent brothers ever could attain.
I suppose myself, then, asking for a sandwich, devouring
Ticonderago, and Philadelphia, while you are making
conquests for Lady Anna Maria,[1] and Lady Priscilla,[2]
passing in review the good kind of men, and good kind
of estates, upon whom your friends might rationally
bestow their sentiments and persons in exchange for
dirty acres and irresistible gold. You are in your scarlet
riding-dress, just dismounted from *Poet*, and I am
hagged with sitting up last night and winning twelve
hundred from as needy a younger brother as myself!

" What shall we talk about ?

" *Madam* begins. Well, Hugh, how do you like
Berlin ?

" *Hugh*. Monstrously ; the tallest grenadiers you
ever saw, the most melodious drums, the sweetest
trumpets, the most delicious artillery, and the loveliest
hussars.

" *Madam*. Are your women handsome ?

" *Hugh*. Prodigious ! Six feet high, six feet round,
as brawny as your chairman : then they eat, and, bless
the pretty creatures, they drink a little too—a set of jolly
dogs, I assure you.

" *Madam*. How do you pass your time ?

" *Hugh*. Harvey and I seldom meet till twelve,
when we go to a lecture on Natural Philosophy : at
one we mount ; Brilliant and the brown horse gallop as
hard as they can lay legs to ground till two, in a beautiful park ; at two, dine, drink one bottle Burgundy,

---

[1] Lady Anna Maria Stanhope.　　　[2] Lady Priscilla Bertie.

success to old England, play at cribbage till four; at
four, go to a lecture on Chemistry; at five, mount the
nags again, or, if there should be a violent supper in
town, dress, arrive there at seven; from seven to nine,
play at shilling whist; at nine, sit down to supper with
forty people, faire l'agréable with amiable neighbour;
to bed at one, and rise next morning with a comfortable
headache, and melancholy reflections upon high living
and poverty," but of Madame Verelst's "fairest daughter,"
not one word !!

And now, what was thought of Hugh at Berlin?

Thiébault tells us that at this time arrived "M.
Elliot, homme d'esprit et délié; de plus, assez bel
homme, très-vif, et très-aimable, original sans doute;
on n'est point anglais sans cela;" and then, to prove the
originality of the Minister's opinions, he goes on to
tell us, that one day giving a dinner to some academicians, "il nous soutint" that Shakspeare was sublime,
and much more so than Corneille, while Racine was
never sublime at all.   To these assertions such a flood
of eloquence was replied that the host appears to have
closed the discussion by the assurance that he had
much admiration for Racine, who was one of his
favourite authors.

On another occasion, says the same writer, he undertook to prove to us that the French language, which he
spoke perfectly, was, when compared with any other
modern language, and more especially the English
language, an essentially poor one.

There was certainly some originality in propounding

these views to a dinner party composed of French academicians.

I find among Mr. Elliot's papers a draft of a letter written to a foreign friend at this time,[1] on literary topics, in which the following passage occurs :—" On ne connait pas assez nos bons écrivains dans ce pays ci. Je ne cache pas ma jalousie en voyant chez le Prince Henri, Voltaire, Maupertuis et pas un seul Anglais. Je viens de finir la lecture d'uu livre où mes pauvres compatriotes ont été impitoyablement volés, l'histoire politique et philosophique des établissements par l'Abbé Raynal. I must write in English, because I am angry, and I know one dare not be angry at Berlin with the favourite French literary puppets. A few plodding, bob-wig'd, sensible English traders have enriched their country with some of the leading facts and leading principles of commerce, navigation, and colonies, truth their object, experience their guide, and plain unaffected language their medium for conveying to their countrymen a knowledge of the subject they treat of; they neglected all those impertinent pretensions which are meant to catch admiration for the author at the expense of the judgment of the reader. Not one exclamation to ' Hommes de la terre !' ' Peuples écoutez ma voix, c'est l'humanité qui parle !' They contrived to say in a few words what Monsieur l'Abbé has dressed in all the luxuriance of French superfluities. In the same sentence you have spices, the philosophy of Confucius, the threadbare subject of Monkish Christianity, the natural history of the

---

[1] Berlin, June 1777.

I

globe, and les agrémens du sexe enchanteur; and this
strange lottery of which ideas should come uppermost—
a compound worthy of some hysterical woman with a
bad digestion, passes in Europe for a profound and
original work !"

The first occasion[1] on which my grandfather came
very prominently before the notice of the Berlin public
was one not calculated to improve his position there.
I allude to the seizure of the papers of two American
agents who had lately arrived in Berlin, with the purpose,
as it was supposed, of carrying on secret negotiations with
the Court, promising future commercial advantages in
return for present assistance of officers and money.

The very first official despatch,[2] addressed by Lord
Suffolk to Mr. Elliot at Berlin desires him to watch the
conduct of these " rebel agents," Messrs Lee and Sayre;
and the second despatch describes Mr. Sayre as a man
of desperate fortune.   Mr. Lee was said to possess
higher abilities, and to be most in the confidence of
Messrs. Silas Deane and Franklin.

The presence of these persons at Berlin was announced by the Prussian minister to the English representative, he being at the same time informed that the
King of Prussia had too high a sense of the regal dignity to give his sanction to the rebellious colonies by
receiving their emissaries, who were therefore obliged to
maintain a strict incognito.

Mr. Elliot, however, saw some reason to doubt the
friendly assurances of the Prussian ministers ; and the

---

[1] June? 1777.   [2] St. James's, 9th May 1777.   Cypher.

rest of the story, written at length by himself to the
Prince of Prussia, and to his own government, may be
shortly told as follows:—Certain persons were desired
by Mr. Elliot to watch the proceedings of two soi-disant
Americans lately arrived at Berlin, known to be agents
of the rebel Congress.   Offers were made to Mr. Elliot
to procure him secretly the papers of the strangers, and
to replace them without risk of discovery; which offers
were accepted by Mr. Elliot, and promises of reward
were given to those who made them.   Nevertheless,
nothing came of these proposals, the risk attending on
their execution being found too great.   A German servant, however, in Mr. Elliot's establishment, having been
made aware of his master's anxiety to procure evidence
of the secret objects which the Americans had in view at
Berlin, by overhearing him say at his dinner-table that he
would gladly give a sum of money to any one who should
bring him their papers, waited for no further authorisa-
tion, but in the most imprudent and reckless manner
broke into the apartments occupied by the Americans in
a certain hotel; entering the room by the window, he
forced open the bureau, and carried off, "à toutes
jambes," the papers it contained.

The master of the house instantly accused Mr. Elliot's
servant of the theft, stating that he had been offered a
thousand pounds only a few days before to become an
accomplice to it; several persons belonging to the hotel
were arrested; and the police were pursuing active
inquiries into the circumstances of the affair, when Mr.
Elliot came forward and declared that he considered

himself to be solely responsible for what had occurred. One of his servants, he said, was undoubtedly the culprit, and had been led to commit the act by Mr. Elliot's own imprudence, he having in the servant's presence expressed himself in the indiscreet manner before mentioned. No time had been lost in restoring the papers to their rightful owners, and Mr. Elliot submitted himself entirely to the judgment of the King of Prussia, acquitting his court of any share in so unjustifiable a transaction.[1]

The king gave to this candid avowal a gracious answer, to the effect that he should wish the subject dropped; but Mr. Elliot thought it his duty to advise his own government to recall him from a post where the credit of his court might possibly be impaired by the conduct of its representative on this occasion.

Mr. Liston was sent home at once with letters explanatory of the circumstances, and on the 1st of August Lord Suffolk wrote to Mr. Elliot as follows:—
"It gives me real concern when I find it my duty to convey any intimation of His Majesty's dissatisfaction with the conduct of a minister whose zeal in the public service is as little doubted as his ability; and who, by

---

[1] My attention having been called to the discrepancy between the account given in the text of this transaction and that to be found in the 6th vol. of Mr. Carlyle's *History of Frederick the Great*, I have only to say, that I have translated all but verbatim Mr. Elliot's letter on the subject to the Prince of Prussia, and have accurately copied the most important passages relating to it from Lord Suffolk's despatches and Mr. Eden's letters; and that no papers, public or private, containing any different version from that given in the text, have been preserved in the MSS. of my grandfather.

an excess of the former quality, has been induced to swerve from that discreet regard to his own situation and the dignified principles of his court, which ought on every moment and on every occasion to regulate both his actions and his language."

Lord Suffolk goes on to comment on the expressions which, by Mr. Elliot's confession, he had hazarded at his table—" expressions which, however they might arise in the warmth of conversation without any serious meaning being intended, were highly improper to be used by the representative of a court which disdained, and will ever disdain, to trust the crooked paths of duplicity and treachery."

After stating that the generous behaviour of the King of Prussia on this occasion to Mr. Elliot prevented the necessity of adopting Mr. Elliot's suggestion that he should be recalled, the despatch ends by recommending him for the future to " abstain from vivacities of language, and to control and discourage so criminal an activity on the part of his dependants."   A little later another despatch informs Mr. Elliot that the King of England had entirely overlooked the exceptional circumstances in the business, in consideration of the loyal zeal which occasioned them; and the despatch closes by the announcement that the expenses incurred by Mr. Elliot would be indemnified by the crown.

Mr. Eden, writing confidentially to his brother-in-law—October 1777—tells him that the King of Prussia's feelings on the subject were not quite such as he had been led to imagine :—

" We had the best reason to know that they were by no means quieted to the degree you supposed; when you were told that the outrage was forgiven, we had absolute proof that you were only told so, and that it was likely to be seriously resented. . . . . The information itself we had already obtained through another channel. . . . You have now only to appear, and to be very discreet in your attention, and in all other respects to pursue the engaging conduct that your own nature would dictate."

This letter, most affectionate and friendly throughout, dwells much on the almost parental feeling of Lord Suffolk for Hugh Elliot, on the kindly disposition of the " closet" towards the young minister, and ends thus : " Let me, however, give you one official caution— recollect always that your letters are for the Royal eye, which is so constructed as to be shock'd at any coarse expression. You lately said ' that a certain prince would do anything to ' *get a shilling.*' I altered the three last words to ' gain an advantage for his people.'"

It has been necessary to tell this story at some length, because the subsequent relations of Mr. Elliot with the court of Berlin were affected by it in no slight degree.

From that period he never recovered the ground which he seems originally to have occupied in the king's good graces, nor does he appear to have adopted Mr. Eden's conciliatory advice, nor to have sought to regain the Royal favour by attentions and deference.

The king condescended to " *bouder*" the young

envoy—the latter affected to disregard the king—the king, growing gradually more and more hostile to England, amused himself by twitting her representative with the failures of her policy, and the unsuccessfulness of her arms; and the minister retaliated by replies, of which the sarcasm was equally delicate and sharp.

CHAPTER THE FOURTH.

1777 to 1778.

THE FAMILY.

WHILE Mr. Elliot had been employed, as we have seen, at Berlin, his family had not neglected to keep him informed of what was passing in London. Early in March the Dowager Lady Elliot and Isabella had returned to England, Sir Gilbert and his wife having gone to Paris to meet them.

A curious succession of accidents caused the various members of the family to miss each other, though actually crossing the channel or approaching its shores on the same day; thus Hugh had sailed from Gravesend (for Cuxhaven) a few hours before Sir Gilbert and Lady Elliot arrived there, and they, during a passage of four hours to Calais, crossed Alick on his way to England, while the Dowager Lady Elliot and Isabella, who were travelling leisurely from Paris, were passed on the road by Sir Gilbert and his wife hurrying to join them in the French capital!

The delay of a day in Paris gave the Elliots an opportunity of seeing something of the town—of dining with Lord Stormont and his young wife, and with her sister, the " charming Mrs. Graham,"[1] and also of renewing acquaintance with Madame Du Deffaud. " I saw her, and was charmed and warmed towards her by the sincerity of her concern in me and mine, and all of us."

Hurrying away from Paris, they retraced their steps again to Calais, and there rejoined their mother and sister. " What that meeting was, you may imagine !" writes one of the party.

Returning to England together, they were met at Canterbury by Mr. Eden and Eleanor, and all proceeded to London, dreading, as others have dreaded, the first sight of familiar objects associated with bygone days. In deference to the feeling which made Lady Elliot shrink from returning to the " dark house," the " long unlovely street," the

> " Doors, where *her* heart was used to beat
> So quickly, waiting for a hand,
> A hand that can be clasped no more,"

her children had arranged that she should not revisit her old home, but should be conducted at once to a small cheerful house in Clarges Street, which they had taken pains to prepare for her arrival. There, accordingly, she was soon installed, with some of her children about her, and pictures of the absent ones hanging on the walls; and there she and Isabella remained till summer sent them to look for " charming air, and gardens and green fields—*in Knightsbridge.*"

But before that time arrived, their spirits were further

---

[1] Whose husband became Lord Lynedoch,—a portrait of her by Gainsborough was one of the gems of the Manchester Exhibition.

tried by another painful parting. Alick's leave having
terminated, he returned early in May to India, and his
departure produced a sad letter from his mother to
Hugh. "That your fate and Alick's," she wrote, "notwithstanding all your advantages, require perpetual
absence, is a heavy sorrow. May I not say with the
Duchess of York in Richard—

> " ' But death has snatch'd my husband from my arms,
>   And pluckt two crutches from my feeble hands,
>   Clarence and Edward. O what cause have I,' etc. etc.

You both live, thanks to heaven! but you are both lost
to me; you, perhaps, I may still embrace, though perhaps not, but Alick, I daresay, I have parted with for
ever, his picture is now before me in my snuff-box, and
that is all I have of him who lightened my burdens with
unwearied duty. May heaven bless and preserve him,
but he is gone to a climate which will, I am sure, destroy
him."

Alick himself returned to his distant post full of
energy and spirit, and with what appeared to be a well-
grounded hope that he might live to achieve a brilliant
and useful career; but the event proved ere long that
his mother's forebodings were more truthful than his own
anticipations. He went to India by the overland route,
and from Constantinople he wrote to Hugh that the
various wonderful exploits performed by the latter during
the war on the Danube, were still the theme of conversation in the society there.

During the spring, Isabella and Eleanor both wrote
frequently to Hugh, and in their letters we get glimpses

of many old friends, besides more distinct views of the members of the family group.

Both the sisters agree that " Maria is most loveable and charming, with every good and agreeable quality," worthy even of " my brother." " They are indeed a very pleasant couple," writes the mother.

The letters of the Edens are sunshine itself. " The world still wags on as it did when you was with us," writes Eleanor; " some are happy, some are unhappy, but of the former none are a quarter so happy as votre petite sœur." And her husband tells her brother that " Eleanor is the delightfulest creature in the world— defies and despises politics—and makes preparations of pap !" And then, with the couleur de rose of home reflected on the Foreign Office, he declares " the political horizon of Europe" to be " clearing up, the American broil waxing fainter, and at all events England more resolute and more cheerful than ever."

" Bob," we hear, " cuts his hair à l'abbé, which is the first step in the church," and Isabella gradually returns into a little quiet society, is touched by the kindness of her reception on her first appearance at court, and meets here and there with old " flames" and friends of Hugh's, of whom she makes mention to him :— " Mr. Pitt was very agreeable at the opera last night. Miss North, merry as ever, bids me tell you she is very much in love with one person, and going to marry another; and her brother is at Oxford, ready to hang himself because Miss Egerton has refused him"—" which I believe he is very glad of," adds Isabella. " Lord

Lindsay, outrageous as ever, was so smitten with the sight of Lady Barrymore, just returned from Paris, that he wanted to carry her home instead of the chairman from his mother's party; but Mr. Fawkener, who was to have been his partner, being afraid of the fatigue, he had to give it up; he goes to America, and the poor duchess cries night and day about it."

Lord Suffolk, Hugh's kind and constant friend, married Lady Charlotte Finch in the course of the summer, and this event gave rise to many remarks from both sisters on the charms and merits of the bride— "She is really a very good kind of girl," writes Mrs. Eden, " but no doubt you will infer she is not handsome, as that would have come first, and I will not attempt to describe her, as all the answer I should receive from you in return would be, All the better for her soul—which is all I ever get from you or Mr. Eden if I do not begin by saying, 'She is very pretty, or rather handsome,' when you will listen to other qualifications with tolerable patience.

" However, though I cannot say this of Lady Suffolk, she has qualities which will make his life happy and comfortable, so much so that most of his friends have thought his marriage a subject on which he might with great propriety be congratulated ! Upon my word, Hugh, you are the greatest gig in the world. I daresay you will say that we all know no one can rejoice in his happiness more sincerely than you do, but if you will not even be at the trouble of writing him a letter to tell him so, you must own he is not obliged to find it out."

A description of Mr. Harris making an imposing

figure at Ranelagh—"making love in a box, and eating bread and butter in the regular way"—prepares us for another marriage ; and before the summer was over the "dangling diplomate" had become one of the family by marrying Harriet Amyand, youngest sister of Lady Elliot. The wedding is so graphically described by Mr. Liston, who assisted at it during his visit to London on business connected with the affairs of the rebel agents, that I cannot do better than to insert it here.

" Yesterday (29th July) was a very busy day with your friends here—a marriage and a christening within a few hours of each other ; your niece was baptized by the name of Eleanor Agnes, your mother and sister standing godmothers ;[1] and after dinner, during which many jokes were cut at Harris, the company adjourned to Lincoln's Inn Fields, where they found the bride, her two brothers, Lady Cornewall, your brother Bob, Miss Harris, and Lord Northington. Here a most trying scene ensued. Six o'clock was the hour named for the ceremony. The priest was ready in his pontificals. The young lady sitting anxious, arrayed in virgin white. The bridegroom standing upon the tiptoe of expectation, a frock extremely *galant*, colour of soupirs étouffés,[1] lining and waistcoat bleu de ciel, a very handsome embroidery, beautiful *brandebourgs*.

---

[1] Eleanor Agnes, eldest daughter of Mr. and Mrs. Eden, married in 1799 the Earl of Buckinghamshire. She was my godmother, and one of my earliest and best loved friends.

[2] Soupir étouffé—a pale lilac—was the fashionable colour of 1778.

In Madame D'Arblay's Diary, vol. i., p. 87, it is thus mentioned :—
" We had been talking of colours, and of the fantastic names given to

These were looked at and admired by everybody. Why don't we procced? said some one. The license is not come. Good God! what shall we do? When it came to be inquired into, it was found that they had not had an adequate idea of the possible delays of the law, and had not applied time enough to give allowance for accidents. But the proctor, who ought to have understood that matter, had faithfully promised to be there at six o'clock. After waiting an hour in a very awkward situation, Sir Gilbert went to the proctor's house to inquire for him. He had set out in the morning to wait on the Archbishop, whose intervention was necessary in the case, and who happened to be fourteen miles out of town. He was not returned. When this answer was brought a dozen of suppositions were formed, one more comfortless than the other. The man was robbed. He was killed by a fall from his horse. He had not found the Archbishop at home. As they had not employed the Archbishop's own proctor, it was to be feared *he* had found means to raise some difficulties that might have induced the Archbishop to refuse giving his consent. This uncertainty, than which it is not easy to conceive anything more completely disagreeable, lasted till near ten o'clock at night, when the license arrived and they were at last married. I must do Mr. Harris and his young wife the justice to

them, and why the palest lilac should be called a *soupir étouffé*, and when Dr. Johnson came in she (Mrs. Thrale) applied to him.

"'Why, Madam,' said he, with wonderful readiness, 'it is called a stifled sigh, because it is checked in its progress, and only half a colour.'"

say, they bore it in a way that did them great honour. They both have a degree of patience, or a command of face, much beyond what I can boast of."

Mrs. Harris, who was only sixteen, writing herself to Hugh, says, " Never was so merry a wedding as mine ! We waited four hours for the license ! your humble servant behaving like an angel, or rather like patience on a monument smiling at the ' Bear teas'd by Bees ' on the chimney-piece, the only tolerable sign of grief in the party."

To this letter Mr. Harris appended some lover-like remarks on the lady's beauty, as she appeared on that eventful day, which, however, are not corroborated by other correspondents of my grandfather, who, whenever they allude to her looks, invariably confine their appro- bation to her " very fine hair." Her letters are ex- tremely lively, and in allusion to the vicinity of the rooms which she and Hugh Elliot had at one time occupied under Sir Gilbert's roof, she usually addresses him as " Pyramus," signing herself " Thisbe." On their way to St. Petersburg, the Harrises spent a couple of days at Berlin, which they seem to have found very pleasant ones, and soon after their arrival at their post, Mrs. Harris reports to Hugh the number of inquiries she receives concerning him from his old military friends, Marshal Romanzow among them. " He presented me to his mother, a fine old lady of past eighty, who has seen Louis XIV., Queen Anne, the Electress Sophia, Peter the Great, and the present King of Prussia's grandfather, and talks of them all as we should of

King George and Queen Charlotte. She was in Berlin just after the battle of Pultawa,—she is Dame du Portrait to the Empress, and sits up every morning till two or three o'clock."

Mr. Harris was supposed not to dislike display, and one of my grandfather's correspondents writes at this time :—" He is likely to figure still more magnificently at Petersburg than he did at Berlin ; the lady's taste for éclât being at least equal to his. He has bespoke a sumptuous service of silver plate. He proposed to omit the covers to the dishes as not being absolutely necessary, and as making the difference of £1000. 'Pshaw !' said la petite ambassadrice, ' what signifies a thousand pounds ! have the covers : ' the covers were accordingly ordered."

Shortly after the marriage, the Dowager Lady Elliot went to a house in Knightsbridge, " quiet as Teviotside ;" and Sir Gilbert and Lady Elliot proceeded to Scotland, whence all accounts agree in describing her unbounded popularity, and her thorough enjoyment of Minto. From Mr. Liston we hear of her gaily dancing with the colliers at Lochgelly ; her impressions of Roxburgh-shire let her tell for herself :—

Minto, Sept. 13.—After a few remarks on her sister's late marriage she goes on :—" I don't, however, believe she is half as much delighted with papas and mammas, and uncles and aunts, as I am with the burns, the glens, the rocks, and the Nutbank. I am even partial to Ruberslaw and the Dunion, charmed with Mount Teviot and the *Yielding* (Eildon) Hills, overcome with the beauties of the smooth, green Minto Hill, and in ecstasies

with Denholm Dene.   But all these delights have been
interrupted by Kelso races, which kept us all last week
from home. The meeting was called thin; excellent sport,
and good balls, where I flatter myself with having made
new conquests in an uncommon way, some by talking,
some by laughing, some by dancing, and some by strong
beer; how shocked will you be at this last, it is not at
all sublime or delicate, but purely rustic and natural. I
had the pleasure of knowing the whole time that I was
the object of staring and observation, and the dread of
a drunken husband every evening; somehow or other,
however, he escaped all inconvenient jollity, though
many of the *geniuses* sat up all the three nights, dancing
on tables and climbing up the walls. I can't say how
glad I was when it was all over. We spent a day with
Lady Diana Scott; their place is quite delightful, the
prettiest I have seen except our own, but I like my own
the best.

" We have a ball at Jedburgh in view, so no prospect
of tranquillity as yet. . . . I declare, when I look
back to the last twelve months, it is so full of circumstances, and those of the most material ones in our lives,
that it is quite a dream—that is, like one; God forbid
it should be really so, that would be a bad joke. You
will have the Harrises soon at Berlin; I must in that
respect envy you and them." A few allusions to Bob
wearying over his studies, and to Alick broiling under a
tropical sun; to Eleanor's anxieties about her baby, and
to Lady Elliot's melancholy state of feeling, occupy the
remainder of the letter, which terminates thus :—" And

K

when I look round I find no one without distresses but
myself." Had they been written at the time, she might
have quoted the words of Longfellow—

> " And only the sorrow of others
> Throws its shadow over me."

The chief event of the autumn, in the estimation of
the family, was the first public appearance of Sir Gilbert
Elliot in the House of Commons, of which Isabella thus
writes (Nov. 28) :—You will, I am sure, rejoice to hear
that my brother has made his first appearance in the
House of Commons, with very great approbation. He
seconded the address, and though he was vastly terrified
when he went down to the House—poor soul! he was
as cold as ice—notwithstanding so great a disadvantage
everybody joined in giving him the highest degree of
praise, and there was the greatest disposition possible
in the House in his favour."

On the 16th of December Sir Gilbert wrote to his
brother a description of the scene which ensued in the
House on the receipt of the disastrous intelligence of
General Burgoyne's surrender. "The House of Commons sat the very day on which the news from Canada
was received. It was a singular moment. Lord George
Germaine very shortly, but in a manly way enough, told
the story to the House; Opposition began, by the most
extravagant expressions of deep sorrow, from which
there was a pretty sudden transition to violent rage,
mixed here and there with a spice of triumph; and the
patriotic grief which opened the debate had soon de-

generated, as all other topics and feelings generally do
in the House, into invectives against ministers, threaten-
ings of impeachments, and motions for immediate inquiries into their conduct. The House, although deeply
affected by the loss of our army, and by the share of
dishonour which must for a time fall on our arms, were
perfectly steady, and betrayed no marks of weakness.
They refrained from coming to any resolution whatever
that day, both for want of evidence, and because we
were not quite cool enough for deliberation. In general,
however, although all acknowledged the event as a
heavy calamity, yet the idea of considering the fate of the
nation as depending on it, or that Great Britain should
stand or fall by the success or failure of a single expedition, was rejected with proper spirit. Preparations are
carrying on with more vigour than before. Both fleet
and army are to be augmented, and, I believe, the plan
of the war changed. It is said the commanders too.
The country has not altered its tone. Manchester,
immediately on the receipt of the bad news, offered to
government to raise and equip a thousand men. I
believe some declaration will, at the same time, be made
of our claims on America, that the ultimate question
we are fighting for may be somewhat more definite, and
the Americans may not have their uncertainty on this
head to plead in aid of their cause. For my own *private*
part, I could have wished that this declaration, if it is
to be made, had come at any other time. Lord North
has, however, pretty much committed himself on this
point in the House." Mr. Eden, writing from Downing

Street on the same day, by the same mail, says, " The story" (of Burgoyne's disaster) " is mortifying and embarrassing enough ; but the nation is steady, the parliament temperate, the administration firm. We have full conviction, indeed, that the Americans are no cowards, but that is no reason with us against fighting them, and all the world, if necessary, in a just and honourable cause."

Such were the views of politicians. Mrs. Eden probably described with tolerable accuracy the general impression produced on the more frivolous part of London society by the evil tidings from the colonies. " News is arrived from America," she wrote, " which Government people say is nothing, and the Opposition say is very bad."

Similar differences of opinion have been seen in our time between *ins and outs*, and go far to justify sensible women in " defying and despising politics"—betaking themselves to preparations of pap !

The letters which were written to Hugh by his family during the winter of 1777 and 1778, confess a melancholy fact, which might have been surmised from the rarity of his mother's letters among his correspondence of the preceding summer—namely, the existence of a partial estrangement between herself and her favourite son. Misunderstandings appear to have existed on both sides, and to have dated from the time of Hugh's last return to his father's roof—that time of re-union so joyfully anticipated, so sad in the reality, so painful in the retrospection.

If the renewal of personal intercourse had not tended
to strengthen the sympathies of mother and son, subsequent neglects of punctuality in correspondence, which
led to suspicions of reserve and of diminished confidence,
had served to increase these mutual discontents, till at
last Sir Gilbert openly alluded to them, and in his usual
tender manner assured his brother that on the side of
the family there was no diminution of the warm affection all had ever borne to Hugh.

He writes—" My idea is that you, in the course of
last summer, conceived that your family and friends
here had in some respects neglected you, and had perhaps permitted your absence to cool their affection and
love for you; and that you have farther conceived that
some circumstances in your public conduct may have
deprived you of a share of your favour with those in
Government, with whom you are more particularly connected.   You see I state a subject which, between any
other two men might seem a delicate one, quite plainly.
The fact is, that no subject between us can be delicate,
because you know my heart and its sincerity as well as
I do myself, or as if it were in your own breast.   I have
mentioned this apprehension of mine merely to assure
you that if you have in fact, as I suppose, admitted such
fears, you may and must immediately dismiss them.
With respect to myself, eternal absence, and even eternal
silence on both our parts, would make no difference in
the truth and warmth of my admiration and affection
for a character which I know thoroughly.   I can make
the same assurances for every one with whom blood or

friendship has connected you; with respect to the other
part of the apprehension which I have imputed to you,
I have made it my business to inquire, and can assure
you with truth that your conduct has given entire satisfaction, and has not only been approved but applauded.
Before I quit this subject, let me ask you if there is not
an awkwardness between my mother and you—you
know the powers of her imagination; trifles light as
air, etc."

> " Alas! how light a cause may move
>   Dissensions between hearts that love,
> Hearts that the world in vain had tried,
>   And sorrow but more closely tied ;
> That stood the storm when waves were rough,
>   Yet in a sunny hour fell off,
> Like ships that have gone down at sea
>   When heaven was all tranquillity !
> *A something, light as air*—a look,
>   A word unkind, or wrongly taken ;
> Oh, love that tempests never shook,
>   A breath, a touch like this hath shaken."

Sir Gilbert's appeal could not fail to meet an immediate response from so warm a heart as his brother's,
and accordingly Hugh must, on receiving it, have written
to his mother in a strain which produced from her the
following reply :—" My dearest and well-beloved son—
Your letter has touched me with the most lively emo-
tions of joy, tenderness, and affection. These proofs of
affection from a beloved child are the rewards of
parents for all they have suffered on their account."

The mists which had hung between them were
dispersed, and during the short remainder of her life

they never formed again,—and it would have been needless to refer to what was so transient in duration, except to explain certain allusions in the correspondence.

There is something sad and striking in the change of relations which had produced this passing misunderstanding between a parent and child so full of reciprocal affection ;—a few short years ago, and Hugh was to her " her dearest joy," her " best comforter," her " darling child," who took away with him the brightest light of home; the years went on, the boy became a man, " with whom," she writes, " it would be but a parent's foolish dotage to interfere, for manhood is the best judge of its own conduct and affairs, and expostulations make unpleasant society."

Absence, in giving to each independent interests and pursuits, had worked its usual effect; for as my grandfather himself wrote to one of his foreign correspondents[1] about this time :—" Le genre humain est une si maudite race que sans l'habitude de se voir, on perd l'habitude de se chérir, et l'intimité la plus parfaite passe à la politesse, aux phrases, et aux compliments ; de là il n'y a qu'un pas à l'oubli." The remark is intended only to apply to ordinary friendships—often no more than habits of personal intercourse accidentally formed and carelessly broken ; but in a modified degree it holds true in the case of even the earliest and tenderest affections when no care is taken to counteract the baneful influence of time and separation. The

[1] Count Montréal.

adage, "Let well alone," is no safe guide in matters of
this nature,—let them alone, and they soon become
anything but *well*. There are perhaps no more painful
surprises in life than those which attend the reunion
of long-parted friends, whose affections have rested on
what once was, but is not, and who find out too late,
that to suit each other always, they should have grown
with each other's growth, nor should have allowed the
influences which moulded the one to leave the other
unchanged.

To grapple with adverse circumstance was not one
of my grandfather's characteristics; but, if his mother
knew better than her son how to hold love fast, perhaps
it was harder to her to let go unrepiningly the feelings
she had no power to retain. The parent's destiny
seemed too hard for her; not to be loved less, but to
see others loved more; to resign such sympathies and
confidences as belong to similar ages, and tastes, and
pursuits; and to rest satisfied with the conviction that
in his sadder hours he would surely return to seek that
comfort in her love which belongs to him "whom his
mother comforteth."

From the time of her husband's death, Lady Elliot's
health, which had never been strong, showed symptoms
of rapid deterioration; perfectly conscious herself that
such was the case, her letters about this time bear
evidence of a disposition to put her house in order
before setting forth on the journey whence there is no
return. Her counsels to her son read like farewells.
Her remarks on the prospects of her other children

are in the tone of one whose own future is not of this world.

Writing to Hugh, in January 1778, of the actual situation, and the probable future of her children, she thus expresses herself concerning her eldest son Gilbert :—" Nothing can exceed the excellence of his heart and head ; all he wants is a further stimulus to exertion. . . . His appearance in Parliament has raised him high in opinion, or rather in expectation, for it must be followed by subsequent ones, which I hope it will this session. . . . He is in a degree independent, and I am sure very much unconnected, except with the King and Lord Suffolk. At the same time I hope that politics—that waning inconstant planet—will never be his principal object, having a so much greater, and as I think, nobler and more independent one, in the certainty of law, if once he take root in that great field. I suppose you would differ from me in this opinion, and would prefer the other line; but I speak and know from experience the difference there is to a man of spirit between what depends on his own actual strength, and on the fluctuating conditions of faction, intrigue, or favour. . . . Therefore, I most devoutly wish the bar to be my son's ultimate object. His domestic happiness in his wife is as great as it is possible to desire. She is indeed a charming creature, and is to me the greatest possible comfort. Her love for her husband will make her conform to every circumstance that is for his interest and honour. It is impossible for two people to suit more entirely."

Isabella's situation, which at her mother's death would become one of painful loneliness, or of dependence on others, weighed heavily on her mother's mind; and though Sir Gilbert and his wife urged her in the most tender terms to entrust them with the charge of their sister, Lady Elliot strongly felt, that "to fix the point of their living together would be unwise, in spite of the reciprocal affection subsisting between the parties; for manners, tastes, and tempers, must all correspond to make living together agreeable; and should it be once determined on, and then given up, a quarrel is supposed to be the cause, which is an injury to the peace of both. Therefore, I think, a certain time should be specified, and it may be prolonged at pleasure."

Lady Elliot's uneasiness on this score was subsequently removed by a kind offer, on the part of the Queen, to provide for Miss Elliot, by attaching her, when the occasion should arise, to the household one day to be formed for the Princess of Wales.

Long, however, before it became needful to take any steps for the arrangement of such a household, poor Isabella Elliot had been laid in her grave; but the comfort which her mother found in the belief that an independent and agreeable position was secured to her favourite child, served to remove her chief cause of distress from the last moments of her life.

Public affairs never lost their interest for Lady Elliot; though she wrote, " I can give you little intelligence about them.

" A French war is much believed; I see no end of

that but one, the loss of credit, and consequent confusion. . . . It is curious to see a thoughtless
pampered people beginning to wake from their fallacious
dream of security, which they believed scarcely Heaven
itself could overthrow.[1] The first result is the spirited
raising of regiments for the service. I do not believe,
if the storm comes, the Premier will face it. Lord
Chatham is thought the most likely, but that can *only
come from a hard necessity.*"—(Jan. 28.)

On the 2d February Lady Elliot wrote again, under
the impression that a union had been effected between
Lord North and Lord Chatham, that the latter "had
offered his services at this crisis and had been accepted.
His expression, I hear, to the king was, that he ' would
go to the other side of the Atlantic for His Majesty's
service.'[2] I do not pretend to judge," she proceeds,
" but it seems to me that Lord Chatham has made a
false step in this affair, and from impatience for power
and office has ruined himself with his friends by coming
among his enemies, unsupported but by one man in the
cabinet, and if his policy is unsuccessful *he will be the
sacrifice at last.*"

Rumours of Lord Chatham's recall to office were rife

[1] Mr. Liston had been struck the year before by " the sang froid
with which people talk of entering on a war with the whole House of
Bourbon."

[2] Compare with this speech, attributed to Lord Chatham by some of
Lady Elliot's courtly friends, that which Walpole, with probably just
as little truth, puts into his mouth a few months later. "The king
made new overtures to Lord Chatham. He said he would not meddle
with the dirty people of the Court. If the king liked dirty company
he might keep it."— *Walpole's last Journals*, vol. ii. p. 244.

through London in the first weeks of 1778; the gloomy
aspect of public affairs had given rise to a general desire
that he should resume the reins of power; and when it
became known that an attempt at negotiation with
Lord Chatham on the part of the Rockingham party
had failed, owing to the antagonism of their views on
American policy, which made a common action impossible, the world immediately decided that Lord Chatham
was preparing to support Government against those who
were for giving way to the Americans.[1]

Gossiping stories were also afloat concerning an
alliance between Lord Bute and Lord Chatham, which
had no better foundation than an interchange of complimentary messages between the two veteran statesmen.
To these reports Lady Elliot could hardly lend an ear,
remembering "the perpetual endeavours that were
exerted to preserve his[2] union with the king in the end
of last reign and the beginning of this, and the jealousy
and coldness this produced from our first connections."

The policy of Lord North's ministry had been so
uniformly unsuccessful from the time of their advent to
power, that the most sanguine of their supporters
began to feel disheartened. Uncomfortable misgivings
clouded the cheerful confidence of Mr. Eden:—"The
short and plain truth," said he, writing from Downing
Street, January 9, "is, that the poor old island is in a
devilish crisis, and the embarrassments in which she is

---

[1] Vol. iv. of *Chatham Correspondence.* Letter from Lord Rockingham, Lord Mahon's *Hist. of Eng.* vol. vi. p. 212.

[2] Lord Chatham's.

involved become every hour more numerous and more complicated; nevertheless, there is a zeal, loyalty, composure, and firmness in the general class of the people that exceeds anything ever known in history. Our naval force, too, is immense, and our money resources by no means deficient. We want soldiers, and what is equally material, we want generals. It has so happened, whether by necessity or misconduct I know not, that the navy has for the whole summer been sacrificed to the army, and the army has as yet done nothing towards the main business. Burgoyne's catastrophe we criticise, of course, because we are disappointed. I fear, however, there is too much cause for criticism; and it is not the least part of my censure, now the mischief is done, that he indirectly throws the blame on his orders, which orders were settled personally with him, and in part actually dictated by him; those orders, too, at the same time that they tell him to make the junction his main object, left him a discretion according to circumstances; and if they had not, I understand it must have been implied in every military construction of orders to be executed at that distance. Besides, he capitulated in the act of retreating, after saying that his orders left him no power to retreat.

"Whether the expedition was ill conceived, or ill executed, or not, the event is very unfortunate to this country, and has given a considerable degree of firmness and consistency to the rebellion. We have, however, no alternative, we must go on; the rebels, in their present disposition, would not return even to a submission of the slightest kind.   France and Spain pretty openly encourage them.   Prussia does the same secretly. The measures which such conduct induces keep us every moment on the edge of war, but we are stout."

On the 10th February Sir Gilbert wrote—"Of the public I have little to say; the prospect of recovering America by war is certainly at an end.   The people are, I doubt, pretty unanimous; the country would defend itself almost without troops, and they have large and well-disciplined armies to oppose to ours.   All that can be said in our present situation is, that if new exertions have but a chance of recovering any part of our authority in America, and of redeeming the honour of our country, it is our duty to make them."

A subsequent letter by the same writer gives a sketch of the conciliatory measures proposed by Lord North, the debates on which are fully given in *Walpole's Last Journals;* and early in March it was known that Lord Carlisle, Mr. Eden, and Mr. Jackson, were to be the commissioners appointed under one of the new acts to treat with the Americans for peace.

On the 13th of March M. de Noailles delivered to Lord Weymouth a declaration from the King of France, acquainting his Britannic Majesty of the conclusion of a treaty of commerce and amity with the independent states of America.   On the 31st Sir Gilbert wrote to his brother — "We consider war as certain, and it is not easy to one unacquainted with the etiquette of public transactions to know why the declaration of war is delayed.   France and England are making the first

hostile salute, which fencers do before an assault, who
present their foils, take measure, stamp with their feet
and take off their hats to each other and to all the spectators.   They have sent us messages, to which we have
given angry answers.   Both our ambassadors are at
home; we have detained each other's ships, and are
making mutual preparations for war.   The militia is
called out, and there is a spirit among the gentlemen to
take part in it.   I rather think we wish for an invasion.
The militia is only between 25,000 and 30,000 men."

Throughout the island went the call to arms.   The
Duke of Buccleuch offered to raise 2000 men in the
south of Scotland for the defence of Scotland; "1000
were accepted, others are preparing to do the same; and
the king will be able to withdraw the regular troops
from the north, and we undertake to take care of ourselves.   This is so much at my own door, and I so
entirely love and approve the motive of the plan, which
is purely public spirit, that I shall have a hard battle
with myself if I resist it.   As to me, the state of the
question is this, it would at once knock up my law."[1]

"The bustle is beyond all description," wrote Isabella (17th March).   "Every creature, from high to
low, is full of nothing but the war, and the thought of
beating the French is very popular and pleasant to the
people in general, who hate them heartily; but I cannot
help feeling the horrors of bloodshed which now only an
arm of the sea parts from us.   The House of Commons
will sit this, and almost every night this week, till three

[1] Sir Gilbert to Hugh.

or four in the morning. It was reported to-day that the
war would be declared at Charing Cross to-morrow; but
this is certainly not so. London appears fuller than any
town I ever saw, and the buzz in the streets, and the
faces of the people, are beyond description. The whole
world are in red coats; most of the militia look very
' *bourgeois*,' but are fond of showing themselves off in
Fop's Alley."

A month later (April 20th) Isabella described
London as empty, " and many people not intending to
return through summer, as the militia were to be encamped in various places. Lady Derby, Lady Cranbourne, and many other ladies, intended to follow the
camp, but this the king has absolutely forbade, as it
would have been such a scene of amusement; so their
camp equipages, uniforms, etc., are of no use. There is
no chit-chat at present; people are very sober and
settled, except what is called the fine set, who are too
much above humanity to interrupt their pleasures for
any earthly or heavenly reason, and they make the conversation of the rest of the world, which is not worth
repeating by letter." Isabella is, as usual, the chief
chronicler of the gossip of the town—Mrs. Eden occasionally assisting with a droll account of somebody's
love affairs, prosperous or otherwise; but ever persistent
in her contempt for politics. "I hear," she wrote, "you
are in doleful spirits about the nation—so is everybody.
We shall be ruined and undone; but, as it cannot be
helped, I shall not make myself unhappy about it—
though I sincerely wish the war were over, that so many

people might not be killed, and that my dear sweet husband might not have so much business, as it makes him very thin."

In Isabella's letters of last year (1777) we read that Lord Lindsay was on the point of setting out for America. Early in the present year (1778) she mentions him as returned from the seat of war on leave of absence, during winter, "wild and agreeable, and handsome as ever; decidedly improved, but making the rhino fly in a sad way." He returned to America in April, with Colonel Stewart, Lord Bute's son, married to "the fortune," Miss Bertie, only a few days before his departure. Other newly-married couples were under the same sad necessity of an immediate parting. The Duke of Hamilton had undertaken to raise a regiment, and was to go to America as captain in it, "which perhaps will be more to your taste than his. He is going to be married to Miss Bur-rell, who is a pretty little girl, very shy, and quite un-known to most of the world, as she is very young, and the fine ladies are all a little displeased; but *le coup est porté*, he is to go six weeks after his marriage"—a step which Mrs. Eden remarks on as "*most wonderful*."[1]

Another marriage on the *tapis* occupied some space

---

[1] Miss Burrell was a daughter of Peter Burrell, Esq., called *Lucky Burrell*. Her sister married Lord Piercy, her brother Lady Priscilla Bertie, daughter of the Duke of Ancaster, who, at her husband's request, changed her name from Priscilla to Elizabeth. Lady Priscilla, at her brother's death, inherited great part of the Ancaster property, and the hereditary office of High Steward. "I wish," said Mr. Eden on that occasion, "that Lucky Burrell commanded the Channel fleet in the place of Sir C. Hardy."

in the letters of both sisters—one projected between
Lord Shelburne and Hugh's former love Miss Molesworth; "he is at least eight-and-forty; she not above
twenty, handsome and rich." But the sequel of the story
contained the remarkable feature in it, and it is thus
related by Isabella :—" Your divine Miss Molesworth has
surprised the world by breaking off from Lord Shelburne.
She dined at his house, and sat at the head of the table,
and was seen to cry all dinner-time. Her aunt, when
she came home, asked her what was the matter. She
made no answer, but ran up stairs to her own room, and
sent Lady Lucan a letter to tell her she found she had
an antipathy to Lord Shelburne, and begged she would
break off the detested match; which was accordingly
done, by showing his Lordship the letter. He was
angry, as you will believe, to lose £40,000 and so pretty
a wife, but put a good face upon it, and said it was
proper the ladies should settle those matters. So the
coast is clear again for your Excellency."

The appointment of Mr. Eden as one of the commissioners to America, and the preparations for his
departure, and for that of his wife, are the chief subject
of the letters written in April. "Eleanor, poor soul!"
had been bemoaning her hard lot, "in having to sit
patiently all the winter listening to the fiddles;" but
the condition of her health seems never to have occurred
to her as a reason for not accompanying her husband on
a long sea voyage in time of war. She writes herself—
" As to my staying behind him, it was an idea that could
never have entered my head for a moment, and I flatter

myself was never an instant in his. Had he proposed such a thing ever so gently I could never have forgiven him; and it is my pride, comfort, and boast, that he would have found it as hard a matter to leave me behind, as I should have found it an impossible one to let him go without me. As to any dangers or hardships I may meet with whilst with him, I think I shall have but little fear; few accidents can happen to one which will not be common to both; and whilst that is the case I am content. So good bye, and God bless you, dearest and most beloved Hugh."

But another parting was inevitable—that with her baby; and it was with a sharp heart-twinge that Mrs. Eden confided it to the care of her mother and sister. The Edens set out early in April.

"Eden concealed from us the day they were to go, and she did not even know it herself. She was playing with her little girl on Monday morning, when Mr. Eden desired her to come down to take leave of Lady Suffolk. She went out and the chaise was waiting in Bridge Street: when she saw it she guessed how it was, and fell a-crying, but got in, and was drove off. It was a great shock, but on the whole the best way. I brought home the little girl, and she amuses my beloved mother and me with her little pretty innocent looks."[1]

Isabella tells Hugh that it was thought very ridiculous of Mr. Storer to join the party, "merely out of affection for Lord Carlisle, and crowding the ship sadly." And before they left St. Helen's, "Storer and Eleanor

[1] Isabella to Hugh, April.

had a quarrel. He has carried a pianoforte with him to charm the Americans, and found out that Eleanor's cabin would be the best place for it; but as she is not fond of music, she begged to be excused; and they were both very warm upon it, so Governor Johnston begged they would take the *piano* and leave the *forte*."[1]

These small difficulties at starting must soon have given way, for Mr. Eden, writing off St. Helen's, April 16, says—" The Captain[2] has exerted himself in contrivances for our comfort. Eleanor has a regular dressing-room and toilet. We have sailed ten miles in a delightful morning, through a fleet consisting of 33 ships of the line, completely ready for sea, exercising guns, etc., the group much improved by frigates and Indiamen."

On the eve of his departure from England, Mr. Eden wrote to his brother-in-law Hugh a long and kind letter, from which the following passage is an extract: —" And now allow me the liberty of a sort of death-bed to give you a little advice. You have the affectionate friendship of our Principal, and the favourable opinion of his Principal; but they have each a notion that you have a predominancy of the Hotspur vivacity in your

[1] Lord Carlisle is described by Walpole as a young man of fashion and pleasure. Mr. Storer was a well-known *maccaroni*, and an agreeable man.

Governor Johnston had replaced *Jackson*, who had been originally appointed to the commission. Sir G. Elliot says of Jackson, that "his universal and detailed knowledge was never of use to him, and left his opinions as undecided and more confused than those of the most ignorant."

[2] Captain John Elliot, son of the Lord Justice-Clerk, and brother of the late Sir Gilbert.

character. This would do well in many stations, but in yours it gives alarm. Be of good heart, and take heed, my dear Hugh, and you cannot fail of acting an eminent, honourable, and important part on the great stage of the world."

The summer of 1778 found the Edens sailing on the high seas; the Dowager Lady Elliot nursing her failing health in strict retirement, cheered by the society of her children and grandchild; Sir Gilbert preparing to put aside his wig, and to stick a cockade in his hat; Isabella living "with a few friends," of whom she says—"The Duchess of Ancaster, Lady Grimston, Lady Priscilla, and Mrs. Lockhart make the chief part. Lady Priscilla sang last night like an angel; and Lady Stormont like a human being!" and the rest of the world allait toujours son train. "Lord North and Lord G. Germayne have a great deal of abuse to bear this session." "There are more bankruptcies in the fine set than ever; executions in private houses, and maccaronis flying abroad."

CHAPTER THE FIFTH.

1777 to 1778.

BERLIN.

IT is probable that the sense of a change in his relations
with his family was one of the causes for the deep
depression which hung over my grandfather's spirit
during the winter of '77 and '78; but the sole cause it
was not, for money difficulties constantly harassed him,
and were all the more sensibly felt as his attachment
for the fair Mademoiselle de Krauth took a deeper and
more serious character.   Writing to Mr. Pitt,[1] who
had lately visited Berlin on a tour to the northern
Courts, he says—" I believe you doubt of the reality
of my reasons of uneasiness, and attribute to nerves
and temper a state of mind occasioned by anxiety and
distress respecting objects over which I have no command, and that ought not to affect me more than the
rest of mankind.   Whatever be the cause, I know the
effect, and rather than submit to it would burst this
embryo of existence, and, in the words of the poet,
spring to light, or sink to darkness, as I think either
better than the long tedious glimmering of the feeble

---

[1] November 1777.

lamp of life, which throws such false shades over every
image within the verge of human comprehension. But
I acknowledge Hamlet's dread of the dream that may
follow; and although six feet underground may be an
asylum for all the passions, inquietudes, misfortunes,
and pain which have seized upon the surface, yet what
other base, cursed fiends may await us in that fathom-
less abyss, to which the grave is the only entrance, who
has ever emerged to tell? My coward soul recoils at
the brink, nor dares to plunge. Do not think I am
seriously weighing *to be or not to be.* You know a
sufficient reason why I can never determine for the latter;
but if that reason did not exist, I verily believe I should
let go my hold, and drop without further struggle to
that common centre which attracts all our species. I
began this letter with an intent to make excuses for the
continual gauntlet your spirits, gaiety, and gallantry run
through my battalion of spleen, disappointment, and
satire. I believe, however, they are too tough to have
been sensible of the efforts of my feeble and dispirited
garrison."

Such was the mobility of my grandfather's temperament, that barely a month before he wrote this gloomy
letter he had described himself to some of his correspondents as thoroughly enjoying an agreable and
brilliant position; and to Mr. Brydone he had written
that of all places he had ever seen he liked Berlin
best—" a great victorious monarch with a numerous
army! I would not change for Etna with all its
eruptions."

Rapid variations of mood have been ever accepted as a lover's normal state, but, in the present instance, they may, perhaps, be no less naturally accounted for by the disordered condition of Mr. Elliot's health, which about this period began to show symptoms of long-standing and serious derangement.

The year 1778 was spent by him entirely at Berlin; and, to judge from the letters he wrote and received, its course was one of checkered light and shade.

He continued at times to exult over the *agrémens* of his life; at others, to lament the manifold expenses into which these led him. We find him at one moment writing admirable philosophy to his friends on the employment of time, and the adoption of the highest motives for action; and at another, laying himself open to their retorts by his own inconsistencies and waywardness. Heaven is just—it gives to some the power of reasoning, and to others that of acting conformably to reason. My grandfather, at this period of his life, shone pre-eminently in the former class.

The spring found him attending on the death-bed of his old friend, Lord Marischal, as he was commonly called. This remarkable man, who to the end of his days retained the titular dignity to which, as head of his family, he had an hereditary right, was the eldest son of Lord Keith, hereditary Earl Marischal of Scotland. Born in 1685, he lived to within seven years of a century; having in his youth served under Marlborough, he died in the reign of George the Third. A devoted adherent of the Stuarts, he left his native land on the

accession of George the First; passed with some other
Jacobite officers into the service of Spain; and only left
those more genial skies to settle at Berlin, when his
younger brother, Marshal Keith,[1] entered the service of
Frederick the Great.   From that time he was frequently employed by the King of Prussia on missions of
importance, but finally returned to spend his last years
in his adopted country, where he lived and died in a
cottage built for him by Frederick the Great, close to
the palace of Sans Souci.   Gay, courteous, and agreeable, as well as worthy of all respect for more essential
gifts, Lord Marischal appears to have been generally
loved and lamented.   The king, with whose philosophical tastes he had much sympathy, lived with
him on terms of the most familiar intimacy; and the
general estimation in which Lord Marischal was held
is thus described by my grandfather in a letter to his
brother :—

"Experience gained in the school of adversity, great
penetration, sound judgment, retentive memory, made
him equally instructive and entertaining.   He will long
be cited in this country as a model of wisdom, benevolence, and virtue.   I sincerely loved and honoured him.
I have just learnt that an accident destroyed lately a
considerable part of his correspondence, which would have
thrown great light upon the principal characters of those
times, when, to use his own expression, 'we were fighting
for a king and not for an empire.'"[2]

A few days before his death, Lord Marischal sum-

---

[1] Marshal Keith was killed in 1758.   [2] Hugh Elliot to Sir Gilbert.

moned my grandfather to his bedside. "You may, perhaps," he said, "have some commission to give me for Lord Chatham.[1] I shall see him in a day or two!" While in attendance on his dying friend Mr. Elliot wrote the following note, probably (for it has no address) to Mr. Hervey :—

"*Wednesday, May.*—Lord Marischal's existence is astonishing; were it not for a feverish pulse and a labouring respiration, his body would be, in all respects, a corpse. There is only enough life left in his animal frame to allow him at intervals the faculty of showing that the mental powers have survived the corporeal. When he musters up strength to express a few words, he discovers more clearness of judgment and memory than I thought it possible nature would permit so exhausted a frame to possess. If it were worth while to form any wish concerning so indifferent a circumstance as the manner in which one would chuse to take leave of a scene that flies from us, 'Que je meurs comme ce juste,' would be mine. As you are not fond of contemplating death, I do not advise you to come here; as I, on the contrary, wish to have as much intercourse as possible with a gentleman, who will one day force himself on my acquaintance, I shall remain here to contemplate him in his most engaging form; it will make me less loth to obey his summons when called upon. Adieu. Spring has spread its fairest tint on the beauties of Potsdam; Lord Marischal alone excepted, all nature revives."

---

[1] He had died a fortnight before.

The position of England at this time was one which could not fail to give uneasiness to all lovers of their country. At open war with her colonies, on the verge of war with France, without such commanders for her fleet and armies as could alone make her military operations effective, and distracted in her counsels by interminable struggles for power between half-a-dozen political leaders, her history during the first twenty years of the reign of George the Third is one little calculated to thrill the reader's breast with patriotic pride.

Hugh Elliot, young, spirited, and full of military ardour, had many a mortification to devour in silence, while acting as England's representative at a court of whose sentiments he thus writes to Lord Suffolk :—[1]

" As to this Court, it is composed of individuals thoroughly ill inclined to Great Britain; but too sensible of their own situation not to know that the day is perhaps not far distant when the existence of their power may depend upon its assistance. It is much to be regretted that there are no means of curbing the licentiousness of our public prints—I believe I should say of our public speakers. The Duke of Richmond's speeches, translated into every foreign gazette, are fatal to negotiation. I beg your lordship's excuse for mentioning a circumstance which may appear trivial in England, but which is certainly of bad consequence abroad."

To a more familiar correspondent he wrote that, " Though the wild rumours of England and its news-

---

[1] 5th June.

papers are treated at home with the contempt they deserve, abroad our politicians are too greedy not to swallow everything. I wish it were possible to publish every week an authentic negative gazette, for instance :—

"Gibraltar is *not* taken.

"The French are *not* landed on the coast of Sussex.

"Ministry have *not* resigned.

"The fleet is *not* rotten.

"The Duke of Richmond's and Fitzpatrick's speeches are *not* gospel.

"For my own part I am silent, and keep my breath till I can join in the chorus with the British lion. One roar will drown all this impertinent clamour, and frighten Europe into its senses."

To another friend he exclaims in despair—"For God's sake tell me what you think of Old England; from this distance she seems old indeed, sans eyes sans teeth, sans everything."

About this time Isabella was writing to her brother that "there was a very comical scene at the opera last night. Lord North came into the house for the first time this winter, and was very soon sent for; upon which the whole people here were led to believe that the French had landed on the Sussex coast, and that there was a rebellion there. The story gained credit, and before the end of the opera, you never saw such an excitement. However, the gentlemen in their militia uniforms seemed very brave, and ready to kill Frenchmen by dozens; and the whole foundation for the report was some smugglers that had refused to enlist in the militia."

To Mr. Eden, the news of whose nomination to be one of the commissioners to treat for peace with America had reached him some time before, my grandfather gave his views of the probable results of the negotiation in the following words :—

" The love of glory, that last infirmity of noble minds, must be set aside by our philosophic country till some dear, daring half-madman once more directs our thunder, or tramples on prudence, and on what people, who think themselves wise, call *reason*. This is too mad a world to act sensibly in. The same line of conduct that brings either an individual or a state into a scrape, often pushes them through it. Had we never engaged in a war with America, it might have been better for us. As it is, 1 fear we have stopped short at the very moment we ought to have risked everything. My conjectures are, that their terms will be haughty and overbearing. In time the natural interests of Great Britain and her colonies will trim the balance, which at present hangs so uneven. But had it been possible to have added the weight of 10,000 men to your commission, I should have had better hopes of your obtaining a peace acceptable to a nation unaccustomed to temporise, and whose spirit is more able to struggle with all the difficulties of debt and war, than to brook disgrace and dishonour."

However great may have been his secret misgivings as to the ultimate results of the war between Great Britain and her colonies, Mr. Elliot invariably main-

tained an appearance of the most serene composure
when the subject came under discussion in the society
of Berlin.

Thiébault says, " Souvent dans la société on parlait
de cette guerre à M. Elliot, et ceux qui cherchaient à
lui plaire en paraissaient quelquefois effrayés, surtout
après que les Français se furent déclarés pour les
Américains. Jamais il ne répondait qu'en montrant une
parfaite sécurité.

" ' Tout ce qui peut nous arriver de pire,' disait-il à
la fin, ' c'est qu'au lieu d'être le premier peuple du monde,
nous serons le second.' "[1]

In this state of suppressed irritation, my grandfather
no doubt hailed the departure of the court and garrison
from Berlin as a welcome relief from the presence of
those whose ill-concealed triumph over England's humiliation was a daily trial of his patience.

It is impossible to over-estimate the self-control
required from a man who, in a moment of national
humiliation, is living abroad among governments or
nations hostile to his country. Though in secret he
may acknowledge her blunders, and lament her policy,
to him she is still " an ill-favoured thing, *but mine
own ;*" and when her bitterest enemies can triumphantly
appeal in support of their assertions to the words of
Englishmen at home, it is not unnatural that he should
find himself in a position of antagonism to all who, from
whatever motives, are unveiling her errors, and proclaim-
ing her weakness. Party tactics, however indispensable

---

[1] Thiébault, tom. xi. p. 309.

to the working of parliamentary Governments, are ill
understood on the Continent. Foreigners attach more
importance to the statements made in the course of a
debate than to the arguments deduced from them, or
the ends to which these are directed; and when an eloquent Opposition has clearly demonstrated that England
has neither admirals nor generals, fleets nor armies, that
her counsels are distracted, her people disheartened, and
that a state of universal rottenness exists, foreigners are
slow to perceive that a mere change of *standpoint*, as
the Germans say, will often suffice to make the most
despondent of our political seers burst forth into a song
of thanksgiving :—"How goodly are thy tents, O Jacob :
and thy tabernacles, O Israel!"

We have so many grounds for gratitude to our
national institutions, that we can afford to put up with
some inconveniences which arise from them ; but it is *a
bore* that they forbid us to act on Napoleon's advice, to
"laver notre linge sale en famille." Europe assists at
our periodical lustrations (which generally usher in our
greatest undertakings), and when the heat of the struggle
is over, and the clouds of steam have evaporated, we
are surprised to find her quoting us against ourselves,
and proving to demonstration that we have "written
ourselves down asses." In the innocence of our hearts
we exclaim, "Qui te l'a dit?" No such surprise, however, awaits him who has watched the progress of events
from a foreign land.

The war known as that of the Bavarian succession

broke out in July 1778; and on the 14th of the month Frederick put himself at the head of his army and entered Bohemia.

All the princes of the blood were also in the field. Rheinsberg was left to solitude and silence; and, in the absence of royalties and warriors, the diplomatists found themselves in unusually advantageous circumstances to *faire l'agréable.*

How far Mr. Elliot profited by these may be guessed by the more frequent mention in his correspondence of the fair Mademoiselle de Krauth.

Letters from travellers returned home inquire tenderly for " la belle des belles," or more irreverently refer to Hugh's taste for " cabbage."

" Beware of Miss Cabbage," writes one, " for she is artful, and knows very well you love her." " If you feed on sprouts," says Sir J. Harris, from the distance of St. Petersburg, " you will find them hard of digestion." Alarming rumours reach the family in England, and produce good advice from Sir Gilbert, who warns his brother against asking a spoilt young beauty to share with him an income which had never sufficed for him alone! It seems to have been a peculiarity of my grandfather's, that whenever he found he had not enough to live on, he invariably proposed retiring upon nothing; and accordingly his letters at this time abound in plans for giving up a luxurious world, and betaking himself to goatskins, locusts, and wild honey.

The letters to which I have been referring are, with many more on the same subject, filed and docketed by

Mr. Elliot himself. They are by no means the sweepings of desks, or the overlooked contents of portfolios, but, strange as it may seem, have been carefully arranged, and are bound in calfskin in their chronological order, with the date of the year, in gilt letters, on the back of each volume.

Stranger still, we find bound in similar manner the subsequent congratulations of the same writers on his marriage; and, strangest of all! there are among these volumes copies of his own letters containing his first impressions of Mademoiselle de Krauth, when regarding her merely as a beautiful girl, *with the manners of Berlin*—which, from his pen, was not a complimentary description.

It is impossible to guess the motives which led to the preservation of such letters as these. Perhaps some of them may have appeared to their receiver as counsels of perfection worthy to be kept, though too hard to be followed. Perhaps the shrewd and caustic remarks on "Miss Cabbage," contrasted subsequently with the respectful homage of the same writers to the charms and merit of Madame Elliot, may have served to elucidate some philosophical theory on the worthlessness of human testimony.

Possibly these letters may have been preserved to be read in penance for the slighting of so much sense, or as proofs that first impressions are best. At all events they *have* been preserved, and those of my friends who are scared by a simple suggestion that even in this world all secrets may become known, should take comfort from the reflection that very few people are at so much trouble as was my grandfather to ensure that none of his should be hid.

That the subject of marriage, though in his mind, was not at this moment contemplated from what we should now call an " *earnest*" point of view, may be gathered from a congratulatory note to his friend, Marquis de Bombelles, who had lately married.

" Tout le monde se marie—je commence à être honteux de mon célibat. Dans le siécle où nous sommes il faut ou détruire ou procréer. Il y a des risques à courir dans les deux métiers, nos ennemis gagnent par nos pertes dans le premier, nos amis gagnent quand nous sommes malheureux dans le second."

About this time [1] he wrote to Countess Thun in the following lively strain—" Je n'ose pas me vanter d'être parfaitement heureux; peut-être y at-il de ma faute; mais malheureusement cela ne console pas. Je suis moins philosophe que je ne l'ai été, au moment qu'il me conviendrait fort de l'être. Je crois que c'est assez le sort de tous les philosophes. On surmonte toutes les passions, toutes les difficultés, quand on n'en a pas; on succombe tout comme si on n'était pas philosophe quand on en a.

" Berlin me plait infiniment; on a du loisir, de la liberté, et peu de bruit. La société y est mêlée comme partout ailleurs, il y a du bon et du mauvais, en général la bonhommie y règne plus que la vivacité et l'esprit. Les femmes sont sans talens, sans beauté, et sans graces. Elles n'en jouent pas moins constamment au

[1] July 15th.

whist, au manille, et savent rester quatre heures à souper, au beau milieu de l'été, sans s'apercevoir si leur voisin mange ou dort, cela dépend de lui. On n'est pas du tout obligé d'être aimable, et rien n'est plus commode pour un Anglais; de tems en tems un officier français nous arrive, la jambe en l'air, chantant, voltigeant, contant toutes les plaisanteries de l'année passée à Paris. Nous en sommes enchantés, nous chantons, nous voltigeons, et nous contons à notre tour, un peu moins légèrement il est vrai, mais on est assez bon pour nous trouver charmants ce jour là et pour en citer l'agrément le reste de l'année. D'ailleurs nous avons des personnes d'une société bien douce, et nous avons des beautés qui le seraient en tout pays."

Writing more confidentially to an English friend, he says :—" I wish I could tell you that any favourable crisis had taken place in my affairs; they are deep gone in a consumption, and can only be saved by a hearty infusion of *metals*, which are not to be met with. Greatly falling with a falling state is the *devise*; it is, however, a poor comfort. I am in Cobentzel's house, perfectly well pleased with it. I am on a very good footing with the world in general; and, though not a little criticised, am, I believe, as well as need be. On the whole, I am more and more attached to Berlin, and shall be very sorry when circumstances oblige me to leave it. The town is very empty and very pleasant."[1] The letter closes with his speculations on the probable conduct and possible consequences of the war between Prussia and

---

[1] September.

Austria, of no interest at the present date; from the scene of war he heard but little, since no officers ventured to correspond on military matters with foreign ministers. That he himself set no store by the partial and scanty information he received, is plain by the following extract from a letter to a friend in the camp of Prince Henry :[1] —"Votre campagne fait aujourd'hui le sujet de toutes les conversations. On en parle à tort et à travers. Sans trop savoir ce qu'on dit, j'ai justement assez de connaissances militaires pour croire que ceux qui ne savent pas *tout*, ne savent *rien;* et nous autres Berlinois et Berlinoises qui nous avisons de tracer vos marches et de décider de vos opérations militaires, méritons parfaitement le mépris avec lequel vous traitez nos savantes discussions."

The distinction gained by the Prince of Prussia in this campaign was particularly grateful to Mr. Elliot, who always experienced cordial kindness at his hands. He says—"The Prince seems to have greatly distinguished himself, and to have merited and obtained a perfect reconciliation with the king—a great event for this country, whose existence depends upon the abilities and harmony of its princes."

No amount of pre-occupation concerning things nearer at hand diverted my grandfather's attention from the fluctuating fortunes of England; and his letters to his old friend, Mr. Pitt, and to Lord J. Clinton, show how keenly his interest was directed to affairs at home. Mr. Pitt had spent the greater part of the year at the northern courts, studying the governments and manners

[1] To Baron Kaphengst, aide-de-camp to Prince Henry, Nov. 1778.

of other nations, with a view of presently taking an active part in public life at home. "I cannot help thinking," wrote Mr. Elliot to him, "that you devote too much time to a very barren soil. Your own country never was in a greater crisis than at present—never was a moment when more was to be learnt or done. My dear Pitt, with your application and desire of getting information, London will afford more objects worth your attention in one day, than the Goths and Vandals in years" (Nov. 6).

On another occasion he wrote to the same friend :— "I have had a variety of English of all sorts and sizes. The more I see of them the more I am convinced of the practicability of the *grand design*.[1] The stuff is there, and recruits come in. I sincerely congratulate you upon the final conclusion of your Continental excursion. Perhaps I am wrong, but I am every day more and more convinced that the wear and tear of such fatiguing journeys are not balanced by the profit of knowledge acquired, applicable to the theatre of England. We are a world apart. It requires a life of perseverance and application to know that world, and it requires uninterrupted habits of its manners, and constant residence in its atmosphere, for the ablest to act in it. As Rousseau says of himself that he does not pretend to describe whether he is better or worse than other men, but he is certain *qu'il est autre*—so may we say of our country.

[1] See 1st chapter. The *design* referred to was to form a band of "*true patriots*," who should devote all their energies to the furtherance in Parliament of certain grand objects, such as Catholic emancipation, internal reforms, etc. etc.

I now consider you as on the point of mounting your
great horse; I wish you may manage him as you intend."

Mr. Pitt's share in this correspondence leads one to
suppose that he was possessed of good sense and
industrious habits, rather than of remarkable abilities.
His letters are chiefly interesting from the light they
throw on the character of his friend; and though they
occasionally savour slightly of a mentor's tone, and
confess their writer to have been of opinion that his
correspondent might be improved by acting "a little
more like other two-legged creatures," they, nevertheless, testify to his sincere regard and admiration for
Hugh Elliot.

The comments which Mr. Pitt makes on his opinions
and manners give a lively impression of the inconsistencies which alternately attracted and provoked his
friends. A passionate lover of glory, he held in contempt the applause of the little world in which he lived.
"You carry your contempt of the Qu'en dira-t-on too
far," said Mr. Pitt. "I agree with you in despising
actions performed for the sake of obtaining applause;
but the good opinion of our friends and countrymen
ought to be grateful to us."

Disregarding the good fortune which had placed
him, at the age of twenty-six, in a great and responsible
situation, he scarcely affected to conceal his disgust
with the manners of the society to which that situation
introduced him; and this very dislike to the general
tone of society threw him all the more readily into a
small clique of clever, well-bred, but unprincipled

people, to whom his imagination lent perfections which they never possessed.

So indolent were his bodily habits, that his friends talk of his sofa as part of himself; yet his activity of mind was unfailing; all intellectual subjects had an interest for him. Politics never spoilt his taste for literature and science; and his powers of conversation made his society to be sought after by many of the most distinguished persons of his time. His spirits seem to have been equally uncontrollable in their glee and their depression—" spirits," says Mr. Pitt, " such as when, on hearing of that great and total defeat of Gates's army by Burgoyne, you threw a whole basin of milk over me"[1]—spirits such as those which, when excited to anger, had led to his enforcing a practical application of England's power on a triumphant and insolent foe.

The story is told thus :—A vulgar Frenchman who had just heard of the acknowlegment by France of the independence of America, came up to my grandfather, and thrusting his face in that of the English minister, said with a sneer—" Voilà un fameux soufflet que la France a donné à l'Angleterre." " Et voilà le soufflet que l'Angleterre rend à la France par ma main !" exclaimed the representative of England, accompanying the words with a stinging box on the ear.

[1] On the 19th September 1777 General Burgoyne attacked Gates's army on Behmus heights, and forced their position. This was probably the action reported at home as a great and decisive victory. Mr. Pitt was averse to the American war.

Mr. Brydone had, in Ratisbon days, remarked on
Hugh Elliot's singular power of communicating to others
some of his own high spirit and ardent desire to serve
his country.

That he continued to urge on his friends the duty of
exertion in public life, is shown in the following extract
from a letter to Lord J. Clinton, who was just com-
pleting a tour of the chief capitals of Europe, having,
according to the regular routine, assisted at Prussian
reviews, Viennese assemblies, and Parisian balls, and
fallen desperately in love with Princess Frederick of
Brunswick :—" My dear Lord—Rank, fortune, abilities,
are yours; do not run the dull, idle, tasteless course of
your contemporaries; the times, your country, ask for
exertion.   Pray, remember that Britain is your theatre,
and your situation enables you to play the part on it
you are fitted for—that of a warm, steady, and judicious
patriot.   *We* are exiles without influence; you may
touch the mainspring."

Lord J. Clinton's letters are easily and pleasantly
written, but do not display any conspicuous talent.   On
the 8th December, soon after having taken his seat in
Parliament, he writes—" As I have attended my duty
to Parliament some days, I can give you some little
account of our miserable situation.   Opposition paint it
in very strong colours.   Government allow that it is
critical.   Charles Fox, with his usual vehemence of
oratory, declares that he sees the inconvenience of
clogging the wheels of Government by Opposition at this
moment; but at the same time says he thinks it his

duty so to do, that we may by this means get rid of
such a weak, wicked, etc., ministry. Government is
daily excessively abused, but at the close of the debate
has always a very considerable majority; people have
not a better opinion of Opposition than of Government,
and therefore choose to side with the latter; perhaps
also, the loaves and fishes make converts. Yesterday
there was a debate in the House of Lords, during which
Opposition used every argument to encourage America.
. . . I will now tell you what I think of our manner
of living here. I cannot say that I much like it; people
look so very cold and uninteresting, that I never go
into company without returning de très mauvaise humeur.
The women are very beautiful, but few of them have des
physiognomies intéressantes; and they know they are
handsome, and expect great adoration.

"I wish you were here; absence is the most powerful cure for love. Some other object presents itself,
and what with politics and present occupations, you
grow by degrees much cooler for the one that is miles
distant. You will say, 'This man does not know
what love is!' I maintain, however, that my way of
treating the subject is the pleasantest and the most
philosophical."[1]

After hearing of the debates which had lately taken

---

[1] Lord John Clinton is mentioned in Madame d'Arblay's diary
among the frequenters of Mrs. Thrale's society; and is described in
1780 as "a very well-informed and modest-mannered boy, ugly, lively,
and amiable." He died of consumption at Lisbon in 1781; and it is
hinted in the letters that his fate was hastened by a disappointment
in love.

place in Parliament, on the conduct of Admiral Keppel and Sir Hugh Palliser, and of General Burgoyne and Sir H. Clinton, Mr. Elliot wrote to this correspondent as follows—" I am surprised at the weakness of the minister, in permitting talking generals and wrangling admirals to lower the dignity of the House in the eyes of all Europe, by making it a mere receptacle of abuse, peevishness, disappointment, and jealousy. What a perversion of the nature of the House, to make it a court of appeal to judge of the propriety or impropriety of Burgoyne's being admitted to an audience in presence of the King![1] Burgoyne's want of conduct as a general is so apparent, that I am at a loss to account for his not being dismissed the service. Can anything be more trifling in this important moment than to throw away time in cavilling about signals, and wakes, and a sea-cannonade, which, by its consequence, does not deserve the name of a battle?[2] Nothing, in my idea, can be more trifling, except the learned and humane discussions of Opposition on the degree of mercy we are to show a victorious enemy![3] There is too much wrangling at home. Our most sacred, or what ought to be our most sacred secrets, are sacrificed to what is called the *honour* of a few individuals. Courts-martial and inquiries are the best spies foreigners can wish for."

" It is a remarkable feature of these times," says

[1] In a debate on the 26th May.—*Walpole's last Journals*, vol. ii. p. 272.

[2] Debates on the conduct of Admiral Keppel and Sir Hugh Palliser.

[3] Debate of 4th December—Lord Rockingham's motion on Sir H. Clinton's proclamation.

Lord Mahon, "that the leading admirals and generals of the war were also, for the most part, members of Parliament; that throughout the spring of 1779, we find not only Admiral Keppel and Sir Hugh Palliser, but also Lord and Sir William Howe, and General Burgoyne, able themselves to allege their grievances or defend their conduct. In some of these cases there were committees of inquiry, and examination of witnesses, but in none any clear or positive parliamentary result. These altercations, in the full details, could not fail to interest, because they inflamed the party spirit of the day."

CHAPTER THE SIXTH.

1778 to 1779.

In the course of 1778 the Dowager Lady Elliot's illness took so serious a turn that her life was despaired of. She, however, rallied sufficiently to be removed to Bristol, where it was hoped that the air and waters might produce temporary amendment, though recovery was no longer deemed possible.

Writing from Clifton in September, Isabella says— " The summer has passed very calmly and serenely. We are living in a beautiful country, and I have learnt philosophy enough neither to reflect too much upon what is past, or look too much into futurity. Bob is of the greatest consolation to us. You will hear with pleasure that he has been preaching with great success here. He preached at the cathedral (of Bristol), and acquitted himself so well that the mayor desired him to preach the assize sermon, which is their great day in the year. His sermon was a very good one, and his manner and delivery were much admired; but I own it seemed not a little strange to me to hear Bob lecturing the judge and corporations with just dignity."

Bob was a poet as well as a preacher, and some of

his effusions were at this time offered to the acceptance
of the goddess of Bath-Easton.[1]

In the course of September arrived letters from
America, which give so interesting an account of the
first impressions made by that country on the minds
of Mr. and Mrs. Eden, that I shall insert them at full
length.

[From Mr. EDEN.]

" *Philadelphia, June* 15, 1778.

" My dear Hugh—After a six weeks' voyage between
the anchorage off St. Helen's and that off Cape Hen-
lopen, we arrived in the Delaware on the 2d instant,
and at this place on the 6th. I have hitherto seen no
more of the country than appears in the passage of 150
miles up the river, but I have seen enough to regret
from the bottom of my heart ten thousand times, that
our rulers, instead of a tour through the enervated and
worn-out countries of Europe, had not finished their
educations with a visit round the coasts and rivers of
this beautiful and boundless continent. The scale of
everything here makes me fancy myself in Brobdignag.
The English rivers and mountains are mere rills and
molehills. This city has the appearance at present of
nothing better than a wide and very opulent village;
but it is so situated that a few years hence will turn it
into a magnificent metropolis. There are not above
23,000 inhabitants left here, and about 16,000 troops,
the British part of which are agreed by all the military

---

[1] Lady Miller, who lived at Bath-Easton. See *Walpole's Letters.*—
Memoir of Mrs. Delany.

men, however differing in other points, to be, in every
respect of dress, discipline, health, activity, and alert-
ness, the finest fellows ever collected in the world.
Washington's camp is about twenty miles from us upon
the Schuylkill, and by the best account he has about
10,000 men. . . .

"We mean to leave this to-morrow and to proceed
to New York; after which this city will be immediately
evacuated. . . . Near 300 ships will sail about
the same time that we do—a fine sight, though, on
recollection of all circumstances, not a flattering one!
. . . I am not at liberty to enter into the subject
of what we are doing on this side of the Atlantic.

" . . . And now, before I conclude, I must say
something of our excellent Eleanor. She had occasion
on the voyage to see every little incident of alarm that a
ship of war can show, and went through the whole with
all the courage of the commodore himself, and indeed
with more composure, as he was often alarmed for her.

"We had some exceedingly rough weather; we had
a lightning and thunder night on this coast too, which
exceeds anything that you can form an idea of in Europe;
we had frequent occasion to clear the vessel as if for
action, and sometimes to fire signal-guns in the middle
of the night. At one time an immense wave broke
upon the side of the ship, and forcing the windows of
Mrs. Eden's cabin (where she was lying on the bed,
there being too much motion to sit or stand), completely
ducked her. The commodore and I were present, and
did not like the situation at all; but Eleanor was seized

with a very hearty fit of laughing at her own figure, and
at the commodore's coat-pockets, which stood open, and
were full of water."

In a letter of the same date, and containing nearly
the same matter, addressed by Mr. Eden to Sir Gilbert,
the following passage occurs :—

" I cannot with propriety enter into any detail of our
politics. On my arrival here I found that some measures
had been taken in England (above three weeks previous
to my departure), which, contrary to all good faith and
good sense, were concealed from me, and which, in other
respects, affect both my public and private feelings. At
present I will intimate what I have now written to you
only to the Duke of Marlborough, the Solicitor-General,
and Sir P. Yorke. I find my colleagues perfectly
honourable, steady, and right-headed."

The measures referred to were the evacuation of
Philadelphia and retreat to New York—of which the
commissioners were in perfect ignorance when they
arrived in the Delaware.

Considering the relations which had so long subsisted between Lord North and Mr. Eden, considering
too the very delicate negotiation which had been confided to him immediately before he left England, the
reticence practised towards him seems incomprehensible.

[Mrs. EDEN to ISABELLA.]

" *Philadelphia.*

" My dearest Sister—After a pleasant six hours' sail
up the river, I arrived at Philadelphia, quite out of my

senses with joy at finding myself once more on dry land; and what added not a little to my satisfaction was, the seeing women walking about the streets with children in their arms—a sight I have not seen since I left England. I really could have ate them up almost, I was so delighted to find anything that brought my little angel so strongly to my mind.

"I found the account we had heard of so much apparent distress in the town perfectly false; indeed, it is quite impossible to believe, by the people's faces, and the extreme quietness of the town, but that you are not in a city perfectly at peace, and at ease. As to security, I feel quite as safe here as if I was in my own dressing-room in Downing Street. We have got into a most excellent house, and very civil obliging people. I cannot help pitying them most sincerely for being obliged to receive us, which is the case, as they are desired to furnish us so many rooms—of course their best—and they retire into a corner. However, that does not seem to hurt them. My landlady likes it extremely, as she informs me. She is fond of company, and so I receive all mine in her room. The people's spirits were much raised by the arrival of the commissioners, as they flattered themselves it would put an end to the alarming report of the town being to be evacuated. The women here talk nothing but politics; and indeed it is impossible they should do otherwise, as the whole welfare of their families, fortunes, and lives, depends upon the turn affairs may take. The ladies tell me that they much fear the commission will do no good now. They say, if Philadelphia is left and given up to the rebels, that independence is declared, and America lost; and that they who have been friends to Government are in a most dreadful situation. It appears certainly a most melancholy thing to desert this large city, which very far surpasses any idea I had of it; and all the country is most beautiful.

"We have left Philadelphia, and are once more on board the Trident in the river Delaware. To-morrow, I suppose, we shall weigh anchor and proceed to New York. I shall be delighted to see my uncle's family. I hear he is beloved by all parties. I passed all the night before last in an open boat, and had no place to lie on but the boards; nevertheless I am not one bit the worse, though I was much afraid now and then, as we were so near the enemy's shore. We could hear the people on the watch calling to each other, and every little while I thought we should have been fired at. All the vessels are this moment sailing by the cabin-windows, at such a rate, that I suppose by this time the town is deserted by our army. You cannot conceive a more beautiful, nor a more melancholy sight, than the one at present before me. Imagine the most beautiful view you ever saw, fine woods on each side—the richest country in the world. Imagine this river covered with vessels in full sail, as thick as possible, crowded with people leaving the city where they have been born and bred, flying from an enemy—which enemy may consist of relations and friends—leaving their whole property and all their

N

fortunes but what they can carry with them. It is indeed a most horrible scene!

P. S. (apparently added at New York).—" Beef and mutton are 2s. 6d. per pound ; porter, 3s. a bottle. In short, how the poor inhabitants live I cannot imagine; indeed, description would fall far short of it all."

[Mr. EDEN to HUGH.]

" New York, July 15.

" We are blockaded by a French fleet, which at this moment is immeasurably superior to ours. The spirit, however, of our people, in this mortifying moment, is very comforting to a civil observer like me.

"The soldiery are all running to the navy, with the leave of the commander-in-chief; and our fleet, such as it is, is most completely manned. Before these armaments separate, if we can give the account of these perfidious and profligate Frenchmen that we hope and wish, our honour and interests may once more be established on this side of the Atlantic. We have 26,000 troops in these islands. It is well you are not here; Eleanor says you would be mad. Your uncle, the commodore, is second in command under Lord Howe. Your other uncle, Mr. Andrew Elliot, is a very sensible and respectable man; he has a beautiful place about two miles from this town, where Eleanor and I occasionally sleep. He has a very numerous family, and will be totally ruined if we cannot recover our affairs; yet he is perfectly cheerful."[1]

---

[1] A short time after the date of this letter, Mr. Eden's second daughter was born—Catherine-Isabella.

In so far as they relate to private concerns, these letters are full of cheerfulness, and the hope that their writers would soon be restored to their own country gave a further stimulus to the spirits of the Dowager Lady Elliot and her daughter.

In November they moved to Bath, where they were soon joined by all the members of the family in England. It was the final gathering before the scene dropped. For some time previously, Lady Elliot had been pained by her inability to write to her absent son Hugh. Once more, however, about a fortnight before her death, the effort was made, and the result is a very long and tender letter, which conveyed to him the last expressions of his mother's love, before it was silenced for ever.

On New Year's Day 1779, Sir Gilbert wrote to his brother, that on the 28th of the preceding month their mother's spirit had passed away. Grievously afflicted with bodily ills, " she, nevertheless, waited with composure for the last stroke. At times she conversed pretty cheerfully with her family, and informed herself with wonderfully minute solicitude of all that could in the smallest matters concern those whom she loved. Her conversation was strong and lively; her Christian faith and submission perfect. My poor sister was never from her heart; and if anything still attached her to life, and made the hour she looked for otherwise than joyful, it was the pang of parting with her. I need not tell you that she often talked of you."

Another era in Hugh's life was closed. Much love and much happiness were in store for him in future years; but the all-enduring, all-hoping, all-believing affection, which had sheltered his childhood, and gloried in his youth, was gone from him for ever.

Isabella went home from Bath to her brother's house, and "nothing," she wrote, "can exceed their tender kindness to me."

Shortly afterwards Sir Gilbert was suddenly summoned to Scotland, in consequence of an announcement that Lord Robert Kerr would stand for the county at the next general election; but the Duke of Buccleuch continued to give his support to Sir Gilbert, who in no long time was able to write to his brother, that it was "singularly fortunate that circumstances, not to be commanded by me, have given me an independent seat for this county, in the midst of such enormous estates and so powerful interests."

In the course of the spring Isabella, resuming in some degree the usual style of her correspondence with her brother, tells him of the marriage of her friend Lady Priscilla Bertie to Mr. Burrell.—"The Duke of Ancaster returns again to America, to the great grief of his mother, who, if he was not so wild, would be quite happy at the marriage of Lady Priscilla to Mr. Burrell, which was so violent an inclination as totally to engross their hearts. I believe he is a very good kind of man, but somewhat coxcombical in his habits. Miss Julia Burrell, the only sister unmarried, is shortly to be married to Lord Piercy, who has resigned the staff. Lord Harrington died last night, which makes a great change to Lord Petersham, whose mar-

riage with Miss Fleming has been deferred on account
of his great debts. She has behaved vastly well—she
pays all his as well as Mr. Stanhope's debts. I think,
however, one may use the scriptural expression on this
subject—' That it is better to give than to receive.' Lord
Cathcart is going to marry a daughter of Mr. Andrew
Elliot, a pretty, sensible girl, with whom he fell in love
at New York. There has not been one tolerable or
endurable play or poem this winter. There is a charming pamphlet called ' Anticipation,' which was published
some time ago, and if you have not seen it it will amuse
you. Keppel has been at Bath, and has led a procession of old ladies from one end of the town to the
other, has marched with them, and they had all blue
flags in their caps, and music playing, and gave him a
ball, which must have been ridiculous enough—he is
the hero of the mob this winter, and many windows
have been broken in his honour."

The news of a " drubbing" given to d'Estaing's fleet
off St. Lucia, and the success of an expedition to Georgia,
produce a letter from Mr. Eden, who, with his wife, had
returned to England in December (before Lady Elliot's
death, but not in time to see her). " The Opposition,"
he says, " are sincerely sorry for this good news—they
confess this in private without reserve—and in public,
during the two last days' debates, have not once named
either St. Lucia or Georgia."

In April 1779 arrived the unexpected intelligence of
Alick's death in India. A putrid fever carried him off
while on a journey to Nagpore, the capital of the Mah-

rattas, where he had been sent on a political mission of
importance. His death was a severe blow to his family,
who had conceived the highest hopes of his future
career from the singular combination of mental and personal qualities which formed his character.   To abilities
calculated to make him play a leading part on the
political stage, he united a strong will and a sweet
temper. His untimely fate called forth unusual expressions of regret, and a glowing tribute to his distinguished
qualities was paid by Mr. Burke in the House of
Commons.

This second bereavement, so soon following on the
death of his mother, came with overwhelming force on
Hugh, who had in the short interval between those two
events been deeply though less severely tried by the loss
of two of his friends—Lord Suffolk, whose kindness had
never flagged, and Mr. Harvey, his most intimate companion. "These two last years have robbed me of
father, mother, brother, patron, and friends.   I am sixty
years old in losses of everything dear to me !"

Thus deprived of the objects of his earliest affections,
he began to feel all the more the necessity of forming
new ties.

" M. Elliot," says Thiébault, " était devenu éperdu-
ment amoureux de Mademoiselle Krauth;" her mother
was supposed by him to object strongly to her marriage
with a foreigner, and with one whose uncertain prospects
and small private fortune had been disclosed unreservedly to her by himself. In the course of the previous
year several notes had passed between them on the

subject of his attentions to her daughter, but the line of
argument adopted by Madame de Verelst to dissuade
him from their continuance seems singularly ill fitted
to attain its ostensible object; she repeatedly requests
him to avoid her daughter's society, on the ground that
the young lady was becoming seriously attached to him,
and that the strength of her feelings for him had already
made her unhappy, and had prevented her from accepting an excellent "*parti*" which her mother had in store
for her! Other notes dwell on the remarks to which
his open devotion had given rise, and which were "*com-
promettant*" for her daughter. Madame de Verelst may
possibly have thought the young Englishman a model of
prudence and of self-abnegation; he was, however, unfortunately more remarkably distinguished for a romantic
and chivalrous nature, upon which the arguments she
used were certain to produce an opposite effect from
that which she professed to desire. If anything had
been needed to rivet his chains, it must have been the
assurance that Mademoiselle Krauth was unhappy, "pour
lui et par lui."

Early in July he wrote to Sir J. Harris to announce
his immediate return on leave to England, for the purpose of preparing his family for the declaration of his
marriage, which, in order to provide against all possible
machinations during his absence, took place privately,
without her mother's consent, before his departure from
Berlin. The withholding of Madame de Verelst's consent may have been intended to deprecate the king's
displeasure when it should become known that a mar-

riage had been contracted between her daughter, a Prussian subject and an heiress, without his previous consent—for it does not appear that their marriage was ever a secret from her. However this may have been, Mr. Elliot wrote to Sir James Harris[1] as follows :—" I am married in private, without the mother's consent, to the Krauth; after the éclât of my attachment to her, I had the choice between folly and dishonesty—my affections pleaded for the first, my conscience forbade the latter. On my part there is very sincere affection, bad health,[2] poverty, and the other defects of character which nature has bestowed on me, and which art has never tried to conquer; on hers, there is youth, beauty, and strong parts. My project is to keep the matter secret till the king's death.[3] The Prince of Prussia, Prince Henry, etc., are as much my friends as princes can be. I despise the world too much to fear its vicissitudes, and think her worth sacrificing life and fortune to, if necessary."

[1] 9th July 1779.

[2] Mr. Elliot's constitution had never thoroughly recovered from the effects of the fever which had attacked him during his Danubian campaign in 1773 ; since which time he had been liable to severe fits of illness, which baffled for a time all medical treatment. After one of these he wrote to Mr. Harris, 5th March 1779 :—" Physicians, that universal distemper, have proved the efficacy of their art in increasing suffering. I believe my original distemper cured long since. . . . I have learnt from the double capacity of foreign minister and invalid that in physic and politics the practitioners are usually blind and presumptuous. The health and happiness of mankind are lavishly sacrificed to quack ministers and quack physicians.''

[3] He was certain to object to her fortune passing into the hands of a foreigner.

He did not question that the idol was one to whom the incense of such sacrifices would be as sweet perfumes.

" Prudence, reason, calculation of possibles," wrote my grandfather to some one else at this time, not, however, with any other than a mental reference to the subject of his marriage,—" these are the crutches with which feeble minds halt through life. I have but one rule—to do that which my conscience says is right, let the consequences be what they may." Unluckily, when the first steps were taken in this unhappy business, my grandfather's conscience seems to have been " en bas de l'escalier," as a Frenchman said his wit was when most wanted, and prudence and reason had taken to flight before it appeared on the scene.

His friends at St. Petersburg and at home certainly believed that the marriage had been desired by the young lady's friends from the first moment of Mr. Elliot's arrival at Berlin, and that he himself never shared in this opinion, and that Madame de Verelst succeeded in gaining and in preserving his entire confidence and esteem, are arguments which in no wise affect the view of the matter entertained by his friends, since all the trust and confidence which he withheld from persons indifferent to or distasteful to him, were reserved to be added to the brimming measure which he gave to those he loved. Clear-sighted to a fault, even suspicious of the motives of the generality of the world, he was credulous as a child where his affections were concerned ; his correspondents perpetually warn him not to believe and confide in precisely those whose society he affected the most.

The summer and part of the winter of 1779 were spent by Mr. Elliot in England; we therefore lose sight of him for a while, except in the letters written to him by Isabella and Sir Gilbert from Minto, many of which show them to have been anxiously expecting him there, but the meeting did not take place till winter recalled the Elliots to their house in Lincoln's Inn.

My grandfather's absence from his post brings Mr. Liston again on the scene, and we find him very soon at his old employment, remonstrating, pacifying, excusing, and receiving confidences from all sides.

Having done all he could to prevent the marriage, he now did his best to make it happy. " It is impossible to make her believe she has no just grounds of complaint; she cannot understand that a man will make the greatest sacrifices for her sake, and yet cannot overcome his habitual indolence."

" Si j'avais un amant qui voulut de mes lettres tous les jours, je romprais avec lui ! " said Madame de la Fayette. Mr. Elliot would have been a lover after her heart, but unhappily the lady of his love was not of the same mind ; and when, as too frequently happened, the English post came in without anything for her, she was at first distressed and then provoked. Mr. Liston pacified her with explanations of his own invention, not probably venturing to interpret to her what Sir Gilbert calls the " family paradox—how possible it is to neglect abominably those we love truly and dearly ;" but to his chief Mr. Liston wrote almost sharply on the mischief which his indolence might cause.

" Le vin est tiré il faut le boire jusqu' à la lie," he wrote on one occasion, explaining further that by the lees of the matrimonial draught he understood "a constant and regular correspondence, and other *petits soins,* which, in all other instances at least, cost you much more than other people,—*and an abstention from perilous adventures.*" As sea-fights for instance ! for the last sentence was undoubtedly called forth by a letter from Mr. Elliot, dated Plymouth, 29th August, in which it was stated that he was about to embark on the Southampton frigate at Plymouth, in the hope of joining Sir Charles Hardy before the action that was then expected to take place.

In this hope he was disappointed, for the English and French fleets did not meet, but he was able to write Mr. Liston an account of Sir C. Hardy's intended operations, closing it with the remark that, after all, at sea " he placed his faith much less in tactics than in English resolution and close quarters."[1]

[1] "On the last day of August Sir Charles Hardy endeavoured to entice the enemy into a narrower part of the channel, but they declined a combat," etc.—Hughes' *History of England,* vol. ii. p. 339.

Among Mr. Elliot's papers there is one, dated Plymouth, August 1779, containing various suggestions as to what should be done to defend the place against a threatened descent of the French. It is apparently addressed to a person in military command, and enters into considerable details concerning the arrangements proper to be made. Mr. Elliot's youngest son, Frederick, remembers to have heard his father tell a story of his having been arrested as a spy in Devonshire—an adventure which no doubt occurred during the visit to Plymouth,

Luckily for us, Mr. Liston wrote of other things besides the domestic affairs of his chief. The following extracts from his letters are selected as containing characteristic anecdotes of the great King. On the 29th May, he describes the King's return to Berlin from the army: —" The King arrived here on Thursday at three o'clock; came in by the Königs-strasse, and drove straight to the palace. The people made little or no noise, because they knew he does not like it. They pretend a woman threw herself on her knees before him, as he stepped out of the coach. 'Was will sie?" said he; no answer. She caught hold of his coat, and burst into tears. 'Was will sie denn?" no answer. He then asked a third time. 'Ich freue mich,' said she. He made a bow to her and seemed affected, as were the spectators. A few Frenchmen, standing at the bottom of the stair, called out, 'Vive le Roi!' on which he turned about, smiled, and said, '*Bravo!*' All the foreign ministers, nobility, etc., had been assembled from ten o'clock to wait for him. He did not go into the room they were in, but joined his generals and Prince Ferdinand in the other room. After embracing his brother, and saying a few words to three of his generals, he retired and ordered dinner immediately. After dinner he stood nearly three hours in one of the windows with Schulenburg, looking over papers and doing business. A great crowd gathered together in the *Place* to stare at him. He wrote to the Queen, saying he could not see her that day, he had so

and investigation of her defenceless state described in the paper referred to.

much to do, but that 'il lui demanderait à diner le Dimanche.' Yesterday he went in his pristine *state*-coach to visit Princess Amelia. I saw him pass under the trees; he looks much better than when I saw him last; and, they say, enjoys perfect health and spirits. Prince Henry arrived yesterday; the King received him, contrary to the general expectation, with great cordiality, and talked long to him with perfect good humour. The King speaks of the Prince of Prussia with great cordiality and affection; he is expected every moment."

The Sunday dinner at the Queen's residence of Charlottenburg, mentioned in the foregoing letter, produced the following anecdote :—" When the King asked all the royal family to dine with him at Charlottenburg, he invited (or he was understood to invite) all the grandes maitresses at the same time; so that Madame de Kannenberg, Madame de Blumenthal, etc., went. Princess Ferdinand having no grande maitresse, carried Madame de Stockhausen; and Mademoiselle de Viereck went by way of gouvernante to the little Princess of Prussia. The Queen and Madame de Kannenberg were there some time before the rest. 'Mon ancienne et bonne amie,' said the King to Madame de Kannenberg, 'I am very glad to see you; but'—observing the two ladies who had just entered—'who are these?' She told him, 'Stockhausen, Viereck.'—'Je ne connais point cela moi. Qu'est-ce-que cela vient faire ici? c'est de la contre bande; elles ne peuvent pas diner ici, ces femmes-là. Je n'ai voulu avoir que les grandes maitresses, qu'elles s'en retournent: qu'on les renvoie.'—' Mais Sire, elles sont venues avec les Princesses, elles n'ont point de voiture, elles ne peuvent pas s'en aller. Si votre Majesté le permet, on leur donnera à dîner dans un autre appartement.' ' A la bonne heure ;' and this was accordingly done. ' Eh bien, Madame de Kannenberg,' said he, when dinner was done, ' qu'avez-vous fait de votre Madame de Stockhausen et de l'autre.' ' Sire, je les ai mises dans l'anti-chambre.'—' Ha ! ha ! ha ! elles sont fort bien là—à leur place.'"[1]

This trait of discourtesy is followed by a graver charge of harshness, carried to extremes, which produced a fatal result in the tragical death of a certain Major Appenbourg, who commanded last campaign the grenadiers, composed of the battalion of Guards and of the regiment of the Prince of Prussia. " They were at Jägerndorff in winter, and there was considerable desertion.   The King, before leaving Silesia, found great fault with this, and the major decided upon returning to Berlin, but was often heard to say, *his resolution was taken.* On his arrival, his Majesty said some harsh things to him ; on which he went home, wrote a letter to the King, which he left on his table, and shot himself. The letter was carried to the King, who is said to have been much shocked. It had been a long premeditated affair. He has left everything in excellent order."

A visit of Mr. Liston's to M. de Hertzberg's country residence affords some curious details concerning the simple, though peculiar tastes and manners of a favourite minister of the great Frederick. M. de Hertzberg had, at various times, conducted important diplomatic trans- actions; and at the time of my grandfather's residence at Berlin, was associated with the venerable Count Finckenstein in the administration of foreign affairs. Frederick held him in high esteem, as he was one of the few personal friends of a sovereign who was more admired than beloved. During the King's last illness M. de Hertzberg attended him, and held him in his arms at the moment of death. It is said that the new King, on arriving at the deathbed of his uncle, was so touched by the unaffected grief of the old and faithful friend attending there, that his first act of sovereignty was to take from his own breast the order of the black eagle, which he habitually wore, and to place it on the neck of M. de Hertzberg, who very soon afterwards became his first minister, and was accused by the French party of fostering *anti-French* sentiments in the new King's mind.

"*July* 27, 1779.—I have spent a day with M. de Hertzberg, who was here, and am exceedingly pleased with his farm and his farming, which is on a large scale, and is conducted (with a view to profit) with all the minuteness of attention required in agriculture, and so seldom found in any but those who have been bred to the business from their youth. He knows every cow by her name, and how many quarts of milk are sold every day.[1] The manner in which he talks to his boors, and

---

[1] The milk was sold daily by dairymaids on the flight of steps leading to the entrance-hall.

the familiarity and bluntness with which they answer him, depose strongly in favour of his good nature; and the manner in which he lives leaves no doubt of his opulence. . . . He had no company with him, and his housekeeper and servants did not seem to think it probable I was to have the honour of dining with him, as I arrived on foot; so that we sat down exactly to the dinner prepared for *him*, which was sufficient to satisfy appetite, but as homely as I should have found it at one of my neighbour farmer's houses in Scotland, and the cloth hardly so clean. The drink, brown and white beer of his own brewing, and one single glass of wine. His dress[1] was still plainer than it is in town, and a small round hat, his hair hanging loose and without powder. Nothing ever brought so strongly to one's memory Curius Dentatus roasting his turnips, or the Dictator ab aratro. But I could have wished that these stories had not been so conspicuously painted in his apartments, for it has the appearance of comparing himself to those men, which would not do. When he touched on politics it was with his usual openness. He regretted not having been sent to make the peace of Tetschen, in which case he thinks many things would have been more favourable to Prussia. There is no doubt of his favourable disposition to us, but he is, like others, led away by Maltzahn's opposition accounts of the distracted state of the ministry and the nation, and by the false views held up in the 'Courrier de l'Europe'

---

[1] Usually manufactured of silk spun by the worms on his own mulberry plantations.

and other foreign gazettes, and seems to wish rather than to hope that we may be able to extricate ourselves." In other letters Mr. Liston describes the sentiments entertained by the Prussian nation towards the French as anything but friendly, in spite of the well-known dispositions of the court; and he mentions having been charged by various persons to send them the earliest news of any success which the English might obtain at sea over the French.[1] As for society, he says, "There is nothing new under the sun—Monday a pique-nique, Thursday an assembly. The same parties arranged at cards; the tables placed on the same individual spots as when you last saw them; the same figures dancing. But of these, if you were here, you

---

[1] Mr. Elliot was ever ready to encourage the well-wishers to his country's cause. Writing to M. d'Arnim from London, August 1779, he said—"Were I to enter upon the present state of Great Britain, I could write volumes without exhausting an unfathomable subject. History does not contain a more singular epoch in the annals of any nation. Torn by the violence of faction, weakened by a most expensive, bloody, and unnatural civil war, attacked by the combined force of the House of Bourbon, loaded with a debt unparalleled in any age, unsupported by foreign allies, deserted even by fortune, at variance with the winds and waves, we have not lost courage, and I am one of those who believe that we shall rise again superior to every enemy, and be what we ought to be—a curb to the ambition of the House of Bourbon, and the defenders of the liberty of mankind, which is in more danger than you seem to apprehend, if France and Spain succeed in outnumbering and crushing our marine." The accession of the maritime force of Spain to that of France was not viewed with unmixed satisfaction by the adherents of the latter Power on the Continent. "The Prince of Prussia (August 1779) expressed a fear that the French had too much baggage to encumber them. 'What baggage, Monseigneur?' 'Les Espagnols.'"—*Letter of Mr. Liston.*

would take notice of none *but one.* That one in public behaves so as to give satisfaction to the most jealous lover, though she certainly does not give equal satisfaction to the poor devil who happens to be her partner. She often speaks to him with such coldness and such nonchalance, that I, an indifferent spectator, am apt to be angry. There are the usual dinners at this minister's and at that minister's—who has seen one has seen all. If I look under the trees I see Pons or Fontana stalking along to go out to the park, or Dolgorouki strangely sticking on the top of a horse; or the very same figures crowding out on a Sunday, which we have looked at a hundred times."

Before the year closed Mr. Liston had it in his power to tell my grandfather a story which was the nine days' wonder of Berlin at the time, and became the subject of discussion and criticism throughout Europe. It will be found at length in the 2d vol. of Thiébault's *Memoirs*, page 20; but to make the following letters intelligible it will be necessary to give it shortly here :[1]—A miller named Arnold, residing in a village in Pomerania, had presented a memorial to the King some year or so before, in which it was stated that he, the complainant, rented of the King a water-mill for 300 rixdollars, but that in consequence of the stream having been directed from its natural channel by the orders of Count N——, the miller's works were stopped, the rent was not forthcoming, and the man was starving. The King sent the

---

[1] Lord Dover's *Life of Frederick the Great.* Thiébault's *Souvenirs de 20 Ans à Berlin.*

memorial to the chancellor, with the order that justice should be done to the miller; the cause was tried, and the miller lost it. The following year a second memorial was presented by the miller to the King, stating that though his case had been lost, the facts were nevertheless as he had stated them. Again the King referred the document to the chancellor, with the command that the cause should be tried before the second tribunal, and that justice should be done—the second trial had the same result as the first; and a third time the miller in despair appealed to the King. Frederick upon this determined to inquire for himself into the facts of the case; aud on the report of persons carefully selected, to verify on the spot the statements of the miller, the King became convinced that an act of gross injustice had been committed, and what ensued will be told best by Mr. Liston.

"On Saturday last His Majesty sent for the chancellor (M. le Baron de Fürst) and the three counsellors who presided at the Court of Appeal, and after reprimanding them very severely for their judgment, he told the chancellor he was dismissed from his office, and that his place was disposed of. The counsellors were sent to the prison of the Carlshof, which you will remember is the *Newgate* of this part of the world; Fürst wanted to speak, but was ordered to be silent and to withdraw. "*Marschirt ab*" was the word, and none of the civilest. Some say the King's illness has made him peevish; others, that his patience had been exhausted by the examples he had lately seen of the quirks and chicanery of the law, to which he had vainly hoped by his former regulations to put a stop.

"To be sure if the case were exactly as the king represents it, it would not bear an argument. A person lets a mill to another, situated on a stream mentioned in the agreement, and afterwards turns aside that stream for other purposes, and still insists on the same rent—nothing more unjust; but they say the fact is, the small portion of water turned aside did no essential harm to the tenant's mill; that the possessor of another mill, a little higher up on the same stream, makes no complaints, and carries on his business as formerly; that the miller is a *mauvais sujet* who wanted to quarrel with the proprietor, etc. etc. The chancellor talks in a very manly way on the subject; he says he cannot blame the King, as he acts as he thinks he ought to do, and considers the judgment given as unjust; but that he cannot help saying His Majesty pretends to judge of matters he does not understand, and decides without having weighed the circumstances of the case. The president and counsellors of the chamber of Cüstrin, who judged in the first instance, are sent for by a detachment of troops, and are to meet the same fate. The president is Count Finckenstein's son. The King has written to Count Finckenstein [1] saying he was sorry to be obliged to dismiss his son for an act of injustice, but that an example was necessary. He could have wished it might have fallen on another family rather than his. The Count is reported to have said, ' Je plains les honnêtes gens; je plains le Roi.'

[1] Minister for Foreign Affairs.

" What is very remarkable in a country like this, is, that the whole town have been to pay their compliments of condolence to Fürst and M. de Finckenstein, even Prince Henry and Princess Amelia sent."

In his next letter Mr. Liston says—" In any other country such a story as I told you in my last would produce some effect; here they talk pretty freely for a few days; and that is all. Words indeed are not spared by the country gentlemen and the nobility here—' precipitate, unjust, despotic,' fly about. The vulgar admire. The King is better, in good spirits, et se moque du qu'en dira-t-on."

Thiébault tells us the sequel of the story thus—" Six months after the events above related, Frederick discovered that he had been in error; the stream in dispute having been diverted below the mill by a proprietor residing on its banks; the miller had therefore no just grounds of complaint, and law and justice had been equally outraged by the interference of the king. But, though convinced of his error, Frederick made no other sign of being so than by withdrawing the magistrates from their prison, reinstating them in their places, and dropping the prosecution of the proprietor supposed to have injured his humble neighbour."[1]

Mr. Elliot made his marriage known to his family on his arrival in England. Sir Gilbert and Lady Elliot heard the news with their usual affectionate kindness,— whatever doubts they may previously have entertained of the wisdom of the step which Hugh had taken, now that

[1] Thiébault, Séjour de 20 ans à Berlin.

it was irrevocable, they were ready to say, " What must
be we cannot change, and will not fear." A cordial welcome was promised to " Charlotte " when she should
come to claim a home among them, and Sir Gilbert
entered warmly into his brother's dreams of future rusti-
cation among the glens and burns of Scotland. Poor
Berlin beauty ! how she would have shuddered had she
heard these projects of burying her *au fond de l'Ecosse*
with a husband and his family *pour tout potage*. " I
long to see your wife," says Mrs. Eden, " but how am I
to talk to her? I cannot speak French !" " Ah, Hugh !
Hugh !" wrote Mrs. Harris from St. Petersburg ; " do
you remember four years ago how you used to abuse all
women, and say if ever you married you would live in
St. James' Street, and your wife in Berkeley Square ?"

Isabella, of all the family, was perhaps the one most
affected by her brother's marriage,—alike in their dispositions and tastes, and full of romantic admiration for
each other, they had kept up a constant correspondence
with the most unreserved confidence ; and while Hugh
formed no closer ties, Isabella could feel that her affection
and sympathy were no less necessary to him than they had
ever been. Poor Isabella's part was a hard one ; she
had been the object of her mother's fondest love,—" It
was," wrote one of the family, " an idolatry calculated to
ruin any character less sweet than hers ; " and from this
exclusive devotion she had now to decline on the affections of those warmly attached to her indeed, but the
first place in whose hearts was not theirs to give. Such
changes have embittered many ; but whatever were Isa-

bella's secret feelings, she came forward, warmly and cheerfully, to welcome her new sister, and quietly dropping
out of her correspondence to her brother those half-uncon-
scious self-revealings which are never written for more than
one, she continued in her usual cheerful, pleasant strain
to tell him of all things likely to interest him and his
wife.　Every now and then a passing remark that her
" letters are dull because she knows nothing now,"—
" no one tells her anything now,"—falls sadly on the ear,
but she passes lightly on, and writes fully and frequently
of the affectionate thoughtfulness for her manifested by
all the family.

A letter of Mr. Pitt's at this date alludes to a circumstance too characteristic of my grandfather to be
passed over.　" With regard to the payment of your
debts, your ideas upon the subject of your wife's fortune
are completely ridiculous; for, take the case *e converso*,
and suppose that the fortune is on your side, and that
from imprudences the other party is involved in considerable debts, whom, notwithstanding her want of
fortune and perplexed state of affairs, you had, by
marrying her, proved yourself to prefer to all woman-
kind.　It is not only an equitable request, but the other
party ought to insist upon it if your romantic head leads
you to refuse it."　" Credit your house accounts,—let
system manage your expenses ;" is always the burden of
Mr. Pitt's advice; henceforth there were to be two to
spend, and no one to keep the accounts.

CHAPTER THE SEVENTH.

1780 to 1781.

BERLIN.

My grandfather returned to Berlin in the spring of 1780 —returned, as he says, to find " nature buried in sand, and mankind in slavery ;" and with so many regrets for the " clear streams, green fields, and stirring interests of English life," that, had the " attraction to Berlin been less powerful than it was," he might have found it a hard task to tear himself away from home. " Would that men could be turned out to grass like horses, and that I had been wicked enough to have been sent a-grazing with Nebuchadnezzar !" On his way back to his post he stayed a few days in Paris to consult doctors, and writes of the impression he received there, to a friend at home, in the following words :—" I never made so interesting a visit to the capital of our enemies. They are perfectly disgusted with the war and their ministers. The name of an Englishmen has again risen to its sterling value ; and were it not for the trust they put in our divisions at home, I do not believe they would continue the war six weeks.[1] You have no idea of the avidity with which ils s'arrachent le ' Courrier de

---

[1] Before the year closed, M. Necker, "as the leading minister in

l'Europe,' and the admiration they have for le grand M. Bourique,[1] and his system of economy. I breakfasted every morning with the flower of the young men of Paris, at the Marquis de Voyer's, where politics were the constant theme, and everything they knew was débité avec toute la franchise et toute l'étourderie qui leur sont propres. I saw several of the officers who were at Savannah, and who have the greatest respect for our *sans culottes* ever since that business. Noailles is a d—d coxcomb, says everything civil in the presence of an Englishman, and is, I understand, one of the most barefaced liars of the many France is blessed with. . . . As for myself, I fear nothing in France but the dark eyes of the Countess Jules."[2]

How soon the public acknowledgment of his marriage followed upon his return to Berlin, and what was the sensation it created, are circumstances of which we are left in ignorance; but in his letters, written in June 1780, he talks openly of his wife and of his plans of life; and towards the autumn his house seems to have become the point de réunion for a very agreeable society. 1780 and 1781 are marked as *white years* in my grandfather's

Paris, addressed a secret letter to Lord North expressing a strong desire to treat."—*Mahon's Hist. Eng.* vol. vii. p. 80.

[1] Burke.

[2] Countess Jules de Polignac, the favourite friend of Marie Antoinette. After Mr. Elliot's return from Paris he filed among his papers notes from Baron de Grimm; from L'Abbé Raynal, asking him to go with him to dinner at M. Necker's; from Comtesse Schouwaloff, begging him to meet d'Alembert and La Harpe; from the Duc de Guines; from d'Argenson, de Saussure, etc.

history; they were spent entirely at Berlin, except
during very short excursions in the neighbourhood; and
we gather from almost every letter that he was happier
than he had ever been before. " Berlin is dull and in-
sipid," he wrote, "but that is nothing to me. I have
at home all that I require." His unusual regularity as
a correspondent is remarked on by his family and friends;
and they in their turn are desired to write frequently of
pleasant things to amuse "Charlotte." "My wife is
so fond of your letters," he wrote to Sir Gilbert, "that
I can think of no better way of teaching her English
than by begging you to write to her often, and to make
her answer in English." Her picture was painted for
Sir Gilbert, and great were the discussions as to the
backgrounds and hues of drapery which should do most
justice to her blue eyes and brilliant skin. " If you take
half as much charge of your wife's appearance as you
did of mine," said Mrs. Eden, " I pity her from my
heart." Whether the family ever received this picture
or not remains untold; but an unknown miniature found
in a desk of my grandfather's, and given to me last year,
agrees so entirely with the description in his letters of
the looks and dress of his wife, when sitting for her
portrait at this time, that we can have no doubt any
longer as to whom belonged those long fair curls and sky-
blue draperies. The picture, in a curiously-worked gold
frame, is well preserved, but the back has been removed.
It probably once contained hair, or a name or date.

In looking over such a correspondence as this, the
map of a whole life is unrolled before one. The starting-

point and the goal, the sunshine and the rain-cloud, are
seen together. The same glance shows us the cause
and consequence of action, the visions of hope, and the
experiences of reality, the growth and decay of friendships, the rapid succession of gladness and grief; and
thus, looking " before and after," and pondering over
what might have been, what has been, and what may be
again, the thought rises in one's mind, that, if there be
in other spheres spectators of these shifting scenes of
life, they see few sadder sights on earth than the dawn
of human joy.

Mr. Elliot's home, with its beautiful young wife and
its pleasant society, seems somewhat to have effaced the
visions of cots beneath a Lowland hill, among purling
streams and green bowers, for in the course of 1780 he
wrote in very dissuasive tones to a brother diplomatist,[1]
who, like himself in former days, entertained notions of
throwing up his foreign appointment to rusticate at home :
—" Permit me to advise you to go to England before
you resolve to ask for your *retraite*. Except you are
master of £2000 per annum, believe me, England is no
place to be idle in. The very wear and tear of society
is necessary, and you will be miserable in any society but
the best. There is no medium. All those I saw who
had left the foreign line regretted it. I repeat it
—England is not the country for an idle man ; an idle
duke with £20,000 a year s'y ennuie à périr ; judge how
much more an idle gentleman with a mere sustenance
must languish."

[1] To Sir T. Wroughton.

Berlin was at this time a very dull residence for any one seeking the pleasures of society. The growing infirmities of the King had increased the natural irritability of his temper to a degree which made him an object of dread to all who came within reach of his sudden outbreaks.

Of the foreign ministers, as many as could kept at a distance from the Court; and when to general ill-humour was added a particular dissatisfaction with England,[1] Mr. Elliot found himself singled out for special marks of the King's ill-will.

On the 23d *May* he wrote to Lord Stormont:— "The King has been on horseback these three last mornings before five o'clock, in the coldest weather ever known in this season; I never saw him more active or in better spirits. Yesterday, at the levée, he addressed himself principally to the French minister; and, after asking the news of the day, told Admiral Byng's story last war with more humour than I imagined that tragical event could have admitted of. The King, in his private conversation, often treats the fatalities our naval officers ascribe to winds and weather as mere excuses for their own misfortunes or misconduct: ' Si j'avais une flotte, je chasserais les vents de la mer,' is an expression his Majesty made use of several times this winter, when he read the complaints of both sides against an enemy he believes often called in to the assistance of an unable or

---

[1] The late successes of the Court of Vienna at St. Petersburg were supposed, at Berlin, to be in part due to the "machinations" of Sir James Harris, English minister there.

unwilling admiral. Yesterday he repeated that he did not conceive how it sometimes happened that both French and English ' trouvaient le vent contraire' in their naval engagements."[1]

"No one can tell," wrote my grandfather,[2] " the misery of appearing in public here in moments of disgrace and defeat. In my public despatches I dwell less upon the general ill-humour of the King, and his particular dissatisfaction with England, than I might be warranted to do, were it not an ungrateful task to expose the weakness of humanity in prey to the infirmities of age and an irritable constitution. It is sufficient to say that sudden starts of passion hurry him (the King) beyond the bounds of reason. In one of these Maltzahn was recalled; and since the Chancellor's disgrace none of His Majesty's ministers count upon the stability of their places."

The recall of M. Maltzahn from London, and the appointment to that post of an " ill-conditioned fellow, merely to spite the English cabinet," gave occasion to one of Mr. Elliot's happiest repartees. " What do they say of —— in London?" asked Frederick, tauntingly.

---

[1] Captain Elliot, writing to his nephew Hugh about this time, says, " I always admired your king as a general, and, from what you tell me of his sayings, I cannot help thinking he would also make a most excellent admiral. I wish to God he would come here and command our fleet ; I would serve under him with more pleasure than any British seaman. I think we should be better, too, if he had the command of both our Houses of Parliament, for our d—d boasted constitution will sink us to the bottom of ——."

[2] To Lord Stormont, July 1780.

" Digne représentant de Votre Majesté ;" replied Mr. Elliot, bowing to the ground.[1]

That the King's ministers were justified in their opinion of the precariousness of the tenure by which they retained office, was proved in the course of the following year by the sudden dismissal of Baron de Borck —an event which caused a great sensation at the time, and is thus related by my grandfather :—

" During my absence"—he and his wife had been on a visit to the charming Prince and Princess of Anhalt Dessau, who are quoted by him and others as models of every virtue—" during my absence a singular event took place.   I called on Baron Borck the night of my return to ask what news.   ' None of consequence to the public,' replied he, ' though there is a bit of news not a little interesting to myself—I this morning received my dismission.'   Judge of my surprise !   He was at that moment supposed to be in great favour, and was destined by the voice of the public to be named Minister of State. His ingenious wife had scraped together a motley troop of comedians who acted in his coach-house.   Upon this theatre Baron Borck's fortune split.   The king wrote to him : ' Si vous voulez être comédien vous ne pouvez rester à mon service ; il faut opter entre le théâtre et votre poste. Réponse—' Sire, Les incommodités de ma femme l'ayant obligée de se renfermer chez elle, elle avait assemblé quelque acteurs qui donnèrent des representations sur un théâtre dans ma maison à des sociétés particulières.'—On ajouta qu'on les avait renvoyés, et qu'on se flattait que Sa

Majesté excuserait une inadvertence dont on n'aurait pas été capable, si on avait eu lieu de croire qu'elle aurait été désagréable à Sa Majesté. *Seconde lettre*—' Je vous prie de prendre votre congé au plus vite." To another correspondent Mr. Elliot says :—" On assure que le Président de Police avait donné avis que les ministres étrangers payaient; cette Hydre qui renait à tout instant à Berlin malgré tous les efforts pour l'exterminer. Cependant je crois qu'il est avéré qu'ils n'ont jamais payé que de leurs personnes."

Priests and academicians were made to feel the force of the royal will. On the 30th May 1780 the first were ordered to perform a mass, and the second to assist at it, for the repose of the soul of M. de Voltaire !—a solemn satire, at which the spectators, struck with a sense of its absurdity, " observed neither decorum nor decency."

The army came in for its share of the royal displeasure. In June 1781 Mr. Elliot wrote—" The heat of this warm season causes severe suffering among the troops. The King has been less satisfied this year than usual with the garrison of Berlin, and has ordered them to be more severely exercised. An old officer lately threw himself in the King's way and asked for support. Infirmities and age had driven him out of the service. He could no longer bear the fatigue which had broken his constitution. The King answered that he must have recourse to his talents, and if these did not suffice, to the humanity of others. ' Vous voudriez que je demandasse l'aumône ? Hé bien ! je commence par m'addresser à Votre Majesté ;' and, at the same time, stretched out

his hat in a suppliant posture. The King answered,
' J'aurai soin de vous, mais ne le dîtes à personne.'
Indeed, the number of those reduced to the like circum-
stances is incredible."

The heats of summer passed, but the king's temper
did not cool; and Mr. Liston, in the course of the
autumn, wrote somewhat disrespectfully of His Majesty,
as follows :—" The old fellow was in perfect good humour
the first day, and as cross as the devil the two last days
of manœuvres. He was particularly severe on the gens-
d'armes—told them they had done nothing but *Schweine-
reyen*, that they were a parcel of *Windbeutels, Berlinische
Hofleute*, and so forth. They say his ill-humour was
much owing to a letter he received by the Friday's post
from Russia, in which the Empress begs, or rather insists, he will give regiments to the two princes of Wurtemberg. He does not wish to comply, and does not
know how to refuse." [1]

The absence of the usual splendours of a Court, and
the extreme difficulty of even obtaining a sight of the
King,[2] deprived Berlin during the last years of Frederick
the Great of the attractions which had drawn so many
young Englishmen to Germany in Mr. Elliot's early
days.

Of the group of gay young men who had met together

---

[1] Mr. Liston, at Berlin 25th September 1781, to Mr. Elliot at
Dessau.

[2] No presentation could be made to the King except through the
interest of some member of his small court at Potsdam. A foreign
minister residing in Berlin could only give a letter of introduction to
one of these.

at Munich in the summer of 1775, three[1] were already
sleeping "the sleep that knows no morrow;" and the
two survivors, Mr. Elliot and Mr. Pitt, were *settled down*
to the serious business of life—the latter as a pains-
taking M.P., the former as a rangé père de famille; the
services of Lacoste, that merriest of Scapins and best of
hairdressers, were no longer required; and a good English nurse was found to be the most important person in
the household. In April 1781 Mr. Elliot's first child
was born—a daughter—to whom the Princess of Prussia
and Lady Harris became godmothers. The Prince and
the Princess of Prussia showed constant kindness to my
grandfather; and there are several letters from her in
this correspondence, all very kind and gracious, but with
one exception, scarcely interesting enough for insertion.

Lady Harris's lively answer to a letter from her old
friend Hugh, which he had apparently written in somewhat solemn strain, to ask her sponsorship for his little
daughter, is worth transcribing :—

St. Petersburg, May 5th-16th, 1781.

My dear *Brother*—I received your epistle yesterday
to my very great and agreeable surprise. This is, then,
No. 1 of our correspondence; God knows whether we
shall ever get out of the teens, or indeed into them. I
look upon your letter to be very much in the style of the
Prodigal Son the two or three first days he spent at
home. 'Tis written as if you had just returned from
confession, and with all the humility of a sinner who has

[1] Mr. Harvey, Mr. Stanley, and Lord Lindsay, afterwards Duke of
Ancaster.

P

just been rebuked. You have, however, too bad an opinion of yourself, for you have too good a heart (and, indeed, a head not amiss when it takes a right turn), not to be a good husband and a good father, as you have always been a good son, brother, and friend, though now and then a teazing and a *chagrining* one. I readily accept the offer of your daughter; she cannot fail of being handsome, and, above all things, I flatter myself, *will have your nose,* my dear old friend. I sometimes think over past times, and reflect that if anybody had told us when we sat upon my couch, you at my sick feet by my fireside in George Street, that in four years I should be writing to you from Petersburg, to you a *married* man at Berlin, that we should have looked upon them as worthy of a strait waistcoat. All I can say is, that I can never be more attached to you, and wish you more sincerely well than I did then, and that this attachment will ever continue the same, and as truly as if you were my own brother. Your wife will always, as such, be entitled to my regard. I do not doubt that she does not want that motive for me to bestow it upon her. You are really very modest about the Princess of Brunswick, for 'twas your cruelty drove her to admire P——; I fear his constancy is not so great as hers, indeed the object is not so worthy on his side. I write this, spending a solitary evening at home, a thing which appears very extraordinary to me who am little used to it. I have been ill a few days of fièvre de fluxion, *et le volage* Harris is gone gadding for an hour or two. In general one sees a great deal of the world and its vanities in this place, and I believe 'tis a better method of disgusting with them than all the common precepts. You ask me if England is my passion; I answer, more so than ever, and my ambition a small circle of friends, and a great part of that small number *Elliots*—I admit willingly the *domesticated* ones. . . . Your brother is, as you well know, the most perfect of human creatures; he is one of the high finished works of the Creator. Maria is a good girl, but most excessive thoughtless and wants keeping in order. As to His Excellency, you may recollect we have talked him over now and then; he is the same wolf, and I the same lamb as ever, but our friendship is notwithstanding as well cemented as that of those animals was in the golden age. Odd as we all are, we shall be very happy to spend a great deal of our time together.

"The Cobentzels[1] are naturally well received here. They continue the same aversion for soap and water, and especially the gentleman, who since his mourning[2] has been more ugly and dirty than ever. They give a number of great dinners and suppers, and think to stop people's mouths, as house-robbers do mastiffs', by filling them. She is extremely clever in her way; but it is not a merciful one, and like justice, spares neither friend nor foe. We live daily a great deal together, as indeed all the body are much united. The Frenchman is not for Sir James, but by a mutual convention (you see I

---

[1] M. de Cobentzel had been the Austrian minister at Berlin, and had lately gone from thence to St. Petersburg.

[2] Probably for the Empress Queen.

make use of technical terms), his children come here, and I, Sir James's *child*, go to his house. The Ambassadors are forbidden fruit; though, if that our mother Eve ate of was as little tempting, her faux pas was inexcusable indeed. Numbers of the Russians inquire after you with the greatest regard—Count Michel Romanzow, Count Simon Woronzow, M. de Barbarodka, and a hundred others.

" My children are well; the boy begins to talk, and will be able to say soft things before your daughter can understand them. My girl is charming for nine months. God bless you! Je vous charge de bien des choses de ma part à Madame Elliot; pour ce qui est de M. Harris, je lui laisse le soin de parler de lui-même. Si vous *politiquez* autant que lui, elle trouvera n'avoir épousé qu'une vieille gazette.—Ever yours most affectionately,

"H. M. HARRIS."

In the course of the summer of 1781, Sir Gilbert paid his brother a visit of a week, on his way through Berlin to Petersburg, whither he was hastening to escort his sister-in-law, Lady Harris, back to England, her presence being required there on matters of family business. This visit was a great pleasure to both brothers, and many allusions occur in the subsequent correspondence to the pleasing impression made on Sir Gilbert by the beauty and agreeability of Hugh's wife, and the happiness of his home. Of Sir Gilbert Hugh wrote, " He appeared to me quite a giddy young man, at least ten years younger than myself, so prudent and steady have I become." Perhaps his account of himself in a

letter to Lady Harris, in which he answered some playful remarks on his former ways, was quite as near the
truth :—" After all," he said, " I find nothing is so like
an *unmarried* man as a married man."

The paucity of English travellers in Berlin during
the summer of 1781 is commented on by Mr. Elliot
with some satisfaction—more than one legacy, in the
shape of bad debts and dishonoured bills, having been
left him in the previous year by his travelling countrymen; but two travellers passed through Berlin in the
summer, who made no small sensation—the Bishop of
Osnabruck (Duke of York), " full of health and spirits,
prodigious handsome, and very civil;" and Baron Dimsdale, physician to the Empress of Russia, who came to
Berlin by her desire, for the special purpose of inoculating
the children of the Prince of Prussia.

Mr. Elliot tells the Baron's curious story in a letter
to the Baronne de Wrech :—" Un homme singulier a
quitté cette capitale avant hier—né Quaker, il rêva une
belle nuit qu'il deviendrait *Baron;* qu'il recevrait en
gros et en détail vingt-trois milles livres sterling, et cinq
cent livres sterling par an; qu'il dinerait avec des Em-
pereurs et des Impératrices; qu'il serait membre du
Parlement d'Angleterre; qu'il porterait bourse et épée,
et qu'il ne dirait plus ni *Tu* ni *Toi.* Les Quakers, ses
confrères, lui dirent.—Mon ami, tu n'es ni beau ni blanc,
ni jeune ni grand; tu radotes, ne conte plus tes rêves.
Le rêveur a cependant eu raison. Le Baron Dimsdale
vient d'arriver pour la seconde fois de la Russie, chargé
de toutes les richesses dont la magnificence de l'Impéra-

trice l'avait fourni. De plus il portait une lettre pour le
Prince de Prusse, le recommandant comme l'homme le
plus digne d'inoculer les héritiers de cette monarchie."

Luckily for the Prussian dollars, the children had
been inoculated, and the Baron's services were not
required.

While Berlin offered so little to amuse my grandfather and his lively gossip-loving côterie, letters from
abroad were particularly welcome ; and, before coming
to the more interesting ones from England, it may be
worth while to glance at the correspondence he kept up
at this period, with unusual regularity, with some of his
brother diplomatists at foreign courts.

From Sir James Harris he heard constantly. I have
already transcribed some passages from the letters they
interchanged while Mr. Elliot's matrimonial affairs were
pending, and the more serious and official portions of
the correspondence are of little interest now ; but the
general opinions entertained by so clever a man as Sir
J. Harris of the Russian court and country are curious
and entertaining, more especially as he was personally
au mieux in that court, treated with distinction by the
Empress, and high in the confidence of Potemkin.

After writing on private concerns, he goes on, in one
of his letters, as follows :—

" Now for a word on this country : You know its
extent, its high reputation—nothing but great deeds are
done in it.

" The monarch is an arrant woman—a vain, spoilt
woman—with more masculine than manly virtues, and

more female vices than weaknesses. The men in high life, monkeys grafted on bears; and those in lower, bears not inoculated. Religion, virtue, and morality, nowhere to be found; honour cannot be expressed in this language. There is no reward for good actions, though immense liberality, ill bestowed; no punishment for any crimes. The face of the country in this neighbourhood is a desert; the climate never made to be lived in. The Russians are, in my opinion, very great, because they are inaccessible; and from the mere local advantages of being able to furnish other nations with more articles than they need receive from them. You will naturally suppose living here not very comfortable; but I am sure of good society at home. Knaves and fools are as good company in a crowd as saints and philosophers."

In other letters he talks of the magnificent dimensions of the apartments, and the reckless expenditure of the court and nobility—the profuse splendour of their grand entertainments, contrasting painfully with the utter want of finish and of comfort in their every-day habits and arrangements, and the squalid poverty meeting one at every turn. " Force pierreries, peu de linge" might have been the motto of the Russian empire at this period.

In the autumn of 1780 the Prince of Prussia had been sent by his uncle to St. Petersburg, in the hope that his soldier-like presence and manners might efface the impression which had been made on Catharine by the graceful appearance and somewhat romantic air of the Emperor of Austria, who, as Count Falkenstein, had visited the Imperial Court some time before. These hopes were, however, frustrated, and Sir J. Harris wrote to Mr. Elliot, on the 12th September 1780, the following amusing account of the Prince's want of success :—

" He appears to her heavy, reserved, and awkward, and her reception struck him as but formal and unpromising. The Empress, usually very talkative, took no further notice of him last evening than decency and common attention required. He has too much good sense to believe those who would make him believe he has no cause for dissatisfaction. He has no confidence in his suite, and justly considers them as spies set out about him by his uncle.

" On Sunday she broke off abruptly her card-party, and, as I was sitting next her, gave me to understand it was because she was worn out by the silliness of the Prince of Prussia, who sat on the other side of her.

" The Prince de Ligne,[1] on the other hand, is received with uncommon distinction.

" The Prince continues to be a dead weight on the Empress, and she has at last ordered her private secretary to tell M. de Panin very plainly that he must contrive to get him away soon, as she felt that if he stayed much longer she might say something rude to him. However strange this may appear, I can assure you it is fact, though I believe no one but myself is acquainted with it. In public she treats him with a coolness and reserve quite foreign to her character."

Another Imperial Court furnished more cheerful

---

[1] Austrian Minister.

subjects for description; and the letters of M. Clément, minister of Saxony at the Court of Vienna, written in the course of the autumn of 1781, seem to have been welcomed with especial favour by the family party (which included Mr. Liston) at Berlin.

For Vienna and its society my grandfather always retained a sort of *first-love* sentiment. " Je vous avoue," he said, " que je n'ai jamais trouvé de séjour depuis où je me suis autant plu qu'à Vienne, peut-être aussi vu par le médium de la santé, de la gaieté, et de la jeunesse. Parlez-moi des plaisirs, des promenades, des femmes, pour plaire à la mienne." To this letter M. Clément replies—" Les grandes villes se ressemblent si fort par le genre et le ton de la société qu'il n'y a rien de piquant ou d'extraordinaire dans celle où je me trouve. Les hommes d'ici, généralement parlant, sont encore fort en arrière pour les lumières et les agrémens de l'esprit. Leurs conversations sont par conséquence fort sèches— elles roulent sur le jeu, sur les plus misérables nouvelles du jour, sur les chevaux, et, parmi ceux qui veulent faire les entendus, sur les arts. Les hommes les plus dignes d'être connus se trouvent dans le militaire, et sont pour la plupart des étrangers. L'étât civil n'en offre que très peu. Les femmes valent infiniment mieux. Sans avoir beaucoup de fonds elles ont pour la plupart ce vernis qui les rend agréables, intéressantes même pour la société. Les dames qui donnent le ton dans la bonne compagnie de la première classe sont très aimables. Il faut vous nommer Mesdames de Thun, Pergen, la Princesse Fran- çoise Lichtenstein, la Princesse Charle Lichtenstein, la

Comtesse Ernest Kaunitz, etc. etc., qui toutes possédent des qualités essentielles et brillantes. Parmi les jeunes dames il n'y en a guères qui seraient des prodiges par la beauté. Je ne saurais vous en citer aucune qui ait partagé de Vénus la forme et la ceinture comme la beauté qui fait le bonheur de vos jours.

" D'ailleurs il règne dans toutes les sociétés beaucoup d'aisance. Point de roideur, ni de hauteur ni d'etiquette, moins même que dans la capitale de Brandebourg, si vantée par sa philosophie et son triomphe sur les préjugés. L'on ne peut en accuser que quelques-unes des Princesses de l'empire qui se trouvent ici, et que l'on nomme d'après une grande autorité par dérision ' *les Nous.*' Les assemblées ont lieu tous les jours dans les maisons de la grande noblesse, où tous ceux qui y sont présentés ont la permission de se rendre, dommage que lorsque trois personnes sont assemblées dans un endroit, l'on ne peut se dispenser d'avoir les cartes à témoin. Il est vrai que la conversation ne se soutiendrait guère, il y a si peu de personnes qui y fourniraient quelque chose. Il n'est jamais question de souper, mais tous les jours un certain nombre de personnes est invité à diner. Au reste, cette société est la seule qui peut passer pour véritablement intéressante ; elle n'est proprement composée que du corps diplomatique et d'un certain nombre des personnes de la ville et de la cour, les deux tiers du reste de la société n'y paraissant jamais. L'on fait en général une très grande dépense ici—l'intérieur des maisons, le nombre des chevaux et des domestiques, surtout les officiers d'hôtel, demandent de fortes sommes."

After describing the beauties of the Prater, the Augarten, and other places of resort at Vienna, M. Clément goes on, " Pourtant, le nombre des promeneurs et promeneuses n'est pas considérable ici—les femmes étant occupées le matin de leurs toilettes et de la dévotion, et obligées d'être habillées les après diners pour aller se montrer le soir aux spectacles ou aux assemblées, leurs bijoux sont superbes."

In another letter M. Clément describes the arrival of the Count and Countess de Nord :—" Nous possédons depuis huit jours M. le Comte et Madame la Comtesse du Nord.[1]   L'Empereur n'épargne rien, ni en dépenses, ni en attentions délicates sur tout ce qui puisse les amuser et les intéresser.   Son projet est de ne pas les accabler par une foule turbulente de parties de plaisir, et de leur laisser *some part of their time to be spent in a comfortable way.*   Le Grand Duc et la Grande Duchesse sortent souvent seuls pour voir les choses les plus remarquables dans cette capitale.   Toute étiquette et gêne est bannie de leur manière de vivre ici.   Il n'y a point de cour chez eux, il ne s'est pas même fait des présentations en règle des personnes d'ici et des étrangers. Le lendemain de leur arrivée tout le monde a passé à la porte du Comte et de la Comtesse du Nord, pour y porter des cartes.   Suivant l'intention de l'Empereur, ces visites ont été rendues de même, M. le Comte du Nord ayant passé à quelques portes lui-même, et ayant envoyé à d'autres ses cartes.   Le jour du bal paré l'Empereur a présenté à ces Altesses Impériales les Ambassa-

[1] Grand Duke Paul of Russia, and his wife a Princess of Wurtemberg.

deurs, Ministres, Généraux, etc. Les Altesses Russes
et Wurtembergeoises dinent et soupent régulièrement
ensemble—l'Empereur et l'Archiduc Maximilien sont
quelquefois de la partie. Enfin tout va comme il plait
au Seigneur—sans faire beaucoup de projets et d'arrangement, et tout le monde est content excepté quelques sots
huppés, qui font les importants, et ne se trouvent pas
assez distingués dans cette occasion. Les Ministres
étrangers du second ordre ne sont pas des mieux traités
—il n'est nulle part question d'eux, il n'y a que les Am-
bassadeurs auxquels on fait un peu finesse. Ils ont soupé
au dernier bal de Schoenbrunn, à la table de l'Empereur,
où se trouvaient les principautés de Russie, de Wurtemberg, et celles de l'empire—c'est-à-dire, des premières
maisons, telles que Saxe, Mecklenbourg, etc. Cette fête
était belle—l'illumination, la quantité et la qualité des
plats, des vins, et des rafraîchissements, tout était dans
le meilleur ordre possible. Il y avait plusieurs quadrilles
composés de différentes sociétés de la ville, habillées en
matelots, en guerriers, en Hongrois, en Cossaques. Les
guerriers l'emportaient sur les autres par la beauté et les
agrémens des femmes qui se trouvaient dans cette société; Myladi Derby en était. L'intention de l'Empereur
de n'admettre à ce bal que des personnes d'un dehors
agréable n'a pas été tout à fait remplie. Au reste, il y
manquait aussi cette tournure gaie sans laquelle ces
fêtes n'amusent pas jusqu'au bout."

Of the Emperor Joseph, M. Clément writes:—" Son
gouvernement est digne de la plus grande attention.
L'Empereur donne les plus belles ordonnances pour

l'économie de ses finances, pour l'administration intérieure, et pour la propagation des lumières parmi sa
nation. Il n'y a rien de plus franc, et de plus popu-
laire, que sa manière de vivre et ses conversations.
Toute contrainte et toute étiquette est bannie de sa cour.
Il n'y parait en public que les Dimanches matin en
sortant de la messe. Il n'y à plus de réceptions à la
Cour où les dames assistent. Il vient de choisir, parmi
les 1325 chambellans de sa cour, 36 qui resteront atta-
chés à sa personne, et jouiront de quelques prérogatives
que les autres n'auront pas—c'est une distinction qu'il a
voulu marquer à ceux qu'il a nommés."

In these letters of M. Clément there are many passages which show the estimation in which Mr. Elliot's
society was held by those who had opportunities of
living in it: " Où retrouverai-je le charme de nos entre-
tiens ?—La société délicieuse de la chère famille anglaise
à Berlin ne se retrouve nulle part;" and such expressions are not peculiar to M. Clément, for among masses
of letters from English travellers, Russian princes,
German and French diplomatists, soldiers and savans,
there are few in which no allusions are made to my
grandfather's remarkable superiority of mind, to his
powers of conversation, and his charm of manner; while
Mrs. Elliot's beauty, and Mr. Liston's good sense, are
not forgotten. Wit and gaiety, and kindness and ease,
combined to make society delightful under the roof of
the English legation at Berlin.

CHAPTER THE EIGHTH.

1780 to 1782.

LONDON AND BERLIN.

THE two years which had been spent by my grandfather in the tranquillity of a happy home had not been uneventful ones to his family in England. The first letter written to Hugh by Sir Gilbert, a few days after the former had set out for Berlin, told him of Rodney's victory off Cape St. Vincent (16th January 1780), and of the distinction gained by Captain Elliot[1] in the action; and the same letter describes the effect produced on the writer by Mr. Burke's great speech on the alteration of the Crown Revenues—" a speech worthy of a true patriot." The naval action has been recorded in all subsequent histories of the time, and it is hardly needful to repeat here the rumours, the fears, and the hopes, which agitated the public mind in rapid succession before the event had been fully ascertained, or to dwell on the triumph with which the first five prizes were hailed as, under the charge of the *America*, they hove in sight off the Lizard. Burke's great speech on the alteration of the Crown's Revenue and influence was a triumph of another kind, no less well-known to all students of

---

[1] John Elliot, son of the Lord Justice-Clerk.

English history; but, on account of its subsequent influence on the political sentiments and connections of the
two brothers, it may be less rapidly passed over here.

At the time of their father's death, Gilbert and Hugh
Elliot had formed no political connection of their own;
Gilbert had come into Parliament a very few months
before; Hugh had already for some time been resident
on the continent. The former was following the law as
a profession, the profession of the second removed him
from the influence of English politics, but kept him in
relation with the party in power. Hugh, high-spirited
and full of zeal for the military honour of the country,
naturally sided with those politicians who were determined to resist to the last any dismemberment of the
empire, and who spurned a policy of conciliation arising
out of the necessities of our position and our military
failures. Gilbert, on the other hand, was not formed by
nature to be a thorough-going party man. Like Tre-
vanion in "The Caxtons," he was apt to see the gold
side of the shield, while his party were still swearing it
to be silver. When a "patriotic Duke" spoke to him,
with evident glee, of the disasters of our army in
America, he felt disgusted with the factious spirit which
looked for parliamentary triumph in the humiliation of
the country. But when Charles Fox made one of his
splendid orations, when Burke brought all the power of
his great intellect to the exposition of liberal principles,
Sir Gilbert could not, like Hugh, look on these men as
mere checks on the action of Government, or, like Mr.
Eden, as *outs* trying to be *ins*.

A gradually-growing despair of the home policy with regard to the colonies, an ever-increasing distrust in the capacity of the men who guided the counsels of the country, a distaste for the tone and views of the supporters of Government, became more and more apparent in his letters. But, on the other hand, the party in power was the only one which, in defiance of failure, still professed to believe in the possibility of recovering the colonies, and refused " to tarnish the lustre of the empire by an ignominious surrender of its rights."[1] While under the influence of these doubts and misgivings Sir Gilbert seems to have held somewhat aloof from the more active portion of his brother M.P.'s, and this had long been matter of regret to his friends ; but the speech of Mr. Burke, on Economical Reform, in the opening of the year 1780, decided him at once to " take part in a business with which," he wrote, " I am captivated ;" and from that time his relations with Burke became those of the most cordial intimacy. In the summer of 1780 the Gordon riots took place, and in Mr. Eden's opinion they produced a more general desire for union, *coalition*, than he ever remembered to have seen before. The German story of the imps who would not be re-conjured into their bottle had received some practical illustrations during the scenes of riot with which London for days had been filled; and while there were military encampments in the parks to keep the people quiet, many notable leaders of parliamentary strife were disposed to mutual forbearance, rather than to further agitation of the public mind.

---

[1] Last speech of Lord Chatham.

Parliament was dissolved in October, and long before
that the Elliots had set off for Minto; but not this time
with Isabella. She, who in brighter days had thought
the annual visit to Minto "a great breach of society,"
now remained in London in a pied à terre which she
took for herself in Chesterfield Street. "Though I shall
now be under a roof of my own, I shall continue to find
in the society of my brother and Maria my best happiness when they are within reach. My house is the
sweetest small place in the world, neat and elegant, and
seems made purposely for me; and I have the Edens
always close at hand."[1] But before the year closed Mr.
Eden was appointed to the Irish Secretaryship, and went
with his family to reside in Ireland; and in the following April, 1781, Isabella writes that "they are living, by
their own account, in the greatest bustle for five days of
every week, and the other two they shut themselves up
in a house they have in Phœnix Park, and see not a soul
but themselves, the children, the dogs, and cats, and
poultry. They are very well liked in Ireland." London
was not without its share of bustle too, the Opera-house
filling to overflowing by the attraction of Vestris's wonderful dancing. "The Queen has given two balls, which
were confined, in point of ladies, to the peerage. They
were, I am told, very pleasant ones, but a vast deal
of dancing. They began at nine and did not finish
till five in the morning; and every creature was obliged to dance every dance both up and down. I saw
somebody the next day, whose feet were so blistered

[1] Isabella Elliot to Hugh Elliot.

Q

that she could hardly stand. Cumberland House is open to everybody who chooses to go. The Duchess is very much liked, and will, I daresay, be a popular character."

While Isabella was thus writing to her brother of the amusements of London, Sir Gilbert was on the road to Berlin, where, as we have already seen, he visited Hugh on his way to St. Petersburg to escort Lady Harris to England; "a bit of knight-errantry" which his sister was slightly disposed to laugh at. However, this trip gave Isabella an opportunity of congratulating Hugh on the charming impression which Sir Gilbert brought home of his new sister, of Hugh's home, and of the baby "Isabella," who promised to be a brunette, and to have a nose as straight as Hugh's.

Sir Gilbert had no doubt much to see, to hear, and to tell at Berlin; and before the brothers parted they had an opportunity of comparing their more brilliant lots in life with that of poor Bob, from whom they received at this time a "tragi-comical epistle," describing his country living as "the most solitary place in the world—not a soul to converse with, the only disturbance to my meditations the barking of a dog, and the cawing of a rookery; a supper of cold mutton and roasted potatoes." He was in despair, and "could think of nothing but matrimony with some woman who could. talk," to find whom he was going instantly to York, where he had heard of such an one, "very fat and good-natured—to have in time a good deal of money." It is described, "on the whole, as a very moving letter."

Parliament met in November, and, as usual, was the
signal for a general move to London. Sir Gilbert, Lady
Elliot, and Lady Harris, settled themselves together
under his roof in Park Street. Isabella returned from
visiting various old friends near London, and re-established herself in her tiny house, where her many pursuits, and the society of her family and friends, made her
quiet life a contented and cheerful one.

Early in December a debate, which ensued on a
motion of Sir G. Lowther's, proved the House to be
agreed on the war in America, and that though it might
continue some time longer for other reasons, no further
attempt would be made to recover the dominion or
resist the independency of the Colonies.

Towards the middle of the month a gleam of cheerfulness was thrown over the political horizon by the
intelligence that Sir Eyre Coote had won a great victory
over Hyder Ali—news not the less grateful to the English
minister at Berlin, because the late successes of that
potentate had given rise to a passage of arms between
himself and the King. " For some time the relations
between England and Prussia had not been cordial, and
Frederick showed his bad humour by not addressing a
word to Mr. Elliot at several successive levées. Mr.
Elliot was indignant and burning to be revenged. When
at length, on the arrival of intelligence that Hyder Ali
had made a successful and destructive inroad into the
British territories in the Carnatic, Frederick broke his
long silence, asking—' M. Elliot, qui est ce Hyder Ali
qui sait si bien arranger vos affaires aux Indes ?' Elliot

promptly replied—'Sire, c'est un vieux despote qui a
beaucoup pillé ses voisins, mais qui, Dieu merci, commence à radoter.' Mr. Elliot related this anecdote to
my informant with much exultation, adding—'Sir, it
was a revenge that Satan might have envied.'"[1]   And
Satan's envy might have reached its acmé when the
news of Hyder Ali's reverses produced an ebullition of
spite from the King which gave Mr. Elliot an opening
for a second and no less ready rejoinder.   Commenting
on the expressions of gratitude to Providence which
accompanied the official narrative of Sir Eyre Coote's
victory, the King remarked—" Je ne savais pas que la
Providence fût de vos alliés."   " Le seul, Sire, que nous
ne payons pas,"[2] was the reply.

The first news of Admiral Kempenfeldt's action with
the French fleet off Brest was hailed in London as a
great naval victory; but though he had succeeded in
carrying off part of a convoy bound for the West Indies
from under the guns of a French fleet far outnumbering
his own, yet, when subsequent details were known, it
was found that the success was a partial one, and that

[1] I am indebted for this anecdote to the kindness of Sir John
M'Neill. The late Lord Fortescue used to tell the story, with some
slight differences, as having been related to him by his father, who, I
believe, was present at the scene.

[2] This repartee has been attributed by Thiébault to Sir Andrew
Mitchell, the predecessor of Mr. Harris at Berlin. I have always, however, been told that Thiébault had been in error, and that it was said
on the occasion described in the text. Thiébault's memory was sometimes at fault. Thus he places the mission of Mr. Elliot between those
of Sir A. Mitchell and Mr. Harris, whereas Mr. Elliot succeeded Mr.
Harris.

the action, by leaving the French fleet unharmed, could have no effect upon the war.

The following letter addressed to Sir Gilbert, and enclosed by him to his brother, may be read with interest, as having been written by a very gallant sailor who took part in the battle.

" Edgar, 14th December 1781.

" My dear Sir Gilbert—I have only time to write you a line to say that I, and everybody in this ship, are perfectly well after being shot at half-an-hour by the Triomphant (they say); except a few shots in our masts, sails, etc., the only misfortune that attends us is, the poor cow has lost her milk. On the 12th, at daylight, we saw a large fleet of ships, which we stood for, and found one squadron of them, four sail of the line, with a great many ships under their convoy. A few miles to the seaward of them there was a fleet of the line regularly drawn up; we stood in between the two fleets, and took twenty or thirty of the transports, victuallers, etc., but, from the badness of the weather, the shortness of the day, and, above all, the nearness of the enemy's line, we could not take possession of them all, nor do we know how many we have; nine is the most we have seen at a time, though, as several of our own ships are amissing, we are in hopes we shall have several more. The time I had the action with the Triomphant was when the convoy pushed down to join the line. I think the commander-in-chief did wondrous well to get a part of the convoy from so superior a force, for they are what you see endorsed—we, twelve of the line—viz. six of three

decks, four of 74, a 64, and a 60; out of the line—one
of 81, four frigates, and a fire-ship. All the 13th we
continued in sight of each other, the two lines ma-
nœuvring; and if we had not got the inclosed list from
the prisoners, I believe the admiral would have engaged
them. If we had, we must have had a bad hand of it,
as they were nearly double of our force, for there were a
great many frigates and armed ships not mentioned in
the list—one we took of 24 guns.—J. ELLIOT."[1]

"*Park Street*, 18*th December* 1781.

"My dear Hugh—In addition to the enclosed letter,
I must add that Sir Richard Pearson, who is in town
from the fleet, says that the Edgar, by her situation in

---

[1] In 1760 Captain Elliot had greatly distinguished himself by the
capture of the "pigmy fleet" of M. Thurot, who, in the command of
three privateers, had made descents on the coasts of Scotland and Ireland, burning two of His Majesty's ships. Captain Elliot, and the
frigates under his command, came up with the invaders in the Channel,
captured them, and took them into the Isle of Man. H. Walpole,
writing to Sir Horace Mann, March 4, 1760, says—"You will see the
short detail of the action in the Gazette, but, as the letter was written
by Captain Elliot himself, you will not see there that he, with half
the number of Thurot's crew, boarded the latter's vessel—Thurot
was killed." One of the guns taken from his vessel is now preserved
at Minto.

The following letter from the bailiff at Minto to the then proprietor,
the Lord Justice-Clerk, father of Captain Elliot and of Sir Gilbert
(afterwards third baronet of Minto), shows the estimation in which
their services were relatively held by some of their countrymen.

"*Moffat*, 5*th July* 1762.

"My Lord—I got to this place on Friday last, and as I passed Lin-
ton I joined company with three merchants from Westmuirland, and
travled with them to Moffat. After asking one another our places of
abode, they asked me if Capt. Elliot was any freind of your Lor* ;

the line, was the leading ship, and considerably ahead
of the rest of the fleet, that she came, in following her
course, directly on the Triomphant (Chevalier de Van-
dreuil), a three-decker, which, on her approach, prepared
to rake her, but that Captain Elliot, by a manœuvre,
received the broadside on his bows in such a manner as
to leave little damage, and then ran immediately close
under the counter of the Triomphant, and poured his
whole broadside into her in such a direction, and so near
to her, as to do her extraordinary damage.   The rest of
the engagement with this ship I cannot describe; Captain Elliot, you see, says nothing of what he has done
himself.   The Triomphant is understood to have suffered
extremely, some of her masts said to be carried away.
She was got into the midst of the French fleet, and thus
protected from further action, etc. etc.—G. ELLIOT."

Several of the transports were afterwards retaken by
the French, and only five are said to have arrived in
England.

The year 1782 began in gloom in the political world,
and my grandfather's own private bark was rapidly drift-
ing into troubled seas.   Thiébault, perhaps, is our best
guide here, though he only gives the gossip of Berlin
when he talks of the clouds which, at an early period of

after telling them that he was your son, one of them said that he believed
you had another son in the Treasoury who made a figour in the House
of Commons, I told them that you had, and that he was as usefull a
man in his way as the Capt., 'Dam it,' answered one of them, 'he may
speake all his days befor he can serve his counterie as much as Capt.
Elliot has done, especially in his taking Thourot.'   .   .   .
"THOS. TURNBULL."

Mr. Elliot's married life, began to obscure the light of home—"Heureux par sa femme," he says, "il ne fut d'abord occupé que du soin de la rendre également heureuse, et il eut recours pour cela à tous les moyens que sa fortune et ses réflexions lui fournirent; il lui procurait les agrémens de la société les plus convenables, il choisissait et variait les compagnies qu'il rassemblait autour d'elle; mais en même temps il cherchait à lui faire acquérir quelques talens, et à lui former l'esprit et le cœur. Par malheur, cette jeune dame si belle était bornée, capricieuse, et entêtée, autant que vaine et coquette. Les leçons l'ennuyèrent, et elle finit par ne plus recevoir qu'avec humeur et dureté les representa- tions les plus amicales." Mr. Elliot's own letters show that he, who had been used to the companionship of women with both heads and hearts, had early formed the project " de lui former l'esprit et le cœur." But unluckily Mrs. Glass's famous receipt is as invaluable when dealing with hearts and heads as with hares; and my grandfather sat down to prepare a dish, of which he had still to catch the main ingredients. The child seems to have been a source of pleasure and amusement to both; and its sayings and doings are recorded very fully for the benefit of relations at home, though they can by no means rival in quality or quantity the nursery tales sent out to Berlin by Mrs. Eden, whose rapidly increas- ing family of daughters occupied most of her time and thoughts.

In March 1782 the ménage of Berlin was momentarily increased by the birth of a second child, a boy, who died almost immediately, to the great grief of Mr. Elliot; and, while still suffering from this disappointment, and from anxiety about his wife's state of health and spirits, political events in England were preparing for him the most severe check which he had yet met with. Early in March he received the following letter from his brother :—

"*Park Street, 5th March* 1782.

"You will have observed the gradual progress of the propositions for peace, at least with America, since the capture of Lord Cornwallis. Such an event would have been a very poor reason, if it stood alone, for determining a nation to give up its purpose, especially a purpose so just and so essential as the recovery of America. But so many years' war with so little success had already produced their effect on opinions here, and this last signal event became the occasion, although not the cause, on which those opinions began to show themselves pretty generally. Accordingly, in the debates nothing more was heard from any quarter of the hope or even possibility of succeeding in the American object; while several persons considerable in the administration began to speak plainly their disinclination to that war, and the despair of its issue,—such were Rigby, and the Lord Advocate for Scotland. Lord G. Germaine prepared his retreat, as I think I mentioned to you at the time, and the symptoms of a general revolution in measures become so manifest, that, without inspiration, you will find by turning to my former letters, I have been a true prophet. I then told you my own opinion, and on that opinion I have since acted by voting for General Conway's first address, which was rejected by a majority of one in a very full House, and by voting and speaking for the second, which was carried by 19. There are, I think, some objections to that address; but there were reasons, too, which may be left to your own conjectures, which did, in my opinion, render an explicit declaration of Parliament and of the nation extremely necessary, and which, I think, outweighed the general objections to such a measure, and the particular defects of this one. The spirited declarations of a people at the commencement or during the progress of a war, produce good effects on the prosecution of the war itself; but it must be confessed that complaints of burthens, and impatience for peace, produce the contrary effects on a negotiation for peace. This observation is made stronger by the wording of General Conway's resolution and address, and ten times more so by the resolution voted last night (4th March); and this is the more to be regretted, as I think Parliament might have avoided this evil without losing the proposed effect of their measures; but I daresay you remember England well enough to know how difficult it is to frame any measure free from objection, when twenty persons are to be the authors of hardly so many words.

"Pray tell me whether this concession to America may not make a change in the politics of Europe. In some quarters of Europe we have had fair words; but I confess I brought home the idea that *all* Europe favoured the independency of America, and looked to the chance of some advantage in such a revolution. . . .

You ask me what will be the effect of all this at home. I really do not know, and I assure you, upon my honour, I have not thrown away a thought on the subject.

" The grand principle of distinction and separation between parties (the American dispute) is now removed. There is at least an opportunity, therefore, for coalition, without the sacrifice of former principle on either side. That the opportunity may not be lost by the damned intricacies of arrangements, private interests, and personal considerations, should be the prayer, morning and evening, of every true lover of his country. *All* the ability of the country united to direct *all* the resources of the country to one good end, is a prospect which I hope is not quite out of sight; but which, I fear, both requires too much virtue, and promises too much happiness, for this latter age to look for with certainty."[1]

A month later Sir Gilbert wrote :—" The change in Government happened immediately after, and indeed as an immediate consequence of the American votes. A very slight consideration will account for it. The true and fundamental cause of the removal of the late ministry was their long and uniform want of success, and the state of despair to which the daily calamities of the country had reduced the most sanguine. This cause, although it became stronger by every day's continuance of it, yet, it will be said, might have been expected to produce its effect much sooner; and this is true. One circumstance only prolonged the power of the administration, which, without it, must have fallen in a much

---

[1] Letter to Sir J. Harris, enclosed to Hugh Elliot at Berlin.

earlier period of our disgraces. It was the wish of Great
Britain to recover America. Government aimed at least
at this object, which Opposition rejected. Those, therefore, who thought the war with America just and practi-
cable, however much they might be dissatisfied with the
abilities of the ministers, or disgusted with their mis-
management or misfortunes, had yet no choice left them,
for they were the only men who would attempt the
recovery of the colonies. This I take to have been the
true bond between Parliament and the late ministry,
and the true key to its otherwise unaccountable longevity.
For, if it had had more lives than a cat, they must all
have dropped some campaigns ago, if the cause I have
mentioned had not preserved them. I remember when
it was said Saratoga would overset them. It was afterwards foretold, that if we should be drawn into a war
with France, ministry could not stand. The necessity
which produced the commission to America, and all the
humiliating concessions which Parliament made, in a
sort of panic, would have destroyed any other government. The same may be said of the Spanish, and after
it of the Dutch war; and there is hardly a gazette
during the last five or six years which would not account
for a change of government. But, in fact, the principles
of the ministers respecting America were agreeable to
the people, and those of Opposition were offensive to
them.

"I speak this language the more confidently to you
now, as you must recollect the time, and that not a
very late one, when I had a strong inclination to side

with those who wished for a change, and that I refrained
from it only on the consideration I have just mentioned;
and whether I and the rest of the nation have been wrong
and foolish on the American question, either from the
beginning, or in its progress, is a point which the purblind-
ness of human reason can probably never see through.

"I must own, however, that events and experience
do very strongly shake my past American principles to
their foundation; and although I could name many
blunders in policy, both civil and military, and many
miscarriages of mere fortune, which might perhaps have
turned the scale against us, and may perhaps be sufficient
of themselves to account for the utter loss of our object,
and the addition of many heavy calamities, yet I must
also admit that the possibility of what has happened
may have happened as the natural and necessary consequence of our measures, independently of blunder or
accident. This is a question of mere curiosity now, so
far as America is concerned, for necessity has already
decided, if not our principles, at least our future conduct
with regard to her. But it is perhaps a great lesson in
political wisdom, applicable to other subjects, which we
ought to study deeply, and which I shall study for one,
without that prejudice at least which belongs to an
obstinate attachment to former opinions. The moment
America was out of the question, Samson lost the lock
of his strength, and the natural weakness of the ministry
appeared immediately. Questions of censure were rejected by very small majorities, and questions for removal
ran still nearer; and would in fact have been carried if

the resignation of the ministers had not preceded their
dismission. . . .

"The chancellor[1] actually remains, but I am not
clear that all the accession of ability which he brings
can compensate for the discord which his difference of
opinion with his present colleagues on their favourite
measures of reform must introduce into the cabinet, and
for the appearance of weakness which a divided government on any capital object must throw upon it.

"The change has been complete; it is generally
said to have been forced on the King, and I cannot
undertake to admit or deny this; but I am more apt to
imagine that the resolution of Parliament respecting
America was the greater violence of the two; and whatever may have been the first impressions, on dismissing
old friends and servants, and receiving into his closet
new and hitherto adverse men, yet there seems to me
to be an impression likely to yield to more knowledge
of these men, and to habits of doing business confidentially with them. You will hardly need to be told
that I voted for the removal of the late ministry. I
refused, however, to concur in the vote of censure, to
which I could not, without an impression of something
disgusting to myself, as well as of injustice, give my
consent in the moment of their fall. I shall support the
present ministry with more cordiality, and therefore I
hope with more exertion, than I ever could the last.
The reforms, with which their government opens, you
know I formerly approved. I think this is a happy

---

[1] Thurlow.

moment for gaining to the constitution some great and
valuable improvements; and I like them the better for
the facility with which they may now be carried, without
those convulsions which could have alone produced
them as the measures of an Opposition, and which naturally, and I think deservedly, gave great scandal when
they were attempted before to be forced on Parliament
by the means of popular distraction, during a war which
rendered all distractions fatal."[1] ..

The advent of the Rockingham party to power gave
rise to immediate speculations on the probable changes,
abroad as well as at home, which would naturally ensue
from a change of policy at head-quarters. Before Mr.
Elliot heard officially of his recall, it was rumoured at
Berlin; and in his first letter home, he says—" There
are two circumstances too flattering to myself not to
mention them to you. The Prince of Prussia, who
came to town on Sunday last, and was at court, took me
aside, and said he hoped what he heard concerning my
change of situation was not true. I told him all that
I had learned upon that subject as yet was from my
friends, but that I had every reason to think it fixed. He
then asked me if I knew the reason; I answered, that I
had been told from home that it was understood that I
had not had the good fortune to be personally agreeable
to the King of Prussia. His Royal Highness answered—
' This is what I have heard; and what surprises me the
more is, I can assure you, that within these very few
days his Majesty a publiquement fait votre éloge; en tout

---

[1] Sir Gilbert to Hugh Elliot, 22d April 1782.

cas je me flatte que nous vous reverrons ici.' I was the more struck with this from his Royal Highness, as there is scarcely any example of his expressing himself so strongly to any individual in his present circumstances. On the other hand, Prince Henry has sent to me to know if it would be agreeable to me that he should write to the Duke of Richmond, with whom he is personally acquainted, to ask that I may be continued at Berlin. The Prussian ministry have been so warm in their expressions of regard, and of regret at my departure, and so positively deny any official interposition from hence, that there is reason to suspect, that if any ministerial step has been taken, it may have proceeded from Count Lusi's own private disinclination; and I should wish this inquired into."[1]

Madame de Verelst, Mr. Elliot's mother-in-law, writing from Prince Henry's residence at Rheinsberg, says—"Votre rappel d'ici ne peut vous être désavantageux; vous êtes aimé de tous les membres de la famille Royale, hors de Sa Majesté, qui ne vous connait pas, et qui a le préjugé de croire que vous êtes guidé par Milord Bute. Les Ministres verront par la suite où ces ménagements les conduiront. Monseigneur me charge de vous faire mille compliments, et de vous témoigner combien sincèrement il est affligé de votre rappel."[2]

In the course of May my grandfather received the following letter from his brother, showing that the

[1] Hugh Elliot to Sir Gilbert Elliot.
[2] Madame de Verelst to Hugh Elliot.

rumours current in Berlin respecting Mr. Elliot's recall,
and the grounds for it, had been better founded than
such rumours often are :—

"*Park Street, 4th May* 1782.

"My dear Brother—I have seen Mr. Fox twice on
your account since my last letter, and have refrained
from writing you till I could tell you with certainty what
to expect. Your recall is determined on the ground of
your being disagreeable to the King of Prussia. This is
the true and only reason for this measure, which I am
happy to inform you is not attributed in any degree to
any part of your conduct, but to its real cause—namely,
the prejudices which had been by some means or other
given to the King of Prussia respecting your supposed
connection with Lord Bute.[1] I believe that Mr. Fox is
really concerned, as he says he is, to find this measure
necessary. * * * I have some reason to think, although
he did not tell me so, and although I have it not from
the office, that the King of Prussia's wish on the subject
has been directly and officially signified to him. I have
no doubt that, whatever the consequences may be to
your future situation, you will with manliness and candour acquiesce in the propriety of your removal in these
circumstances. It remains to know what is now to be
done. I conversed pretty freely on this subject with
Mr. Fox to-day, and I am expressly authorised by him
to assure you that it is his wish and his intention, as

---

[1] The King of Prussia had never forgiven Lord Bute his share in
the Peace of Paris, by the terms of which he considered himself
aggrieved.

well as that of the King, to give you another Court as
soon as an opportunity or vacancy shall occur.   He said
the King mentioned this of his own accord, as soon as
he had informed him of the propriety of your quitting
Berlin.   He says, however, he does not know of any
immediate vacancy, but that he will look for it, and take
the first occasion which offers.   I am authorised by Mr.
Fox to tell you what you have read."

A little later Sir Gilbert wrote again, that in spite of
the assurances made by Fox in the interview described
in the preceding letter, two vacancies in the foreign line
had occurred and had been filled up.   Mr. Stanley,
Lord Derby's brother, coming in over Hugh's head, had
been appointed to Dresden.   "I own I cannot bring
myself to suspect Mr. Fox's sincerity; in the first place,
it would be contrary to his general character, and in the
next place, why should he use any art with me, whom
he certainly cannot fear?   Yet I cannot help feeling
that the present appointments in your line have the
marks of yielding to importunity.   To importunity I
have myself an insurmountable reluctance and aversion,
and if the business is to be decided on those principles,
I fear I shall be an unsuccessful agent; yet I will certainly represent, as it strikes me, the fair claim you have
for a preference to strangers in your profession.   *   *   *
What will you do in the meanwhile?   Your return home
with your family must naturally be uppermost in your
thoughts and wishes."

To these letters my grandfather replied that their
effect on him might be best described in several

expressions of Jaffier:—" The feigned story of his
embarrassments is more than realised in my fate."   He
does not particularise the expressions, but one can fancy
that to the order of " Home, home, I say !" he may have
mentally replied—

> " Yes, if my heart would let me—
> This proud, this swelling heart ; home I would go,
> But that my doors are hateful to my eyes,
> Filled and damm'd up with gaping creditors ;
> I've now but fifty ducats in the world,
> Yet still I am in love, and pleased with ruin.
> O Belvidera ! Oh ! she is my wife—
> And we will bear our wayward fate together,
> But ne'er know comfort more."—*Venice Preserved.*

The moment at which Mr. Elliot's recall took place
was peculiarly ill-timed as regarded his private affairs,
for there were questions pending concerning his wife's
estates which could not be decided until she should
attain her majority, of which she still wanted some
months ; and while they continued unsettled it was
believed that her absence from Prussia, together with
that of her husband, might be exceedingly detrimental
to their future fortunes.   My grandfather's own means,
too, had been greatly embarrassed during the previous
two years, owing, it appears, in some measure to his
having sustained heavy losses at play during the winter
which preceded his marriage.   The côterie of Prince
Henry, which Mr. Elliot frequented very constantly,
chiefly because there he was certain of meeting with
Countess Verelst and her daughter, was very much
addicted to high play ; indeed, at that time on the

Continent, as in England, gaming was the passion of
the day.   It was not, however, a passion of my grandfather's, who is always described by his friends as
preferring conversation to the card-table; but at a
moment when harassed by mental disturbances, doubts
as to his own course, and as to the feelings of others, it
was not unnatural that he should have sought *des
distractions* in what constituted the chief interest of
the society in which he lived.   Bets, too, he made; and
as they were generally staked on the success of some
English admiral or general, he was not unfrequently a
loser.

May passed without any further intelligence from
England on the point of a future employment for Mr.
Elliot, but Sir Gilbert still wrote—" I assure you
sincerely that I have the most entire reliance on the
former assurances of Mr. Fox; but, should no mission
be found for you at present, I must repeat to you and
my dear *Belvidera* the most affectionate welcome, and
the most earnest invitation to all we can share with
you in town or country, in point of society, convenience,
accommodation, or more substantial assistance, which
your occasion or my abilities can point out."

Belvidera, unfortunately, was not at all disposed to
exclaim with her prototype, " If love be treasure, we'll
be wondrous rich!" and the "unkindest cut of all"
that my grandfather had at the moment to endure was
the utter heartlessness displayed by his wife.   Tears
and reproaches, and a declared resolution never to leave
her native country, were followed up by a line of

conduct which made her the subject of general remark, and many of his friends went so far as to recommend a separation; but this was a course which his own feelings made impossible, and her youth, her inexperience of the world, and the irritable state of nerves which had followed on, and continued since, her last confinement, were pleaded by him as reasons for redoubled forbearance and tenderness; to which Sir Gilbert replied—" Even without these pleas, no man is for a larger portion of indulgence from mortal to mortal than I am; if she only loves you half as well as you do her, she is sure of a warm place in my breast; consider me and mine, town and country, at your disposal in this crisis." And then, referring to the separation which had been advised, he ends by saying, " I am not for making a man happy by breaking his heart."

For this time the domestic storm blew over, and Mr. and Mrs. Elliot proceeded to pass the summer at a *château délabré* in the vicinity of Rheinsberg. While there, he received a letter from Prince Henry, which begins as follows, apparently in answer to an invitation from the ex-minister:—" De Rheinsberg, 13 Juillet 1782—Monsieur, Sous quelque titre, sous quelque nom, qu'on vienne vous voir, c'est toujours sans autre dessein que celui de jouir de la société de l'aimable, de l'instruit, et de l'honnête Elliot." Then follow some, at the present date, unintelligible remarks on the proceedings of the French and English fleets in the Channel, and the letter ends thus—" l'idée de votre successeur m'est aussi amère qu'elle l'est d'ordinaire aux souverains lorsqu'ils envisagent le leur. Je ne saurais vous peindre une plus forte antipathie; elle est fondée sur mon amitie et sur la haute estime avec laquelle, je suis, Monsieur, votre très affectionné ami,   HENRI."

That my grandfather did not acquiesce in the propriety of his removal from the court of Berlin *on the grounds given for it,* appears plainly in the following letter to his brother :—" I am convinced," he wrote, "that had I been at any other court of equal importance, some cogent reason would have occurred to have made my removal at least plausible in the eyes of the world. You may remember what my sentiments were when I was last in England; and as things have turned out, I must acquiesce in the propriety of my removal from a post of confidence by those who must have considered me as by no means coinciding with them in principle or action."[1] This view of the case was, however, one which Sir Gilbert would by no means accept; and though he " could not prove that his brother's removal had not been made in order to clear the way for a friend of Mr. Fox, still he did not believe it, and remained unshaken in his confidence in the sincerity and friendliness of Mr. Fox."[2] The true grounds of

[1] Hugh Elliot to Sir Gilbert, 2d July 1782.

[2] The mission to Berlin had been offered first to Mr. Stanley, and secondly to Lord Cholmondeley, of whom Lord Holland says— "Lord Cholmondeley had much impaired his fortune by dice and dissipation, and, though an associate of Mr. Fox and his friends, thought it a better game to attach himself to Shelburne."—See the

my grandfather's removal from Berlin are probably to be found in part in the reasons assigned for it by Sir Gilbert, and in part in those supposed, and "acquiesced in" by his brother.

The dislike of the king, as represented by Count Lusi (digne représentant de Sa Majesté), was a sufficient reason for Mr. Elliot's removal from Berlin; and most probably the representations made to Mr. Fox derived additional weight from what must have reached him from other quarters concerning Mr. Elliot's habitual modes of thought and of expression when dealing with political questions. The warnings and remonstrances written to him by his family to Munich had been frequently renewed since his appointment to Berlin; his unguarded readiness in expressing his opinions in mixed society, without due consideration of the impressions they were likely to give; his strong condemnation, *when among his countrymen*, of certain political characters at

rest of the note by *Lord Holland—Correspondence of C. J. Fox*, vol. i. p. 318.

Walpole says—" I have said that the new ministers were distressed for want of places to satisfy their friends. . . . In these difficulties Lord Rockingham behaved with more zeal and decency than Lord Shelburne. An instance of the latter's impolitic insensibility occurred in the case of Lord Cholmondeley. . . . Lord Cholmondeley had peculiarly attached himself to him."—*Walpole's Last Journals*, vol. ii. Nevertheless, Lord Cholmondeley's claims were not overlooked by Lord Shelburne's colleagues, as he was appointed by Mr. Fox to succeed Mr. Elliot at Berlin. Mr. Liston, writing on the 21st of July, mentions the receipt of a letter from Lord Cholmondeley, in which, on the dissolution of the Rockingham Ministry, he announces that "he has resigned the honour of being His Majesty's envoy at Berlin."

home; the vehemence of his feelings in all points relating to the military reputation of his country, which at one time had nearly led to an open rupture with his old friend General Burgoyne—all these were well known traits of character, which not only justified his recall, but probably inclined Mr. Fox to consider the King of Prussia's feelings for Mr. Elliot from a point of view somewhat analogous to His Majesty's. On the other hand, if the same vehemence and the same powers of satire and of irony had been directed towards another political party than that of Mr. Fox, it is possible they might have been viewed with as little disfavour as the pointed and pungent sayings of the Fitzpatricks and Hares, and might have obtained indulgence from a minister whose own tenure of office was by no means agreeable to the King of England.

The death of Lord Rockingham in the month of July dissolved the ministry of which he was the head, and the immediate consequences are too well known to need repetition. On the 5th July Sir Gilbert wrote:—" With the opinion they (Lord J. Cavendish, Fox, Burke, etc.) entertain of Lord Shelburne's character, they could do no otherwise with dignity or credit; for myself, my choice between the two is easily made. My opinion has been, since the American business was over, that the country looked to the abilities of Mr. Fox, and the high character and integrity of his and Lord Rockingham's friends, for their salvation. I know little personally of Lord Shelburne or of his immediate retainers, Dunning, Barré, and Alderman Townshend, but the little I do know,

added to the voice of the world, is decisive with me. I
fear we shall have a repetition of our old distractions in
the struggle; I think it cannot, however, hold long. In
the meanwhile, the present Government is gaining
strength wherever it can, and has made a valuable
acquisition in William Pitt, to whom, at the age of two
or three and twenty, Lord Shelburne offered either the
Chancellorship of the Exchequer or the Secretaryship
of State, as he pleases."

On the 8th August he wrote again on his brother's
affairs, and reiterated his belief that Mr. Fox would
have performed his promises in Hugh's favour :—" This
I am confident he would have done, merely on the
apparent justice of the thing, without any motives in
my favour.[1] I feel a strong confidence that these
ministers will take the same view of your claims " (either
for employment or for an allowance in the interval—a
sort of half-pay which was usually given in those days),
" on the ground of their justice. I shall, however,
certainly not bring myself under any obligation to them,
and I have openly and explicitly declared myself on this
subject. Lord Shelburne sent for me a few days after
he became minister, and with a profusion of flattery,
and of promises of office, or anything else I could wish,
desired my support. I told him frankly that I preferred
his rivals. My mouth is therefore stopped, but I own
that I do not conceive party can be allowed to go so

---

[1] In an earlier letter Sir Gilbert had said, " I make no pretensions
to any *weight*, though I hope and believe I have the good opinion of
those whom I must respect."

far as to rob you because I am become obnoxious. Crying wrongs are not so frequently done by Governments as they are complained of, and I cannot despair of your finding justice even when favour is against you. Your case is simple—after many years of approved service in a profession which withdraws you from all others, and from any other road to fortune or advancement, or even subsistence, you are recalled without any alleged fault of yours, but for reasons entirely foreign to your own conduct."

Early in September Lord Grantham notified to Mr Elliot his appointment to the Mission at Copenhagen, and on the 29th Hugh wrote to his sister Isabella that he had accepted " an offer which, considering the circumstances of the times and my brother's political line, I think exceedingly handsome on the part of those who made it. I was very humiliatingly treated by the demigod of the blackguards. . . My brother seemed most decidedly convinced of the rectitude and ability of a set I neither loved nor approved. He is the creature on God's earth I most love and admire ; but I think he, like many others, has been led away by the false glare of a meteor, in which there is neither consistency nor a spark of heavenly fire—a mere blaze kept up by the foul breath of faction and desperation."

The last letter of Sir Gilbert, from which I have made extracts, terminates with the remark, that he is suffering from a very severe cold, and very shortly afterwards such grave symptoms showed themselves as to cause serious uneasiness to his friends. On the 29th

October he and Lady Elliot, though her confinement was close at hand, crossed the Channel on their way to Nice, but they had proceeded no further than Lyons, when their progress was arrested for some time, for there their first child was born.[1]

While they are proceeding to the south, and my grandfather, who had with difficulty resisted the strong impulse to join his suffering brother, is preparing to take possession of his new post at Copenhagen, we may turn from them to some of the letters which the former received during this year of turmoil from the Edens, Isabella, and others.

[1] Gilbert, second Earl of Minto.

CHAPTER THE NINTH.

1782.

ISABELLA—THE EDENS—MR. LISTON.

ISABELLA'S first letters in the spring of 1782 are full of
anticipations of pleasure from a visit which it had been
arranged she should pay to her brother Hugh and his
wife in the course of the summer—a project that came
to nothing, owing to the disagreements in the Berlin
ménage, which became known to the family in England
early in the current year. The letters of his family must
have been less painful to my grandfather after they
knew the sad state of things, than when they were
written under the impression that his home was like his
brother's and sister's—a scene of happiness and affection.
One wonders whether all the tender passages to " our
sister," and the kisses to the baby, were ever delivered.

On the 5th March 1782 Isabella wrote—" My
brother's speech on Wednesday last, on General Conway's motion, was very much approved, both as to matter
and manner. You would be all agitation, I am sure, if
you were in this island now. You remember how much
you used to be agitated when it was not so general as it
is now; every creature is full of conjectures. As to the
ladies, they go about to balls, operas, assemblies, as

usual; and there are this month enough of them, just what you may remember—Almack's, and so forth. Eleanor writes to me very often; her last letter was just after the birthday, which is kept some time in February. It was very fine and very full; and she says she grows quite thin, from being obliged to see and visit such a number of people." Isabella's last letter in 1782 (December 18) excites our sympathies, by being written in "a fog—an absolute darkness," the more to be deplored, as it even checked her ardour in setting out to see the "new actress, Mrs. Siddons, who is quite the rage; and people go to dine at the Piazzas in Covent Garden, at three o'clock, in order to get places. All the gentlemen cry, and the ladies are in fits; and in short, nothing of the kind has met with such universal applause since Garrick. I have only seen her once, in Jane Shore, and outlived it. She is certainly very fine, and much improved since even you saw her. I have seen Morton Pitt and his wife; she seems a very pretty, sweet girl, and he is vastly happy."

Whatever might be the political fortunes of the Edens, the sunshine of their private life was never for a moment dimmed; thus, while in Walpole's Journals we hear of an infuriated and disappointed politician, we find Mr. Eden himself, writing with all the fortitude of a Cincinnatus from his farm at Beckenham, and with an unaffected enjoyment of simple pleasures and rural life, which I believe to have been quite unknown to any attitudinising old Roman.

Writing from Beckenham, Kent, on the 8th of

August 1782, he says :—" Our farm is beautifully situated, and well circumstanced in every respect ;" he then goes on to describe the house, gardens, and shrubberies, the possible profits to be derived from his farm, and continues—" We have dismissed our coach-horses, and our carriages are oiled and locked up, as is also our plate-chest. We have two spare beds and many visitors, indeed some who never came to us before; and our only difficulty has been to prevent them from clashing with each other. As to your situation, I did not conceal my feelings when Gilbert told me you was to be recalled. He was not, nor is he at this hour, disposed to think anything wrong that Charles Fox could do ; and his politics are so pure, that no individual interests can exist in their atmosphere. The pretence taken for putting your talents under an extinguisher does not palliate the injury. Lord Derby wanted an employment for Mr. Stanley, who was first meant to be named, but was not sufficiently skilled in languages ; Lord Cholmondeley was next named, and went out with the minister that named him. Lord Hyde is now talked of; you know him. I do not enlarge on these subjects ; the reflections which occur to me upon them cannot escape you. Gilbert and I are personally on very kind terms, but I never talk politics with him. The world may misjudge him; but his conduct towards the close of Lord North's Government was, in its appearance most unsteady, and in its effects most unkind to his natural and old friends and connections. His subsequent conduct has been inefficient; for whether he had acted right or wrong, he certainly was entitled to expect

from the Rockingham ministry immediate and solid protection, both for you and for Mr. Elliot of New York.

"Having now disposed of ourselves, it is most in the
order of things to advert to the public. I do not think
(and men of weight and wisdom agree with me in the
opinion) that the present administration is strong enough,
either in numbers or efficiency, to be permanent, and
every effort is using to obtain some pacification in the
course of this autumn, and Mr. Fox and his friends
would be in some degree pledged to the conditions of
it, however dishonourable or inexpedient, but success
even in that great object would not preserve the present
Government in its present form; there must be new
fermentations; we shall see what they will produce.
The game would be completely in the hands of Lord
North and his friends, if Lord North were formed to
manage such a business. The King's situation is undoubtedly much enfranchised. It was not ill said by Mr.
H. Walpole, that 'the crown devolved to the King of
England on the death of Lord Rockingham.' Hare says
that his friend Fox is promoted from the service of the
King of England to that of the King of Egypt (Pharaoh).
Their remark on the Duke of Richmond's defection was,
that His Grace would not *go out* with any man.

"Upon the whole, you have thought us always unlike
any other people under the sun, and every line of our
history shows it.

"Eleanor and your four nieces desire to be affectionately remembered to you.   W. E."[1]

[1] Mr. Eden to Hugh Elliot.

The loss of the society of Mr. Liston was one of the most serious grievances which fell upon my grandfather in the course of 1782. Mr. Liston himself could hardly have been more eager and anxious than was his friend to see him placed in a situation more suitable to his age (he was entering on his 40th year), and more capable of affording a scope for his abilities, than that of secretary to my grandfather, which he had continued to hold since Mr. Elliot first entered the foreign line. Urgent representations had been frequently made on his behalf by Mr. Elliot to the Foreign Office; and in the course of the summer of 1782 he was appointed secretary to Lord Mount-Stuart's embassy at Turin. He was so old and true a friend, and had been so entirely, from Mr. Elliot's boyhood, in his confidence, that nothing could make up for his loss at a moment when anxiety and distress were pressing heavily on his chief's mind; and, though parted, their correspondence continued to be of a highly confidential character. The letters he wrote from Vienna on his way to Venice and Turin, and from Turin itself, are amusing, as the following extracts will show.

After remarks on the prosperous appearance of the Austrian peasantry, the cultivated and cheerful aspect of the country, and the beauty of Vienna and its environs, Mr. Liston thus proceeds to describe his impressions of the society :—

" *Vienna, 14th August* 1782.

"Sir R. Keith has been extremely civil to me. What I consider the greatest mark of it is, that he has pressed me to stay till Sunday next, that he may have an oppor-

tunity of presenting me to the Emperor. . . . I have
stared at the faces of the society of Vienna at Madame
de Hatzfeld's, and at Prince d'Auersperg's assemblies,
and have dined and supped with some of the corps
diplomatique, and have been introduced to Prince
Kaunitz, of whom I think there is even a chance of my
becoming a favourite, if I were to remain here. When
Sir Robert first carried me to the Prince's house, he
very prudently advertised me that my reception depended upon the humour he might be in; that he might
speak to me, and might not; that if he did, I *must let
him speak*, which I seriously promised. Sir Robert was
at great pains to procure me a favourable reception; and
with this view recommended me to the Prince as having
been long attached to Sir Andrew Mitchell at Berlin
(who it seems was a favourite of the Prince), etc. etc.
I observed the injunction, of 'letting everybody speak,'
so faithfully, that I even allowed this to pass without
any other contradiction than a broad stare in Sir Robert's
face. All attempts to make me be spoken to were long
ineffectual; and I was so mindful of my lesson, that M.
de Kaunitz at last asked Sir Robert if I spoke French.
Upon being answered (by Sir Robert) in the affirmative,
he asked me how long I had been at Berlin. I answered
five years, and so the audience ended. This to be sure
is no favourable entry on the road of favour, but, the
day after, I received an invitation to dinner (in consequence, I suppose, of Sir Robert's management with the
Countess Clari). At dinner he did but once address
himself to me, but now and then stared at me, which I

s

returned as you used to do the King of Prussia's looks on certain occasions. When dinner was half over he asked Sir Robert how my name was spelled, and expressed his joy to find at last an English name of which the orthography was reasonable; and so the dinner ended. Still this is not a gigantic stride towards favour. After the ceremony of washing the teeth, and our removal to the other room, I happened to stand near Madame de Clari's card-table, where he also was, and looked attentively at his coat, which was of singularly fine English cloth. This gave rise to a conversation, which was continued so long afterwards (and adjourned to a window), as to excite the attention of a good part of the company. Princes and Princesses came respectfully up and bowed, and attempted to attract his attention in vain; and to Sir Robert Keith's great surprise (who was not present at this scene) I was asked again to dinner to-morrow."

On the 17th of August he wrote again—"I continue to be a kind of favourite of Prince Kaunitz, and dine there every third day. Sir Robert also carried me to Madame de Thun's, who is extremely civil. She talks with great feeling and affection of you, and says she knows your motives for upholding Mrs. Elliot (contrary to the opinion of the world); that you never did anything wrong except from excess of virtue, and that this is also the case at present. Sir Robert Keith, too, has spoken of this subject. After I had told him your motives, he said, 'Well, his conduct, to be sure, is not what is thought *wise*, but it is perhaps better than wise—*it is a better thing.*' They are infinitely uneasy

here on the subject of republican politics. It is
reported that the Austrian interest at Petersburg is in
the last stage of a consumption, and that the Emperor's
declining to join the Empress in her rage against the
Dutch is likely to make it give up the ghost. My
reception by the Emperor was, as Sir Robert informs
me, extremely civil. His conversation consisted in
questions put to me, very much in the common style,
concerning my stay at Berlin, my change of situation
to Turin, the difference of climate in the two countries,
etc., and contained nothing remarkable, unless it may
be considered as remarkable that he seemed perfectly
informed of our connections, of the situation you had
been in at the Court of Berlin, of your marriage, even of
the last éclat. He spoke of you, au reste, with the
highest praise."

Mr. Liston reached Turin on the 1st of September,
and wrote a few days later to Mr. Elliot in raptures
with the beauty of the beautiful plain of Lombardy
with its magnificent wall of mountains; Turin, too,
came in for a full share of praise, and those who, from
the terrace of the Capuchin convent, have looked upon
it as he did, in all the splendour of a September sunset,
must agree with him that earth has few scenes to show
more fair. " I felt myself," he says, " transported into
the third heavens." The chief drawbacks to his comfort in his new situation consisted in the number of
social engagements into which he found himself obliged
to enter; and he writes feelingly of the number of royal
personages on whose fête-days he must appear in a gala

dress, each new one costing £20 sterling. "How I am to get to the end of the year I know not." Three times a-week the ministerial receptions began so early in the morning that "one has to be dressed all day, which perhaps is less hard on me than on most John Bulls"—I suppose on account of his habitual orderly attire, the neatness of which he sometimes refers to in fun; but Mr. Liston's most serious misfortune appears to me to have consisted in a certain appearance of honesty and common sense, which disposed everybody to confide in him; his hands were perpetually full of other people's love affairs or money matters. My grandfather made him his confidant, Lord Mount-Stuart intrusted him with his accounts, and in those days it appears that a secretary held a very different position in the house of his chief from what is at present the case, since, bon gré, mal gré, Mr. Liston was forced at Turin to divide his time between the duties of a Diplomatist and of a "Comptroller-General."

The early part of the winter of 1782 found Mr. Elliot at his new mission at Copenhagen; his wife had urged upon him so strongly the danger to her own health and that of her child, which might arise from a winter journey, that he had consented to leave her till spring under the charge and roof of her mother. A generous nature would have felt grateful for the trust implied in a compliance with her wishes on such a point, but hers was light and arid as her native sands, susceptible of the slightest impression, and of the deepest retaining no trace.

Madame de Verelst wrote to him constantly after his departure, and always with ample details of her daughter's looks, health, etc.   That her letters were scarcely of the kind likely to satisfy a sentimental disposition may be gathered from the style of a note which contains hardly anything but the following passage :—" Ma fille se porte bien, s'occupe de sa musique, et bien plus longtemps de sa toilette ; je ne crois pas qu'elle vous aime comme par le passé—non ; mais je me flatte qu'elle a de l'amitié pour vous ; elle sentira qu'une femme n'est estimée qu'autant qu'elle est bien avec son mari."

Mrs. Eden's hair must have stood on end if she had read the above specimen of German sentiment.   Under these circumstances the winter passed.   The very beginning of spring was signalised by the unfortunate events which made my grandfather's private history the nine days' wonder of half the capitals of Europe.   Thiébault, in his *Sejour de* 20 *ans à Berlin,* tells the whole story at length, and with tolerable accuracy ; but it is even more graphically told in the letters lying before me.

When the time approached for the reunion of husband and wife, Mrs. Elliot positively refused to leave Berlin ; and the letter in which she stated her determination, containing many calumnies and misrepresentations, was so worded as to leave little doubt on her husband's mind that she had written under dictation ; at the same time he heard of her misconduct from various sources, and was even warned that the thoroughly unscrupulous person who had obtained so great an

influence over her was known to consider her infant
child as the chief obstacle to the dissolution of her
marriage with Mr. Elliot.

On this hint Mr. Elliot started at once for Berlin.
Performing the journey in a shorter time than it had
ever been accomplished before, he passed through the
gates of Berlin under a feigned name, and arrived at
daybreak at the house of a friend, whose letters to Mr.
Liston, describing the events which ensued, were forwarded by him to Sir Gilbert, and among his papers they
have been preserved. The letters are written in French;
and, as they are very long, it will be advisable to con-
dense and translate the greater part.

Within a few hours of his arrival, Mr. Elliot was in
possession of an intercepted letter from his wife to her
cousin, the contents of which justified his intention of
removing the child from her charge; and he immediately
proceeded to make the necessary arrangements for so
doing.

Having learned from the same source that his wife was
engaged to sup at Prince Frederick's in the evening, he
ordered six post-horses to be in readiness, and on the
return of Mrs. Elliot's empty carriage to her house, the
coachman was ordered to drive to the post-house; the
horses were harnessed; the child, who had been brought
there also in a hackney coach, was embraced by her father,
and, with her servants, placed in the berline; and, in less
than twelve hours after Mr. Elliot entered Berlin, his
daughter had passed the gates on her way to Copenhagen, without a soul in her mother's house having had

a suspicion of the adventure. Mr. Elliot accompanied the carriage through the Porte d'Orangebourg, and came back on foot to the residence of the writer of the letter. Together they proceeded to Mr. Elliot's own house, where he possessed himself, without difficulty, of his wife's papers, among which he found the draft of the letter he had so recently received, in the handwriting of her cousin Baron Kniphausen. Assembling the men-servants, he positively forbade any one of them to cross the threshold during twenty-four hours, under penalty of being " hâché en piecès; " which expression, we are told, he accompanied " d'un air d'Alexandre," and with a hand on his sword; and having thus secured himself against any immediate communication between his wife and Baron Kniphausen, he returned to his friend's, and spent the night with him in examining the correspondence which they had seized. " Had you been with me, my dear Mr. Liston," says the writer, in English, " que de dou-ceurs vous auriez lu." Poor Mr. Liston being, as usual, the *patito* in his chief's domestic troubles, and no doubt never having been forgiven for his early discovery of the lady's dispositions. Next morning Mr. Elliot visited his mother-in-law, to calm her distress, and in her presence he wrote the following note :—

" Monsieur, ce qui est differé n'est pas perdu. La necessité de mettre ma fille en sureté m'oblige de partir d'ici sans remplir la promesse que je vous ai faite à Rheinsberg l'année passée. Maitre de toute votre cor-respondance avec une malheureuse qui a succombé à vos ruses, je serais à même d'obtenir de la justice du

Roi et des Loix une satisfaction égale à vos crimes. Le motif pour lequel vous animez une fille contre sa mère et une femme contre son Mari est clair. Mais sachez que jamais je ne consentirai à punir ma fille pour les égarements et les folies de sa mère, ni à seconder vos vues de vous emparer des Biens dont mon enfant doit seul heriter. Si vous souhaitez de prevenir les disgrâces que je vous destine il vous sera aisé de me trouver. Je serai toujours prêt à vous ceder ma vie ou à vous arracher la vôtre comme le sort des armes en décidera. Votre insolence vis-à-vis de ma belle mère qui mérite ma protection, est la raison principale pour laquelle je souhaite trouver l'occasion de vous en punir comme vous le méritez. H. ELLIOT."

His letter written, Mr. Elliot ordered four horses to his phaeton, and drove out of Berlin through the gates by which he had entered; but this time under his true name and designation—" Elliot, ministre plénipotentiare de S. M. le Roi d'Angleterre près le Roi de Danemarck."

The small vessel which he had hired to bring him from Copenhagen to (illegible) was waiting there for him, and among the *suite* he rejoined on board, his faithful dog is specially mentioned.

Having taken this journey at a moment's notice, for the purpose of securing the safety of his child, but at the imminent risk of ruining himself by a step for which he had neither precedent nor authority, he now made a regular demand for leave of absence to return to Berlin for the arrangement of his affairs. The first of these

was the chastisement of Kniphausen, against whom all
his wrath was directed, for in not one of his letters does
he ever refer to his wife except as an object of pity.

On the 12th of July the same correspondent as
before wrote to Mr. Liston at Madrid the sequel of the
story. Mr. Elliot having written to a friend in Berlin
that he proposed shortly to arrive there, " when his cane
would be more eloquent than his pen to answer the impertinent letters he had received from Kniphausen," the
latter, "fit le glorieux," practised pistol-shooting daily, and
endeavoured to secure the services of a second. " Mais,"
says the letter, " malgré les offres qu'il fit jusqu'à 100
Louis d'or il ne pût réussir." A rumour having got
abroad that he had found a second in a gentleman of
the Court, this gentleman was arrested and carried
before Count Hertzberg, the prime minister, and obliged
to give his word of honour that he would not act as
Kniphausen's friend. The baron himself was dismissed
from the service of Prince Henry, and was also threatened with arrest, to avoid which he passed into Meck-
lenburg; and there Mr. Elliot, who, in ignorance of all
that had been passing at Berlin, had sought his enemy
in vain at Rheinsberg, finally came up with him at
three in the morning at a small road-side inn, where,
stopping for a moment to make inquiries, Mr. Elliot
was refused admission, on the plea of the whole house
having been retained by a single traveller who had
lately arrived there. This cautious proceeding convinced
him that he had found his man. Armed with swords
and pistols, and a good cane, he entered the baron's

room and demanded instant satisfaction, which being
refused, he lost all self-control and fairly broke his cane
over his enemy's shoulders. This operation completed,
Mr. Elliot conceived that nothing remained but to fight;
but after many pour-parlers concerning seconds, dis-
tances, etc.—Mr. Elliot being for five paces and his
adversary for twenty—the Baron "beau comme Apollon,"
but not so brave as he was beautiful, demanded a delay
until more regular arrangements could be carried out.
To this Mr. Elliot replied by giving him four days for
his preparations, leaving him the choice of time and
place. The interval was spent by Mr. Elliot at Hop-
penrade, from whence he wrote to a friend at Berlin :—

"My dear Sir—I have only time to let you know
that I broke my cane upon M. de Kniphausen in Meck-
lenburg without his offering to return the blow; he has
declined fighting till another opportunity.—Yours ever,
                                        "H. E."

In the meanwhile, the Baron was writing to his
relation Count Hertzberg, to the Maréchal de Wrech, to
the Baron de Keith, etc., "that Mr. Elliot had come to
him in Fürstenberg, and, accompanied by four armed
men, had fallen upon him in the most cruel manner,"
etc. etc.

When these misrepresentations reached Mr. Elliot,
he wrote again to the friend to whom he had previously
announced the fact of the encounter at Fürstenberg:—

"My dear Sir—Pray send the enclosed to Hertzberg;
before this reaches you I believe the town of Berlin will
be undeceived as Rheinsberg is already, and as to

writing to anybody till all is settled, I am resolved 1 will
not. Kniphausen's story is a lie from beginning to end.
I have been waiting all day for his challenge, and have
not yet received it. I have given him four days to ap-
point a place and hour. Tell Juel[1] the truth, and tell
him to be sure that they do not write anything false to
Copenhagen. Kniphausen, nor nobody else, ever offered
to touch me with one of their fingers. He took his
caning in good part, and not a sword nor pistol was
shown till he went to take up his from the table; and
then I showed him a pocket-pistol, telling him to let his
lie, which he did. God bless you, and be sure all is right,
and will remain so till the end.—Ever, etc. H. E."

The four days expired, but only to bring new excuses
on the part of Kniphausen, till at last Mr. Elliot, wearied
of writing, went to Berlin and occupied himself in taking
steps for his divorce. He also called on the ministers and
the corps diplomatique, and so thoroughly explained the
situation between himself and his antagonist, that the
latter was advised by his friends to seek no further delay,
and he accordingly challenged Mr. Elliot to meet him
at Baireuth, a village on the frontier—where they finally
met, and the end of the story must be told in the
writer's own words :—" K. demande à tirer le 1er à 20 pas
de distance et donne pour signal de mettre la main au
chapeau quand l'un on l'autre sera satisfait. Le
second de K., nommé Copick, jadis officier dans ce service,
mésura le terrain. O'Connell, second d'Elliot, trouve
que les jambes de Copick sont plus longues que les

---

[1] The Danish minister.

siennes, bref, les pistolets se chargent et sont remis en mains des antagonistes. E. montre sa poitrine à découvert. K. en fait autant. Elliot était en bas, K. en bottes. Elliot n'avait qu'un léger froc, et K. avait un surtout pardessus son habit. K. tire son coup et manque. E. en mettant en joue, le pistolet se décharge de lui même. K. tire son second coup tout aussi inutilement que le premier. E. à son tour tire et si bien que l'air de la balle fait détourner la tête à K. et va frapper contre un arbre en ligne droite avec lui à 20 pas plus loin. Ces deux coups tirés, K. porte la main au chapeau dans l'espérance de quitter le champ de bataille. E. s'y oppose disant qu'il n'est point satisfait—que l'un ou l'autre doit rester sur la place et que la distance ne doit plus être que de 10 pas—à moins que K. ne lui fasse des excuses par écrit de ses propres impertinences, de la lettre qu'il lui avait écrite en date du 19 Avril, de la fausse accusation de sa conduite à Furstenberg, etc. etc. Là dessus les seconds entrent en negociations, qui durèrent près de deux heures. K. fit des propositions. E. ne fut point content. Tout devenant inutile le combat recommença, mais à la même distance, vû que le second de K. dit que comme on était convenu de 20 pas d'abord il ne permettrait pas qu'on changeât. K., le pistolet à la main, cria, que dès qu'il y'en aurait un de blessé, il signerait tout ce qu' Elliot avait exigé. E. fut satisfait. K. tire son coup. E. sans le plus petit mouvement de tête et encore moins du corps, porte la main sur la poche de son habit. On lui dit : Vous êtes blessé? Non, répondit il—ce n'est rien. O'Connell lui dit de tirer

son coup. Mais K. repétant que s'il était blessé il
signerait, E. lâche son coup en l'air avouant d'être
blessé et effectivement la balle avait percé la poche de son
habit—sa culotte—avait éffleuré la peau—et était res-
sortie par un trou qu'elle fit au bas de la ceinture de
son habit. Elliot, avec un sang froid inconcevable, ne veut
point se faire visiter ni laver la place jusqu'à ce que tout
soit fini. Après quelques moments employés à changer
ou adoucir les expressions convenues, K. écrit sur la
place ce qui suit—

" ' M. Elliot après avoir été blessé à mon troisieme
coup et ayant tiré son coup en l'air, je lui fais la déclara-
tiou de mon propre mouvement que je suis fâché d'avoir
eu des torts envers lui, et lui en fais des excuses, de
même que de lui avoir écrit une lettre outrageante le
14 Avril.

" ' Je déclare encore que les bruits sont faux que M.
Elliot m'ait attaqué avec des gens armés à Furstenberg.

(Signé)   ' KNYPHAUSEN.

" ' Le 3 Juillet 1783.'

" En outre il promit sur sa parole d'écrire une lettre
d'excuses à Mad^{me.} la Comtesse de Vérelst.

" Quand M. Elliot fut muni de ces papiers, le second
de K. voulait que les deux ennemis s'embrassassent d'autant que K. dit ' Actuellement notre querelle est vuidée.'
Sur quoi Elliot mettant son chapeau à la main, s'adressa
en Allemand à K. lui disant :—'Monsieur, je vous souhaite
toute sorte de bonheur ; mais quant à ce qui est d'amitié
ou de relations entre vous et moi—il n'y en aura jamais.
Pour vous, Monsieur,'—se tournant vers le second

de K.—' vous vous êtes conduit dans cette affaire comme un galanthomme, et je me ferai un plaisir de l'avouer publiquement—et dans toutes les occasions.' Après quoi E. fit bassiner la blessure et se remit en voiture pour revenir à Berlin.

"Mercredi matin toute la ville sçut l'histoire, ce ne fut qu'un cri d'éloges pour Elliot.   Toutes les cours lui envoyèrent des félicitations—le Prince et la Princesse de Prusse, le Prince et la Princesse Ferdinand, la Princesse Amélie, le Prince de Brunswick.   Le Prince Ferdinand lui écrivit la lettre la plus flatteuse.   Vendredi matin le Prince Henri lui fit écrire combien il était charmé que l'affaire se fut terminée si honorablement de sa part, et le fit prier de passer par Rheinsberg à son retour, ajoutant qu'il le rencontrerait à Meisbourg si pour quelques raisons inconnues E. ne voulut point se rendre à Rheinsberg.   Le Roi apprenant l'affaire s'écrie, ' N'avois je pas raison quand je disais qu'il ferait un excellent soldat !'   Hier matin Elliot est reparti, couvert de gloire—dans huit ou dix jours son divorce sera fini. Voilà donc mon cher envoyé, la pure et exacte vérité de toute cette histoire qui a fait plus de bruit ici que jamais le siège de Troie n'en fit.' "

An English friend, writing to himself, says, " The whole garrison of Potsdam is delighted with you."

The Baron having written himself down a libeller and villain, and his conduct throughout the whole transaction having been cowardly and base, as well as unprincipled, the society of Berlin turned its back upon him.   Prince Henry dismissed him from his ser-

vice, Prince Ferdinand (the King's youngest brother)
addressed Mr. Elliot in the following terms :—

" Friedrichsfeld, 9th July 1783.

" Monsieur—Permettez-moi de vous féliciter d'avoir
heureusement terminé votre différence avec le Baron de
Kniphausen. La manière dont j'apprends que vous
vous êtes conduit vous couvre de gloire, et elle justifie
la bonne opinion que j'ai toujours eu de vous ; la grandeur d'âme que vous avez témoigné envers votre adver-
saire fait votre éloge. Je me réjouis de savoir vos jours
conservés, etc. etc. etc.—Votre très affectionné ami,

" FERDINAND."

And, in still warmer language, the Princess of
Prussia wrote for herself and her husband—

" Potsdam, 12th July.

" Vos malheurs étaient faits pour vous attirer la
compassion de toute âme sensible, et la noblesse de vos
procédés l'admiration et l'estime de tout le monde.
Vous y avez réussi parfaitement ; le Prince (Royal) vous
rend toute la justice possible. J'embrasse ma filleule,
parlez lui de moi. Mille grâces de ce que vous me dîtes
touchant la naissance de mon fils ; ayez de l'amitié pour
lui, celle d'un ami galanthomme ne peut que lui être
précieux dès qu'il saura l'apprécier. FRÉDÉRIQUE."

But while royal princes and ministers hurried
to offer him expressions of sympathy and of approbation,
he was laid prostrate by a severe attack of illness, from
which he had been suffering at the time of his departure
for Berlin, and of which he had been totally unmindful

during the late agitations; for some days he was seriously ill.

In the letters which he wrote home during these painful transactions, he confined himself to the facts which it was necessary to tell, and passed over in silence the feelings which filled his breast. To those who knew his naturally expansive nature and almost feminine tenderness, such silence must have told more plainly than speech of the struggle it caused him to contend against affections not withered but crushed. To us, half a page in an old pocket-book gives a glimpse into his secret thoughts when on the eve of meeting what seemed an impending fate, and though the lines written there have no pretensions to poetical merit, the occasion which suggested them lends them an interest of their own :—

" July 8, 1783.   Before going out to fight a duel.

" When youthful ardour led me to the field,
  My youthful sword a blooming Laurel won,
  When sacred friendship glowed with equal warmth,
  My hand propitious gave that friend success ;
  With fiercer flame, when Love had fired my soul,
  That flame, soon mutual, lighted Hymen's torch ;
  The Laurel, Friend, the Wife—these gifts were mine.

———

" To teach the vanity of earthly good,
  From War I brought disease and years of pain ;
  From Friendship's ashes learnt that man is frail ;
  And Hymen's torch but lights me to my tomb."

Below these lines the following sentence is written :—

"*P.S.*—I entirely acquit Liston of the least coolness or change of sentiment.

"H. ELLIOT, 8th July 1783."

The reflection on Mr. Liston probably rested on some misconception, or emanated from that mood of mind in which "all the world appears unkind." Its almost simultaneous retractation was doubtless due to a sudden consciousness that it might cause pain when explanation would have ceased to be possible.

During Mr. Elliot's stay in Berlin the necessary steps were taken for his divorce, and, when his health was re-established, he returned to Denmark on the best footing with his mother-in-law, with Prince Henry, and all his old Berlin connections. His wife subsequently married her cousin, and both lived in strict retirement until her death, which took place in a few years after these events.

Thus again Hugh Elliot stood alone in life; his household gods lay shattered round him; the mother who would have mourned over him was gone; and though his family sorrowed for his sorrows, it was with a feeling not unmixed with congratulation at the sever-ance of so deplorable a connection. "Thank God," says Isabella, after his return from Berlin, "you have got safely away from all those strange people."

What was thought at home of the first act of this uncommon romance in diplomatic life, may be gathered from a letter written by Mr. Liston from London, shortly before he went to Spain:—

"*London, 23d May* 1783.

"The day before yesterday I had an audience of

T

leave of the King (as they mean to despatch me immediately). He kept me (I believe) pretty long, and went through many subjects, among others your journey, with which I was amazed to find him so well acquainted. The first accounts he had had of it were from a German gazette; then from the Leyden paper; then from your two private letters to Mr. Fox,[1] both of which were shown to him; and he must also have heard of it from other quarters, from the particulars I found he knew. I told him that it[2] was a measure of absolute necessity, and that you could not possibly do otherwise; which he seemed to assent to, and I was very happy to find him speak with so little rigidity on the subject. Both the courts concerned have used friendly language. The opportunity I had of talking so long with the King has had the same effect with me as the successive conversations you have had used to have on you; that is, to convince me of his extensive knowledge of many things one would not expect him to be master of, and of his sound good sense in many others. I know not from what circumstance it was, but I felt myself inspired with more courage to speak to him than I usually have to people that are placed even one step above me."

[1] The Coalition Government came in in March 1783.

[2] This refers to Mr. Elliot's hasty journey, *without leave*, from Copenhagen to Berlin.

CHAPTER THE TENTH.

1782 to 1785.

COPENHAGEN.

THE first letters which my grandfather wrote from Copenhagen in the winter of 1782 and 1783 give an agreeable account of his impressions of the place. Even through the clouds and mist of winter he gazed with pleasure on a fertile and undulating country, a sea alive with shipping, and a handsome capital surrounded by country residences standing in wooded and picturesque parks. The contrast offered by such scenes to those he had lately left was sensibly grateful to him; and when in July 1783 he returned from the painful agitations of Berlin to his beautiful villa at Christiansholm, it seemed to him like "a haven of peace to a shipwrecked mariner."

He appears to have been at once cordially received into the society of the Schimmelmanns and Reventlows,[1] families allied by ties of blood and by congenial tastes and pursuits, and frequent mention is made by him of their delicate kindness to himself, and of the resources he found in their attractive society.

[1] The readers of the *Memoirs of Perthes* will be familiar with several accomplished members of the above-named families.

Other friendships he owed to his intimacy with
Countess Bentinck—a very remarkable old lady—who
resided at Hamburg, and whose unblemished life and
strong mental powers had made her the respected centre
of a distinguished circle. My grandfather had made her
acquaintance during the many visits to Hamburg which
in the early years of his residence at Berlin had afforded
him rest and relaxation. She had been the confidant of
his love-story; in her later letters she confesses that
often, while sitting with him in her garden at Elms-
büttel, listening to the delicious pictures of an ideal
happiness of which he, " le cœur rempli d'un espoir bien
doux," anticipated the realisation in his future home,
she had asked herself, with fear and trembling, if it were
indeed possible that a female character such as that
described to her could " come out of Nazareth ?" and had
prayed that even such a miracle might be worked in
favour of her friend—" un être composé d'esprit et de
cœur."

When Mr. Elliot first learned the circumstances
which made the immediate removal of his child from
his wife's care a matter of urgent necessity, it was to
Countess Bentinck that he turned for help and assistance, and, throwing himself on her generosity, he
implored her to give his child temporary protection
should anything happen to him, or should obstacles be
raised to his removal of her from the country. This
appeal was received by his venerable friend as a most
gratifying proof of the confidence with which her
character had inspired him; for not only did he know

her to be a near relation of the man who had so sorely
injured him, but to be connected with him by other
ties—Baron Kniphausen's mother having, on her death-
bed, left him, with others of his family, to the tender
care of the Countess Bentinck, whose sister, I believe,
she was. Mr. Elliot's trust was amply justified by the
tenderness with which Madame de Bentinck responded
to his request; and not only did she promise his child
such love and care as she would have given to her own,
but she placed her château of Doorwerth, in Guelder-
land, at his disposal, should he think it a safer refuge
than Hamburg for his infant daughter.

As we have seen, however, Mr. Elliot succeeded in
carrying her out of Prussia without coming into collision
with the Prussian Government, and Countess Bentinck
tells him in one of her letters, immediately after his
return to Copenhagen, that the King not only did not
blame his conduct, but that, on the contrary, he had
said:—" Qu' Elliot étant père, était louable d'en avoir
les entrailles," and that all the royal indignation was
directed against the officer in charge of the gates who
had been taken by surprise by Mr. Elliot's sudden
revelation of himself. Hence a very severe *ordonnance*
had been published, to the vexation of all subsequent
travellers, who were to be submitted to " une inquisition
de Goa " before passing the gates of Berlin.

To Countess Bentinck's good offices, Mr. Elliot was
indebted for the friendship of her nieces, Countess de
Wedel and Countess de Holstein-Letraborg. Of the first
of these ladies she says, " Elle a des qualités rares dans

toutes les cours, et serait digne d'être Angloise—ou
même Romaine par son caractère serieux et digne." Of
the Countess of Holstein she gives a more elaborate and
very charming portrait. " Once a charming girl, she is
now an incomparable wife and mother, living only for
her family and friends. She goes rarely to Copenhagen,
and it would be as hard for you to wean her from her
happy simple tastes, as for the Spaniards to take Gibraltar from the keeping of your kinsman." She had a
peculiar claim to the interest of an Englishman, having
been strongly attached to the unfortunate Queen Matilda,
who selected Countess Holstein for the painful duty of
attending her in her terrible journey to Stade. The
Countess, though barely three weeks had passed since
her confinement, would not disobey the orders of a princess whom she adored, though she could not always
approve, and together they nearly perished by the way
in a violent tempest. "Elle s'est fait sa gloire," says her
aunt, " of being the last Danish lady who conformed to
the royal prohibition against wearing the order by which
Queen Matilda had decorated the ladies whom she
especially distinguished by her favour."

The first court reception, or " appartement " as it was
called, at which Mr. Elliot assisted, is described by him
as brilliant and striking, though on general occasions the
vast apartments were ill lighted and worse filled—neither
courtiers nor candles being sufficiently numerous for
their large dimensions.

The Royal family consisted of the King, Christiau
VII. (who had married and divorced Matilda of England,

sister of George III.), of his stepmother, Juliana Maria
of Brunswick-Wolfenbuttel, widow of Frederick V., of
her son Prince Frederick and his wife, and of the young
Prince Royal and his sister—children of the King and
of Queen Matilda. The Prince Royal was, at the time
of Mr. Elliot's arrival in Denmark, a slight slim boy of
fourteen, of noble and easy carriage, "very like his
English relations." The Princess, "a little fairy, having,
at the age of ten or eleven, possessed herself of all graces
and all charms, dancing, talking, and holding her circle
in perfection."[1]

The circumstances under which my grandfather made
his début in the society of Copenhagen were not such as
to dispose him towards taking an active part in its
pleasures; for "when the stormy rain was past, the drops
remained still."

Dispirited and suffering in body as well as in mind,
he held aloof as far as was compatible with his position
from the world around him, and occupied himself with
"his child, his books, and his thoughts." He relates
with pride the growth of his little girl's vocabulary, and
the increasing intelligence of her remarks; and the "dear

---

[1] She was born a few months before the Revolution took place which
cast her mother from the throne, and the nursing and rearing of this
infant had been the only comfort of Queen Matilda during her melancholy confinement at Cronburg. She afterwards said that the parting
with her child was the severest pang she felt, when removed from Denmark to a safer and more dignified prison in her brother's castle of Zell.
Some years after her death, Coxe, the traveller, was told at Zell by an
eye-witness of the fact, that the Queen constantly apostrophised and
wept over the portraits of her two children, for whom she retained to
the end of her life the warmest affection.

pretty little Bella" becomes a prominent personage in the letters he writes and receives.

To his family he describes himself as resuming old studies for her sake—learning, that he might instruct.

It is very probable that the idea of collecting and of preserving his correspondence occurred to him at this time.   He frequently says in his letters that his thoughts are turned to the past; that he is busied in studying it by the light of experience; and as the collection of letters which I have described as chronologically arranged, and bound in volumes, terminates with the correspondence of 1784, it seems not unreasonable to suppose that its formation was one of his chief occupations during the interval of quiet and leisure which followed on his return to Denmark, immediately after his divorce.   The work was not ill suited to his frame of mind; it was an attempt to keep a waif from the gallant bark which had set out in "life's morning," with "youth at the prow and pleasure at the helm."

Ten years had elapsed since his first going forth from home, and, as he reviewed their flight, what varied scenes must his memory have recalled!—the Cossack tents on the Danube, his hairbreadth escapes by land and water, the brilliant courts of Warsaw and of Vienna, where he left so deep an impression, that years afterwards travellers found, in the title of his friend, a passport to the best society; the gallicised Munich, gay, vicious, and superstitious; the barrack-like Berlin, where everybody not on parade was carousing and gambling, and whence philosophy failed to banish ennui and indigestion; but where, across every scene, there flitted a phantom with fair face and golden hair, like the treacherous nymphs of her country's fables, luring the traveller on to trouble and sorrow.

One can fancy him in whom, as Lord Stormont said, the " elements were blended," dreaming over these things in the beautiful solitude of Christiansholm, while, half in tenderness and half in mockery, and wholly sad, he set himself to " weigh the weight of the fire, to measure the blast of the wind, to call back the day that was past !"

While thus occupied, public events seem to have lost much of their interest for him. " It is our destiny to fall into a Pit(t), or be caught by a Fox, unless Boreas should take us up again," he wrote ; and none of these things excited him—disheartened and disenchanted, the world to him was a stage, and all the men but players.

In the meanwhile his letters from England bore no trace of any such *indifferentism*. The last letters which I have quoted were written during the short government of Lord Shelburne,[1] to be so soon succeeded by the ill-fated Coalition—the strongest of governments as regarded parliamentary support, the weakest in the favour of the King and people. Mr. Eden, as is well known, was one of the active promoters of the Coalition ; and neither he nor any other of my grandfather's correspondents had any misgivings as to its success when it should be once fairly launched.

[1] Lord Shelburne came in in 1782, and was turned out by the Coalition in March 1783.

While the new ministry was in process of construction, Isabella wrote feelingly of the mischief done to London society by the excess of party strife.

" At present," she wrote on March the 6th, " this country is much like the sea that surrounds it—nothing settled, and party running very high. Eden's friends and my brother's faction of last year have joined forces, but what the result will be is not yet determined. . . . Nothing can equal the strangeness of the scene here for the last twelvemonth—balls, assemblies, etc. The Prince of Wales goes to all the great houses, and there is a ball every Tuesday night for him, where he gives the list."

A month later she wrote again—" I continue to live as usual, very quiet, and am surrounded by bustle, which, this last six weeks, has been of a most unpleasant kind. Had you been in England, you would have agitated yourself to death. Indeed, the most phlegmatic characters were so. The Coalition are now what is called *in;* and I own I am a sufficiently good subject to wish there may never again be such a scene. However, I make no reflections on what is called politics, as being able to determine what is really the good of the country is quite out of my reach. Mr. Eden kisses hands on Friday, on being made Vice-Treasurer of Ireland. He got credit for having been the means of uniting the two parties. During the crisis the union was wonderful. Time will show how it will turn out. Your principal [1] has great knowledge and power of reading character, with an unbounded genius; what the rest of his character may be

[1] Fox.

I do not know, but all his greatest enemies are now much attached to him; the scene is very perplexing. However, I think one goes more along with him in it, than with the persons who united with him. Nancy Elliot[1] is going to marry Sir David Carnegie, a Scotch gentleman of a very good character and large fortune."

The India bill, which was foreseen to be a danger, passed through the Commons triumphantly, and Sir Gilbert (who had returned in the summer from the Continent in renovated health) wrote a detailed account of the measure to his brother, under the impression that he was to be one of the parliamentary directors (the seven kings) to be appointed under Mr. Fox's bill. The fate of the India Bill, and the part taken by the King and the House of Lords, are so well known, as to make it useless to give extracts from the letters which relate to these events, since they throw no new light on the subject.

The party who had a large majority in the House of Commons had ceased to govern, and the minority furnished a ministry.

The House of Commons passed a strong resolution denouncing a dissolution, though, as Mr. Eden wrote, "after all it would be a more constitutional course to pack a Parliament, than to govern in defiance of one."

The minister was, in the eyes of his opponents, an inexperienced boy, and his great talents could not be

[1] Daughter of Mr. A. Elliot, and grandmother of the present Earl of Southesk. She died in 1860.

expected to compensate for the entire dearth of ability
in the greater part of his colleagues. "Habits of
business make men of business," wrote my grandfather,
not very much distressed by a change of government
which excluded Mr. Fox from office. "I cannot agree
with you there," said Mr. Eden, "for who ever had such
habits of business as some of our friends during a series
of years, and yet"—

The defeated majority had no doubt that a very
short interval would suffice to restore them to power.
Confidence and glee were on the side of Opposition.
Sir Gilbert was keener than he had ever been; "If,"
wrote Mr. Eden, "his passions were equal to his
abilities, he would play a leading part." The result of
the general election dashed their hopes to the ground,
and they learned that the people and the King were
equally averse to the rule of a party who had compro-
mised their principles to establish their power.

One consequence of the general election was to
deprive Sir Gilbert of a seat, an event less deplored by
himself than by his friends. "My philosophy or my
indolence," he said, "makes me well satisfied with the
prospect of some leisure for self-improvement," etc.;
and he proceeded in the ensuing summer to enjoy the
sea-breezes at Swanage, and the shades of the New
Forest, with all the glee of an emancipated school-boy.
In the autumn he and Lady Elliot accompanied Lady
Harris to Bath, and from thence he wrote a letter to his
brother, in which he describes a visit from their old
schoolfellow Mirabeau.

"I was lately agreeably surprised by a note dated *Hatton Street, Holborn,* from our old persecuted school-fellow Mirabeau, who has fled to England for safety, and has nothing but his pen to trust to for support. I found him as ardent a friend as I left him, and as little altered as possible by twenty years of life, of which six have been consumed in prison, and the rest in personal and domestic troubles. He is very much ripened in his abilities, which are really considerable, and has acquired a great store of knowledge. . . . . . Mirabeau is as overbearing in his conversation as awkward in his graces, as ugly and misshapen in face and person, as dirty in his dress, and withal as perfectly *suffisant*, as we remember him twenty years ago at school. I loved him, however, then, and so did you, though, as he confesses, you sometimes quarrelled with him, being always somewhat less patient in admitting extreme pretensions than me. His courage, fortitude, spirit, talents, application, and, above all, his wrongs and sufferings, should rather increase than weaken our affection for him, and I am really happy in welcoming and perhaps serving him here. I brought him with me the other day to Bath, where he made such hasty love to Harriet, whom he had little doubt of subduing in a week, and where he so totally silenced my John Bull wife, who understands a Frenchman no better than Molly housemaid, where he so scared my little boy with caressing him, so completely disposed of me from breakfast to supper, and so astonished all our friends, that I could hardly keep the peace in his favour; and if he had not been called unexpectedly to town this morning, I am sure my wife's endurance, for I cannot call it civility, would not have held out another day. He says he shall sell his estate when his father dies, settle for good in England to be naturalised, it being absolutely impossible to live in France with any sort of security. In the meantime he is writing books and pamphlets for bread."

In the course of the autumn of 1783 my grandfather had had some communications with Mirabeau, which arose out of a conversation held by Mr. Elliot with a passing traveller at Berlin; and a very characteristic letter from Mirabeau will be found in Appendix No. II. It cannot fail to interest a student of that remarkable man's history, though it is too lengthy to be inserted here.

While the Elliots and Harrises had been spending their summer together, Isabella had remained in the neighbourhood of London, occupied in preparations for a journey to Copenhagen, where, at her brother's request, she proposed to pass the winter. She had actually taken her passage (Aug. 1784) when she was attacked by a violent fever, which left her entirely prostrated in mind and body. For some time her life was despaired of, and, though after a time she rallied to a considerable extent, her nervous system never recovered the shock. In the preceding year she had suffered from severe illness; and while in weak health, her warm affections and acute sensibilities had been greatly affected by the troubles and prolonged absence of her favourite brother; the separation from him, the loss by death of those members

of her family most tenderly united to herself, and, farther
back still, certain painful recollections connected with
her last summer at Tunbridge (previous to her mother's
death), had undermined her once gay spirits. A sense
of duty, a naturally sociable temper, and plenty of resources in herself, enabled her for a long time to combat
the despondent feelings which occasionally arose in her
mind; but a healthy body is needed to struggle with a
sick heart, and when her health failed her spirits gave
way. The short remainder of her life was spent in retirement from the world, though she continued to see
her family, and occasionally to write to her brother Hugh
in a cheerful and uncomplaining tone.

Happily for him, the sad tidings of her illness reached
him at a moment when his mind was occupied by events
of considerable political importance, then enacting in
the capital of Denmark, to explain which, together with
the share he bore in them, it is necessary to give a slight
sketch of the internal politics of the Danish Court at the
time of his arrival there in the autumn of 1782.

The revolution, as it was called, of 1772, though in
point of fact it had no greater result than to substitute
the authority of the Queen Dowager for that of the
Queen Consort, had terminated in the banishment of
Queen Matilda, and the execution of her favourite, Count
Struensee. From that time the Queen Dowager, stepmother of the King, had attained uncontrolled influence
over him, and with it the entire direction of the Government of the country.

The King, who in 1782 is described in Mr. Elliot's

letters as hopelessly insane or imbecile, was nevertheless
made to go through the pageantry of a part, for the
realities of which he was utterly incompetent. The constitution of the country was purely despotic; the King's
will superseded law. When the King in Council uttered
the words " Le Roi le veut," a close was at once put to
discussion; a royal order, with the sign-manual affixed,
was absolute; and this, particularly distinguished by the
appellation of an order of cabinet, was the instrument
by which Denmark had been governed for many years.
Persons devoted to the interests of the Queen Dowager,
and of her son Prince Frederick, were placed about the
person of the King, in the highest offices of state, and
the Prince Royal, the King's son, was held in a state of
pupillage, which, in the case of an heir-apparent, was
unusual in that country, even at his early age.

By the laws of the land it was enacted that a Prince
of the blood might be confirmed at the age of thirteen—
that ceremony entitling him to take his seat in Council;
but in the case of the Prince Royal, the period of minority was protracted till he had attained his sixteenth
year.

Mr. Elliot was not long at Copenhagen before he
discovered that the existing system of government was
odious to the majority of the people, that the principal
nobles were disaffected, and that the most considerable
men in the country were secretly conspiring to effect its
overturn, so soon as the young Prince should have attained his majority.

With the internal affairs of Denmark the English

minister could have nothing to do; but the ill-will of Frederick the Great, the flickering friendship of the Empress of Russia, and the great maritime power of the house of Bourbon, made the English government, whether that of the Duke of Portland or of Mr. Pitt, attach considerable importance to the preservation of friendly relations with the Scandinavian kingdoms.

These relations were greatly imperilled by the state of affairs in Denmark. The Queen Dowager and her party were entirely devoted to Prussian interests, the King of Prussia, by constant attentions to the Queen and her favourites, having succeeded in establishing a powerful influence at Copenhagen. He was, in fact, the *Deus ex machina* of the Danish cabinet.

Count Bernstorff, whose position, fortune, and character had enabled him to carry on a powerful opposition to the Government, and whose condemnation of the policy of the Neutral League had given great offence to Frederick the Great, had been banished at that king's instigation, and he was the first person of note and consequence who broached to Mr. Elliot the projects in formation for making the young Prince Royal the instrument of his grandmother's downfall. At the time of Count Bernstorff's dismissal, the young Prince, then a boy, promised him his future support; and such confidence was placed by the Count in the steadiness of the Prince Royal's character, that from henceforth they corresponded constantly on the most important subjects. For two years before the Prince attained his majority, Count Bernstorff furnished, in secret, daily instructions for His

U

Royal Highness's guidance, which he implicitly followed ; receiving the letters by means of a trustworthy valet, and always consigning them to the flames immediately after having read, and committed their contents to memory.

The certainty that a change of government would be advantageous to English interests led the Prince's party to make the English minister their confidant; he of course stated the fact to his Government, and received from them strict orders to take no part in any of the steps proposed, simply to watch and wait.

The extreme youth of the Prince Royal, who in 1783 was only in his 15th year, made Mr. Elliot very distrustful of the success of an enterprise which depended on the discretion and resolution of so young a Prince; nevertheless signs of spirit and tact were not wanting in his conduct.

The Queen Dowager had endeavoured to inculcate in him sentiments of deference and submission to his uncle Prince Frederick, and the public had remarked with disapprobation that the Prince Royal was made to kiss his uncle's hand when joining him at the theatre or on other occasions. The Prince himself disliked the ceremony, an unusual one in Danish families, and had quickly perceived the impression it produced on others ; having therefore determined to get rid of this act of homage, he, one evening that Prince Frederick presented him his hand to kiss, threw it from him with such violence as nearly to overturn his uncle, who was both weak and deformed. Other and similar actions gave the people an insight into the feelings which the young Prince, in spite of occasional ebullitions, held under stern control.

As the period of his majority approached, the situation of the Prince became extremely critical, but in proportion to the increase of difficulty was the increase of resolution on his part. Besides the correspondence which he had kept up for two years with Count Bernstorff, he communicated personally and by letter with some of the leading men of the country, in spite of being surrounded at the time by spies and creatures of the ruling party.

About a week before the Prince came of age, the Queen Dowager appeared to have conceived a suspicion of his correspondence with Count Bernstorff, and put some hard questions to him, which he answered with so much unconcern and adroitness as to dispel every suspicion. An unexpected summons to Court of one of the conspirators threw the whole party into unfounded alarm; and the very evening before the revolution took place, M. de Schach-Rathlow, second only to Count Bernstorff in the direction of the movement, but who still ostensibly acted with the Queen Dowager's party, was engaged in conversation with one of the ministers, when a servant brought and delivered to him a packet of most important and secret papers. On the minister showing some surprise, M. de Schach-Rathlow with great composure drew off his attention, and pocketing the papers, contrived presently to leave the room. He told Mr. Elliot a few days afterwards that

these were the very papers to be signed the next
evening by the King in council, which by an oversight
were thus conveyed to him in the middle of an assembly.
This scene was witnessed by Mr. Elliot. On the 14th
of April, the Prince Royal took his seat in Council, and
at once rising in his place desired to read a memorial
which he drew from his bosom.

This instrument contained the reasons he alleged
for a total change of government, together with a
list of the persons he entreated his father to call into
his councils. A second memorial followed, by which
the King was urged to enact that no future orders by
himself in the cabinet should be valid without the
countersign of the Prince Royal. So dignified and
firm was the attitude of the Prince, and so great the
surprise of all present, that no serious objections were
made. Those faintly urged by Prince Frederick were
silenced with warmth by his nephew. The King signed
the documents presented to him, and the Prince Royal
at once delivered to M. de Schach-Rathlow his credentials as minister.

The Prince then waited on the Queen, and acquainted her himself with what had passed in the council; and " as her passions were violent, a scene of considerable confusion ensued in the palace."

Nevertheless, he insisted that a court-ball, which
was to take place that night, should not be postponed,
and assisted at it himself with the utmost composure.
So secretly and quietly had these important transactions
been conducted, that many of the Danish nobility were first

made aware of what had occurred by the arrival of one of
the new ministers at an assembly given by Count Moltke.
On the evening of the same day a despatch was sent to
Count Bernstorff, summoning him to Copenhagen and
to the post of Minister of Foreign Affairs; but unluckily
it found him laid up with a fit of the gout, and seventeen days elapsed before he arrived, during which the
state of affairs was most critical.

So many interests were affected by this unlooked-
for change of government, such bitter resentments and
violent passions had been excited, that the Prince's
personal safety was not deemed secure in the palace;
and for several nights his partisans guarded his door.
"The person," wrote Mr. Elliot to Lord Carmarthen,
April 24, 1784, "who has principally the ear and confidence of the Prince Royal, has made no secret to me
of his apprehensions; and declared that it was the
determination of their party rather to perish than
to abandon the young Prince again into the hands of
people whose passions are now too inflamed to know any
bounds.

" For my own part, I have thought myself under the
necessity of taking a decision without waiting for any
instructions from home, as there was no possibility of
their arriving before the conclusion of this important
transaction. I therefore desired this gentleman to let
his Royal Highness know, that should the opposite
party have come to any overt act of violence, I should
have asked leave to appear openly in his defence;
and, by the fortunate arrival of a number of English

ships at this critical conjuncture, there was little doubt but that I might have procured essential assistance from their crews and other persons attached to me in Copenhagen.

" Thanks be to God, the personal resolution, constancy, and prudence of the Prince Royal have alone overcome every obstacle."

The most remarkable feature in this revolution is the part taken in it by the Prince at the early age of sixteen, after two years of careful and secret preparation for the final blow.

The English Government expressed great satisfaction with the conduct of their minister throughout these events.

Lord Carmarthen remarks that the singular degree of confidence reposed in him by Count Bernstorff, from his first arrival in the country, proved the high opinion which that eminent person had conceived of Mr. Elliot's ability, judgment, and secrecy.[1]

[1] I have already alluded to the friendship Mr. Elliot had formed on arriving at Copenhagen with the families of Count Reventlow and Count Schimmelmann ; and closely allied with these by relationship, by political sympathies, and by social tastes, were the families of Count Bernstorff and of the Counts Stolberg. It was in the intimacy of this domestic circle that Mr. Elliot first became known to Count Bernstorff. To give an idea of the intellectual pursuits which occupied much of their attention, I need only make an extract from one of many letters written by Countess Augusta Bernstorff, née Comtesse de Stolberg, to Mr. Elliot, during his visit to England in 1785 :—" Je lis à présent Butler (l'Analogie) que vous avez eu la bonté de me donner, et je le lis avec un plaisir, un interêt infini, me disant souvent que c'est à vous que je dois ce plaisir. Je lis aussi the *Life of Ciceron*, by Middleton—that is a charming book ; and

The King highly approved of the line taken by his representative, and the policy now inaugurated by the new Government in Denmark, combined with the warm feelings entertained by the young Prince for his English relations—" Am I not half an Englishman ?" he said— gave every hope of a cordial alliance between the two crowns.

All my grandfather's private letters mention the warm approval which his conduct, during these delicate transactions, had met with at home, "from the King downwards." Sir J. Harris observed—somewhat in character—" that Hugh Elliot had not made half enough of his share in them ;" and Mr. Eden wrote from Beckenham a letter of cordial congratulations.

It was the last which my grandfather received from him before he returned on leave to England in 1785 ; and it gives a bright and pleasant picture of the family, under the impression of which we may leave them. Of himself, Mr. Eden says—" Whatever may be the ups and downs of my political career, my cheerfulness will never suffer." His orchard was " a garden of the Hesperides,"

besides Akenside, que j'aime beaucoup, et que je ne connaissais pas encore. He seems fond of nature, and then I am fond of him ! Mille graces du cher, cher Young, que vous m'avez envoyé au moment de partir, et des lignes infiniment trop flatteuses que vous y avez ajoutées et que je ne sçaurais m'approprier. Quand reviendrez vous ? Pray don't forget Blair's *Rhétorique*, Gray's *Letters*, and Mason's works.—Farewell, my dear sir.

" Souvenez vous de moi qui vous suis bien sincèrement attachée,

" AUGUSTA C. DE BERNSTORFF,

" Née C. DE STOLBERG."

This lady was a friend and correspondent of Goethe's.

where a band of merry handsome children plucked fruit all day long; his farm, strange to say, was profitable, and all the time which Mrs. Eden could spare from home and children was spent in trying to make others as happy as herself. The marriage of Admiral Digby to one of Mr. Andrew Elliot's daughters gave her great satisfaction. " The Admiral," wrote Mr. Eden, " is a good man, and as rich as Pactolus; he does not consider a set of features or the tincture of a complexion as essential ingredients in matrimony. Mr. Andrew Elliot has had luck in the marriages of Lady Cathcart, Lady Carnegie, and Mrs. Digby. I am glad of it, for he has great merits."[1]

Mrs. Eden was, however, sometimes called upon for condolence instead of congratulations; and the frequent mortifications which her brother Robert met with were confided to her sisterly ear, but without obtaining much pity from Mr. Eden—" Poor Bob has a rage for matrimony, and offers himself so suddenly to every young woman that they are quite frightened, and scream " No!"

I have now completed the task which I originally proposed to myself—namely, to draw from my grandfather's correspondence a sketch of his early career.

It appears to me that no fitter moment could have been found to review the story of his youth, than that

---

[1] Lady Cathcart and Lady Carnegie were the daughters of Mr. Elliot by his second wife, an American lady, Miss Plumstead, who had been sought in marriage by General Washington before she married Mr. Elliot.

at which I believe him to have collected the materials
of which I have made use; that he should have done so
when he did, was one of those incidents, unregarded at
the time, which derive from subsequent events a deep
significance.

Already the friends of his early days, or most of
them, were gone—father, mother, brother, had passed
away—Isabella's days were numbered—the new ties he
had formed for himself were dissolved—the most intimate of his companions and correspondents were dead,
and those who remained had been long separated from
him, and had settled down into lives in which he had
borne no part. Louis d'Yve had ceased to write of "his
too amiable aunt;"[1] and Mr. Pitt of his patriot band.

The Elliots and Edens continued to be as dear and
as tenderly attached to him as of old, but time, distance,
and constant separation, could not fail to tell on the
frequency of their correspondence. Sir Gilbert, always
an indolent letter-writer, found an excuse for protracted
silences in the monotony of his country life. Mr. Eden,
busily occupied both at home and abroad in important
political transactions, had no time for the cheerful,
pleasant letters which in idle days at Beckenham he
used to write for himself and his wife.

When family letters cease to be records of our daily
paths, and become occasional *cartes du pays*, their charm
is gone; we learn the general features of the country over
which our friends are travelling—we see its outline, but
lose the colouring, the distinctness, which familiarity with

---

[1] Countess Neipperg.

details alone can give. My grandfather may possibly have been of this opinion, since he ceased henceforth to bestow any care on the arrangement of the letters which he from time to time received from his relations.

The most interesting portions of his correspondence, subsequent to 1785, relate to political transactions connected with the affairs of the Court at which he was for the time resident, and are for the most part confined to official papers or to memoranda made by himself. From these I have been induced to select such portions as will fitly blend into a few slight sketches of his public career. The last years of his mission to Denmark were perhaps the most eventful of his diplomatic life.

CHAPTER THE ELEVENTH.

1785 to 1790.

SWEDISH CORRESPONDENCE.

In 1785, as I have said, Mr. Elliot came home on leave; and during his stay in London he had several interviews with Mr. Pitt, with whose great abilities he was much struck. He returned to Denmark in 1786, naturally impressed by the views of the minister, the great object of whose policy at that time was the preservation of the balance of power. The transactions to which the papers preserved by him, under the title of the "Swedish Correspondence," relate, did not take place till 1788.

On the breaking out of the war between Russia and the Porte in 1787, Gustavus III.[1] of Sweden, who had

---

[1] Gustavus the Third succeeded his father in 1771. He received the news of his accession to the throne at Paris, where he was passing a winter under the incognito of Count Haga. And Madame du Deffand alludes with pity in her letters to " ce pauvre prince royal, qui pour être devenu Roi est obligé de s'en retourner dans son triste pays." His agreeable and rather courtly manners procured him much greater success in the polite society of Paris than was obtained by another royal traveller, Count Falkenstein (Joseph the Second). Shortly after his return home, he effected a revolution in the Swedish state, by which

married a sister of Christian VII., set himself with assiduity to cultivate the friendship of the Court of Copenhagen, and to impress on that government the importance
of seizing a moment when Russia was involved in a great
and distant war, caused by her own ambition, to weaken
her power in the North by some decisive blow which
should effectually check her insidious and over-reaching
policy. To effect this object, the closest union between
the two northern kingdoms, and their common action,
became necessary, and trusting to the influence of his
personal qualities, which had already contributed to the
most brilliant successes of his reign, the Swedish king
determined to pay a neighbourly visit to his Danish
relations, with the confident hope of inoculating the
young Prince Royal with his system of policy.

Supple and adroit, yet daring and persevering, his
personal advocacy of his views was calculated to produce considerable effect on those with whom he came in
contact; and the gift of eloquence, which he possessed

he greatly extended the royal authority; and he introduced considerable changes in courtly etiquette, and even in the national costume.
His love of pomp and ceremonial, with the fatigue of a day at court,
are amusingly described in Coxe's Travels, vol. iii. In a private letter
to Mr. Elliot, dated August 1784, Coxe, after descanting on the king's
extraordinary powers of conversation, says—" Nevertheless, I must say
of him, as you did of another king, that he is 'very meretricious.'"
Coxe was presented, at a royal reception, to the king's son, a child of
six years old, who addressed him as follows—"M. le Capitaine—Je
suis enchanté de vous voir, vous avez fait un long voyage." The Englishman stared; but Count Sparre, the Prince's preceptor, explained with
pride that *he* had suggested the appropriate compliment to the great
navigator, betraying that he had taken Coxe for Cook.

in a singular degree, joined to something brilliant and romantic in his appearance and address, made him precisely the character likely to influence a young man.

Not only, however, did the king fail in converting the Danish ministers to his views, but the Prince Royal, though possessing great admiration and affection for his uncle, did not for a moment listen to his schemes. Denmark was bound to Russia by treaties[1] and by interest, and her policy was one of peace.[2]

Baffled in his design of creating a strict alliance with Denmark, Gustavus determined to cast the die alone, but not till, in the spring of 1788, he had again

[1] In 1773 Russia ceded Schleswig and Holstein to Denmark in return for the Duchy of Oldenburg and the promise of naval and military aid under certain specified contingencies. This last article appears to have been secret.

[2] The following dispatch will illustrate the state of feeling between Denmark and Russia alluded to in the text :—

"*Copenhagen, 25th March* 1788.

"My Lord—Paul Jones has been treated with very singular marks of distinction at this court.

"Soon after his arrival, Count Bernstorff invited him to dinner with the foreign ministers, but he could not profit of that invitation on account of an indisposition.

"He was presented by the French minister to the Royal family, and supped at the same table with the King of Denmark and the Prince and Princess Royal,—an honour conferred, before, only on officers who rank as generals, or on foreigners of high birth or elevated situation.

"At the sacred concerts performed at Court, he occupied one of the chairs usually assigned to foreign ministers.

"As the public express equal surprise and resentment at this extraordinary conduct towards a person notorious as Paul Jones, and who had committed acts of piracy within the limits of the Danish

personally, and strongly, but still unsuccessfully, urged
upon his nephew, the Prince Royal, the importance of a
close and active alliance between the Courts of Copenhagen and Stockholm. The Prince Royal, who was at
the time in Norway, occupied in reviewing the troops
commanded by Prince Charles of Hesse,[1] replied to
these representations by enforcing the wisdom of a
pacific policy, and offering his services as mediator
between Sweden and Russia; and, on his return to
Copenhagen, the Prince gave his suffrage in council for
maintaining the treaties with Russia, a course which

dominion, I found great difficulty in forming any plausible conjecture
for the reasons of so undignified a proceeding, till I learnt yesterday
that the Russian minister avows that this adventurer is to be employed
in the Empress of Russia's navy in a high rank. I therefore now
attribute this glaring deviation of the court of Denmark from its usual
decorum to its unbounded deference, or probably even fear, of the court
of St. Petersburg. Paul Jones, I am assured, says that he has received
proposals from the Empress to command the squadron in the Black
Sea.

"Baron la Houze, the French minister, left his name with a card
signed le Commodore Paul Jones at my door. Not having returned the
visit, the French minister asked me at court, in the presence of a
numerous circle, if I knew he had been at my door with le Chéf
d'Escadr⁺ M. Jones, I answered that I was not ignorant of that circumstance and desired that he would be pleased to observe that he had not
been admitted. · To this he replied, ' Pourquoi ?' and I again answered,
' Qu'il ne le seroit jamais chez moi en pareille société.'—I have the
honour, &c.   H. ELLIOT."

Paul Jones may possibly be better known at the present day to the
readers of fiction than to students of history; Fenimore Cooper having
made him the hero of a popular novel called *The Pilot*.

[1] Prince Charles of Hesse was brother-in-law to the kings of Sweden
and of Denmark.

finally determined that of the Danish ministry. It
afterwards appeared that, during all these negotiations,
Denmark never gave the slightest intimation of those
articles in the treaty of 1773 by which she was bound to
lend military aid to Russia if attacked in the north ; and
this concealment gave rise to a charge of treachery,
which was subsequently brought by the King of Sweden
against the Prince Royal, and with some semblance of
justice, since the King had scarcely joined his army in
Swedish Finland,[1] whence he proposed to commence his
land operations against Russia, when the Court of
Copenhagen published a declaration to the effect that,
within a month from its date, Prince Charles of Hesse
would invade Sweden on the side of Norway with the
stipulated number of auxiliary forces. A mutiny among
the officers of Gustavus' army, many of whom were
averse to war with Russia, and were even in secret correspondence with that Court, broke out almost simultaneously with the announcement of the military preparations
of Denmark. Nothing could well seem more desperate
than the position of the Swedish King ; he was a prisoner
in his own camp, while a treacherous enemy threatened
his kingdom, and while the Swedish Senate itself, which
had been deprived of its powers and reduced to a mere
cipher by the revolution of 1772, showed symptoms of a
disposition to take advantage of the King's difficulties
to repossess itself of its lost authority, at the expense of
the kingly power.

---

[1] At the Peace of Abo, 1743, the river Kymen formed the limit of
Russia and Sweden.

Before, however, any decisive steps had been taken, Gustavus contrived to escape from Finland, and appeared unexpectedly at Stockholm, where, knowing the nobility, who were numerous and powerful, to be generally indisposed towards him, he threw himself at once upon the support of the citizens, and of the people at large, over whom he possessed a great ascendency. He dispatched every soldier from the capital to the frontier, and, with all the thrilling eloquence which he knew so well how to wield, he entrusted the guardianship of the Queen and her children to his people.

Nothing could exceed the enthusiasm of the citizens, who themselves manned the batteries and works; and, on the return of the officers from Finland, the public feeling was so strongly displayed against them, that it became unsafe for them to appear in public in their uniforms.

At this moment of imminent danger to Sweden, the influence of two great Powers made itself felt on her behalf.

After the accession of Frederick William to the throne of Prussia, and the appointment by him of Count Hertzberg to the post of First Minister, the Courts of Berlin and of St. James' had drawn together.

The new King and his Minister were in policy and personal feelings as much opposed to France and Russia as Frederick the Great had been to England; and England, Prussia, and Holland, had lately entered into an alliance, the object of which was the preservation of the balance of power against the encroachments of Catherine

II., and of the House of Bourbon. The English ministry
had, throughout the year, impressed on their Minister
at Copenhagen their determination not to let Sweden be
destroyed by any combination of powers against her.
The English Minister at Berlin, Mr. Ewart, wrote
strongly, in the same sense, of the views entertained by
the Prussian Government, and it was on the urgent
representations of Count Hertzberg, and of Mr. Ewart,
and also with the full approbation of Count Bernstorff,
who appears to have acted a very insincere part, that
Mr. Elliot determined to set out for Stockholm, there
being at the moment no representative of England there,
for the purpose of obtaining a personal interview with
the King, and of prevailing on him to accept the mediation of England and Prussia, instead of seeking, as
he had threatened to do, the good offices of France and
Spain.

" The pressing circumstances of His Swedish Majesty"—wrote Mr. Elliot to Lord Carmarthen (Nov.
1788)—" and the immediate danger to which the
balance of the North was exposed, left me no time to
wait for further instructions than those contained in
your lordship's despatches. Indeed, the very positive
though general instructions given me, to prevent by
every means a change in the relative situation of the
northern nations, invested me, as I conceived, with full
power to act according to the exigency of circumstances."

Before leaving Denmark, Mr. Elliot received from
Mr. Ewart an intimation of the decision of the Prussian

Cabinet for immediate action, and was informed that a
declaration was on its way from Berlin to St. Petersburg
and Copenhagen, announcing that a body of 16,000
troops would enter Holstein simultaneously with the
advance of the Prince of Hesse in the dominions of
Sweden.

Mr. Elliot, on arriving at Stockholm, found that the
King had departed for Dalecarlia, where, after the
example of his great predecessor, he had descended to
the bottom of the deepest mines, and, by his spirited
appeals to their loyalty, had excited the rough Dalecar-
lians into a fever of enthusiasm. Armed with their
implements of labour, and, in some instances, with
antique and rusty weapons preserved among them for
centuries, they formed an uncouth and grotesque but
devoted body-guard to the King.

" On my arrival in Sweden, after a search of eleven
days I traced the King wandering from place to place,
endeavouring to animate his unarmed peasants to hope-
less resistance. His very couriers were ignorant of his
abode. At length, exhausted with fatigue and illness, I
reached the King at Carlstadt, upon the 29th of September. Here I found his carriage ready to convey him
to a place of greater security; without generals, without
troops, and with few attendants, he was devoid of every
means of defence. The King's own words were, that ' I
found him in the same situation with James the Second,
when he was obliged to fly his kingdom, and abandon
his crown.' He was on the point of falling a victim to
the ambition of Russia, the treachery of Denmark, and

the factious treason of his nobility. In the sincerity of
distress the King also added, ' to the mistakes of his own
conduct.' Backed as I presumed myself to be by the
joint concert of the Kings of Great Britain and Prussia,
I did not limit the expressions dictated by the animating
conviction of the reality of my powers, and replied with
confidence—'Sire, prêtez-moi votre couronne, je vous
la rendrai avec lustre.' On further explanation, the
King consented to adopt all those measures which I
thought most suitable to his situation."

In other words, the King, upon the assurances given
him by the English minister of the support of Prussia
and England, resigned all idea of accepting the mediation
of France, and placed himself unreservedly in the hands
of Mr. Elliot. Gothenburg, the most important fortress
in the kingdom, was already threatened by the Danish
forces. By Mr. Elliot's advice, the King of Sweden
now resolved to throw himself at once into the place,
and there to make a determined stand; while the
English minister undertook to proceed to the head-
quarters of the Danish army to open a negotiation
with the Prince of Hesse, having for its object the aban-
donment of his designs on Gothenburg, the arrangement
of an armistice, and the final withdrawal of the Danish
troops from Norway. Mr. Elliot had joined the King,
as we have seen, on the 29th of September, at which
time no suspicion of the Prussian declaration had been
entertained in Sweden.

On the 2d of October the King, while on his way to
Gothenburg, received a courier from Berlin with the infor-

mation which Mr. Elliot had already derived from Mr.
Ewart, of the Prussian determination to come to his assistance by marching troops into Holstein, and the King
wrote the same day to Mr. Elliot, giving him an account
of the despatches, and continuing as follows:—" Rien
ne pouvoit mieux me confirmer dans la pleine confiance
que je vous ai marquée qu'une déclaration aussi précise.
Je suis cependant bien aise qu'elle soit arrivée après vous
avoir donné la marque la moins équivoque de la foi
entière que j'ai mise à vos paroles. Le zèle que vous
m'avez montré dans une occasion aussi importante ne
pouvoit dans ce moment être mieux payé par moi que
par mon entière confiance.

＊   ＊   ＊   ＊

" Vous ne pouvez douter combien de droit vous vous
acquerrez auprès de moi aux sentiments avec lesquels
je prie Dieu, qu'il vous ait, M. d'Elliot, dans sa sainte
garde.—Votre très affectionné   GUSTAVE.[1]
        " *Mariestad, ce 2 Oct.* 1788."

On the following day the King of Sweden arrived

---

[1] [TRANSLATION.]

"Nothing could confirm me more strongly in the full confidence
which I have testified in you than so precise a declaration. I am
moreover, glad that it arrived after the most unequivocal mark of the
perfect faith I have in your words had been given. The zeal you have
shown in my affairs on so important an occasion can at this time only
be repaid by my entire confidence.

＊   ＊   ＊   ＊   ＊   ＊

" You cannot doubt that you are entitled to be regarded by me
with the feelings which make me pray God may have you, Mr. Elliot,
in his holy keeping.—Your very affectionate   GUSTAVUS.

        " *Mariestad, 2d October* 1788."

in Gothenburg (Oct. 3), where his presence was wholly
unlooked for; with his usual success, he at once infused
a spirit of determined resistance into the inhabitants of
the place.   The herald sent by Prince Charles of Hesse
to summon the town was led blindfold into the presence
of the King, and informed that the place would be
defended to the last extremity.

On the 4th, Gustavus wrote from Gothenburg to
Baron d'Arnfeldt.[1]

" Gothenbourg, ce 4 d'Octobre 1788.

" Je suis arrivé ici hier au soir à onze heures, mon
cher ami, et après avoir attendu une bonne heure au
pont-levis par une tempête affreuse, j'ai été bien dédommagé par ma réception.   J'avois couru la poste depuis
Alengsab, et suis entré à cheval; dès que j'avois passé
la dernière poste, et que j'étois parvenu aux quais, une
troupe de bourgeois me reconnut, et commença à crier
Vive le Roi; à ces cris tout le monde vint aux fenêtres,
et sortit des maisons, et accompagné d'une foule immense,
je suis arrivé à la maison de gouvernement * * *
Gothenbourg n'étoit pas tenable il y a huit jours; aujour-
d'hui il peut tenir quatre semaines, et dans quelques
jours plus longtemps," etc. etc. etc.

" Il faut que le courier d'Elliot ait fait impression,
puisque l'on croit que les ennemis se soient arrêtés à
Uddevalla. * * *

[1] Baron d'Arnfeldt was at the time commanding the King's troops
in Dalecarlia ; after the death of King Gustavus the Baron sent to Mr.
Elliot, in 1798, copies of the confidential correspondence which had
passed between the King and himself during the autumn of 1788.
From this correspondence the above extracts are made.

On the 6th the King wrote again, "Mardi au plus tard, la ville sera investie. Les Princes passeront demain la rivière ; nous ne pouvons leur disputer le passage n'ayant pas de troupes ; il faut les harceler et les inquiéter pour retarder le passage. * * * Elliot arrive, il sera reçu, comme il le mérite, sous tous les rapports imaginables."[1]

The representations which, in the meanwhile, Mr. Elliot had been employed in urging on the Danish leaders, had been by no means successful. The apparent moderation of Count Bernstorff previous to Mr. Elliot's departure for Sweden was repudiated by the conduct of the royal princes at the head of the army ; and, having warned the princes that the consequences of an attack on the King of Sweden's dominions would be a rupture with England and Prussia, Mr. Elliot joined the King

[1] [TRANSLATION.]

"I arrived here yesterday evening at eleven o'clock, my dear friend, and after having waited a whole hour at the drawbridge in a fearful tempest, I was well repaid by my reception. I travelled post from Alengsab, and entered on horseback. When I had passed the last post, and drew near the quays, a troop of townsfolk recognised me, and began to cry 'Vive le Roi.' At these shouts everybody came to the windows and out of the houses, and, accompanied by an immense crowd, I arrived at the Government-house. Eight days ago Gothenburg was not tenable ; now, it may hold out four weeks, and some days longer, etc. etc.

"Elliot's courier must have made an impression, since it is believed that the enemy has stopped at Uddevalla.

"On Tuesday, at latest, the town will be invested. The Princes will pass the river to-morrow. We cannot dispute the passage, not having troops. They must be harassed and disturbed to retard their passage.   .   .   Elliot arrives. He will be received, as he deserves, on every score.'

in Gothenburg (Oct. 6), and prepared to await with him the attack of the enemy. Three days later the town was saved.

"I knew, my lord," wrote Mr. Elliot, in the narrative he subsequently sent to his Government of these events, "how decisive the appearance of an English minister, at that trying moment, would be at Gothenburg—it re-united the well-disposed, and disheartened the disaffected. An early acquaintance with the art of war and science of engineering enabled me to point out the most important positions for defence; and the voluntary offer of assistance from the gallant spirit of the English seamen, then in that harbour, ready to man the batteries under my command, would, I trust, have helped to render the Danish attack of a very doubtful issue, had those very preparations not had the more desirable effect of inducing the Prince of Hesse to treat for an armistice of eight days,[1] in which interval the Prussian declaration arrived, and I was confessed to have been no less the saviour of Holstein than of Gothenburg, Sweden, and its sovereign.   *   *   *

"To so circumscribed a period had the distresses of the King reduced the possibility of retrieving his affairs, that had I reached Carlstadt twenty-four hours later than I did, or been less fortunate in concluding the first armistice before the expiration of

[1] The Prince of Hesse's letter, proposing to Mr. Elliot to join himself and the Prince Royal at Bahus to treat of an armistice, is dated 7th October. That armistice, concluded under Mr. Elliot's mediation and guarantee, was prolonged for a month, and the final convention for the evacuation of Sweden was signed at Uddevalla in November.

forty-eight hours, Gothenburg must have fallen ; and I
have the authority of the King, seconded by the voice of
the whole country, to say, in that case there would have
been no safety for the sovereign in his own dominions,
and that nothing less than a successful war, carried on
by foreign powers, could have rescued Sweden from a
dismemberment by Russia and Denmark."[1]

On the night of the 9th, eleven days after the first
meeting of the King and the English representative, the
former was able to write to Baron d'Arnfeldt that an
armistice was signed, and the firm and cautious measures
of the minister had thus been crowned with success.

> " *Gothenbourg, ce 9 Octobre* 1788,
> " *à* 10 *heures du soir.*

" Je me hâte, mon cher ami, de vous envoyer la convention ci jointe, qui vient d'être signée en ce moment ;
par les arrangements que nous avons pris, Gothenbourg
est hors d'insulte, et j'espère que dans huit jours nous
pourrons parler d'un plus haut ton. Je ne puis assez
louer Elliot ; il vient de faire un grand coup qui fait
honneur tant à son jugement qu'à son courage, et qui,
en sauvant la Suède, conserve la balance de l'Europe et
couvre l'Angleterre de gloire. * * * Adieu, mon bon
ami, ne vous désespérez pas, nous sortirons bien de cette
affaire-ci, et à notre honneur. Je vous embrasse de tout
mon cœur.   GUSTAVE."[2]

---

[1] November 29, 1788. Hugh Elliot to Lord Carmarthen.

[2] [TRANSLATION.]

> " *Gothenburg, 9th October* 1788,
> " 10 *o'clock evening.*

" I hasten, my dear friend, to send you the annexed convention,

On the 16th October the King wrote that the armistice had been prolonged, and that the Prussian envoy, Baron de Borck, had arrived, "aussi chaud pour nos intérêts que le chevalier Elliot même." On the 19th the King tells his correspondent that the Prince of Hesse had announced to Mr. Elliot his intention of retiring into Norway, but, on the 2d of November, he says that the negotiations have been checked by the pretensions of the Prince of Hesse, that he, the King, has in consequence ordered the immediate occupation of two towns lately evacuated by the enemy, and he adds—"Je ne puis assez me louer du ministre de Prusse; il serait à souhaiter qu'Elliot n'eut point diminué de zèle et d'activité depuis que nos affaires ont commencées à se remettre. Il peut avoir raison, mais moi je n'ai pas tort de vouloir tirer parti des conséquences."

It was clearly not the duty of the English Minister to facilitate these views of the King. He represented a neutral power desirous to act fairly by all parties, with the object of maintaining the balance of power in the North, not of allowing one potentate to overreach the other. The Annual Register for 1788 tells the

which has just been signed. By the arrangements we have made Gothenburg is safe from insult; and I hope that in eight days we may be able to take a higher tone. I cannot praise Elliot sufficiently. He has accomplished a master stroke, which does as much honour to his judgment as to his courage, and which, by saving Sweden, preserves the balance of Europe and covers England with glory. Adieu, my good friend; do not despair, we shall come out of this business well and with honour. I embrace you with all my heart.   GUSTAVUS."

whole narrative of these negotiations at length, and
with great accuracy, as may be seen by comparing it
with the original and very voluminous papers preserved
by Mr. Elliot, containing his correspondence with
the King of Sweden, Count Bernstorff, and Prince
Charles of Hesse; and no feature in the story is more
creditable to the English minister than the perfect
fairness of his dealing towards both parties, which was
rewarded by the confidence of the Swedish King on the
one hand, and of the Danish commander, Prince Charles
of Hesse, on the other.

The King of Sweden showed a greater amount of
spirit in facing the unexpected storm which had burst
upon his country than of judgment and forbearance
when he found himself no less unexpectedly relieved
from its dangers.

Encouraged by the loyal and patriotic spirit which
these dangers had raised throughout his people, animated by hatred of the Danes, and by a desire to
revenge on them, with the assistance of his two powerful
allies, the humiliations they had wreaked on him, he
was become less eager to advance the negotiations than
to seek a pretext for a fresh rupture. This disposition
showed itself in various ways, to the great embarrassment of the mediating ministers. It first appeared in
the seizure (12th Oct.), during the armistice, of twenty
Norwegian barks, laden with provisions, stores, and
arms, for the invading army, which were carried into
Gothenburg " with all the triumph of a victory; whilst
the King supported this violence on the ground that

seas and waters were not mentioned in the instrument."

This act of violence and of bad faith produced a joint and strong remonstrance from the ministers of England and Prussia. Mr. Elliot also wrote a separate appeal to the King's sentiments of honour and justice, pointing out the utter impossibility of his continuing to hold the honourable title bestowed on him by the King and the Prince of Hesse, of arbiter between them, should he become a consenting party to such a violation of the engagement drawn up by his efforts. The King having before complimented the minister on the glorious situation he was placed in, an " individual is the depository of the solemn word of a great king, and of a prince commanding an army "— Mr. Elliot now repeated these words in his letter, to recall them to the King's memory. and as introductory to his subject, he then proceeds:[1]— " It was on the acknowledged character of British veracity, stable as the foundation of their island, the underwritten saw a sovereign and a prince rely, to stop the effusion of blood, on the point of inundating the north of Europe. It was on the verbal assurance of a stranger, credited for the faith of his name and country, that two armies, ready to combat, have resigned their hatred, and renewed their ancient ties of amity and confraternity. It is, therefore, in the sacred name of honour and truth, that the underwritten is obliged to declare that, according to his weak insight, the objects contested must be restored to Prince Charles of Hesse. He dispenses with

[1] Annual Register.

entering into a discussion of time and place—he fulfils his task in virtue of his right as umpire."

The King's answer to this letter is among Mr. Elliot's papers, and is sufficiently quaint; it was long in coming, since the date is 2d November:—

"*Gothenburg, 2d Nov.* 1788.

"Monsieur de Bork m'a remis la lettre que vous m'avez fait le plaisir de m'écrire, et il vous rendra conte de ce qui a été résolu entre nous. Je suis si ennuyé d'entendre parler de ces bâteaux que vous ne trouverez pas étrange que je ne vous en parle plus. Une chose plus intéressante c'est d'avoir des nouvelles de votre santé, qu'on m'a dit être bien mauvaise, comme je crains que le mouvement que vous vous êtes donné pour mes affaires soit en grande partie cause de son dérangement, c'est une raison de plus pour m'y intéresser. J'espère que vous voudrez bien me donner de vos nouvelles et si vous souhaiteriez d'avoir mon médecin et que je * * * [illegible] qu'il vous trouvât, je vous l'enverrais. Je vous prie, etc. etc.   GUSTAVE.

"Vous voudrez bien vous charger de mes complimens les plus tendres pour le Prince Royal, et bien des honnêtetés pour mon beau frère."[1]

---

[1] [TRANSLATION.]

"*Gothenburg, 2d November* 1788.

"M. de Borek has given me the letter which you have done me the kindness to write to me, and he will give you an account of all that has been resolved on between us. I am so tired of hearing of these barks that you will not think it strange that I say no more about them. A more interesting thing is to hear of your health, which I am told has been very bad; it is the more interesting to me, because I fear

A few days later, the King, to save himself the
mortification of a restitution to his enemies, determined
to make over the barks to Mr. Elliot, which he did in
the following terms :—

"8 *Nov. Gothenbourg.*

"NOTE, PAR ORDRE DU ROI.

"Pour donner une preuve de l'estime et de la considération que la conduite de M. Elliot, etc. etc., a
inspiré au Roi, et marquer à ce ministre combien Sa
Majesté lui sait gré du zèle qu'il a témoigné pour le Roi
et la couronne de Suède, Sa Majesté fait présent à ce
ministre, et à lui seul, des bâteaux pris et de leurs car-
gaisons,"[1] etc. etc.

"(Signé)   COMTE SPARRE,
*"Lieut.-Général Commandant en Chef
sous les ordres du Roi."*

About the same time that the seizure of the barks
had taken place, the King had published a proclamation, or manifesto,[2] "evidently intended to excite the
greatest possible animosity against the Danes, by most
injuriously and unjustly charging on the Norwegian
army, and of course upon their general, the ruin of the

that the agitation my affairs have caused you may be in a great measure
the cause of its derangement. I hope you will let me hear from you,
and if you wish to have my physician, and that I [illegible] that he
would find you, I will send him. I beg you," etc. etc.

"Give my most tender regards to the Prince Royal, and kindest
compliments to my brother-in-law."

[1] The note goes on to value the cargoes, and to direct that the cost
of stores injured or destroyed should be paid in money.

[2] Annual Register.

Swedish provinces in their possession, by the exorbitances and depredations of which they were guilty."[1] It was to the honour of the English minister that he showed as much zeal in refuting these calumnies, in justifying the conduct and vindicating the honour of the Prince of Hesse, as he had constantly done in promoting and securing the interests of Sweden. This strangely-timed manifesto, which, like the affair of the barks, happened during the first armistice, produced the following note from Prince Charles of Hesse to Mr. Elliot :—

" *Secrette.*

" Je voulais justement vous marquer, mon cher ami, que nous allions penser à notre retraite quand je reçus la lettre du Roi ;[2] je désire fort de vous voir bientôt ici, comme vous me l'avez promis, et régler définitivement avec vous plusieurs circonstances importantes. Je voulais vous proposer de régler une armistice pour continuer jusqu'au 1er Mai, mais je n'ose en ce moment, après la

---

[1] These calumnies appear to have found their way into the English newspapers, for some months later we find the Prince of Hesse writing to Mr. Elliot to complain of an article in the *Morning Chronicle*, in which, among other mis-statements, it was reported that "the Norwegians and the German Prince at their head," had carried *instruments of torture* with them into Sweden. The Prince begs Mr. Elliot to regain for him the esteem of his excellent countrymen, by convincing them that no other instruments than surgical ones had formed part of his baggage. "J'ose espérer de votre amitié Monsieur un recit tout simple et naïf des faits, et que votre nom si glorieux pour votre nation détruira toutes les abominations que l'on se plait en Suède à répandre contre moi. Je vous embrasse de tout mon cœur. God bless you, my dear sir.   CHARLES."

[2] A hostile letter from the king.

belle déclaration de Sa Majesté Suédoise, qui ne me
parait guère disposé pour cet effet. . . . Je vous
embrasse de tout mon cœur.   CHARLES.

"*Bahus, Octbre.*"

The prince wrote a more formal letter after hearing
of Mr. Elliot's spirited vindication of his conduct.

"Monsieur—Si l'incartade de Sa Majesté Suédoise
avait pu me donner un moment de mauvaise humeur,
j'en ai été bien dédommagé par votre chère lettre qui m'a
fait un plaisir infini; agreéz, Monsieur, mes plus vifs
remerciments de la noblesse de vos procédés à mon
égard. Je suis pénétré de reconnaissance. . . . Je
suis dans l'attente du plaisir de vous voir ici. Son
Altesse Royale (le Prince Royal) me charge de vous
faire ses complimens—nous réglerons ensemble les articles d'une armistice prolongée jusqu'au 1er Mai, et tout
ce qui concerne la rentrée du corps auxiliare en Norwège
pour y prendre ses quartiers d'hiver. D'avance j'ose
vous donner plein pouvoir, ne pouvant remettre en des
meilleures mains les intérêts des braves troupes que j'ai
l'honneur de commander. Nous n'aurons alors qu'à
mettre ici la dernière main aux conditions que je ne
balancerai pas d'accepter dès que vous les trouvez
justes.

"Je suis, avec une consideration et une amitié aussi
distinguées que sincères et parfaites—Monsieur, votre
très humble serviteur,

"CHARLES, PRINCE DE HESSE.

"*Uddewalle, 26th Octobre* 1788."

On Mr. Elliot's appearance in the town of Uddevalla, he received a quaint letter from the magistrate, who, in the name of his fellow-citizens, implored the English minister to make interest on their behalf with the Danish general, in order that they may be relieved of a contribution in specie which he had threatened to levy on them.

The letter, signed Anders Aberg, and dated, Uddewalle, 5th November, says—" 'Tis a glory for this town to receive your Excellence, and also for its magistrates to pay their humble attendance. The Swedes in general love and esteem the English nation, but we feel a special veneration and love for your Excellence's high person, who, by the grace of God, is the true and effective man to restore peace and tranquillity to the North. We have the greatest reason to return our humble thanks to your Excellence, who already has mediated, and procured a stop to the cruels of the war, through this most desired and happy suspension of arms. * * * I venture also to advance this my humble petition, that it might please your Excellence to recommend this little town to further gracious treatment, that no contribution may be asked from it. So we will strive as much as in our power to accommodate us to the will and commandment of their Highnesses, as long as their troops live here, etc.

" The magistrates of this town beg leave to have a share in the grace and benevolence of your Excellence, and henceforth to be in your gracious memory included."

The final convention for the evacuation of Sweden, on the 6th of November, was drawn up by Mr. Elliot at

Uddevalla in the presence of the Prince of Hesse, while his Swedish Majesty and the Prussian minister (both at Gothenburg), discouraged by the refusals they had met with, had so completely lost hopes of success, that preparations were making for the recommencement of hostilities.

"Having twice," says Mr. Elliot, in a despatch to his government, "prevented the King of Sweden from breaking the armistice, at Uddevalla I prevented the Princes from recommencing their operations, which they had determined to do in consequence of the ill-timed and violent declaration of his Swedish Majesty."

"The Prince Royal, in the presence of his officers, called me 'l'ami commun du Nord.'

"Six weeks after my arrival in Sweden, a victorious army of 12,000 men, animated by the presence of the Prince, were checked in their progress by my single efforts, were induced to evacuate the Swedish territories, and consented to a truce of six months in order that the mediating powers might have time to establish the peace of the North on a solid basis.

"The courier who is charged with these letters was witness to the marks of attention and respect conferred upon His Majesty's minister in this singular scene. He saw those Princes at the head of their troops, drawn up in order of battle, abandon the great object of their ambition, and, in my presence, give orders to the army to begin their march back to Norway.

"Perhaps in the annals of history there is not to be found a more striking testimony of deference paid by a

Y

foreign prince to a King of England, than that the
Prince Royal of Denmark manifested on this trying
occasion."

On the very day of his departure from Sweden, and
immediately after his parting interview with the King,
Mr. Elliot wrote to His Majesty and to the Prince Royal
of Denmark to acknowledge the courtesy and kindness
which he had experienced from them, and to ask their
pardon for the "*vivacités*" into which he confesses that
an excess of zeal had betrayed him during some of the
discussions he had held in their presence.

The copies of these letters have been preserved, and
in both occur passages which cannot be passed over,
since they are honourably characteristic of a man whose
courage was no less conspicuous in the presence of
powerful individuals than in the treatment of important
transactions.   They may also be taken in evidence of
the imposing position filled by him as umpire between
the two royal antagonists, which entitled him to feel
what Mirabeau was wont to say :—" Ma tête aussi est
une Puissance."[1]   To the King he says—

> " *Gothenbourg, le* 10 *Nov.* 1788.

" Sire—Au moment de mon départ daignez agréer ce
peu de lignes dictées par un cœur rempli de respect, de
reconnaissance et d'attachment.   Pardonnez, Sire, les
torts de l'humanité ; le souvenir des moments où j'ai
pû par trop de zèle manquer à votre Majesté, couvre
mon front de rougeur et remplit mon âme d'amertume.

---

[1] The saying attributed to Mirabeau is given in a private letter of
Sir Gilbert Elliot's.

Daignez, Sire, oublier mes torts, et souffrir qu'en quittant votre Royaume, j'ose encore être *vrai*.

" Je crois prévoir la consommation d'une alliance défensive qui va assurer la tranquillité des états de V. M. et celle des pays voisins. Il ne faut qu'un *sacrifice*, c'est celui de cette malheureuse gloire qu'un Prince ne peut obtenir que par l'effusion du sang. Prenez, Sire, pour guide votre cœur noble, élevé et sensible, et il ne vous dictera jamais la mort d'un homme ni la ruine d'une famille.

" La gloire d'un Prince conquérant ne s'écrit qu'en lettres de sang, et ne s'éternise que par le souvenir des dévastations des Provinces et la désolation des Peuples. Un roi guerrier dépend pour sa réputation de la cohue vulgaire et doit s'adresser aux préjugés et à l'ignorance pour obtenir le suffrage d'un jour, que la plume du philosophe, la page de l'historien bouleversent quelque fois même avant que la mort ait enséveli toutes les facultés mortelles dans le néant d'où elles sont sorties.

" Consultez, Sire, les loix du Roi des Roix, et réconnoissez que le Dieu de l'univers est un Dieu de paix," etc. etc. etc.[1]

---

[1] [TRANSLATION].

" Gothenburg, 10th November 1788.

" Sire—At the moment of my departure deign to accept a few lines, dictated by the strongest feelings of respect, gratitude, and attachment. Forgive, Sire, the failings of humanity; the memory of those moments in which, through an excess of zeal, I failed in respect to your Majesty causes a flush to rise on my brow and fills my soul with bitterness.

To the younger Prince he writes more strongly still :—

" Gborg. 10 *Novbre.* 1788.

" Monseigneur—Au moment de quitter la Suède pour me rendre à Copenhague, permettez, Monseigneur, que je me jette à vos pieds, que je lui renouvelle au nom du Roi mon maitre, au nom du Roi de Prusse, des remercimens pour la noblesse, la dignité, la modération de vos procédés. Je reconnais, Mgr toute l'étendue, toute l'importance des conquètes qui ne pouvaient échapper à la bravoure de vos troupes où à l'habileté de vos officiers. Je sens donc vivement le prix du sacrifice fait à la

" Deign, Sire, to forget my errors, and suffer me, in leaving your kingdom, once more to speak the truth.

" I think I foresee the consummation of a defensive alliance which would secure the tranquillity of your Majesty's states and that of the neighbouring countries. But one sacrifice is necessary ; it is that of this miserable glory which a Prince can only obtain by the effusion of blood. Follow, then, Sire, the guidance of your noble and elevated heart, and it will never decree the death of a man or the ruin of a family.

" The glory of a warrior Prince can only be written in letters of blood, and he can only be immortalised by the remembrance of the devastation of provinces and the desolation of nations. A warrior king depends for his reputation on the vulgar crowd, and must address himself to prejudice and ignorance to obtain the applause of a day, which the pen of the philosopher, the page of the historian, often annul even before death comes to enshroud the mortal faculties in the nothingness from which they came. Consult, Sire, the laws of the King of Kings, and acknowledge that the God of the Universe is a God of Peace."

Mr. Elliot's freedom of speech appears to have had no ill effects on his intercourse with the King, for they continued to correspond from time to time on a most friendly footing, and did so even after Mr. Elliot left Copenhagen.

déférence que V. A. R. a daigné me témoigner pour le
Roi votre oncle et son très auguste allié.   Que ma joie
sera complète si cette première marque des dispositions
de V. A. R. à leur égard prépare la grande conféderation
des Princes vertueux qui feront consister toute leur
gloire à maintenir la paix de l'Europe et à consulter le
bonheur de leurs sujets. . . .

" Accordez, Monseigneur, votre pardon à un homme
qui péche souvent par trop de zèle.   J'ai quelquefois
manqué à V. A. Royale en parlant même du Roi de
Suède.   En me rappellant certaines expressions dictées,
par la chaleur du moment, je sens que j'étais ingrat vis
à vis d'un Roi, qui m'a comblé de ses bontés.   J'ose
assurer V. A. Royale que le Roi de Suède ne désire que
le renouvellement de votre amitié ; j'ajoute Monseigneur,
que le Roi vous aime.   J'ai quitté V. A. Royale envi-
ronné de l'eclât de vos triomphes ; j'ai trouvé le Roi de
Suède quelques heures plus tard, humilié par un
jeune Prince, son neveu, chez qui il avait été l'année
passée à la même époque, pour en rechercher l'amitié.
À peu près à votre age, Monseigneur, ce même Roi n'avait
devant lui que le perspectif du bonheur, des succès et
de la gloire.   Toute l'Europe le flattait, et était rempli
de ses éloges.

" Excusez, Monseigneur, que je risque en honnète
homme de supplier V. A. R. de s'arrêter un instant
pour fixer à jamais dans votre souvenir que le sort des
Princes dépend autant de leur bonne conduite que celle
des individus. . . .

" J'implore la Providence de ne jamais inspirer à

V. A. R. que des sentimens de justice et d'humanité qui vous assureront la bénédiction Divine.

" Pardonnez, Monseigneur, au predicateur Elliot un sermon que la scène dont je sors m'a dicté," etc. etc.[1]

---

[1] [TRANSLATION.]

" *Gothenburg*, 10*th November* 1788.

" Sir—At the moment of my departure from Sweden to return to Copenhagen, permit me, Sir, to throw myself at your feet, that I may renew, in the name of the King my master, in the name of the King of Prussia, acknowledgments for the nobleness, the dignity, the moderation of your proceedings. I acknowledge, Sir, all the extent, all the importance of the conquests which could not escape the valour of your troops or the skill of your officers. I feel, then, keenly, the value of the sacrifice made to the deference that your Royal Highness has deigned to show me in regard to the King your uncle and his very august ally. How complete will be my satisfaction if this first token of the dispositions of your Royal Highness towards them paves the way for the great confederation of virtuous Princes, who will make all their glory consist in maintaining the peace of Europe and in consulting the happiness of their subjects. . . .

" Grant your pardon, Sir, to a man who often errs from an excess of zeal. I have been sometimes wanting in respect to your Royal Highness in speaking of the King of Sweden. In recalling some expressions which escaped me in the heat of the moment, I feel that I was ungrateful to a king who has laden me with kindness. I venture to assure your Royal Highness that the King of Sweden only desires the renewal of your friendship. I add, sir, that the King loves you. I left your Royal Highness in all the glory of triumph—I found the King of Sweden, a few hours later, humbled before a young prince, his nephew, whom he had visited this time last year to seek his friendship. When about your age, Sir, this same King had before him a perspective of happiness, of success, and of glory ; all Europe flattered him, and was filled with his praises.

" Pardon me, Sir, if I venture, as an honest man, to intreat your Royal Highness to pause an instant, in order to fix in your

In different style from both these letters is the one he addressed to the Prince of Hesse, urging on him the duty of tempering the warlike dispositions of the young Prince of Denmark. After expatiating on the Prince's resemblance to his royal uncle the King of England, and on the latter's happy domestic life, he ends thus:—

" Plût à Dieu que tous les Princes de l'Europe trouvassent autant de gloire à faire des enfants qu'à detruire des hommes ! "

To which the Prince of Hesse replied :—" Je vous rends mille graces, Monsieur, au nom de tous les Princes de l'Europe du bon souhait que vous faites pour eux. La guerre et la gloire dont vous faites mention s'allient très bien selon la mythologie ancienne."

On his return to Copenhagen, Mr. Elliot found eight Russian ships of the line, which should have wintered at Gothenburg, lying at their anchorage in the Sound ; and the reception given him by Count Bernstorff, and the Russian minister, prepared him, in some degree, for the intrigues which the discomfited partizans of the Russian and Danish alliance had insidiously conducted during his absence, with the hope of injuring him in the estimation of his own Court.

A young prince checked in the hour of victory, an

memory for ever the truth, that the fate of Princes depends as much on their good conduct as that of private persons. . . .

" I implore Providence ever to inspire your Royal Highness with those sentiments of justice and humanity which will secure to you the Divine blessing.

" Forgive, Sir, the preacher Elliot a sermon dictated by the scene which he has just quitted," etc. etc. etc.

army turned back in sight of a great and easy prize,
a powerful minister baffled and disappointed, furnished
elements of mischief which could not fail to raise a
storm.

The accusation brought against Mr. Elliot by his
enemies, was that of having out-stepped his instructions
—of having declared war against the allied powers of
Russia and Denmark, without the authority of his
government. As soon as he became aware of the
nature of the charges made against him, Mr. Elliot
appealed, in a very spirited and manly despatch, to Lord
Carmarthen. The letters which had passed between
himself and the King of Sweden and the Prince of
Hesse sufficiently attested the accuracy of his assertion, that he had never declared a state of war *to exist*
between England and Denmark; but that he had pronounced it to be the inevitable consequence of persist-
ence on the part of the Danish commanders in their
meditated attack on the first commercial city of Sweden.
The despatches which Mr. Elliot had received at various
periods throughout the year from the English Government, and the letters from Mr. Ewart, together with the
Prussian instructions of M. de Borck, fully justified
Mr. Elliot, in his own opinion, in adopting the course
which he had so successfully pursued; and after stating
this fully and explicitly, he closed his despatch by the
avowal of the extreme disappointment and mortification
with which he found himself under the necessity of
disproving the injurious accusations of his enemies, at
a moment when he had looked with confidence to re-

ceiving, in the augmented confidence of his own government, the due reward of his arduous services.[1]

To this spirited appeal the Duke of Leeds replied as follows:—

"I have the satisfaction of acquainting you, by His Majesty's command, that he highly approves the zeal and ability which you have manifested in the very delicate and critical situation in which you were placed, and in which you came under the necessity of acting, from the pressure of the moment, without waiting for His Majesty's particular orders. His Majesty considers the general tenor of the instructions which you have received, and the peculiar urgency of the situation, as having fully justified you in the measures which you adopted to prevent the mischievous consequences of the extension of hostilities," etc. etc. "You may show this despatch to Count Bernstorff."

The Prussian Government was not less warm in its approval of Mr. Elliot's services to the cause of the Northern alliance.

Mr. Ewart wrote from Berlin, October 31, 1788— "Count Herzberg begs me to repeat to you the strongest assurances of his esteem and admiration,

---

[1] The despatches from which the narrative given in the text of Mr. Elliot's conduct in Sweden has been taken, were all written after his return to Copenhagen, and after he had learned the efforts which had been made in London by Count Woronzow, Russian Minister, and M. de Schönborn, Danish Chargé d'Affaires, to obtain from the English Government a disavowal of his Swedish policy. Hence the tone of self-assertion which may be remarked in his share of the "Swedish Correspondence," and which is foreign to his usual style.

adding that the extraordinary ability you had displayed not only justly entitled you to the appellation of an excellent minister, but to that of a distinguished states-man, since you had acted much more in the latter capacity than in the former, by having directed the whole of the operations entirely yourself.

" His Prussian Majesty, in a long conversation I had with him the other evening, paid the most flattering compliments to you, and to the whole of your conduct on this critical and important occasion.   I don't wonder that Count Bernstorff says he likes you much better as a man than as a minister."

The Annual Register tells us that, during the en-suing winter, Mr. Elliot, "whose ability and address had produced such essential and timely benefit in the foregoing year, still took the lead, on the part of the three allied courts, in all affairs relative to the Northern kingdoms; continuing to exert the utmost zeal in the pursuit of the object which was finally attained—namely, the neutrality of Denmark in the war between Sweden and Russia."[1]

---

[1] A tribute to Mr. Elliot's merits, which will scarcely be suspected of partiality, may be seen in the following letter from the Ambassador of France at Stockholm, a man whose name is invariably mentioned in Mr. Elliot's correspondence with the highest respect.

"*Stockholm,* 17*th Nov.* 1788.

" Vous n'avez fait que paraitre en Suède Monsieur, et votre presence y a retabli la paix et la tranquillité.   Vous avez arrêté dès son principe une guerre entre deux voisins que leur intérêt commun autant que les liasons de sang doivent toujours tenir en bonne intelligence ; et par le succès de vos negotiations vous avez prevenu des malheurs inevitables pour le Danemarc et pour la Suède.   Vous jouissez de cette douce satis-

The story of this curious bit of diplomatic service cannot be more aptly concluded, than by the insertion of the two following letters :—The first from the King of Sweden to George III., and the second from the town of Gothenburg to Mr. Elliot.

"Copie d'une lettre de Sa Majesté le Roi de Suède à Sa Majesté Britannique — datée de Gothenbourg nd 16 Oct. 1788. Conforme à la minute qui se trouve aux archives ministerielles de Suède.

"Monsieur mon Frère et Cousin !—J'ai dans tous les temps mis trop de prix à l'amitié de votre Majesté pour ne pas dans le moment présent, où elle m'en donne des preuves si essentielles, lui en témoigner ma reconnaissance. Votre Majesté a senti la nécessité de conserver la balance dans le Nord. Elle a rendu justice à mes sentiments pour elle. Elle a vu que la Suède seule pouvait arrêter l'explosion de l'ambition de la Russie, et former une barrière pour l'Europe, et Votre Majesté a jugé que, pour effectuer une operation si essentielle pour le bien et la liberté commune, il fallait soutenir la Suède contre le nouvel ennemi, qui, en mêlant la fraude à l'inimitié, menaçait la première ville commerçante de mon Royaume. Avec un ami aussi

---

faction. Elle est plus satisfaisante pour vous que tous les compliments qu'on pourrait vous faire et que mérite votre dextérité à manier deux caractères, qui dans le cours de cette négociation si j'en crois les recits qu'on nous en a fait, n'ont pas toujours été faciles à accorder.

"J'applaudis de tout mon cœur à vos succès," etc. etc.

"MARQUIS DE PONS,
"*Ambassadeur de France à Stockholm.*"

puissant, je ne pouvais qu'être sûr de réussir, mais je
dois à la vérité y ajouter que sans la fermeté, l'ardeur,
le courage, et l'habileté du Ministre de Votre Majesté à
la cour de Danemarck, le Sieur Elliot, vos bonnes intentions n'eussent point eu le succès désiré.   Je lui dois
la justice qu'on n'a pu mettre plus d'activité et de zèle
dans ses démarches qu'il n'a fait pour retenir l'injuste
invasion de mes ennemis, et que, malgré sa santé chan-
cellante et les dangers de toute espèce qu'il a essuyés, il
m'a servi comme il aurait pu servir votre Majesté—c'est
à dire, avec la loyauté et la fermeté d'un véritable
Anglais, et comme je ne puis mieux m'acquitter envers
lui qu'en rendant un fidèle compte de sa conduite à
votre Majesté, et que sa conduite m'est une nouvelle
marque de vos sentiments pour moi, je me hâte par ces
lignes de vous en témoigner toute ma sensibilité, en
vous assurant de tous les sentiments d'amitié, de la
haute estime, et de la parfaite considération avec
lesquels je suis, Monsieur, mon Frère et Cousin, de votre
Majesté, le Frère et Cousin,   GUSTAVE."[1]

[1] [TRANSLATION.]

" Copy of a letter from His Majesty the King of Sweden to his Britannic
    Majesty, dated Gottenburg, 16th October 1788.   According to
    the minute in the Ministerial Archives of Sweden.

    "Sir, my Brother and Cousin !—I have at all times too highly
valued your Majesty's friendship to withhold at the present moment,
when I receive such essential tokens of it, the assurance of my gratitude.
Your Majesty has felt the necessity of preserving the balance of the North.
You have done justice to my feelings towards you. You have seen that
Sweden alone can arrest the explosion of Russian ambition, and form a
barrier for Europe, and your Majesty has judged that, to effect an operation so essential for liberty and the common good, Sweden must be sus-

"Traduction d'une lettre écrite en Latin et addressée au Sieur Elliot par le 1ʳᵉ Magistrat de la Ville de Gothenbourg, accompagnant une médaille en or.[1]

"Monsieur !—La postérité ne pourra sans doute se ressouvenir qu'avec admiration de la reddition merveilleuse de Gothenbourg en l'année 1788, lorsque cette ville était si près d'être attaquée par des forces ennemies, et de subir un joug étranger, et c'est en commémoration de cet évènement que la ville a cru de son devoir et de son honneur, d'en éterniser par une médaille sa profonde reconnaissance.

"Vous, Monsieur, fûtes à cette occasion un témoin oculaire de l'héroïsme et de la sagesse avec lesquelles le Roi sçut écarter des dangers aussi menaçants, et c'est la juste considération de Sa Majesté pour toute sorte de

tained against the new enemy, who, mixing fraud with enmity, menaced the principal commercial town in my kingdom. With so powerful a friend I was sure of success, but I owe it to truth to add that without the firmness, ardour, courage, and talent of your Majesty's minister at the Court of Denmark, Mr. Elliot, your good intentions would not have had the desired success. In justice to him, I must say that no one could have shown more activity and zeal than he did in the steps he took to stay the unjust invasion of my enemies ; and that, notwithstanding his precarious health and the dangers of every kind which he has undergone, he has served me as he might have served your Majesty—that is to say, with the loyalty and firmness of a true Briton ; and as I cannot discharge my debt to him better than by giving your Majesty a faithful account of his conduct, and as his conduct is to me a new mark of your regard, I hasten by these lines to show my sense of it in assuring you of the feelings of friendship, highest esteem, and most exalted regard with which I am, Sir, my brother and cousin, the brother and cousin of your Majesty   GUSTAVUS."

[1] This medal is now in my possession, given me by my mother.

mérite, qui a éclairé la ville sur ses devoirs envers vous, Monsieur, dont le zèle infatigable dans les négociations les plus épineuses contribua si puissamment à leur succès.

"La ville ne pouvant jamais oublier des services si essentiels, ni effaçer le souvenir de vos éminentes qualités personnelles, a cru pouvoir se permettre la liberté de vous offrir un exemplaire de la dite médaille, comme un témoignage des sentiments dont elle est pénétrée, et c'est de sa part aussi bien que de la mienne, que j'ai l'honneur de me dire, bien respectueusement, Monsieur, votre très humble et très obéissant serviteur,

"DANIEL PETTERSSON,[1]

"*Bourgemattre de Gothenbourg.*

"*Gothenbourg, le 9 Février 1792.*"

[1] [TRANSLATION.]

"Sir—Posterity, without doubt, will only remember with admiration the wonderful deliverance of Gothenburg in the year 1788, when that town was on the point of being attacked by the forces of its enemies, and of being subjected to a foreign yoke; and it is in commemoration of the event that the town conceives it due to itself and its honour to immortalise by a medal its profound gratitude.

"You, Sir, were on this occasion an ocular witness of the heroism and the wisdom by which the King averted these impending dangers, and the just consideration of His Majesty for every species of merit, has enlightened the town on its duty to you, Sir, whose indefatigable zeal in advancing these delicate and embarrassing negotiations contributed so powerfully to their success.

"The town, which can never forget such essential services, nor lose its sense of your eminent personal qualities, desires to offer to you a copy of this same medal as a testimony to the sentiments retained for you by the town," etc. etc.

"DANIEL PETTERSSON,

"*Burgomaster of Gothenburg.*"

CHAPTER THE TWELFTH.

1790 to 1799.

PARIS—DRESDEN.

IN 1790 Mr. Elliot came home on leave, and was sent by Mr. Pitt on a secret mission to Paris in 1790 and 1791.

Beyond the bare fact that he was so sent, the correspondence tells nothing of this mission. In one letter only is there an illusion which throws a light upon its nature and success. A brother diplomatist, writing to him some years afterwards concerning a delicate negotiation then pending, says :—" If you could have been sent to conduct it as successfully as you did your mission to Mirabeau," etc. etc.

In 1792 he was appointed minister at the court of Saxony, where he remained till 1802. His mission to Dresden was not apparently marked by events of any peculiar interest.

The house of Bourbon, of which we have heard so much, had fallen, in its most important branch, before a power, of which we have heard nothing! though for many a day to come it was found not ponderable by the statesmen whose scales and weights had been adapted

to the " balance of the North." Revolutionised France
had started into life with a giant's strength, prepared to
use it *like a giant.* And during the ten years passed
by Mr. Elliot in Saxony, his correspondence is occupied
with details concerning the submissions of small powers,
the struggles of great ones, the intrigues of French
emigrants, and the insolence of French agents. A voluminous correspondence with his brother, after the latter
had become Lord Minto and Envoy to Vienna, contains
very little matter of public interest at the present date.
One short note, however, has a trait in which we see
that time and circumstance had not entirely subdued
early predilections in the diplomatist's breast. " Suwarrow," he said, " is at Prague; if it were not for my
family ties, I should be strongly tempted to throw up
my post and have a campaign with my old chief!"[1] A
quarter of a century before he had written from Munich,
his first diplomatic post, " My greatest pleasure is to
shut my eyes and fancy myself in Count Woronzow's
tent on the Danube."

Of his manière d'être at this time of his life Mrs.

[1] " Mr. Elliot was attached to General Suwarrow's staff when the
latter took and destroyed the town of Turticaya, took several cannon,
and made a great number of prisoners. Mr. Elliot was the person
despatched by Suwarrow with this news to Marshal Romanzow. The
general gives the highest encomiums to this young gentleman."—
Letter of Sir R. Gunning, June 15, 1773.

With Romanzow Mr. Elliot corresponded from time to time till
the close of the Marshal's life. In the summer of 1788, the Marshal
acknowledges, in a little note, the pleasure Mr. Elliot had given him
by introducing to him *M. de Blucher,* an officer of whose qualities he
formed a high opinion.

Trench gives a lively description in her charming Journal, on reading which his surviving children declared it to be *himself*.

" Mr. Elliot," she says on one occasion, " was wonderfully amusing. His wit, his humour, his discontent, his spleen, his happy choice of words, his rapid flow of ideas, and his disposition to playful satire, make one always long to write shorthand and preserve his conversation."[1]

The pages in which Mrs. Trench describes the visit of Lord Nelson and of Sir William and Lady Hamilton to Dresden are among the most entertaining in her journal.

Lord and Lady Holland too are mentioned by her among the guests she met at the English legation, and it was probably during this visit that a circumstance occurred which gave rise to the following anecdote of my grandfather, told me by Lord Russell, who had heard it from Lord Holland.

Conversing one day with a Prussian gentleman, whose exaggerated praises of two Princes of that Royal House had somewhat wearied him, he watched his opportunity to get rid of his interlocutor. At last it came :—" Il faut avouer que ce sont deux grands princes ?" said the Prussian, and waited for an answer. " Oui, et deux fort mauvais sujets ! " quietly replied Mr. Elliot, to the great amusement of Lord Holland, a listener to the dialogue.

While at Dresden he and my grandmother had the

[1] Dresden, October 7, 1801.

z

happiness of receiving his brother and Lady Minto under their roof when they passed through Dresden on their way to Vienna, to which court Lord Minto was accredited as envoy extraordinary in 1799. Lord Minto's visit to Dresden preceded his wife's by some months; various family reasons having prevented her from leaving England at the same time with himself. To this circumstance we are indebted for a glimpse into my grandfather's home, preserved for us in the letters of his brother and sister-in-law.

Some years had passed since the brothers had met, and in the interval Hugh Elliot had married a beautiful girl of humble birth, but whose personal qualities justified his choice.

Lord Minto, writing to his wife from Dresden, 1799, says:—" I have, since I have seen Hugh's wife and beautiful children, better hope of his happiness than I ever had before. She is very handsome—her face and head remarkably pretty, in so much that the celebrated Virgin of Raphael in the gallery, one of the finest pictures I ever saw, is her exact portrait; while two of the children are so like the cherubs looking up, that I told Hugh it was a family picture. I find her sensible and pleasant, and they are both generally liked, and on the best possible footing here.

" Hugh's extreme good humour and temper, and his affectionate and cordial manner to every creature that approaches him, in whatever shape, are captivating qualities."

In May of the following year it became Lady Minto's

turn to write to her husband of the household at Dresden, and her expressions of pleasure at being again with Hugh and with his family, are no less cordial than Lord Minto's. " I am delighted with Dresden," she wrote on the 2d May 1800, " with the gallery   .   .   .   with the country, in which there seems so much comfort and so many beautiful scenes. We take long airings every evening, and I know you will be glad to hear that I admire Mrs. Elliot and the children to the utmost." After a glowing tribute to " Margaret's " uncommon beauty and natural pleasing manner, she ends thus—" The children are really charming, and the two groups are hugging and kissing, and intimate friends already."

" It is a happiness to me," wrote Lord Minto to Hugh after this visit, " that for a moment our families have made one family."

CHAPTER THE THIRTEENTH.

1803 to 1806.

MISSION TO NAPLES.

MR. ELLIOT, being at the time on leave in England, was sent to Naples at twenty-four hours' notice, in May 1803, Lord Nelson giving him a passage to the Mediterranean in the "Victory."

War had been declared on the 20th of May between Great Britain and France, and the First Consul had announced an intention of requiring all neutral nations to close their ports against British ships, while foreign courts suspected of leanings to British influences were threatened with an army of invasion. Bonaparte assumed that France was the head of the Southern Confederacy of Europe, and declared that he would not suffer either Spain, Portugal, or the States of Italy to deviate in any degree from the system of politics adopted by France.

At the moment of Mr. Elliot's arrival at Naples (June 1803) a French army was approaching the frontier on its way to take possession of Tarentum and other ports on the Adriatic, which the First Consul

J'ai reçu votre lettre et suis pénétré de Reconnoissance pour tout ce que vous me dites et pour l'interet que votre interessante petite famille veut bien avoir pour moi. Nous avons reçu aujourd'hui le courier de mellau le 26 le Gouvernement s'est passé sans aucun inconvénient et sans la moindre démonstration de satisfaction du publique, on a envoyé les passeports à Vonck, elof pour porter des propositions de l'un de la Rußie et même de l'angleterre, le courier paroit tres consterné Somme voila tout ce que à la hâte je puis vous dire ni Berlin ni le Portugal personne à reconnu le nouveau Roi qu'il vous nous a beaucoup d'honneur. Si vous voulez venir la perdrie à 2 heures soit demain ou apres demain vous etes toujours le maitre et le bien avec bien du plaisir que je vous exprimois des Sentimens de mon eternelle Estime Confiance et Reconnoissance votre Sincere-amie Charlotte

J'ai été tres contente du général Lacy et suis charmé qu'il Conoisse Montfret

claimed a right to occupy so long as Great Britain should hold Malta.

The greatest consternation prevailed at Naples. The King, Ferdinand IV., afraid of admitting the British minister to his presence, had retired to Caserta, leaving the hereditary Prince to represent him in Naples, and only consented with difficulty to return there on the insistance of Mr. Elliot that his credentials should be received by the King himself. " It was right," he said, " to show that the presence of a British minister in the capital of Naples, a British man-of-war in the harbour, and of Lord Nelson's fleet in the Mediterranean, were circumstances calculated to restore confidence to the King."

The Queen, Caroline, daughter of Maria Theresa and sister of Marie Antoinette, " the only spirited character there," possessed great ability, activity, and energy ; but these qualities were so mixed with violence and indiscretion, that her conduct was at the mercy of those who knew how to take advantage of her weaknesses. At the mature age of fifty-two, she had formed an attachment for a French emigrant officer, le Marquis de St. Clair, which had led to her being surrounded by a knot of his countrymen, among whom were some who cloaked dangerous objects of their own under the name of French emigrants—" a title which," wrote Mr. Elliot to his Government, " no longer denotes any real degree of hostility towards the Government of Bonaparte. I must confess that the First Consul cannot make use of any better channel to forward his

own purposes than that of French emigrants at foreign
courts."

"The Queen herself," he wrote to Lord Nelson,
"is well inclined towards us; yet she is continually
drawn into scrapes and inconsistencies by these designing people, who are in their hearts equally hostile to
Great Britain and to General Acton."

General Acton,[1] highly trusted by the King, and in
Mr. Elliot's estimation the only man in the kingdom
capable of forming and sustaining such a policy as would
ensure its independence, had by his constant assertion
of the rights of his sovereigns, and his resistance to the
unjust and arrogant demands of the French Ambassador
at the Court of Naples, become an object of persecution
to Bonaparte, who never failed to insist upon his removal
from the high situation he had held for more than twenty
years. Unfortunately General Acton was old and infirm,
and his opposition to the Queen's schemes for the ag-
grandisement of her French favourites had rendered him
obnoxious to her; while "her experienced management
of every female wile and snare, of which the constant

---

[1] Sir John Acton, Bart. of Aldenham, born in 1726, was for many
years the Neapolitan prime minister and commander-in-chief of the
land and sea forces of Naples. Though he had succeeded to the
baronetcy on the death of a cousin in 1791, he is invariably styled
"General Acton" throughout the correspondence, both in official and
private letters. "General Acton," wrote Mr. Elliot in one of his
despatches, "had in early life passed from the service of the Great
Duke of Tuscany into that of his Sicilian Majesty, for the purpose of
reforming and directing the Neapolitan naval department. His subsequent rise took its origin as much from the Queen's known partiality
towards him as from the King's favour."

practice of a life spent in the pursuits of pleasure and
ambition have made her so consummate a mistress, enabled her to soothe, deceive, and master him whenever
it suited her so to do."

The finances were verging on a state of bankruptcy,
the army was ill paid, the nobility were disaffected, the
people indifferent, the mercantile classes in despair; and,
in hourly expectation of the closing of the ports, some of
the English merchants had taken to flight before the
British minister arrived. Such was the condition of
things at Naples when Mr. Elliot entered on the task
which had been intrusted to him—namely, to sustain, if
possible, the independence of the Two Sicilies, by encouraging the Government to persevere in a system of
strict neutrality, and by aiding them to make military
preparations for resistance in the event of an invasion of
their dominions.

The defence of Sicily was an object of paramount
importance with the British Government, and in case of
danger in that quarter, Sicily was to be defended "with
or without the concurrence of His Sicilian Majesty."[1]

With these objects in view, Mr. Elliot set himself to
gain the confidence of the Queen, to support with all his

[1] "The kingdom of Naples once lost, that of Sicily may be preserved; if Sicily were once lost, the loss of Naples would infallibly
follow. The first, therefore, though a great evil, would still leave an
asylum for the royal family, and would ensure an important security
to the interests of His Majesty in the Mediterranean. The last would
prove the irretrievable ruin of their Sicilian Majesties, and would afford
to the French Government a dominion in that sea, which they have
hitherto endeavoured in vain to obtain."—*Despatch to Hugh Elliot*,
November 11, 1803.

influence that of General Acton, and to instigate the
Government to various military preparations, such as
arming the inhabitants of Calabria on the pretext of
self-defence against Tunisian cruisers, and the restoration
of the defences of Messina under the secret superintendence of English military officers, and by means of English
money.

The natural consequences of this vigorous conduct
ensued.   Acton and Elliot became equally obnoxious to
France, and the drama enacting at Naples was thence-
forth marked by a double plot:—the external struggle
between Bonaparte and the sovereigns of the Two
Sicilies, and the internal struggle between the Queen
and Sir John Acton.

It was Mr. Elliot's opinion that if the Queen had
understood the true interests of Naples as thoroughly as
she comprehended and hated the objects of Bonaparte,
much might have been done to save her country; but
her passions were too strong for her judgment, or, as he
wrote, " the judgment of the sovereign was warped by
the frailties of the woman ;" and to procure the fall of
Acton, she did not disdain to make use of Bonaparte.

In August 1803, two months after Mr. Elliot's arrival,
she desired him to wait upon her at seven o'clock in the
morning, in her private apartments.   " She was much
agitated, and it was some time before she could speak
on public affairs; at length, however, she did so, with
more than usual animation, and, having occasion to
mention Bonaparte, his name was always accompanied
with some appropriate epithet."

Mr. Elliot expressing some surprise that Her Majesty should be so incensed against him at a moment when he had graciously condescended to bear part of the expenses of his troops in the kingdom of Naples, the Queen replied with vivacity—"Mr. Elliot, I must make you the full confidence of what we have received from him, though we have not ventured to show his letters to General Acton." The Queen then led Mr. Elliot into her cabinet, and laid before him three letters, of which he was permitted to send home copies, "to be communicated solely to the King's confidential servants." The first was from herself to Bonaparte, imploring, as the mother of her family and of her people, that he would relieve the kingdom of Naples from the burden of supporting his army; the two other letters were from Bonaparte to the King and Queen. In the second, the most important of the two, he wrote to the Queen as follows :—

"*Bruxelles, le* 9 *an.* 11.

" J'ai lu avec la plus grande attention la lettre de votre Majesté.

" Je la prie de rester persuadée qu'après lui avoir fait beaucoup de mal j'ai aussi le besoin de lui être agréable.

" Dans les conjonctures actuelles, il est de la politique intérieure de la France de consolider la tranquillité chez tous ses voisins; il est de la politique extérieure d'aider un état plus faible, dont le bien être est utile au commerce de la France, mais je veux répondre par une confiance sans réserve à celle de votre Majesté. Com-

ment veut elle que je considère le royaume de Naples
dans ses rapports géographiques et politiques, lorsque je
vois à la tête de toutes les administrations un homme
étranger au pays, et qui a centralisé en Angleterre ses
richesses et toutes ses affections ?

" Cependant le royaume de Naples ne se gouverne
pas par la volonté et les principes du souverain, mais
par la volonté et les principes de ce ministre. J'ai donc
été décidé par une sage prévoiance à considérer Naples
comme un pays gouverné par un ministre Anglais.

" Répugnant beaucoup à me mêler des affaires in-
térieures des autres états, ce n'est que pour être sincère
envers votre Majesté, que je lui donne la véritable
raison, qui justifie toutes les mesures prises envers
Naples et dont elle pourrait avoir à se plaindre.

" Je désire que votre Majesté soit convaincu du
reste du grand prix que j'attache à tout ce qui peut
tranquilliser et ordonner le Continent et contribuer à son
bonheur.

" Je prie votre Majesté de croire aux sentiments de
la considération la plus distinguée.

" (Signé)   BONAPARTE."[1]

[1] [TRANSLATION.]

" Brussels, the 9 year, 11.

" I have read your Majesty's letter with the utmost attention.

" I entreat you to rest assured that, after having done you great
injury, I am now desirous to be agreeable to you.

" At the present conjuncture it is the internal policy of France to
consolidate peace amongst all her neighbours ; it is her external policy
to aid a feebler state, the well-being of which is of importance to
French commerce ; but I wish to respond by a confidence without
reserve to that your Majesty has shown to me.

The Queen commented on the insolence, the perfidy, the ambition, etc., of Bonaparte, and then consulted Mr. Elliot as to what he thought of the plan to remove General Acton from the King's councils. " Who," continued her Majesty, " should be put in his place ? For I am much afraid that if General Acton were to see the First Consul's letter, he would immediately ask for his dismission." Mr. Elliot replied, " that upon an occasion, big with the most important consequences, he could not venture to give a hasty reply." Two days later[1] he sent her a letter in which he informed Her Majesty that he would not consider the letter of Bonaparte as " de lui seul;" but rather as giving expression to the secret desire of many discontented Neapolitans and others

" What must I think of the kingdom of Naples in its geographical and political relations, whilst I see at the head of the administration one who is a stranger to the country, and who has centred in England his wealth and all his affections ?

" Nevertheless, the kingdom of Naples is not governed by the will or the principles of its sovereign, but by the will and according to the principles of this minister. I, therefore, was led by a wise foresight to decide on considering Naples as a country governed by an English minister.

" Disliking much to interfere in the internal affairs of other states, it is only in order to be sincere towards your Majesty that I have given you the true reason which justifies all the measures taken in regard to Naples of which you might complain.

" Yet I wish your Majesty may be convinced of the great value I attach to all that tends to tranquillise and arrange the Continent, and contribute to its happiness.

" I beg your Majesty to accept of my warmest expressions of esteem.
" (Signed)   BONAPARTE."

[1] August 16, 1803.

to be rid of a man who had served the royal family and
country with faithfulness, and whose policy had gained
the support and approval of England.   After urging the
Queen to acquaint General Acton with the nature of
the First Consul's communications, Mr. Elliot went on :—
" Bonaparte se plaint que le Général Acton soit
Anglais, et moi je me flatte qu'il l'est, autant par son
caractère ferme, loyal, et calme, que par sa naissance, et
dans ce cas je promets à votre Majesté, qu'il ne
secondera pas les vues sinistres du Consul par une
obéissance à ses ordres, et par une désertion de son
poste, pour le ceder aux ennemis de son souverain."[1]

The letter ended, after recalling the many encouraging
circumstances in the position of the country which were
attributable to General Acton's foresight and to British
support, by the distinct statement that the moment was
not one for reticence and mistrust, and that if a dyke
was to be constructed against the torrent which threatened to overflow Europe, the basis on which it should
be raised must be solid, and that for himself, speaking
as an honest man and a minister, he should refuse to
take one more step in advance until he had received the
most positive assurances that the insolence of Bonaparte

----

[1] [TRANSLATION.]

" Bonaparte complains that General Acton is an Englishman, and
I flatter myself that he is so, as much so by the firmness, loyalty,
and calmness of his character, as by his birth ; and in this case, I
promise your Majesty that he will not second the sinister designs of
the Consul by obedience to his orders, and by deserting his post to
yield it to the enemies of his sovereign."

should not affect any change in the position of the minister.

The Queen replied in terms of high admiration to what she was pleased to call his "*parfaite lettre.*" As Mr. Elliot had advised, the Consul's letters were shown to General Acton; and the King protested that he would rather give up his crown than sacrifice so faithful a servant. "Had the Consul's letters been kept secret from General Acton, as was originally intended, the King would have been exposed to hear mysteriously and daily all the fears, alarms, and insinuations of the minister's enemies, without his having had an opportunity of combating them."[1] For that time the storm blew over, the monitions of Bonaparte were met with explanations which were accepted, and Mr. Elliot proceeded to write to his Government that he must candidly own he was by no means persuaded that Bonaparte thought the dismissal of General Acton would be disagreeable to the Queen. "H. M. has so many irons in the fire that the natural consequences must inevitably ensue. There are, both in France and Germany, several individuals in habits of intimacy and correspondence with the Queen, who conceive that if General Acton was removed, and the French influence established here, they will be put in possession of the government."

"I flatter myself," he wrote,[2] "that the Queen has so severely felt the inconveniences she has been exposed to by listening with too much complacency to specious and artful insinuations, that Her Majesty will not, for some

---

[1] Hugh Elliot to Lord Hawkesbury—Naples, August 28, 1803.

[2] August 28, 1803.

time at least, be induced to deviate from the direct line, which can alone encourage her real friends to exert their energies in her defence.

" I acknowledge in Her Sicilian Majesty many great and pre-eminent endowments : infinite ability and activity, a degree of courage above her sex, and every quality which may enable her to struggle against difficulties, under whose load weaker minds would sink ; and should these qualities be called into action, she will, I am certain, act with a spirit and decision worthy of her birth and situation. But in all cases that require discretion, self-command, and prudence, Her Sicilian Majesty needs to be guided and controlled."

While taking this bold course in support of General Acton at the Neapolitan Court, Mr. Elliot did not hesitate to join with him in representing to Lord Nelson and Sir A. Ball, Governor of Malta, who desired to place a British garrison in Messina, the inexpediency of committing any overt act which would give the French a pretext for marching into Naples.

He assured them that no grounds existed for any immediate alarms on the score of the French movements, and he warned them not to listen to "the misconceptions of misinformed people, and particularly of our merchants, who are excellent dealers in Newfoundland fish, but are bad newsmongers, and who will continually harass you with the same absurd stories with which my table is also covered, until I get a proper opportunity of consigning the intelligence and alarms of these deep politicians to their proper place."[1]

---

[1] Hugh Elliot to Lord Nelson, September 1803.

To a proposal of Lord Nelson's for blockading the ports occupied by the French, he also "opposed his frank though considerate opinion." "The first consequence of such a measure would be that the French would complain of the impossibility of their getting supplies in the provinces they now occupy, and they would therefore extend their quarters to the districts adjoining the capital—if not upon the capital itself—in which last case, every port of the kingdom would be shut against us, and open to our enemies."[1]

The policy of the English Government at that time was not conducted on any large views; and its agents abroad were sometimes puzzled by the multiplicity of objects pointed out to their attention, and were frequently left to act independently of any instructions at all. The precarious nature of all modes of communication between distant parts of Europe greatly contributing to the uncertainty of diplomatic correspondence.

In the dearth of precise instructions, the civil and military servants of the crown in the Mediterranean were desired to act in concert under various contingencies; but they by no means invariably coincided in their views of the policy to be pursued. In reading the letters of the generals and admirals, of the colonels, majors, and sea-captains, who were desired to correspond with Mr. Elliot, it strikes one forcibly that from Toulon to Turkey, purely British interests were the only ones which they thought it essential to serve. The statesmanlike mind of the minister, on the other hand, perceived

[1] To Lord Nelson, August 16, 1803.

the danger of adopting measures at once short-sighted and selfish, the mere suspicion of which did us infinite damage with our continental allies.

Thus, as we have seen, in the first year of his arrival at the Neapolitan Court, Mr. Elliot had some trouble to prevent Lord Nelson and the Governor of Malta from disgusting Naples, increasing the already existing jealousy of Russia ("always a cold friend to us," said Mr. Elliot), and giving France a pretext for marching on Naples, by throwing a garrison of 1400 British soldiers into the fort of Messina, which was totally unprepared to receive them.

That he took all the necessary steps for the restoration of the defences of Messina is proved by his correspondence, and by the condition in which the works were found by our troops in 1806 ; and until the deplorable events of that winter, the neutrality of Naples was observed, and her ports remained open to English men-of-war and trading vessels, while English officers and English money were actively though secretly employed in military preparations against her hour of need.

When the transactions of the year 1803 became known in England, the Government approved highly of Mr. Elliot's share in them, as will be seen in the following despatch :—[1]

Downing Street, July 3, 1804.

" It gives me particular pleasure to be the channel of communicating to you his Majesty's gracious ap-

[1] From Lord Harrowby to Hugh Elliot.

probation of the prudence and discretion, as well as the zeal and energy, which have distinguished your conduct in a situation peculiarly difficult. The success of your efforts to induce the Government of Naples to pursue a line of conduct which (without making any unworthy or unnecessary concession) has enabled it to avert the immediate danger by which it was menaced, and the measures which, in conformity to your suggestions, have been adopted for the defence of the Calabrias and of Sicily, have been highly satisfactory to His Majesty's Government. They have also excited the warmest sentiments of approbation on the part of His Sicilian Majesty, who has instructed his minister here to express the sense which His Majesty entertains of your meritorious exertions, and his anxiety that you should in future continue to act with the same caution as well as energy by which your past conduct has been so eminently marked. In these sentiments of cordiality and goodwill towards yourself the Russian ambassador has entirely concurred."

The First Consul was crowned Emperor of the French in 1804, and M. Alquier, his representative at Naples, was desired to present his new credential letters to the King and Queen.

It was with the greatest difficulty that the Queen prevailed on the King to grant M. Alquier an audience, which at last he only consented to do in the hope that this concession would, by gratifying the new Emperor, lead to the withdrawal of the French troops from Naples. Nothing, however, could exceed the dryness of the

King's manner, and the only sentence he uttered was probably the most perfectly truthful to which he had ever given expression. "You will assure the Emperor," he said, "that my sentiments towards him will never undergo any alteration." It was observed that the Queen, in her reply to the ambassador's compliment, frequently repeated the expression "the Emperor, *your master*," which was meant tauntingly as being addressed to a person who had always professed the sentiments of a violent republican, and had voted the death of his former sovereign.

Though Mr. Elliot's vigorous support of General Acton and his policy promised to be successful as against external foes, it was not proof against the machinations of the Queen. In June 1804 a fresh plot exploded, which ended with Acton's fall. Having been drawn into a warm personal altercation with the French ambassador, General Acton felt himself so grossly insulted by the language addressed to him that he ordered M. Alquier out of his room. The result was an announcement from the ambassador that he should leave Naples if Acton were not dismissed. The particulars of the interview are not given in the official correspondence; but in a private letter, marked "secret," from Mr. Elliot to General Acton, written apparently on receiving that minister's account of what had passed, the following passages occur :—[1]

"Je suis sans inquiétudes sur les suites de la bourrasque préméditée de l'ambassadeur de France.

[1] Hugh Elliot to General Acton, May 7, 1804.

.   .   .   .   Votre Excellence me permettra
cependant de dire avec la franchise de mon caractère,
et de ma nation, qu'à l'avenir il ne devrait entrer par
aucune Porte, par laquelle on n'aura pas le privilège
de lui indiquer la sortie, quand il lui aura plu de
manquer à toutes les bienséances.

Depuis que l'on reconnait entre les nations
civilisées les convenances dues aux gouvernemens
établis, jamais, je crois, un ministre étranger ne s'est
avisé de présenter une note officielle au ministre du
pays, portant l'étrange proposition d'éloigner ce même
ministre des conseils de son maître, et qualifiant les
corréspondances d'une souveraine du mot d'incendaires."[1]

The "bourrasque" produced graver results than
Mr. Elliot anticipated, for the matter having been
referred to Paris, despatches arrived in due course
from the Marquis de Gallo (Neapolitan minister at the
French court, and, to borrow a phrase of Mr. Elliot's,
"a conquest of Bonaparte's"), which represented in

---

[1] [TRANSLATION.]

"I am not uneasy in regard to the results of the French
ambassador's premeditated outburst.

"Your Excellency, however, will permit me to say, with the frankness of my character and of my nation, that in future he should
enter by no door by which one cannot take the privilege of
showing him out, when it has pleased him to be wanting in
common courtesy. Since the recognition amongst civilised nations
of the respect due to established governments, never, I believe, has a
foreign minister thought proper to present an official note to the
minister of the country containing the strange proposition to remove
this same minister from his master's counsels, and stigmatising the
correspondence of a sovereign as incendiary language."

strong terms the deep resentment of the Emperor, and the grave apprehensions to which it must give rise; while *private letters* from the same source assured the Queen that within forty-eight hours a French messenger was to be despatched from Paris, bearing a declaration of war in case General Acton should not have left the capital before his arrival.

The Queen professed to be overcome with alarm on the perusal of these letters, and, for the first and only time in her history, she pleaded her personal fears to the King as the ground for the immediate departure of the minister; and in spite of the remonstrances of Mr. Elliot, who urged at all events a less indecent flight, General Acton was persuaded to retire before a formal demand for his removal should arrive. He accordingly set sail for Palermo[1] within the time specified by De Gallo—not, however, until the King, at the Queen's instigation, had settled on him and his heirs a pension of £6000 a-year, a measure which, under the circumstances of the case, looked much like a bribe to him to depart.

Acton once out of her way, the Queen professed to regret him, and to have been carried away by her alarms, as Her Majesty was pleased to style her feelings upon this occasion. On the arrival, eight days later, of despatches from Paris, in a much more moderate tone than had been anticipated, she graciously said to Mr. Elliot, "Vraiment M. Elliot j'en suis au repentir, et nous avons été trompés." But in those moments of

---

[1] On the 25th May.

violence and passion, " when alone she was sincere," she
admitted that it was the general's age and weakness, in-
capacitating him for energetic and resolute measures,
which had determined her to be rid of him.

After General Acton's departure the councils of the
court became more than ever distracted and perplexed.
From the distance of Palermo, Acton professed to
direct every department of the administration by the
King's desire, while the Queen appointed her French
friends to high places, and gave the command of the
army to Count Roger de Damas, a French emigrant.

In this strange state of disputed authority between
the Queen and the Minister, " who increase the difficulty of forming a decision respecting the veracity of the
statements of either by continuing to correspond between
themselves, and to load that correspondence with the
strongest professions of mutual regard and esteem,"
Mr. Elliot conceived that " there was but one clue to
guide him out of such a labyrinth of contradiction and
inconsistency"—which was to prevail upon the King
himself to confide to him, from his own mouth, his real
sentiments and intentions. " I believe," he wrote,
" there is no prior example in His Majesty's reign in
which he ever consented to take a step so contrary to
his usual habits, having always had great aversion to
treat personally even with his own ministers." Mr.
Elliot subsequently described the conference granted
him by the King as the most remarkable in . which
he had had a share in the long period of his diplomatic services. Forced to speak for himself, the

King displayed talents and eloquence which took the English minister completely by surprise; but the audience, nevertheless, terminated by the King's desiring Mr. Elliot, on all matters of importance, to address himself solely to the Queen, as the only person in his dominions in whom His Majesty placed any confidence.

" The Queen at present transacts business daily with the heads of all the departments, and acquits herself of so laborious a task with infinite ability. Her Majesty has permitted me to wait upon her every day between the hours of one and three, and communicates to me all the despatches received by the Court without reserve. Her professions of attachment to England are as strong as those of General Acton ; but I mistrust the impetuosity of Her Majesty's feelings, which will ever betray her into acts of imprudence."[1]

The successful result of the machinations against Acton produced in due time a similar attack upon the British minister. The French ambassador spoke with the greatest acrimony concerning the apparent increase of favour shown to Mr. Elliot personally, since General Acton's departure for Sicily.

" Among the extraordinary expressions used by M. Alquier, he said that he had been duped by the apparent concession made to France in General Acton's departure—the influence I had gained over the counsels of this country having been visibly augmented, since I had no longer to struggle against the weakness of the late minister."[2]

[1] Hugh Elliot to Lord Harrowby, 24th June 1804.
[2] November 6, 1804, to Lord Harrowby.

The King of Naples was therefore admonished to abandon his connection with England, to dismiss his minister, and to trust unreservedly to the loyalty of Bonaparte.

A few days later M. Alquier threatened an immediate advance of General St. Cyr's army if the Neapolitan Government would not consent to dismiss Mr. Elliot and close their ports against British ships. The choice of evils presented to them was, however, grave enough to divest even the Neapolitan ministry of some of the " poltronnerie naturelle," of which the Queen accused them.

Mr. Elliot " the likeness of a kingly crown had on." A British man-of-war was ever ready at his command to place King and Queen in security, which their capital might not always afford them. British fleets protected their coasting trade, British fishing-vessels were at the moment unloading at the Mole, British money paid their troops, and the undaunted character of the British minister had infused some of its own courage into the timid.

The Neapolitan ministers replied to the demands of Alquier by the pertinent question—" Are we, when threatened by France, to quarrel with England too ?" The King stood firm; the Queen's courage and resolution were beyond all praise; and on the appearance of a strange squadron in the offing, reported to be the French fleet, she sent for the minister of war, and in Mr. Elliot's presence, desired the batteries to be manned, and prepared to resist to the last. Alquier, who had possibly exceeded his instructions, lowered his tone; and Bonaparte's next despatches informed the Neapolitan Court that he had more important objects in view, and would not insist on violent measures.

The successful resistance of the Neapolitan Government on this occasion was mainly attributable to the firm and wise counsels of Mr. Elliot, and in due course of time Lord Mulgrave, Secretary of State for Foreign Affairs, wrote to Mr. Elliot in terms of high approbation of the conduct pursued by him:—

"*Downing Street, March* 27, 1805.

" I have the greatest satisfaction in communicating to you His Majesty's fullest approbation of the indefatigable zeal with which you have attended to the object of your mission, and of the talent and judgment with which you have acquired so considerable an influence in the councils of the Court of Naples.

*   *   *   *   *

" His Majesty relies on your experienced activity and talents to support the resolution and firmness of the King of Naples, and to assist his councils."

Under the influence of her secret cabal the Queen now entered on a correspondence with Napoleon, in which she offered him an annual subsidy on condition of the withdrawal of the French troops from Naples. To these overtures, the wisdom of which Mr. Elliot had strongly contested, the new Emperor replied in language calculated to arouse the highest resentment of the Queen.

" Madame—La lettre de Votre Majesté m'a été

remise par Monsieur le Marquis de Gallo. Il m'est difficile de concilier les sentimens qu'elle contient avec les projets hostiles, qu'on parait nourrir à Naples. J'ai dans ma main plusieurs lettres de Votre Majesté, qui ne laissent aucun doute sur ses veritables intentions secrètes. Quelque soit la haine, que Votre Majesté paroit porter à la France, comment après l'expérience qu'Elle a faite, l'amour de son Epoux, de ses enfans, de sa famille, de ses sujets ne lui conseille-t-il pas un peu plus de retenue, et une direction politique plus conforme à ses interêts? Votre Majesté qui a un esprit si distingué entre les femmes, n'a-t'Elle donc pas pu se détacher des preventions de son sexe, et peut-Elle traiter les affaires d'état comme les affaires de cœur? Elle a déjà perdu une fois son royaume. Elle a été deux fois la cause d'une guerre qui a failli ruiner de fond en comble sa maison paternelle. Veut-Elle donc être la cause d'une troisieme? Déjà à la sollicitation de son ambassadeur à St. Petersbourg dix mille Russes ont été envoyés à Corfou. Quoi! sa haine est elle tellement jeune, et son amour pour l'Angleterre tellement exalté, qu'Elle veuille, quoiqu' assurée d'en être la victime première, embraser le Continent et opérer cette heureuse diversion pour l'Angleterre? J'avoue que des passions si fortes auroient quelque part à mon estime, si les plus simples idées de raison n'en faisoient sentir la frivolité et l'impuissance. Son neveu l'Empereur d'Autriche[1] ne partage point ses sentimens, et ne veut point recommencer la guerre qui

[1] The Emperor of Austria was the son-in-law of the Queen as well as her nephew.

n'auroit pour son Empire que des résultats peu satis-
faisans.   La Russie même que les sollicitations du
ministre de Votre Majesté ont porté à envoyer dix mille
hommes à Corfou sent très bien, que ce n'est point par là
qu'elle peut faire la guerre à la France; et les dispositions
d'Alexandre Premier ne sont point guerrieres.   Mais en
supposant que la catastrophe de Votre Famille et le
renversement de Votre Trône armassent la Russie et
l'Autriche, comment Votre Majesté peut Elle penser, Elle
qui a si bonne opinion de moi, que je sois resté assez
inactif pour être tombé dans la dépendence de mes
voisins.   Que Votre Majesté écoute cette prophetie,
qu'Elle l'écoute sans impatience : à la premiere guerre
dont Elle seroit cause, Elle et sa posterité auroient
cessé de régner, ses enfans errans mandieroient dans les
différentes contrées de l'Europe des secours de leurs parens.
Par une conduite inexplicable, Votre Majesté auroit
causé la ruine de sa famille, tandis que la Providence
et ma modération lui avoient tout conservé.   Renonce
t'on ainsi à un des plus beaux royaumes de l'univers !
Je serois fâché cependant que Votre Majesté prit cette
franchise de ma part pour des menaces.   Non, s'il étoit
entré dans mes projets de faire la guerre au Roi de
Naples, je l'aurais faite à l'entrée du premier Russe à
Corfou, ainsi que l'auroit voulu une politique circonspecte.
Mais je veux la paix avec Naples, avec l'Europe entière,
avec l'Angleterre même, et je ne crains la guerre avec
personne.   Je suis en état de la faire à quiconque voudra
me provoquer, et de punir la Cour de Naples, sans
craindre de ressentimens de qui que ce soit.   Que votre

Majesté recoive ce conseil d'un bon frère; qu'Elle rappelle
les chefs des milices; qu'Elle ne provoque aucun espéce
d'armement; qu'Elle renvoye les Francais qui l'excitent
contre leur patrie; qu'Elle rappelle de St. Petersbourg
un ministre, dont toutes les démarches ont pour but de
gâter les affaires de Naples et de la mettre dans des
dangers imminens; qu'Elle renvoye Monsieur Elliot, qui
ne trame que des complots d' assassinats et excite tous
les mouvemens de Naples; qu'Elle donne sa confiance
au chef de sa maison, et j'ose, le dire à moi, et qu'Elle
ne soit pas assez ennemie d'Elle même pour perdre un
royaume qu'Elle a gardé au milieu d'un si grand boul-
versement où tant d'états ont peri. Je ne fais pas ma
cour à votre Majesté par cette lettre. Elle sera desagré-
able pour elle. Cependant qu'Elle y voye une preuve de
mon estime. Ce n'est qu'à une personne d'un caractère
fort, et au dessus du commun que je me donnerois la
peine d'écrire avec cette verité. Sur ce je prie Dieu,
Madame ma Sœur et Cousine qu'il ait votre Majesté en
sa sainte garde.   (Signé)   NAPOLEON.[1]

"*Paris, ce Nivose, an. 13.—Janvier* 1805."

[1] [TRANSLATION.]

"Madam—Your Majesty's letter was transmitted to me by the
Marquis de Gallo. It is difficult for me to reconcile the sentiments
it contains with the hostile projects which seem to be nourished at
Naples. I have in my hand several of your Majesty's letters, which
leave no doubt as to your real secret intentions. However great the
hatred that you seem to bear to France, how is it that, after the experience you have had, the love of your husband, of your children, of your
family, of your subjects, does not counsel a little more prudence and
a policy more in conformity with your interests? Your Majesty has a
mind distinguished amongst women, can you not then throw off the

The Queen was so moved on reading this letter, that she described herself, in a note with which she forwarded it to Mr. Elliot, as unable to witness his perusal of it, and she begged him to make himself acquainted with it before they met to consider it. The opening lines of his answer are highly characteristic :—" The first feeling of a gentleman on reading such a letter, addressed to a princess, wife of a sovereign, daughter

prejudices of your sex, and can you treat affairs of state as you would affairs of the heart? You have already lost your kingdom once. Twice you have caused a war in which your father's house has narrowly escaped complete ruin. Do you then wish to cause a third? At the request of your ambassador at St. Petersburg, 10,000 Russians have already been sent to Corfu. What! is your hatred so fresh, and your love for England so exalted, that you wish, though assured of being yourself the first victim, to embroil the Continent and procure thus a diversion in favour of England? I confess that passions so powerful would command some portion of my esteem, if plain reason did not show their frivolity and impotence. Your nephew, the Emperor of Austria, does not share your sentiments, and does not wish to renew the war, which would produce results very unsatisfactory for his Empire. Even Russia—though at the solicitation of your Majesty's minister she has been induced to send 10,000 men to Corfu—knows very well that it is not thus that she can make war on France, and the temperament of Alexander I. is not warlike. But supposing that the calamities of your family and the overthrow of your throne armed Russia and Austria, as your Majesty expects, how can your Majesty, since you have so good an opinion of me, think that I should be so inactive as to fall into a state of dependence on my neighbours? May your Majesty listen to this prophecy; may you listen to it without impatience! At the first war of which you are the cause, you and your family will cease to reign; your children, wanderers, will beg, in the different countries of Europe, assistance from their relations. By conduct so inexplicable, your Majesty will have ruined your family, while Providence and my moderation would have preserved you everything. Will you thus renounce one of the finest kingdoms in the universe?

of Maria Theresa, must be a strong desire to inflict
personal chastisement on the writer. The arm and not
the pen would give the fittest answer."

In the interview which ensued, the Queen, with
bitter tears of grief and anger, lamented to Mr. Elliot
the precipitation with which she had acted in humiliating herself by making overtures to Bonaparte. " In
justice to Her Majesty, I must say that I have seen,

I should be sorry, however, if your Majesty mistook this frankness of mine
for a threat. No ; if it had suited my plans to make war on the King
of Naples, I should have done so on the first appearance of the Russians
in Corfu, as a cautious policy would have required. But I desire peace
with Naples, with all Europe, with England even, and I fear war with no
one. I am in a condition to make war on whoever provokes me, and to
punish the Court of Naples, without fear of the resentment of any one.
Let your Majesty receive this advice from a kind brother, let her recall
the leaders of the militia ;[1] let her not provoke any species of armament ;
let her dismiss the French who excite her against their country, recall
from St. Petersburg a minister, all whose movements tend to injure the
affairs of Naples, and to put her in imminent danger ; let her dismiss
Mr. Elliot, who only frames plots for assassinations, and excites all the
manœuvres of Naples ; let her give her confidence to the head of her
house, and I venture to say, to myself; and let her not be so much her
own enemy as to ruin a kingdom which she has retained amidst so great
an overturn, in which so many states have perished. I do not pay court
to your Majesty by this letter. It will be disagreeable to you. Nevertheless, you may see in it a proof of my esteem. It is only to a person
of a strong and superior mind that I should take the trouble to write
with so much frankness. Rest assured that I pray God, Madam, my
sister and cousin, that He may have you in his holy keeping,

"(Signed)   NAPOLEON.

" *Paris, this Nivose, year* 13.—*January* 1805. "

---

[1] Chefs des milices : Napoleon probably intended chefs de *masse*, as
the leaders of the armed population of the Calabrias were styled.

under General Acton's own handwriting, in a letter to
the Queen, his approbation of the offer made to France
of an annual subsidy of six millions of French livres.
(Sorry I am to add, that from many other parts of
this minister's private correspondence with Her Majesty,
I have but too much reason to observe that both his
temper and his judgment are impaired, from the mortification attending the decline of his influence at this
Court, a circumstance which he ought to have foreseen
as the natural consequence of his ill-advised retreat from
the capital.") [1]

Mr. Elliot's influence with the Queen increased, as
she had occasion to observe the soundness and independence of the advice he gave her. He spent hours
in conference with her and her ministers, and not a day
passed without her writing to him.

Numbers of her letters lie before me, some written
in moments of intense agitation, others on the most
trivial occasions ; but, in almost all there are some
characteristic traits which account for the influence the
Queen obtained over those whom she could not dupe.
She carried into her intercourse with the persons in her
confidence the charm of a kindly bonhommie, of a high
spirit, and of the indiscretion which looks so like, but is
not, trust. Love of children was a marked feature in her

---

[1] In another despatch he says :—" The weakness of General Acton
towards the Queen is such, that I am certain of his laying before her,
in his confidential letters, the substance of whatever I might communi-
cate to him, with any colouring which he might think the most agreeable to her feelings at the moment."

character,[1] and there are not, among some hundred
letters, half-a-dozen without a kindly mention of Mr.
Elliot's youthful family—" Comment vont les chers les
intéréssans enfants ?"   " Que les chers enfants prient
pour moi."   " Mes amitiés à l'excellente Madame Elliot
et à la charmante petite colonie."   " Je suis touchée de
l'amitié des enfants."   These and similar phrases recur
perpetually in letters containing the most important information, and often half illegible from the emotion of
the writer.

Almost as numerous are the words of praise and
affection lavished on Lord Nelson :—" Que fait il, où est
il, mon héros—le brave et digne Nelson ?"   The sight
of an English sloop, a vessel of war, carrying despatches
to Nelson, and beating out of port in a high sea, and in
the teeth of a heavy gale, brought an admiring note
from the Queen :—" Je l'ai suivi avec mes lunettes,
et mes vœux accompagnaient le vaisseau et les matelots
Anglais.   Courage, enthusiasme, sentiments de devoir
sont des qualités qui font un grand peuple."

Queen Caroline attached great importance to personal interviews with all those who, however remotely,
were engaged in her service.   Not content with letters
from Lord Nelson, or with the information conveyed in
his despatches to Mr. Elliot, she frequently chose to see
the officers in command of the vessels despatched by

---

[1] She was the mother of seventeen children, and their birthdays and
fête-days are always mentioned.   " No business to-morrow, because it
is the birthday of my dear little Leopold."   " I suffer in body and
spirit, but I must take the children to Caserta, as they expect it,"
etc. etc.

him to carry his correspondence to Naples. On one
occasion Mr. Elliot informed her the captain would
not be able to wait upon her, having no suitable dress
in which to appear before Her Majesty. Her answer
was short :—" Que me fait l'habit ? Je veux voir l'homme,
présentez le." In one of the Queen's notes she begs
Mr. Elliot to come to her, to hear from herself the
expression of her admiration for the humane action he
had so gloriously performed.

A graphic, and I believe a perfectly correct account
of the adventure referred to, is to be found in Madame
de Staël's novel of *Corinne*, where the hero sees a man
struggling in the waves of a stormy sea, and after
vain attempts to induce any of the lazzaroni to go to
his assistance, plunges into the sea himself, and finally
succeeds in swimming ashore with the man whose life
he had saved; but not until his own strength was so
nearly spent that the bystanders at first believed it
could not be restored.

A note to *Corinne* tells us that the action attributed
to Oswald had been actually performed by Mr. Elliot,
British minister at Naples, and his family possess a
record of the fact in the shape of a small volume of
sonnets, in four languages, composed in honour of what
is termed his heroic conduct.

For a short period there ensued a respite in the
system of bullying by which Bonaparte sought to intimidate Naples, but early in the spring of 1805 it was
intimated to their Sicilian Majesties that the appointment of the Count de Damas to the command of the

Neapolitan army was viewed with grave displeasure at Paris. The excitement which this announcement created at Naples was shortly afterwards increased to the highest pitch by the arrival of an aide-de-camp from General St. Cyr, demanding the disarmament of the levies in Calabria, the cessation of further recruiting for the Neapolitan army, the removal of Mr. Elliot, and the dismissal of Count Damas.

For some weeks ministers consulted, messengers went to and fro; De Gallo was ordered to remonstrate at Paris, Prince Cardito was sent to treat with General St. Cyr, and the Queen's agitated feelings found vent in daily notes to, and interviews with, Mr. Elliot.

"26 *Janvier* 1805.

"Nous sommes une autre fois dans les horreurs menacées des troupes Bonapartiennes. St. Cyr nous a decoché son adjutant, avec l'ordre précis en trois jours, qui s'ecoulent demain, d'avoir une réponse, ayant ordre de prendre des mesures fortes, les points sont : désarmemens, récrutation, éloignez M. Elliot, exilez Damas. Cardito part ce soir pour la Pouille à rabattre les points impossibles, et sa réponse décidera la chose que dans mon cœur et âme je crois décidée. Je vous prie brulez mes lettres car je crains les gentillesses impériales de ces vils esclaves, qui ne désirent que de me compromettre, et se venger sur moi, mais je suis décidée à les braver, et à risquer d'augmenter le nombre de leurs crimes. Je préfère la mort au malheur d'être l'esclave d'un tel être. Mes com-

pliments à Mad^{e.} Elliot et aux chers enfants, et croyez
moi pour la vie votre sincère amie,[1]   CHARLOTTE.

"21 *Fevrier* 1805.

" La réponse de Cardito est arrivée.   St. Cyr a sus-
pendu toute démarche jusqu'à la réponse du Grand
Bonaparte qui ne peut tarder.   J'avoue que je suis
revoltée de ces manières de barbare que l'on se permet
vers nous, et que je ferois volontiers de tout pour nous
en soustraire.

" Enfin nous attendrons encore cette crise que j'espère
s'eventera comme les précédentes; il est affreux
d'être si fort abaissé que de devoir souffrir la loi d'un tel
homme, mais c'est l'ouvrage de ses amis, et encore plus
de ses demis ennemis, et cela me rend la vie et l'existence odieuse depuis longtemps.   Si je n'avais pas
des enfants, et une famille (et je parle à un bon Père
qui me comprend) j'aurais quitté tout, et un trône avili
par celui qui y est monté, mais il faut songer à nos

---

[1] [TRANSLATION.]

" 20th *January* 1805.

" We are again in all the horror of being menaced by the Bona-
partist troops.   St. Cyr has sent his adjutant, with strict orders in three
days, which expire to-morrow, to have a reply, ordering strong measures ;
the points are—disarmament, cease recruiting, remove Mr. Elliot, exile
Damas.   Cardito sets out this evening for Apulia, to beat down the impossible points, and his reply will decide what in my heart and soul I
think decided.   I entreat you to burn my letters, for I fear the imperial
tricks of these vile slaves, who only desire to compromise me and to be
revenged on me ; but I am resolved to brave them and to risk augmenting
the number of their crimes.   I prefer death to the unhappiness of being
the slave of such a being.   My compliments to Mrs. Elliot and to the
dear children, and believe me, your sincere friend,   CHARLOTTE."

enfants, et comme nous n'avons jamais thésaurisés, ni amassé des ressources, il faut souffrir, mourir de peine, pour leur laisser une existence. Pardon, mais la confiance et la plénitude du cœur m'ont fait écrire cet episode," etc. etc.[1]　　　　　　　　　　　" C."

" Je crois que le régicide Alquier veut nous intimider. Je n'aime pas la vie du tout, je ne m'en soucie pas du tout; ils me l'ont fait haïr."[2]

"Je vous avoue que je suis revoltée de vivre ainsi sous le couteau de telles gens et je ferois de tout volontiers pour en sortir.

" Ne croyez aucune nouvelle, aucun propos, on les dénature. Venez à moi toujours avec confiance. Vous

---

[1] [TRANSLATION.]

" 21st February.

" The reply of Cardito has arrived. St. Cyr has suspended all action till the answer of the Great Bonaparte, which cannot be delayed. I confess that I am disgusted by these barbarous manners, which they permit themselves towards us, and which I would willingly do anything to escape. In short, we yet await this crisis, which I hope may be averted like its predecessors. It is dreadful to be so abased, to be in the power of such a man; but it is the work of his friends, and still more of his half enemies, and that has long since rendered life and existence odious to me. If I had not children and a family (and I speak to a kind father who understands me) I would have quitted all, and a throne dishonoured by him who has ascended it; but we must think of our children, and as we have never hoarded nor amassed resources, it is necessary for us to suffer, to die of misery, to leave them an existence. Forgive me; confidence and the fulness of my heart have made me write this episode," etc. etc.　　　　　　　　　　　"C."

[2] " I think that the regicide Alquier wishes to intimidate us. I do not love life at all. I do not care for it at all; it has been made hateful to me."

saurez toujours l'exacte verité; ma loyauté est inchange-
able, autant que mes sentimens sont *pour la vie.*"[1]

Iu one of these letters a remarkable phrase occurs:
—"Dieu préserve le royaume dans les mains de notre
tyran. *On serait étonné avec la bouche béante, hors moi,
des ressources qu'il en tirerait.*"[2]

The French Government at last yielded on three out
of the four points originally insisted on, but they accompanied the concession with a positive command for the immediate dismissal of Count Damas, which even the Queen
could not disregard. The shell has burst—" La bombe
est crevée," she wrote to Mr. Elliot. " Le coquin Alquier
donnera une note officielle si Damas à midi n'est point
parti. L'ordre est venu à St. Cyr pour qu'il prenne d'abord
la position d'Ariano et traite le pays en pays conquis.
Ainsi il faut bien donner un congé à Damas. Je suis
au déséspoir, humiliée, enragée, consternée. Nous re-
tarderons mais n'éviterons point nos malheurs. Adieu.—
Votre amie pour la vie,   CHARLOTTE."[3]

<hr/>

[1] [TRANSLATION.]

"I confess to you that I revolt at living under the knife of such
people, and I would willingly do anything to escape it.

"Do not believe any tidings, any reports, they are falsified. Come
to me always with confidence. You shall always know the exact truth;
my loyalty is unchangeable, as my sentiments are *for life.*"

[2] "May God preserve the kingdom in the hands of our tyrant. *The
resources which he would draw from it would fill any one but myself
with amazement.*"

[3] "The shell has burst. . . . The rascal Alquier will give an
official note if Damas has not set off at noon. St. Cyr has received
orders to take the position of Ariano at once, and to treat the country
as conquered. Thus it is necessary to dismiss Damas. I am in despair,

Prince Cardito was informed by General St. Cyr that
he had orders to seize Count Damas' person whenever
this could be effected by a detachment from the French
army, without paying any respect to the rights of sovereignty of the King of Naples. The alleged offence of
Count Damas was his having used indiscreet language
against Bonaparte; but "it is only just to say," wrote
Mr. Elliot to his government, "that considerable activity
and energy have been displayed in the military department since he was placed at its head."

The representative of Naples at the Court of St.
James' was desired to express his sovereign's sense of
the wisdom and discretion of Mr. Elliot's advice during
the crisis, and for some time the Queen signed her notes
to himself, "Votre reconnaissante amie."[1]

humbled, enraged, alarmed. We may retard, but we cannot avoid, our
misfortunes. Adieu.—Your friend for life,   CHARLOTTE."

[1] During the crisis a messenger was despatched to London "apparently" to ask for Mr. Elliot's recall—an application which produced
the following reply from Lord Mulgrave to Prince Castelcicala :—

"*Downing Street, 3d April* 1805.

" The undersigned has the honour to acknowledge the receipt of the
official note of His Sicilian Majesty's Envoy Extraordinary and Minister
Plenipotentiary of the 2d instant, which has been laid before the King.

" No specified cause of complaint against any part of the conduct
of Mr. Elliot having been stated in the above-mentioned note, His
Majesty would have been at a loss to conceive the ground on which a
request could have been made by His Sicilian Majesty for the recall of a
minister whose zeal, diligence, and distinguished talents in the
discharge of the duties of his mission had merited and secured the
expression of His Majesty's fullest approbation, and whose respectful
attachment to the persons of their Sicilian Majesties had so fully
answered the views and expectations with which His Majesty had

The English minister did not hesitate to advise concession when concessions were inevitable or immaterial,
but he was compelled still more frequently to counsel a
more courageous and straightforward policy than the
Neapolitan Court was prepared to adopt. Their councils fluctuated between rashness and servility, and provoked the indignities which were heaped upon them.

"Les gens timides," he wrote to the Queen, "qui
se croient prudents par excellence, continueront de
crier, Cédez, cédez, tout ce que la perfidie peut demander
comme gage de sa tranquilité. J'avoue que je suis
d'un sentiment différent, et que je crois que l'on risque
moins de voir avancer les français en refusant d'accorder
des concessions disgracieuses et fatales, qu'en faisant
des sacrifices journaliers qui ne font qu'augmenter le
désir d'en exiger d'autres." [1]

conferred on Mr. Elliot the mission to the Court of Naples. The
recent information, however, which has been transmitted to his
Majesty by Mr. Elliot has apprised His Majesty of the source from
whence the demand has arisen."

The despatch goes on to state that while the King would always
comply cheerfully with the genuine wishes of His Sicilian Majesty in
regard to the withdrawal of a minister who might have rendered
himself personally objectionable to the King of Naples, he could
not, consistently with a proper regard to his own dignity, with a just
attention to the rights of neutral and independent sovereigns, or an
adequate consideration of the established laws of nations, consent to withdraw his minister from a neutral and friendly court at the imperious
mandate of an enemy, etc.

[1] [TRANSLATION.]

" Timid people, who think themselves superlatively prudent,
will continue to cry, Yield, yield—all that perfidy can demand as a
pledge of tranquillity. I confess that I am of a different way of

On another occasion, when Bonaparte had shown
an inclination to try the effect of cajolery upon the
recalcitrant court of Naples, the Queen wrote—
"Heureuse Angleterre, protegée par la mer de ce fléau
du Continent."[1] Mr. Elliot replied, "Ne croyez pas,
madame, que l'Angleterre doit son bonheur à vingt et
un milles de mer qui séparent notre isle de la France.

"Nous devons notre bonheur à nos sentiments
d'honneur et de probité, à notre courage, à notre
industrie, et notre nationalité; et surtout à notre
profonde connaissance de la France et de ses habitans.
Nous savons que l'on risque moins à être ses ennemis
ouverts et avoués qu'à être exposés aux dangers de
recevoir de leur part de ces baisers fraternels dans
lesquels ils ne manquent jamais d'emporter la pièce."[2]

The coronation of Bonaparte as King of Italy took
place in the summer; and the determination of the
Neapolitan Court not to acknowledge the new title

thinking; and I think that there is less risk of seeing the French
advance when disgraceful and fatal concessions are refused than when
daily sacrifices are made, which only augment the desire to exact
others."

[TRANSLATION.]

[1] "Happy England, protected by the sea from this scourge of the
Continent!"

[2] "Do not think, madam, that England owes her happiness to
the twenty-one miles of sea which separate our isle from France.

"We owe our happiness to our sentiments of honour and probity,
to our courage, to our industry, and to our nationality, and, above all,
to our profound knowledge of France and her inhabitants. We know
that there is less risk in being her open and avowed enemies than in
being exposed to the danger of receiving those fraternal kisses, whilst
bestowing which she never fails to carry off the prize."

except in concert with the Court of Vienna, brought a
torrent of invectives on their heads. The Emperor
spoke publicly of the Queen of Naples, who was
known to have counselled the policy adopted by the
King in opposition to the advice of his ministers, in
the most violent language, of which she wrote as
follows :—

" 9 Juin 1805.

"En publique, au cercle, l'Empereur-Roi a tenu
des propos indécens sur nous, et moi en particulier, à
nos ministres, au point que Cardito dit ne le vouloir
revoir de la vie, ni s'y exposer plus ; il a formellement
declaré que si pour le 16 de Juin il ne reçoit la Reconnaissance à Bologne où il se trouvera, il cessera toute
communication avec ce pays et nous traitera comme pays
ennemi.

.   .   .   " Nous tenons ferme malgré ces menaces
de ne point reconnaître avant que l'Empereur ne
reconnaisse. Comme nous sommes les deux seules
Puissances en Italie point encore asserviés, je m'attends
de ce Corse enragé et heureux, toutes les folies et
démences, trahisons et violences. Mais que pouvons
nous y faire ? Si ne point provoquer, comme sans
discontinuer, la Russie, Vienne, et l'Angleterre nous
prêchent, signifie plier, il faudra le reconnaître, sauf,
malgré cet avilissement, avoir le sort de Parme, Gênes,
et Lucques.—Croyez moi pour la vie et jusqu'au
tombeau votre sincère amie,   CHARLOTTE.[1]

[1] [TRANSLATION].   " June 9th 1805.
" In public, at the levée, the Emperor-King has made indecent

"On ne parle que des horreurs, des menaces que le forcéné Corse a crié en publique contre moi ; mais il ne sait pas que c'est réellement me décorer de la Légion d'Honneur, que de ne me pas compter parmi le nombre de ses bas et vils adulateurs."[1] In spite of which brave words, the Queen fell ill of rage and mortification; and, while unable to admit Mr. Elliot to her presence, she wrote to him "that she would fly to America with her family if any one would only give her two millions sterling to go there; that she would even prefer to spend her life on the mountains of Scotland than to throne it in Naples as Bonaparte's slave—"esclave de ce maudit Corse—de ce Corse rusé."

remarks on us, and particularly on me, to our ministers, to such a degree that Cardito said he would never willingly see him again, nor expose himself to a repetition of it. He has formally declared that if, by the 16th of June, he does not receive the recognition at Bologna, where he will be, all communication with this country will cease, and he will treat us like enemies.

. . . "We remain firm, in spite of these threats, in not recognising him before the Emperor[2] has done so. As we are the only two Powers in Italy that are not yet enslaved, I expect from this furious and fortunate Corsican all sorts of follies and falsehoods, treasons and violences. But what can we do? If *not to provoke*, as Russia, Vienna, and England preach to us without ceasing, signifies to *bow*, it will be necessary to acknowledge him, lest, notwithstanding this caution, we incur the fate of Parma, Genoa, and Lucca.—Believe me to be for life, and to the grave, your sincere friend, 　　　　　CHARLOTTE."

[1] "Nothing is talked of but the horrors—the threats that the furious Corsican has blustered forth in public against me; but he does not know that not to count me amongst his low and vile flatterers is truly to decorate me with the Legion of Honour."

---

[2] Of Austria.

The institution of the order of the Iron Crown drew from her some sarcastic remarks :—" Josephine aussi crée un ordre—une étoile qui se porte sur la poitrine. Moi je lui donne la devise, Honni soi qui mal *n'en* pense."[1]

The return of Prince Cardito with verbal accounts of his reception by the Emperor gave the Queen a second attack of fever, and she thus describes her ambassador :— " Cardito est revenu exactement comme avec tant d'esprit vous l'aviez prédit—ébloui de la force, de la grandeur de Buonaparte, le trouvant détestable; mais n'y trouvant aucun remède—aucun moyen de le vaincre. Enfin, il est revenu plus Napolitain qu'il n'est parti. Les pauvres gens !—il faut les sauver malgré eux."[2]

All the vials of the destroying angel seemed to be outpoured on Naples in the year 1805. In July an earthquake destroyed more than 4000 of the inhabitants of the kingdom. "Had the oscillations of the earth lasted another second, it is the opinion of persons qualified to form one, that all this great capital would have been destroyed."

The earthquake was felt at ten o'clock at night, caus-

---

[1] [TRANSLATION.]

" Josephine has also created an order—a star which is worn on the breast. I give her this motto for it—'Evil be to him who does *not* think evil of it.' "

[2] " Cardito has returned exactly in the state of mind you predicted—dazzled by the strength, the greatness of Bonaparte, finding him detestable, but finding no remedy, no means of conquering him. In short, he has returned more Neapolitan than he set out. Poor people ! they must be saved in spite of themselves."

ing the inhabitants of Naples to pass what the Queen
called " *une vilaine nuit.*" She wrote the next morning
to Mr. Elliot that the shock had found her at her
writing-table, in the act of fixing an hour on the following day for an interview with him. The King was at
Portici, the Hereditary Prince and his wife at Caserta;
it became her duty, she wrote, to think, as far as the
powers of thought left her allowed her to do, how best
to secure the safety of her beloved children and grand-
children. Calling them around her, they spent the
night together in an open court of the palace, every
moment expecting to be overwhelmed with ruins. At
the British Legation an evening party had been going
on, when floors began to tremble, walls to rock, lights
went out; and in a moment card-tables were deserted,
guests fled, children rushed from their beds, a cripple
found his legs, the instinct of every one leading him
to seek safety in the open street. The thoughts of
many turned to the ships at anchor in the harbour, and
Mr. Elliot lost no time in placing the English man-of-
war at the Queen's disposal, but the sight of the agitated
sea was less re-assuring even than the earth when the
momentary disturbance was past.

In August followed a violent eruption of Mount
Vesuvius, when a stream of lava reached the sea at Torre
del Greco, while two other branches came even nearer to
the town of Naples; and through all the miseries and
alarms of the time the Queen sighed for vengeance, till
at last it seemed within her grasp.

She had ever chafed under the policy of the neutrality,

" que nous prêchent l'Angleterre, la Russie, et l'Autriche.
Buonaparte a un plan fixe, le suit avec opiniâtreté, fermeté, avec ruse, profitant des faiblesses, des sottises des
autres, et les petits en seront les victimes.   Nous, les
premiers; tout cela me met la mort dans le cœur."

Russia and England having formed an alliance against
France in the spring of 1805, had proposed to themselves,
among other objects, the entire evacuation of Italy by
the French, and with this view both Powers despatched
troops to the Mediterranean, with orders to act in concert.   A Russian minister, M. de Tatitscheff, to whom
large powers had been given by the Court of St. Petersburg, arrived in Naples in the month of July 1805.
From that time Mr. Elliot's influence waned.   The
Queen's hopes turned to Russia, as to the Power most
able and ready to strike the blow which she so longed
to inflict.

A long series of intrigues between certain individuals
of her special society, and certain other individuals connected with the Russian nobility, threw the new minister
from Russia into her toils; and it is probable that the
desire of committing Russia to more extensive measures
of hostility towards Bonaparte than were consistent
with the policy of England, led her to foment an amount
of mistrust between the ministers of the two great Powers
sufficient to prevent them from coinciding in a policy
which might thwart her own.[1]   In the beginning of the
year the Queen had placed in the hands of the English
representative, " considering him not so much as a mini-

---

[1] See Appendix, No. IV.

ster as a friend," a secret correspondence with her agents
in Russia, representing that government as full of jealousy
and mistrust of the objects of England in the Mediterranean.[1] At the very time when she was concocting
with M. de Tatitscheff a convention for the employment
of an Anglo-Russian force, her French adherents were
busily employed in suggesting causes of jealousy and
mistrust of England and her representative to General
Lacy, the commander of the Russian force, by whom
these underhand dealings were exposed to Mr. Elliot.[2]

To the Russian Convention [3] Mr. Elliot refused to be
a party, on the ground that its objects went beyond
those which his Government had instructed him to
pursue. Mr. Elliot's efforts, since his first coming to
Naples, where " he had stood alone and unsupported by
the minister of any other foreign power," had been calculated solely to maintain the security of the Two
Sicilies, by yielding as much as possible in every in-

---

[1] This is a very remarkable transaction. The Queen, early in 1805,
placed in Mr. Elliot's hands confidential letters to herself from the
Duke of Serra-Capriola, minister of Naples at St. Petersburg, in which
it was stated that the Court of St. Petersburg thoroughly mistrusted
British objects in the Mediterranean, and warned Naples especially of
England's designs on Sicily. The Queen permitted Mr. Elliot to send
home copies to his Government, on the positive assurance that such a step
would be kept from the knowledge of her own representative in England,
and would be confided simply to the King and his confidential servants.
This information, when received in England, seems to have taken Lord
Mulgrave, Foreign Secretary, completely by surprise.

[2] General Lacy, a straightforward old soldier, of Irish extraction,
and, at the time he reached Naples, of the advanced age of eighty.

[3] September 21, 1805.

stance which might have committed its neutrality, and by encouraging, on the other hand, the adoption of every secret measure for profiting of the internal resources of the provinces with a view to their own defence." The objects of the Russo-Neapolitan Convention seemed to him to be widely different, while it was apparent to him that the very small proportion of English forces to be employed in any combined movements would necessitate their implication in undertakings, possibly in disasters, over which they would exercise no control. Coalitions and contingents were not to his taste; he considered that England, by her fleets, her subsidies, and her counsels which, at all events up to the summer of 1805, had been crowned with success, had done her part towards maintaining the independence of the kingdom of the Two Sicilies; that if military operations on the Continent, and on a great scale, were deemed advisable, Russia, a great military power, bound to Naples by earlier treaties, should take the lead and the responsibility. Unhappily, an Anglo-Russian armament, to be placed under the supreme command of General Lacy, was decided on.

The Russian Convention was signed in September, and, in Mr. Elliot's opinion, it led to all the fatal consequences which afterwards ensued. The King of Naples, who, though in secret, was a party to it, was shortly afterwards forced by the menaces of France to ratify a treaty of neutrality with France, on the faith of which the army of General St. Cyr vacated the Neapolitan dominions; and on the day following that of the ratification of the

French treaty, the King was prevailed on to give M. de
Tatistcheff a declaration under his sign-manual, which
annulled the validity of his prior signature with France,
and by which he called for the disembarkation of the
foreign troops in the kingdom of Naples for the protection of his dominions.

These disgraceful acts of perfidy were kept as far as
possible from the knowledge of Mr. Elliot, who, when
retailing them at a later period[1] to his own Government,
terms them " as disgusting as they were disgraceful.
I have cautiously avoided taking any part in transactions
equally contrary to sound policy and good faith. My
situation has been indeed peculiarly embarrassing, as
there was a manifest inclination in the Russian mission
to ascribe my unwillingness to second these proceedings
to a jealousy of their growing influence, and above all to
a secret view of not opposing the conquest of Naples, in
order to afford a plausible pretext for seizing on Sicily.
Unfortunately, the Queen, who had been goaded by
every species of invective and ill-treatment from Bonaparte, and who was surrounded by individuals either of
mean abilities, or, perhaps, even treacherous incli-
nations, stimulated the Russian minister to precipitate every warlike measure, and carried, by her
influence, the consent of the King, of the hereditary
prince, and the council."

The transactions which to the English minister appeared as foolish as they were unprincipled, were viewed
in a very different light by the Queen, the chief actor in

[1] June 3, 1806.

them. Writing to Mr. Elliot on the day of the disembarkation of the British troops under General Sir
James Craig, she describes herself as prepared, with all
the self-sacrifice of a martyr, to immolate good faith and
honour on the altars of patriotism.

" 20 Nov. 1805.

" Liée à jamais et ouvertement dans ce moment à la
bonne cause, je sens tout le poids énorme d'une respon-
sabilité à travers tant de différentes circonstances, mais
sure du principe pur et honnête comme désinteressé qui
guide nos actions je me laisse blâmer, déchirer, critiquer
pourvu que j'ai le bonheur de sauver à mon epoux et à
nos enfants par l'aide et secours de nos braves alliés leur
patrimoine. Je vous prie d'avoir en moi une confiance
entière. Mon caractère la meritera toujours," etc. etc.[1]

The first news which greeted the English general on
his landing at Naples was that of the capitulation of
Ulm, which had been known there, though carefully concealed from the people, since the beginning of the
month.

On the 4th of November the Queen had written to

---

[1] [TRANSLATION.]

" 20th November 1805.

" Bound ever and openly at this moment to the good cause, I feel
all the enormous weight of a responsibility in so many varied difficulties ;
but certain of the principles, pure and honourable as disinterested,
which guide my actions, I allow myself to be blamed, to be torn in pieces,
to be criticised, provided I have the happiness of saving their patrimony
to my husband and our children by means of the assistance of our brave
allies. I entreat you to place entire confidence in me. My character
will always deserve it."

Mr. Elliot that news of a terrible disaster had reached
them from all quarters; incredible as it appeared, the
Austrian army had succumbed without striking a blow.
She adds—" Le contre coup pour nous sera terrible."

And on the 11th she wrote again :—

" J'ai reçu votre obligeante lettre que j'etais à dîner
avec mes enfants, en famille, pour la fête de St. Martin,
tenant à ces anciens usages du bon vieux temps en
famille, mais mon âme et mon cœur en étaient bien
éloignés.　J'avais reçu un courier de Paris, qui nous
confirme toutes les mauvaises nouvelles, et nous annonce
l'armée Autrichienne détruite.　De Venise on nous dit
qu'il ne passe pas un quart d'heure sans arriver bâteaux
de toutes espèces remplis d'officiers, de soldats qui
évacuent le Vénitien. Nous avons seulement le doute si
c'est à la suite d'une bataille perdue où par la crainte
d'être tournée.

" Masséna est donc libre de se promener où bon lui
semble.　Tout ceci me tient très peinée.　Quelconque
sera mon sort, et celui de ma chère malheureuse famille
je remplirai mes devoirs."[1]

[1] [TRANSLATION.]

" I received your welcome letter when I was dining with my
children, *en famille*, on St. Martin's fête, adhering to the family
usages of the good old times, but my heart and my soul were very far
away.　I had received a messenger from Paris, who confirmed all the
bad news and announced to us the destruction of the Austrian army.
From Venice we learn that a quarter of an hour does not pass without
the arrival of boats of every description, filled by officers and soldiers
who evacuate the Venetian territory.　We are only in doubt whether
it is the result of a lost battle or for fear of being turned.

" Massena is then free to march where he pleases.　All this is very

As is well known, on the news of the capitulation of Ulm, the army of the Archduke Charles evacuated Venetia, in order to share in a combined movement with other portions of the Austrian forces for the purpose of defending Vienna. Consequently, when the Anglo-Russian troops assembled at Naples, they and the army of His Sicilian Majesty were the only forces in the Peninsula opposed to the victorious armies of France.

The only cheering news which reached the Neapolitan Court during the month of November, was the reported victory of Trafalgar; but no details of it were received till the beginning of December, when the fatal intelligence of the death of Nelson produced a note from the Queen, which bears the evidence of genuine feeling (2d December) :—

"J'ai reçu la triste lettre que vous m'avez envoyée. Je n'étais point capable dans le premier saisissement de la douleur de la grande irréparable perte que nous venons de faire, de vous répondre. Donnez-moi tous les détails des évènements qui nous privent du héros que je regretterai toute ma vie. 20 vaisseaux augmentent sa gloire, mais rien ne peut consoler de sa perte. Tant de courage, vertus et modestie, tout cela réuni ne se retrouve plus. Pour lui c'est un bonheur, pour nous un sensible malheur. Adieu. Croyez moi jusqu'au tombeau votre sincère amie,   CHARLOTTE."[1]

painful to me. Whatever may be my fate, and that of my dear un-fortunate family, I shall fulfil my duties."

[1] [TRANSLATION.]

" I received the sad letter which you sent me. I was not capable,

On Christmas day came, along with the news of the battle of Austerlitz and the armistice with Austria, a rumour of the bulletin fulminated by Napoleon from Moravia against the Neapolitan dynasty (25th December 1805).

"Ces bulletins m'ont atterrée," wrote the Queen. "Je veux encore me flatter que ces fatals bulletins n'étaient pas signés — ne soient point authentiques; mais une voix interne me le dit, et me fait reconnaitre la manière de s'exprimer, et me fait trembler de la verité du reste. Si ce debaudage (sic) a eu lieu, si tout cela a été, nous sommes perdus sans retour! . . . À votre digne épouse et à l'aimable petite colonie bien des complimens pour la fête de Noël."[2]

The immediate consequence of this disastrous news was the retreat of the Anglo-Russian force from the frontiers to the neighbourhood of Naples, the commanders of both armies uniting in a declaration to the

in the first shock of grief for the irreparable loss we had sustained, of replying to it. Give me all the details of the events that have deprived us of a hero whom 1 shall regret all my life. Twenty vessels may augment his glory, but nothing can console for his loss. So much courage, virtue, and modesty—all this united iu one individual, is not to be found again. For him it is happiness, for us a heavy misfortune. Adieu. Believe me even to the grave your sincere friend,   CHARLOTTE."

[2] " These bulletins have overwhelmed me. I wish still to flatter myself that these fatal bulletins were not signed—are not authentic ; but an internal voice tells me they are so, and makes me recognise the mode of expression, and makes me tremble that they are true. If this disaster has taken place, if all this has been, we are lost beyond redemption ! . . To your respected wife, and to the amiable little colony, the compliments of the Christmas season."

King that such was the only course they could pursue under circumstances which they stated in detail.

The utter want of any information, beyond that which reached them through French sources, added greatly to the difficulties with which the commanders had to contend.

" I would give £5000 for reliable information," wrote Sir J. Craig to Mr. Elliot, on the 30th December. " My despatches from Lord Castlereagh come no lower than the 16th October, and for anything I can extract from them, either useful or agreeable, they might just as well have remained in his lordship's secretaire to this moment. I cannot comprehend what they are about."

The retreat of the allied force greatly exasperated the Court, and the following note from Sir James Craig to Mr. Elliot, written immediately after the generals had held a council of war, at which it had been resolved that the allied armies should continue for the present to cover the town of Naples, shows what were the feelings of the Queen towards her English allies, and shows too that, under her violent abuse of his countrymen, the spirit of the English minister began to chafe.

" *Monday, 6th January, Naples.*

" I lose not a moment in acquainting you with the result of an interesting conversation which I have this instant finished with General Opperman. . . . For the present we shall remain where we are, and it is probable that, if the French advance, we may gratify —— with the sight of a battle, but that may still depend on a future circumstance. For God's sake do not give up

your connection and influence in that quarter, and take
an opportunity of saying how much injustice is done to
me," etc. etc.

Two days later an aide-de-camp of the Emperor Alexander reached Naples, with positive orders for the immediate embarkation of the Russian troops, and their return
to Corfu.

As soon as Sir J. Craig learned that the Russians
had irrevocably decided on withdrawing from Naples,
he proceeded to embark his own troops, justly considering that the presence of 7000 British troops, unsupported by any reliable force, in the midst of a population
indifferent if not unfriendly, could be no effectual check
to the advance of the French armies. But he offered to
put his force at the disposal of the Neapolitan King for
the defence, in conjunction with our fleets, of the island
of Sicily—a proposal which was received by the Government of Naples with the most violent indignation, while
M. de Tatistcheff distinctly informed Mr. Elliot that the
Russian force would, under no contingency, co-operate
with Great Britain in the defence of Sicily.

Some difference of opinion existed at this time
between Mr. Elliot and General Craig as to the course
to be pursued by the latter under the existing circumstances. The Government of Naples was endeavouring
to obtain from Massena an armistice of forty days, for
the purpose of entering into negotiations with Bonaparte,
on the basis of an abdication by the King, Ferdinard IV.,
in favour of the hereditary prince ; and it was believed`
that such propositions would be supported by Russia and

Spain. The Court believed, or professed to believe, that the presence of their allies in the neighbourhood of Naples would have greatly aided the probability of a successful termination to their negotiations; and when that hope was withdrawn, they strenuously urged on the English minister and general the importance of abstaining from any action in the direction of Sicily which could furnish a pretext to the French for seizing on the Neapolitan dominions.   Mr. Elliot appears to have thought the negotiations at one time promised success; to Sir James Craig they from the first appeared utterly futile; and bearing in mind the instructions he had received from his own Government to prevent, with or without the concurrence of His Sicilian Majesty, the French from effecting a landing in Sicily, he determined to steer his course for the Straits of Messina, there to await the progress of events.   The feelings of the Court on the occasion are fully described in the following letters from the Queen to Mr. Elliot :—

"10 *Janvier* 1806.

" Dans ce moment arrive un courier de Moravie. Je m'empresse de vous l'envoyer et de m'informer de votre santé. Je souhaite un bon voyage au Général Craig, et qu'aucune tempête en mer n'augmente ses craintes, et je n'oublierai de ma vie sa visite.—Adieu."[1]

[1] [TRANSLATION.]

"10*th January* 1806.

" A courier has just arrived from Moravia.   I hasten to send him to you and to bring me news of your health.   I wish General Craig a good voyage, and that no tempest may augment his fears, and I shall not, while I live, forget his visit. —Adieu !"

" 19*th January.*

" Vous serez le maitre de venir quand vous voudrez les mouvemens sont de trop d'importance, pour ne vouloir vous voir. Je vois l'escadre à la voile—j'espère qu'à toute la conduite exécrable tenue envers nous, elle n'essaiera pas d'entrer de violence au Sicile—pour empêcher tout accomodement, nous perdre et notre famille sans ressource. Je viens de recevoir les lettres de Rome du 18. Nous devons nous attendre à toutes les infamies avanies pour prix de la couteuse et courte visite Anglo-Russe. Certes que nos cœurs sont révoltés; jamais on n'a été si loyal, et si digne que nous l'avons été. Combien je plains ceux qui pensent honteusement; et je suis, avec bien de l'estime, votre sincère　　　　CHARLOTTE."[1]

In a despatch of Mr. Elliot's to Sir J. Craig, of the the same date, 19th January, he wrote that he was instructed by the Neapolitan Government to assure Sir James that an attempt to take possession of any part of Sicily without the King's concurrence would be con-

---

[1] [TRANSLATION.]

" 19*th January.*

" You are at liberty to come when you choose. The movements are of too much importance for me not to wish to see you. I see the squadron under sail. I hope that to all the execrable conduct exhibited towards us there is not to be added an attempt to enter Sicily by force —to make all arrangement impossible, to ruin us and our family beyond redemption. I have just received letters from Rome of the 18th. We must expect every infamous insult as the price of the costly and brief Anglo-Russian visit.

" Certainly our hearts are revolted; never has any one been so loyal and so honourable as we have been. How I pity those who think shamefully; and I am, with much esteem, your sincere

" CHARLOTTE."

sidered an act of open hostility, tending inevitably to the
conquest of Naples by the French. That the tone
adopted by the Court was by no means palatable to
the Minister, may be gathered from a letter addressed
to him by the Queen on the 26th January.

"*26th Janvier.*

"L'affligéant silence et absence, que tant comme
ministre d'Angleterre, que comme chévalier Elliot, vous
gardez avec moi, dans des moments aussi affreux, et où
toute notre conduite ne meritait point d'être entrainée,
ce morne silence, je le romps pour vous demander quelle
nouvelle vous avez de l'escadre de Collingwood. Le ciel
dans sa colère nous a privés du respectable ami Lord
Nelson, pour être en but à tous les malheurs. Les
miens sont à leur comble; mais je remplirai mes pénibles
devoirs jusqu'à la tombe. Vous saurez toutes les nouvelles de Rome mieux que moi. Je me borne à vous
demander quelle nouvelle vous avez de l'escadre de Brest
et de Collingwood; et croyez moi, avec bien de l'estime,
votre affectionnée,   C."[1]

[1] [TRANSLATION.]

"*26th January.*

"The distressing silence and absence, which, both as English
minister and as Mr. Elliot, you maintain towards me in this dreadful
condition, into which we did not deserve to fall, this gloomy silence I
now break to ask what tidings you have of Collingwood's squadron.
Heaven in its anger has deprived us of our respected friend, Lord Nelson,
to leave us a mark for every misfortune. My troubles are at their height,
but I will fulfil my painful duty till death.

"You know all the Roman news better than I do. I confine myself
to asking you what news you have of the squadron of Brest and of
Collingwood. Believe me, with much esteem, your affectionate   C."

A few days later, the return of the Duke of San Teodoro with the news of the failure of the negotiations showed that all was over.

> "30 *Janvier*.

> "La journée d'hier," wrote the Queen, "a été pour moi si orageuse et douleureuse que je n'ai été capable de rien.   Le retour de San Teodoro, les infames nouvelles qu'il apporte decident de notre sort et de ce malheureux et beau pays."[1]

On the 4th of February the French crossed the frontier, and on the 11th the Queen fled to Palermo—where the King had already preceded her—and Sir James Craig and his army were put in possession of the fortress of Messina.   "Sir James Craig," wrote Mr. Elliot, "with a degree of patience and forbearance which does equal credit to himself and to his army, conformed to the wishes of His Sicilian Majesty, and not a soldier landed in Sicily before the French had passed the frontiers of the kingdom of Naples.   One material object was gained by this deference to the right of sovereignty of His Sicilian Majesty, that when the British troops took possession of Messina, it was not only with the concurrence, but at the requisition of the King, and neither malevolence nor prejudice can cast an aspersion on the good faith of the British nation."

---

[1] [TRANSLATION.]

> "30*th January*.

"Yesterday was to me so stormy and so painful that I have not been fit for anything.   The return of San Teodoro, the infamous news which he brings decide our fate, and that of this unhappy and beautiful country."

Mr. Elliot accompanied the Queen to Palermo, and how altered were the relations of the Queen and the English representative, may be gathered from a note she addressed to him immediately after her arrival :—

"Je désire savoir de votre santé et de votre intéressante famille, dans le pénible voyage que vous venez de faire. Il m'est très sensible de ne vous avoir ni vu, ni même reçu une ligne de votre part après y avoir été si accoutumée, et cela dans mes affreuses et cruelles circonstances, où je suis navrée, atterée par tout ce qui est fait pour me rendre malheureuse. Ce n'est pas dans ce moment que je m'attendais du Chevalier Elliot, du ministre Britannique un tel oubli. Si la politique ou de fausses idées dont le temps prouvera la fausseté en soit le motif, j'attends de ce même temps qu'il vous force à reconnaître le caractère de celle qui sera toujours votre affectionée et sincère amie,   CHARLOTTE."[1]

The meeting of the Queen and of Acton was a scene of violent recrimination and tears, and the struggle for power between them was as keen as in their better days; but the flight of the Neapolitan army under

---

[1] [TRANSLATION.]

"I desire to know of your health and of that of your interesting family, in the trying voyage that you have just made. I feel very much, neither having seen you, nor even received a line from you, after having been so used to do both ; and this in my dreadful and cruel circumstances, when I am overwhelmed, struck down by all that is done to render me miserable. It is not at a time like this that I expected such forgetfulness from Mr. Elliot, from the British minister. If policy or false ideas, of which time will prove the falsity, are the cause, I expect that this same time will force you to know the character of her who will always be your affectionate and sincere friend,   CHARLOTTE."

Damas from Calabria was for a time decisive against
the influence of the Queen; it was ignominious as
well as disastrous, and as the defence of the provinces
had, like all other warlike measures, been warmly
advocated by her, her influence over the King's mind
was for a moment profoundly shaken. Taking
advantage of this state of feeling to withdraw him
from the Queen's cabal, General Acton and Mr.
Elliot persuaded the King to go with them to Messina,
in order there to discuss with the English generals the
best mode of defence of the island.[1] "The King,"
wrote Mr. Elliot from Messina to his wife on the 5th
April, "was received here to-day by the people with
the greatest enthusiasm, and if one may be allowed to
form any conjecture from the vociferous expressions of
loyalty of the populace, Sicily will make a better stand
against the French than the opposite kingdom did.
The French must sooner or later attempt this narrow
passage, which in some places is certainly not three
miles in breadth. I have passed the whole of this
morning looking through my glass at an attack made
by George Elliot[2] in his frigate upon a French battery
within pistol-shot. As far as I could judge, he silenced
it in about three-quarters of an hour; but as he is

[1] Sir James Craig, a man of first-rate abilities, but of a difficult
temper, was about to resign the command on account of ill-health, to
Sir John Stuart.

[2] Hon. George Elliot, second son of the first Earl of Minto, afterwards Admiral and K.C.B. The notorious Fra Diavolo, escaping from
the French, took refuge about this time on board Captain Elliot's ship,
and was by him carried to a place of safety.

since driven out of the straits by a contrary wind, we have no particulars. Last evening several people were wounded in making a similar attempt with gunboats. So wretched are the arrangements as yet taken here, that although the coast of Calabria does not appear to be twice more distant from Messina than Prince Venti-milia's house is from your Terrace, yet nobody seems to know anything of what is passing on the other side of the water." The letter ends by saying : " I returned from my dinner on board the ' Excellent' at ten o'clock at night. This is already the third time that I have spent four or five hours at a round table, with bottles, glasses, and wine in some cases, dulness in others, and now and then interesting conversation. I cannot but regret so great a loss of precious time at this con-juncture." The king is described as immensely enjoy-ing this episode in his life, giving the parole, " London and St. George," to the British garrison of Messina, pluming himself on his right to be considered as commander-in-chief of the army (7000 British troops), and above all, rejoicing with strange gesticulations and stranger words when from some safe place he watched the artillery practice from the opposite shores ; clapping his hands with glee when a shot struck some miserable vessel hugging the coast, and apparently perfectly un-mindful of the fact that such boats on either side of the strait were manned by his own subjects and countrymen.

We learn from the Queen's letters that she had only been informed of the King's intended departure from Palermo on the day before it took place, and she bitterly reproached Mr. Elliot for having connived at keeping her in the dark. The King had to each party the value of his sign-manual, and no other; though the Queen, to do her justice, had always affected the utmost deference to his will, and in her almost daily letters to Mr. Elliot during the best part of two years, she invariably represented herself as a mere subordinate agent. Mr. Elliot, on the other hand, in the despatches he wrote during the same period, dispensed with any mention whatsoever of His Majesty's name. Times were strangely changed since the previous summer, when the Queen had insisted that General Lacy, in spite of his remonstrances, should open his commission solely to herself, and when Mr. Elliot for the first time incurred her serious dis-- pleasure, by uniting with the Russian general in a representation to the King of the inconvenience arising from the absence of any responsible minister with whom they might confer.[1]

While smarting under the mortification of feeling herself set aside, an event occurred which enabled the Queen to checkmate her adversaries by the preparation of a counter-plot. During the absence of the King, Admiral Sir Sidney Smith arrived in the bay of Palermo with a small squadron, and the Queen at once profited of the occasion to " work on the peculiarities of his disposition," and, according to her own phrase, *de lui monter la tête.* Despising Sicily and impatient to

---

[1] It had been, since General Acton's fall, the practice of the Queen to insist that all important affairs should be treated with herself personally.

regain Naples, she was incapable of calculating coolly
the means in her power for accomplishing so great an
event. "*D'entamer la chose, de faire une explosion
générale,*[1] was what she aimed at, and Providence
seemed to have favoured her designs by the arrival of
Sir Sidney Smith, who was fully as ready to undertake
anything or everything without further consideration as
she could desire."

This officer, who was the *fanfaron* of virtues which
he really possessed—for he was brave, chivalrous, and
enterprising, though under the influence of exorbitant
vanity he enlarged upon his own merits till modest men
felt inclined to doubt them—was now invested by the
Queen's influence with supreme authority over all the
King's forces on land and sea. A proclamation stating
his powers was clandestinely drawn up, without the
slightest communication with Sir J. Stuart, and Sir
Sidney formally accepted the powers conferred, promising the Queen that he would now "dare to do more
than Bonaparte would venture to imagine!"[2]

Five days before this letter was written the battle
of Maida had been fought and won, and in a letter
written a few days later to Mr. Elliot by Sir J. Stuart,
he mentions the fact of his pursuit of the enemy having
been impeded by the action of armed bodies of men
acting under the authority of Sir S. Smith — King
Ferdinand's generalissimo !

[1] Private letter to the Right Hon. C. J. Fox, August 1806.

" "Celui," he says in a letter to the Queen, dated "Pompée, devant
Scilla, 9 Juillet 1806, "Celui qui peut parler en chef suprême peut

That this extraordinary commission given to the
English admiral produced nothing worse than temporary inconvenience, and that a decided rupture between him and the general was avoided, is creditable to
the good sense and good feeling of both parties, and
also to Mr. Elliot, who never ceased his endeavours to
bring about a good understanding between them.

While at Messina Mr. Elliot exchanged some letters
with the Queen. In one of these she informed him of a
report of Bonaparte's death, which had reached her in a
somewhat coarsely-worded note from the Prince of Hesse-
Philipsthal, the brave defender of Gaeta, the only general
in the Neapolitan army worthy of the name, but whose
rough manners had made him disagreeable to the Queen
and her cortége. To Her Majesty's communication Mr.
Elliot replied in the following terms :—

" Je me sens profondément humilié de devoir me
rejouir avec l'Europe entière sur le bruit encore vague de
la mort d'un individu, atroce il est vrai, mais dont les
succès, les craintes qu'il a su inspirer, font l'opprobre du
siècle dans lequel nous avons été condamnés à fléchir
sous les tyrannies d'un aventurier conquérant.

" Je ne blâme point le style du Prince de Hesse.
Partout où je jette les yeux aujourd'hui je ne vois rien
moins noble que la soi-disant noblesse. On ne réussira
plus *que par le peuple;* et au peuple il faut parler son

faire des coups de maitre, et cette unité que Buonaparte conserve dans
ses projets et son action, qui le fait réussir, maintenant je l'ai moi cette
unité de pouvoir, qu'on me la conserve, et j'ose faire plus qu'il n'ose
imaginer."

langage.   On n'est plus général sans être soldat.   Et je
crois que les manières de Suwarrow et du P. de Hesse,
feront fortune auprès du peuple et du soldat là ou l'esprit,
la mesure, et l'addresse qui conviennent au courtisan
viennent échouer complètement."[1]

This letter was probably intended for Count Roger
Damas as much as for the Queen.

Mr. Elliot continued to correspond with the Home
Government throughout the summer, the chief subject
of his despatches being the commission given to Sir
S. Smith, and the invasion of Calabria by Sir J.
Stuart.   He did not the less heartily rejoice over the
victory of Maida, because he had always urged on
the British commanders the futility of all such partial
attempts on the French power in Naples.   Having, as
he said, so lately seen an Anglo-Russian and Neapolitan
army retire from that kingdom before an enemy had
entered it, he refused to believe that a handful of

---

[1] [TRANSLATION.]

" I feel deeply humbled in being forced to unite, with all Europe,
in rejoicing over the still vague report of the death of an individual,
atrocious it is true, but whose success, and the fears he has been able
to inspire, form the disgrace of the age in which we have been condemned
to bow under the tyranny of a conquering adventurer.

" I do not blame the style of the Prince of Hesse.   Wherever I cast
my eyes now, I see nothing less noble than the *soi-disant* nobility.
One will only succeed now by *means of the people ;* and the people must
be addressed in their own language.   One can no longer be a general
without being a soldier.   And I think that the manners of Suwarrow
and of the Prince of Hesse will make their fortune with the people
and with the soldiers, with whom the talent, the suavity, and the tact,
which suit the courtier, completely fail."

British troops would now reconquer it out of the hands
of the French. Sir J. Stuart, writing to him from the
"Camp near Maida," says :—" I did not confide my intentions to you, knowing how strongly you would dis-
approve them," etc.—and Mr. Elliot probably did not
find in the fruitless though brilliant battle of Maida
any reason to change his opinions.

Mr. Elliot was recalled from Sicily in 1806, when
Mr. Fox coming into office appointed his brother, General
Fox, to the command of the forces in Sicily, and to the
post of representative of the Government at the Court
of Palermo—conceiving it for the public interest that
one person should at that critical conjuncture fill both
offices.

When the moment for Mr. Elliot's departure came,
he could not but feel that so strange and full of
anomalies was the condition of things at Palermo, that
he could hardly have remained there with credit or
satisfaction to himself. The King and General Acton
had been quietly laid aside ; the Queen, indefatigable in
weaving nets which held no fish, at one moment egged
on the English commanders to attempt the re-conquest
of Naples ; the next, poured invectives upon them because they resolved to expend all the means at their
command in the defence of Sicily. While the Russian
Government was daily drawing nearer to her great
enemy, she bestowed her fullest confidence on the
Russian minister, whose fatal advice had been the immediate cause of the distress which had overwhelmed her
family. Living in a state of penury, in a *masure*

délabrée, always without complaint, and seemingly
without consciousness of personal discomforts, she, in
the King's name, issued edicts and proclamations to
imaginary forces for impossible exploits; and while prepared for any step which might tend to overthrow the
power of Bonaparte, she was already conceiving the
possibility of opening an amicable arrangement with him
for the barter of Sicily for Naples, and the betrayal of
her English allies.[1]

Mr. Elliot, in writing to his Government, and summing
up the history of his experiences of the Neapolitan Court,
gives it as his distinct opinion that the independence of
the Two Sicilies had fallen not so much before the successful ambition of Bonaparte, as by the intrigues of the
Court; "with an essential part of government in the
hands of a French emigrant, the Neapolitan Court became the centre of the intrigues of a designing set of
persons, who were careless of the interests of Naples,
and inimical to those of Great Britain."

[1] In little more than three years after Mr. Elliot's departure from
Palermo, the Queen of Naples saw, without disapprobation, the marriage of her grand-daughter Maria Louisa to the "Modern Emperor,"
as she frequently called him.

CHAPTER THE FOURTEENTH.

1810 to 1830.

LEEWARD ISLANDS—MADRAS.

ON the termination of his mission to Naples, Mr. Elliot returned to London, and in 1809 he was appointed Governor of the Leeward Islands. The condition of the Continent—from which the success of Bonaparte's armies had all but banished diplomacy—and the risks and expenses consequent on the removal from place to place of a numerous family, decided Mr. Elliot to abandon a diplomatic for a less brilliant, but also a less precarious, career. It was, however, at a great sacrifice of personal happiness that he accepted of a post to which he felt it impossible that his family should accompany him; and the five years that he spent at a distance from them form, perhaps, the most unhappy period of his life.

The numerous letters which he addressed to his wife and elder children from the banishment of Antigua contrast curiously with the family letters written by and to him in his youth. The anxieties which others had felt for him, it was now his turn to experience; and the gay, elastic buoyancy of spirit which had distinguished him in early life, had given way to a sore sense

of the "slings and arrows of outrageous fortune."
Returning to England after years of active and often
of brilliant service to his country, he found that such
service rendered at a distance met with far less acknowledgment than would have been readily bestowed on
political support at home. To save an ally of England
was no doubt good; but to save a vote to Government
was better. Shrewd observer as he was, and versed in
the politics of Europe, Mr. Elliot was struck by the
narrow views and unskilful policy of statesmen whose
mental gaze was contracted to the arena of parliamentary strife; while to their imperfect knowledge of,
and limited interest in, continental politics, he ascribed
the curious selection of their diplomatic agents, and
also some anomalies in the system of procedure towards
them. His general impressions of England are given
in a letter to a friend, written shortly before leaving it
for the Leeward Islands, after a residence of three years
in London.

"The country," he says, "surpasses all my recollections by its beauty, cultivation, and appearance of
prosperity; but my long residence abroad has made me
averse to the general manners of English society, in which
there is less of nature and of good breeding than I have
met with among the same classes of society in any other
country of Europe. The women are sensible, intelligent,
and well-informed; but with the exception of a few
who have had a cosmopolite training, they want the
charm of courteous grace which distinguishes their
semblables in other aristocratic societies. . . . There

is a certain trafficking spirit in English society, and
people seek in it for pleasure less than for advantage;
a prudential consideration for *self* is highly classed
among English virtues, and is conscientiously practised."

Whatever the drawbacks to his enjoyment of English
life, Mr. Elliot's thoughts turned longingly homewards
from the tropical climate and the exceptional condition
of manners and society in which he now found himself.
The cruelties practised upon the slave population revolted
his nature, and in the first year of his government considerable unpopularity was brought upon him by the
publication of some of his despatches to Lord Liverpool,
which treated of the oppressive conduct of the planters,
and the insufficiency of the civil institutions as then
existing to restrain them. Mr. Elliot had been desired
to inquire into certain facts connected with atrocious acts
of cruelty perpetrated by a planter of the name of
Huggins in the island of Nevis—acts committed in the
public market-place, without interference from the
magistracy, and yet so exceptionally ferocious as to have
become the subject of indignant resolutions passed in
the House of Assembly at Nevis—acts for which, when
brought to trial, the perpetrator had been acquitted by
a jury composed of his own friends. In writing to Lord
Liverpool of these horrors, and of the remissness or cul-
pability of those whose duty it was to punish them, Mr.
Elliot gave it as his opinion that the root of the evil lay
much deeper than the conduct of a few individuals.

" It must be accounted for by the defects of a constitution little adapted to the present state of decreased

and decreasing white population of this island, which no longer furnishes a sufficient choice of men fit to fill any public department. The fact is, the governments of the smaller islands were formed in times when many of the proprietors lived upon their estates, and the white population was in some instances, perhaps, ten times as numerous as it now is. Of the few white inhabitants who remain, managers, overseers, self-created lawyers, self-educated physicians, and adventurous merchants, with little real capital or credit, compose the greater part. The acquirements of education among many of this description of persons are very unequal to the task of taking a share in the government. The prevalence of principle, either moral or religious, is also, I fear, not to be calculated from the repetition of the hackneyed expressions of which an ostentatious use is frequently made in addresses, and on all occasions meant to meet the public eye at home.

" To collect from such a state of society men fit to be legislators, judges, or jurymen, is perfectly impracticable. Individual interest, personal influence, animosity of party-feuds, weigh down the scale of justice and direct the course of legislative authority into acts of arbitrary and unjustifiable power, cloaked under the semblance and dignified with the name of constitutional acts. How such defects are to be remedied is a question which requires much minute investigation and serious and dispassionate consideration," etc., etc.[1]

This letter having been read before the House of

[1] November 21, 1810.

Commons, found its way in the newspapers to the West Indies, and a letter from Mr. Elliot's private secretary, Mr. Heydinger, describes the indignation which it had excited :—

" St. Kitt's, September 1811.

" I am told that had the Governor gone to town that evening he would have been pelted.   However that may have been, he went soon after, and goes frequently, without experiencing any difference in his reception.   .   .   . A handbill has been circulated calling on all the managers, lawyers, physicians, and merchants of this island, and of Nevis and Montserrat, to meet and consider the contents of the letter.   .   .   .   The Governor takes no notice of them, and leaves them to talk till they are tired, when he supposes they will give over."

In the following year, 1811, the trial and execution of a planter named Arthur Hodge created a great sensation in the Islands, as, owing to the position and connections of the accused, it was believed that the Governor's veto would intervene to prevent the sentence of execution from being carried out.

Mr. Elliot, writing to his wife, thus describes him :— " A considerable planter in the island of Tortola, named Arthur Hodge, Esquire, a member of Council, and a gentleman well known in England, and connected by marriage with families of distinction there, has been thrown into prison upon the accusation of having *murdered many of his slaves* by severe punishments and various kinds of torture.   His trial is to take place on the 25th, and Mr. Horsford, the Solicitor-General in this

Government, goes with me in the 'Cygnet' as the principal lawyer, to conduct the prosecution. The eyes of all the West Indies are turned towards this cause, and it will create a no less general sensation in Great Britain. My business is to see justice impartially distributed, and that the proceedings shall meet with no interruption on either side. The enormities laid to the charge of this Mr. Hodge are more dreadful than any I ever heard of within the limits of the British Empire. On the other hand, his defendants assert that the accusation is founded in a foul conspiracy to deprive the prisoner of his life and his honour. In the meantime, the state of party at Tortola is said to be violent and inflamed, and the Island is in fact without any regular force whatever, which can act upon an emergency for the support of the civil power or of tranquillity. The law must take its course in this disagreeable business, and God grant that it may be directed to its proper object, that the guilty may suffer and the innocent escape."

His next letter to his wife tells her the result of the trial.

"*Tortola, May* 9, 1811.

"My dearest Margaret — In my letter from St. Christopher, by the 'Duke of Kent' packet, I told you I was to proceed to Tortola upon a business of the most disagreeable nature. I accordingly arrived here upon the morning of the 26th April, and am lodged in a tolerable house situated on an eminence about a mile and a half from the town. The trial of Arthur Hodge, Esq., one of the members of the Council of

Tortola, for the murder of several of his slaves, was put off till the 29th ult. He was indicted in the first instance for the murder, by severe treatment, flogging, etc., of only one slave named Prosper. After a trial which lasted from ten o'clock of the forenoon of the 29th April till five o'clock in the morning of the 30th, Arthur Hodge was found guilty, and was condemned to be hanged on the 8th of May. By a majority of the jury he was recommended to mercy, and that mercy it was in my power to have granted by suspending the execution of his sentence till the King's pleasure should be known. But alas! there were no grounds which could justify me in acceding to the strange recommendation of the majority of the jury. Neither could any of the judges second it. The unfortunate man would have been tried upon five other indictments, some of them still more atrocious than the one upon which he was found guilty, and his general character for barbarity was so notorious that no room was left for me even to deliberate. His victims have been numerous; some of them were even buried in their chains, and there have been found upon the bones taken from the grave chains and iron rings of near forty pounds weight. Judge of the distress I have been exposed to the whole of this last week by the petitions of the prisoner and the personal applications of his relatives. Yesterday the fatal sentence of the law was carried into effect, and thus perished a man born to affluence, connected with families of distinction in England. He had been three times married, has left several children; he had been in the army, had a

liberal education, and lived in what is called the great
World. His manners and address were those of a gentleman. Cruelty appears in him to have been the effect
of violence of temper, and habit had made him regard-
less of the death and suffering of a *slave*. God grant
that this severe example may teach others in the West
Indies to dread a similar fate, should they forget that
slaves are their *fellow-creatures*, and that their lives are
protected by the laws both of England and the colonies.
The state of confusion in which I found this part of the
government has made it necessary for me to take several
strong measures to maintain public tranquillity, and to
prevent any interruption being given to the course of
justice. Thank God, I consider everything now as
finished, and have the satisfaction to say without the
appearance of tumult or disorder. The militia are dis-
charged from duty, and the country is in its ordinary
state, so that I hope the rest of the time I have to remain here will be quietly passed. Never were my
feelings more harassed than during these last eight days,
not even, I may say, when I lost sight of you and my
children. Think of a young family deprived in one fatal
moment of their only surviving parent, and think of the
struggle it must have cost me to do my duty upon so
trying an occasion. O my dear Margaret, shall I ever
again forget among you all the pangs I have endured for
all your sakes in the West Indies? whose climate,
manners, and principles, war with my body and mind.
May God's goodness one day reward me and mine for a
period of much uncomfort to myself!"

In a despatch to Lord Liverpool describing these events, he mentions that the majority who recommended Hodge to mercy were seven in number. After strongly recommending the vigorous conduct and noble eloquence of Mr. Horsford to the attention of Government, he goes on to say that " until a British legislature shall think it expedient to define with precision and benevolence the extent of the rights which one individual can exercise over another, the condign punishment of Arthur Hodge will serve to warn many that death ensuing to a slave from severity of punishment will be considered in the eye of the law as heinous and atrocious murder."

The sufferings of the slave population by no means absorbed the whole of his attention, as is proved by the energy with which he urged the claims of the free coloured people of Antigua to more liberal treatment than they received under the existing system of colonial law and usage ; pointing out the mischiefs of granting civil rights with one hand, and of neutralising them with the other (for example, though enrolled in the militia, they could never be promoted); and showing himself, in every word he wrote, just and humane in his feeling towards the people of colour, and profoundly conscious of the truth, that to concede popular rights and despise popular affections is a ruinous policy for those who govern.

His conduct on many occasions was warmly approved at home, and in 1814 he was recalled from the Leeward Islands to receive the appointment of Governor of Madras.

After a stay of barely four months' duration in

London, he left it again at a moment of almost unexampled interest in the annals of his country. England
was about to receive the sovereigns and warriors who
had at last won the cause which she alone had never
deserted; and it is not to be wondered at that the
younger members of the family shrank with dismay
from the dire necessity of departure. Their father,
however, had learned, in the solitude of his West Indian
life, to regret nothing while left in the enjoyment of his
family circle. To use his own expression:—" At his
age his heart required rest, which was alone to be had
in the society of those his eyes doated upon — his
children and their mother."

On the 14th of May 1814, he, having first been
sworn a member of His Majesty's Privy Council, sailed
for India, accompanied by all his family, with the exception of two boys left at school. His departure from
Plymouth had been delayed from day to day, in the
hope that the ship bringing home his brother, Lord
Minto, late governor-general of India, would arrive at
that port, where she was already due, before he should
have left it. In this expectation he was unfortunately
disappointed, and the brothers, who had not seen each
other for years, never met again. Lord Minto died a
few weeks after his arrival in England from the consequences of a chill caught at the funeral of Lord Auckland. Lady Auckland also died during her brother's
absence in India, and these repeated losses in his family
account for the meagreness of his private correspondence during his Indian career.

His government at Madras was unmarked by any events of conspicuous interest, or at least by any in which he individually bore a part; for the period of his government was that of the close of the Mahratta war.[1] His private life was, however, brightened by the acquisition of many valued friends, some of whom bore names which, as those of Munro and Malcolm, will live in the history of India.

The last year of his residence at Madras was rendered one of gloom by the death of his wife. " No words can describe," wrote one of his family, " the loss of her who was the centre of all our affections and of all our pleasures."

Mr. Elliot returned to England in 1820, with his family. On their way home they were detained for some time by stress of weather at St. Helena, where, He who had " dropt from the zenith like a falling star," was wearing out the term of his existence. Living at the Governor's house, they had daily opportunities of witnessing the agitated existence of Sir Hudson Lowe, constantly haunted as he was by fear of his illustrious captive's escape; while the satisfaction with which these alarms were viewed, and the skill with which they were heightened by the French society at Longwood, were no secret to Sir Hudson's visitors :—

---

[1] The Mahratta war was finally terminated at the battle of Mahidpore, 21st December 1817, when the army of Holkar was routed by the army of the Deccan, under the personal command of my father, General Sir Thomas Hislop, for which victory he received the thanks of both Houses of Parliament.

" Hardly ever did we get through dinner without his starting up to inquire if all was safe." The agreeable qualities of the guests were by no means unappreciated by the French residents in attendance on Napoleon, and many efforts were made to induce Mr. Elliot to ask for an interview with him; but this he persistently refused, saying that he considered Bonaparte to have been the greatest enemy his country had ever had, and a curse to Europe; and for his own part he had no desire to see him.

The spectacle of fallen greatness affected him less than the contemplation of the Nemesis which had worked the fall—bringing to a far Atlantic Isle the man whose unrivalled career the united nations of Europe had barely sufficed to check, the noise of whose armies had banished peace from the quiet gardens of Dresden, and thoughts of peace from the lovely terrace of Palermo.

For the remainder of his life Mr. Elliot resided chiefly in London, where some still survive who remember the charm of his society. One who knew him well described his conversation as " a shower of pearls and diamonds," so sparkling and so spontaneous; but whatever the felicity of his talk, or the grace of his manner, by his descendants he is best remembered for the gifts of heart and mind which made him beloved by a large and devoted family.

He died on the 2d of December 1830, and was buried by the side of his brother in Westminster Abbey. A few weeks before his death he visited my mother at

Boulogne, where he, who had seen the Revolution of
'89, had an opportunity of witnessing a review of the
National Guard of 1830. The earliest public event he
is said to have remembered was the funeral of George II.
He lived to see the accession of William IV.

His surviving children at the time of his death were five sons and
three daughters. Henry, Lieutenant-Colonel in the Army, died 1842.
Edward, for many years Police Magistrate at Madras, died 1866. Gilbert, Dean of Bristol. Charles, Admiral and K.C.B., Governor of St.
Helena. Frederick, Assistant Under-Secretary of State for the Colonial
Department. Emma, died 1866. Harriet Agnes, died 1845. Caroline,
god-daughter of the Queen of Naples.

Mr. Elliot's daughter by his first marriage, Isabella, married at
Dresden, in 1801, to George Payne, Esq., died in 1826. And a son
by his second marriage, Maximilian, died in India in the same
year.

APPENDIX.

—◆—

I.

"*Camp at Boston, Aug. 7, 1775.*

" My dear Friend—I know it will give you pleasure to hear that I arrived safe here in good health last Sunday, after a very tedious passage of near eight weeks ; in short, we had not four-and-twenty hours of fair wind from the time we left England till we got here.

" I shall now attempt to give you some little description of our present situation ; I can't say that our affairs wear the best face possible, but there is an old saying, that when things are as bad as they can be they must mend. We are in a town almost deserted by its inhabitants, situated upon a peninsula with a very narrow neck of land that runs into the country ; this neck we have very strongly fortified ; on all other sides of us are small arms of the sea, where our men-of-war and transports, for they are all armed, lie at anchor. Opposite our lines, upon the heights, and indeed all round us, the Americans are

2 F

encamped to about the number of 30,000, and have flung up some of the strongest works I suppose ever seen, so that we are totally blockaded by these rebellious scoundrels. We every now and then make little excursions and attack them, and burn a few of their houses, but not having sufficient force, never venture out into the country. There was a very serious affair happened the 17th of June, which I suppose you have heard of; but in case you should not, here it is. Opposite this town, on the other side the smallest arm of the sea, lay Charlestown, a very pretty well-built town. One morning early the 'Lively' frigate, which is stationed there, discovered a work that the rebels were working very hard at, and had nearly finished, upon the heights of Charlestown. They had then mounted four pieces of cannon, and meant the next day to have battered, Boston about our ears. The vessel gave the alarm, and the troops were ordered to land and attack them. The ships covered our landing, and by all accounts there never was so severe a fire kept up for about an hour and a half as that day. We had a very high hill to march up, upon the top of which was this strong redoubt, where the enemy were covered up to the chin. All the way as the troops came up the hill were large rails, so that the men were obliged to ground their arms to get over them, and exposed all this while to the enemy's fire, and to the fire from Charlestown, which was lined by them, and which lay upon our left flank. Our men behaved remarkably well, and everyone says there never was a more glorious day for the officers known.

After three hours our troops made themselves masters of the redoubt and cannon, and General Howe, who commanded, now remains master of the ground, where he is encamped, and has fortified himself very strongly. We had about 1100 killed and wounded, of which number 93 were officers. The rebels lost an amazing number. They talk of attacking us every day, but I don't think they dare. I wish they may, for we are well prepared. I forgot to say that we burned the town of Charlestown to the ground. Our wounded men recover very slowly, as we have nothing to eat but salt pork and peas, and now and then fish. I have tasted fresh meat twice since I came here. Adieu. Write to me soon, etc. etc.—Ever yours, Thos. Stanley."

II.

LETTER FROM MIRABEAU.—P. 286.

"*Par Aix en Provence,* 14 *août* 1783.

"Mon âme a dès longtemps deviné la votre, mon cher Elliot, et je ne sais quel instinct me présageoit vos vertus avant que l'âge les eut développées et m'eut mis à même de les apprécier. Mais lorsque vous m'inspiriez les premiers sentimens vifs et profonds que j'aye connus, lorsqu'au printemps de notre jeunesse je vous chérissois d'une amitié si tendre, qui m'eut dit que je vous devrois un jour toute ma reconnoissance, tout mon dévouement pour les vœux et les efforts que d'un bout de l'Europe à l'autre, après tant d'années de silence et d'absence, vous feriez pour mon salut et mon bonheur?

"Je reçois une lettre de Londres; celui qui me l'écrit est un françois estimable, ami du chef des représentans genevois (Clavière), mon intime ami, qui est venu recueillir en Irlande les fruits de la générosité de votre nation. Voici les propres mots du françois dont je vous parle :—

"'Un de mes amis qui voyage par toute l'Europe (M. Brac), ami de la vérité, admirateur de vos ouvrages, a vu en passant à Copenhague M. Elliot, ministre plénipotentiaire du Roi d'Angleterre; je copie ce qu'il me marque pour vous. *Je suis chargé par M. Elliot de savoir ce qu'est devenu M. de Mirabeau le fils, auteur des lettres de cachet. Virchaux m'a assuré qu'il étoit votre connoissance, votre ami*—(j'espère l'être un jour quand les circonstances nous auront rapprochés)—*il l'a été jadis de toute la famille de cet honnête Anglois dont je vous parle qui voudroit le fixer en Angleterre pour le soustraire aux horreurs qu'il a subies depuis. J'avois avec moi son ouvrage ; il vouloit le lire ; il y reconnut la chaleur et le stile de son ami, il m'a prié de lui offrir, au cas qu'il fût libre, un asile en Angleterre, et des moyens de courir avec lui la carrière de l'Ambassade si ce métier lui plait. Écrivez lui son adresse, et des détails sur son existence. En consequence j'ai écrit à M. Elliot,'* etc.

" Le françois qui m'écrit ainsi s'appelle Brissot de Warville. Il vous sera fort aisé de croire, mon cher ami, que cette lettre m'a touché jusqu'aux larmes. Je n'aurois pas été si malheureux si je n'étois pas né très sensible ; voilà ce que prouve ma vie entière, et jusqu'à mes fautes. Je vous ai reconnu ; et je me suis dit à moi même qu'il est doux de chérir un ami dans un bienfaiteur ; il n'est, comme je le mande au françois à qui je dois cette précieuse nouvelle, que votre nation qui offre de tels traits d'amitié et de générosité ; mais, dans cette nation même, il doit être très rare qu'un jeune homme, jetté dans la carrière de l'ambition, s'attendrisse à l'idée des maux qu'a souffert un ami de Collége qu'il n'a point revu et qui ne lui a point écrit depuis 17 ou 18 ans ; et veuille arracher au despotisme une victime étrangère à sa patrie ;

je ne serois pas l'objet d'un sentiment si noble, d'une pensée si haute que je serois enthousiaste de l'homme qui l'a conçu ; jugez ce que vous m'êtes, mon cher et digne ami ; jugez si je me sens pressé du désir de vous serrer dans mes bras. Mais mon ami, voici ma position, jugez la, et conseillez moi.

"Je ne vous ferai pas mon histoire. Le détail en scroit immense ; et les détails constituent seuls la vérité des faits. Qu'il vous suffise de savoir aujourd'hui que ma destinée a été un orage continuel, et ma vie un roman ; qu'asservi sous le double despotisme de mon père et du gouvernement provoqué par lui, j'ai fait de graudes fautes et éprouvé de grands maux ; que ces fautes ont tous laissé mon honneur intact, et que quelques unes même ont beaucoup relevé mon caractère moral ; que ces malheurs ont abrégé mes forces et ma vie, mais n'ont flétri ni mon ame ni mon énergie naturelle. Croyez enfin, homme noble et généreux, que je ne prendrois pas encore le nom sacré de votre ami, si j'en étois indigne.

"A l'âge de 22 ans je fis un très grand mariage en perspective, nul au moment pour les ressources pécuniaires. Mon père, armé de sa dureté ordinaire, n'y suppléa pas. J'eus la folie de me déranger considérablement, et de resserrer ainsi ma dépendance que j'avois déjà très aggravée par mon mariage. Une aventure honorable et d'éclat, mais qui heurtoit le gouvernement dans son opération favorite, la révolution parlementaire, me fit tomber sous le glaive le plus terrible de notre gouvernement. Une lettre de cachet me frappa. Elle servoit trop bien mon père qui toujours m'a voulu perdre. On diroit en vain que la nature n'est point ainsi faite— mon histoire a trop prouvé qu'un père envieux, et une courtisane adroite échappent à toutes les combinaisons dans la marche de leurs haines et de leurs complots. Sept années entières m'ont vu baloté d'ordres arbitraires en ordres arbitraires ; de châteaux en châteaux. Un tel régime n'était pas fait pour assouplir mon ame indépend- ante et fière. Elle s'est aigrie ; deux fois j'ai brisé mes chaînes et aggravé mon crime *d'esclave révolté.* Deux fois j'ai été repris en pays étranger. La Hollande a eu la lâcheté de me rendre au moment de la guerre ; j'avois été par mille obstacles arrêté dans le projet de passer en Angleterre ; j'ai cruellement expié la faute d'avoir mé- connu le seul asile de la liberté ; le Donjon de Vincennes tel que je l'ai peint m'a servi de tombeau pendant 3 ans $\frac{1}{2}$ et 10 jours. Mais là même j'ai prouvé que les esclaves volontaires font plus de tyrans que les tyrans ne font d'esclaves forcés. Le gouvernement a fini par forcer mon père à briser mes chaînes. Il est vrai qu'alors je n'avois point écrit contre *les lettres de cachet et les prisons d'état.*

" Vous vous demandez sans doute ce que faisoit Ma- dame de Mirabeau pendant ce temps là. Elle jouoit la comédie, elle donnoit des fêtes ; elle faisoit le métier d'his- trione sur la cendre de mon fils. J'ai tout dissimulé, et suis revenu en Provence redemander ma femme, bien moins pour la ravoir, que pour faire tomber par son acqui- escement, ou par une discussion judiciaire, les horribles calomnies que les collateraux de ma femme, intéressés à ce que nous n'ayions point d'enfans, n'avoient cessé de vomir contre moi, pour mieux consolider ma perte, et m'empêcher toute réunion.

"J'ai demandé Madame de Mirabeau. Elle a plaidé en séparation, elle a plaidé avec atrocité; j'ai plaidé avec noblesse. Trois de vos compatriotes, tous trois mes amis, Lord Peterborough, Sir Bisset, et le Major Baggs, ont été témoins de cet odieux procès, et peuvent rendre témoinage à la vérité; non que leur déposition comme celle de mes amis ne soit suspecte; mais ils peuvent dire s'il y a deux opinions dans le public sur ce procès.

" Certainement s'il eût été en mon pouvoir de réaliser la plus petite partie de la fortune que je dois avoir un jour, je n'aurois pas soutenu ce procès; et la vue et le contact d'une terre esclave ne m'auroit pas souillé plus longtemps; mais lié par la double tyrannie du plus étrange de tous les pères et de la plus impérieuse des nécessités; entravé par le dérangement de ma première jeunesse, il m'a fallu viser à l'indépendance par la seule route qui put m'y conduire; et dont les bourbiers infects qui la parsemoient m'auroient cependant écarté sur le champ, si mes adversaires n'avoient pas eu l'insigne maladresse de compromettre à chaque pas mon honneur dans la discussion de ce procès.

"Je l'ai perdu; mais je l'ai perdu comme on n'en perd point en France. Surchargé de chaînes de toute espèce; écrasé de dettes qu'on auroit pu arranger par le seul emploi de mes revenus, ce dont on s'est bien gardé, tout en ôtant le pouvoir de le faire moi même; investi des préventions qui dans le pays le plus méchant de la terre ont résulté du manège et des relations officieuses des intéressés à ma perte ; entouré d'ennemis, mal servi par mon père, désagréable au gouvernement, je suis arrivé dans une province où il me restoit peu de parens, peu d'amis secrets, et presque pas un avoué, pour lutter contre la famille la plus étendue, la plus accréditée ; contre le particulier de la ville d'Aix, qui en fait les honneurs, et qui passe pour avoir la société la plus aimable, les plus puissans amis, le meilleur cuisinier. Quand je suis arrivé tout le monde me fuyoit ; j'étois l'antechrist. Je me suis conduit irreprochablement et j'ai été assez heureux pour concilier beaucoup de fermeté et de sagesse. J'ai parlé en public quatre fois ; mon ame a élevé mon génie, et j'ai eu le plus grand succès. C'est avec raison que les anciens du talent de la parole avoient fait un dieu. Le public toujours extrême s'est rangé de mon côté jusqu'à l'idolatrie. Les battemens de main m'ont poursuivi au palais, aux promenades, au spectacle. Un arrêt m'a condamné par un complot abominable. L'arrêt a été hué. Le parlement même s'élève contre les cinq juges qui l'ont déshonoré, dit-il, car sur neuf j'en avois quatre pour moi, et les seuls d'entre ces neuf qui soient estimés. La faveur du public a augmenté. La scène s'est ensanglantée. J'ai été obligé de régenter un insolent colonel. Le peuple a été prêt à le lapider ; enfin, je suis devenu comme le démagogue de la Provence, et le vainqueur du procès est en fuite, tandis que le vaincu est hautement proclamé, *l'illustre infortuné.*

" Je n'avois assurément mérité ni tant de sévérité,

ni tant d'indulgence ; et vous croyez bien que ces tristes
succès ne me tournent pas la tête, d'autant qu'une insur-
rection n'est jamais rien en France, et que je n'en serai
qu'un peu plus odieux à toutes les autorités. Mais ils
m'imposent une sorte d'obligation de faire casser l'arrêt
qui est un véritable attentat aux mœurs et à l'ordre
public, et qui d'ailleurs, selon notre mode françoise,
n'étant point motivé, peut laisser croire au loin qu'aulieu
d'être fondé sur un ridicule ergotage de palais, il l'est
sur les imputations atroces dont on avoit voulu m'écraser.
Mon honneur est donc intéressé à la radiation de cet
arrêt après laquelle je suis bien éloigné du désir de
raviser le procès comme je le pourrois—première entrave
qui s'oppose à ce moment à mon expatriation ! Et c'est
en vérité la moindre ; car que me sont tous ces motifs
secondaires pourvu que je sois bien avec ma conscience,
et que je puisse vivre avec des hommes courageux et
libres ? Ces motifs d'ailleurs ne sont point sans objections, car mon séjour à Paris est loin d'être sans dangers
extérieurs et sans inconvéniens domestiques ; on me
menace que le ministre s'opposera à mon voyage dans la
capitale—ce me scroit assurément une raison de plus d'y
aller, si j'avois d'après cela le moindre espoir de succès
dans la révision de l'arrêt ; attendu que j'en regarde la
poursuite comme une espèce de devoir de citoyen. Mais
en est-il de ces devoirs où il n'y a point de patrie ? et ne
rendrai-je un plus mauvais service à la vérité et à la
justice en la faisant échouer une seconde fois, qu'en lui
laissant purement et simplement la vengeance de l'opinion
publique ?

" Mais, mon cher Elliot, voici des considérations
d'une toute autre nature ; je vous l'ai dit, bien loin
d'arranger mes affaires, mon père a eu l'odieux machia-
vélisme de les laisser dans un très grand désordre. Son
compte de tutelle bien appuré, il se trouve me devoir
40,000$^{liv.}$; 70,000 ou 80,000 au plus payeroient toutes
mes dettes. Il m'avoit donné par contrat de mariage
8500$^{liv.}$ de pension annuelle. Il les touche maintenant,
sous prétexte de payer mes dettes ; n'en paye aucun
créancier, et prélève seulement une pension alimentaire
de 2400$^{liv.}$ qu'il m'abandonne très en rechignant. Je n'ai
pas pu parvenir encore à changer cet état de choses. Je
n'ai pas pu obtenir qu'il me permit d'emprunter pour
éteindre en bloc toutes mes dettes, et m'assurer ainsi un
revenu indépendant. Mon oncle, qui lui prodigue son
bien et ses épargnes, n'a pas eu plus de crédit que moi
même à cet égard. Il a subvenu à tous les frais de
l'affaire actuelle ; mais grandbailli de Malthe, riche
seulement en viager, épuisé par son frère, lié par des
devoirs de reconnoissance envers des entours auxquels
il ne peut laisser que de l'argent—cet honnête homme
qui n'a de défaut que son invincible foiblesse pour son
frère, ne peut pas beaucoup, et sa volonté est découragée
par l'inutilité de ses efforts.

" Vous sentez, mon cher ami, qu'il ne me convient pas
d'être à charge à personne. Il me paroit impossible que
j'obtienne aucun emploi dans un pays aussi étranger que
le votre à tout françois. Rappellez vous que dès l'âge
de 16 ans je voulois n'avoir d'autre patrie que ce noble
pays de la liberté, et que votre honnête Liston m'en

détourna par ce motif. D'ailleurs je ne prendrois certainement pas de place indigne de moi, ni d'une certaine subalternéité. Je suis capable (et j'ai été mis à cette épreuve) du courage necessaire pour gagner ma vie, mais je n'aurois pas celui d'être le stipendié d'un grand seigneur quelconque. Ajoutez que je ne laisse pas que d'être connu en Angleterre (le nom de mon père y a de la célébrité) que je le serois bientôt davantage par la nature des amis de votre nation que je me suis faits en France, et que j'y serai nécessairement un homme de convention ; il ne me sera point permis d'y être l'homme de la nature, et c'est un grand malheur pour quiconque se sent un peu audessus des rêves de la vanité humaine.

"Voilà bien des inconvéniens, mon cher Elliot. Il y en auroit beaucoup de sauvés, je l'avoue, si vous aviez assez de crédit à la cour de Copenhague, ou chez tel autre prince du nord que ce puisse être pour me faire obtenir quelque emploi. La carrière est moins brillante qu'en Angleterre sans doute ; mais elle est moins exclusive. En Angleterre il faut être Anglois ; dans le Nord il ne faut souvent qu'être françois.

"Au reste, je conviendrai naïvement avec vous, mon cher ami, que toutes ces objections me pèsent peu en comparaison de la liberté garantie, et de la possibilité de me livrer à mon énergie naturelle ; deux avantages que je ne puis guère trouver que loin de mon déplorable pays. Mais la nécessité ! la nécessité ! qui sait vaincre cet ennemi ? peu d'hommes en ont le courage, et il ne me manque pas. Mais la possibilité ? je ne la vois pas. Le bonheur ? je suis payé pour ne pas compter sur le mien.

" Parlez moi donc desormais, mon cher Elliot, en conseil et en guide, après m'avoir appellé en ami et en bienfaiteur. Que me conseillez-vous ? quelles avances me seroient nécessaires ? quelle marche dois-je tenir ? je puis espérer de mon oncle une somme d'argent qui m'aideroit à une expatriation ; quelle doit-elle être ? Mais je ne crois pas pouvoir raisonnablement compter sur une amélioration de fortune du vivant de mon père. Il est si dur et si dérangé, que ce seroit présumer que de s'en flatter. Il aime beaucoup mieux garder les 6100$^{liv.}$ qu'il retient sur mon revenu que de me payer les 40,000$^{liv.}$ qu'il me doit, et au moyen des quels n'ayant plus que 2000$^{liv.}$ d'intérêts à supporter sur mon revenu pour me mettre en regle vis à vis de mes créanciers, j'aurois 6500$^{liv.}$ annuelles, et avec cela l'on vit dans tous les pays du monde, surtout quand on a plus de 60,000$^{liv.}$ de rente substituées sur sa tête. Comment remédier à cela ? En plaidant contre mon père ? c'est une extrémité bien déplorable, et très loin d'être sans danger. Il faut donc se résigner, et combien cette résignation me seroit payée si j'achetois la liberté à ce prix !

" Ecrivez moi surtout ceci, mon cher ami, et pardonnez de bien longs et fastidieux détails et un fatigant griffonage. Vous n'auriez pas pu me conseiller si vous n'eussiez pas exactement connu mon état de situation ; et sur cette ébauche rapide, à peine, et bien à peine, pourrez vous en juger. Parlez moi nettement, et dites moi quelles ressources vous prévoyez pouvoir me ménager dans le pays quelconque où vous m'appellerez. Si vous me conseillez de partir, je partirai ; ce sera ma manière de vous remercier, et c'est la plus éloquente du moins pour mon coeur. Le votre est dès longtemps à l'unison, et vous n'aurez pas de peine à croire que celui, qui vous a tant aimé quand il n'étoit que votre polisson de camarade, sent doubler son dévouement pour vous, quand vous enchaînez toute son estime et toute sa reconnaissance. Vale et me ama.

" MIRABEAU fils.

" Donnez moi des nouvelles de votre respectable père, de votre aimable frère, et du bon Liston; si il vit, il ne vous est sûrement pas étranger. Prenez la voie la plus courte pour me répondre, et adressez moi par duplicata, 1ère enveloppe à M. Boyer, receveur des droits du greffe à Aix en Provence, et dessous, pour le Comte de Mirabeau ; et au Duc de Mansfield, votre ambassadeur à Paris, avec prière de m'adresser le paquet à Aix en Provence, si je ne suis point à Paris, rue de Seine à l'hotel de Mirabeau. Donnez moi votre adresse direct.

" Si vous me faites partir, prescrivez moi ma route, et dites moi quelle sorte de lettres de recommandation il me faut pour Copenhague, ou pour Londres."

In the commencement of the foregoing letter the circumstances are related which caused it to be written. Mr. Elliot, however, appears to have understood from its contents that the writer had believed himself to be addressing Sir Gilbert, for in his reply, dated Copenhagen, 1st October 1783, he says :—

" J'ai reçu, mon cher Mirabeau, votre lettre en date du 14 Aout.

J'y réponds avec la franchise de notre première

jeunesse. Vous avez cru écrire à mon frère, à l'ainé des deux qui étaient vos camarades à la Barrière St. Dominique. Vous l'aimiez mieux que moi, et vous aviez raison. Il était dans ce temps là le meilleur des enfants, il est aujourd'hui le plus estimable des hommes," etc. Mr. Elliot then goes on to explain to his friend how infinitely more limited were his own powers of helping another man to a political career than Mirabeau had been led to suppose them; that the nature of the English constitution did not admit of the bestowal of political appointments on foreigners; and that he had simply proposed to offer his friend a refuge under an English roof, though in a distant corner of Europe, from the persecutions to which he had been so long a victim.

The first result of M. Brac's visit to Copenhagen, and subsequent communications with Brissot de Warville, himself destined to become a conspicuous figure in the revolutionary drama, was a letter from Brissot to Mr. Elliot. In this letter, dated No. 1 Brompton Row, 17th July 1783, he says—

"Je ne puis vous dire rien de positif sur le sort de ce jeune homme plus connu par ses longs malheurs que par ses écrits. * * * Je désirerois bien qu'il acceptât l'asile en Angleterre; c'est la seule contrée où il puisse donner l'essor à son âme. M'y fixant moi même j'aurais l'agrément d'y jouir de sa conversation," etc.

III.

EXTRACT FROM A LETTER OF THE KING OF SWEDEN
TO MR. ELLIOT, PARTLY GIVEN AT P. 308.

" J'AI envoyé des ordres si sévères au Gouverneur de
Gothenbourg qu'il n'osera pas se rendre; après demain
le régiment des Gardes arrivera et le 8ième de Jeutland.
La garnison sera alors de trois milles hommes. Je pars
pour m'y rendre, et pour animer par ma présence la
Bourgeoisie. Je n'y resterai qu'un jour, et j'irois m'éta-
blir à Skara où à Alingsas où je vais faire assembler les
troupes que j'ai. Je crois avoir dans trois ou quatre
jours deux mille hommes de cavalerie," etc.

The King must have drawn a somewhat flattered
picture of his military resources in this letter to the
English minister, for on the same day, the 2d of October,
he wrote to Baron d'Armfelt, that " in *about a week*
from that time he hoped to collect a garrison of 3000
men in Gothenbourg. On the 4th he wrote to the same
correspondent from Gothenbourg that the Guards and
other troops expected were still to come. On the 6th
he described himself as having *no* troops at all, but
added, that in eight or ten days he hoped to assemble

some 2000 men. Mr. Elliot, however, joined the King on that same day at Gothenburg, and the letter of the Princes, consenting to treat, is dated the 7th.

Baron d'Armfelt caused the original letters of the King to be copied by his daughter, Marie Auguste Armfelt, and sent them in 1798 to Mr. Elliot, accompanying them with a letter, in which he says that these were all he had been able to find (they are eight in number) among the mass of papers which formed the only relics left him of his "lost friend and master." He adds, that he believes there were two or three others, in which mention was made of Mr. Elliot, "the man who had saved both King and country."

IV.

RUSSIA AT NAPLES.—P. 380.

THE Queen's policy in endeavouring to foment jealousies between England and Russia is incomprehensible, as the existence of her throne appeared to depend on their mutual good understanding. In July 1803 she informed Mr. Elliot that Count Woronzow, the Russian minister in London, had desired Count Rosomowsky (Russian minister at Naples) to put the Queen and Court on their guard against Mr. Elliot, as being a *très mauvaise tête*, very dangerous, and likely to bring them into some serious scrape if he were listened to. The same language, Mr. Elliot was told, was held to General Acton, accompanied with warnings against the ambitious views of England with respect to Sicily.

That headlong impulse as often as state-craft governed Her Majesty's conduct is curiously shown in some transactions which occurred in the month of May 1805. By her orders, a Russian traveller, Prince Scherbatow, was suddenly arrested in his bedroom at night, and conveyed under an escort across the frontier. No notification of so extraordinary a circumstance was made to the Russian Chargé d'Affaires for twenty-four hours after the arrest had taken place, when the head

of the police waited upon him with the information that
Prince Scherbatow having formerly killed, in a duel on
the frontiers of Bohemia, the Chevalier de Saxe, a relative of the King, it was thought expedient to expel
him from the kingdom. The King and the Minister for
Foreign Affairs were subsequently proved to have known
nothing of the event until some time after it had taken
place.

The Russians in Naples were naturally extremely
indignant at the unceremonious treatment their country-
man had received; and before the unfavourable impression produced by this incident had passed off, another,
stranger still, occurred. The English man-of-war, the
'Excellent,' which was stationed at Naples, having sailed
from that bay to the Bay of Baja for the purpose of
exercising the crew, the Queen became suddenly possessed by the preposterous notion that the departure of
the British ship had been contrived to give the Russian
ship of the line at anchor off Naples an opportunity of
seizing the Neapolitan frigate, the 'Archimedes,' as an act
of retaliation for the insult to Prince Scherbatow. She
sent orders to all the Neapolitan frigates in the road,
or within the mole, to be upon their guard, and the
'Archimedes' was actually prepared for action, the men
kept through the night at their quarters, and another
frigate was ordered into the road for the purpose of supporting the 'Archimedes.' Fortunately, Mr. Elliot, on
hearing of these extraordinary proceedings, was able at
once to see the Queen, and he easily succeeded in unde-
ceiving her, but not till much ill-feeling had been pro-

duced. In the despatch which relates this strange story, Mr. Elliot says—" Your Lordship will be able to judge from this statement of the great inconveniences which daily occur from the Queen's unhappy susceptibility, and from the mischievous suggestions made to her by designing persons." [1] The despatch closes by the information that Her Majesty had suddenly been laid up with a violent attack of fever; and Mr. Elliot was persuaded, from the events of the last fortnight, that the Queen had been in a state of unnatural excitement and agitation.

[1] May 21, 1805.

FINIS.

Printed by R. CLARK, *Edinburgh*

ERRATA.

Page 29, 8th line from top.—*For* "rentrez," *read* "entrez."

Page 40, 3d line from foot, and afterwards where the name occurs.— *For* "Lord Lindsay," *read* "Lord Lindsey."

Page 49, 11th line from top.—*For* "Ou," *read* "On."

Page 64, 11th line from top.—*For* "Guards," *read* "Army."

Page 107, 2d line, page 109, 13th line, and page 213, 18th line from top.—*For* "Wrech," *read* "Wreich."

Page 201, Note 2, last line.—"D'Argenson" should be preceded by "Voyer." The Marquis Voyer d'Argenson is the person intended.

Page 217, 1st line.—M. Clément was not minister of Saxony ; he was sent to Vienna by the Elector of Saxony on a secret mission, and had no diplomatic rank.

Page 263, last line.—*For* "serais," *read* "serai."

Page 267, 3d line, 2d paragraph.—*For* "writing," *read* "waiting."

Pages 284 and 285.—Date at top *should be* "1784," *not* "1783."

Page 291, 4th and 10th lines from foot, and page 292, 11th line from foot.—*For* "Schach-Rathlow," *read* "Schack-Rathlow."

Page 301, 6th line from top.—*For* "possessing," *read* "professing."

Page 308.—For remainder of King of Sweden's letter, *see* Appendix III., page 432.

Page 309, 9th line, and page 312, 10th line from top.—*For* "d'Arnfeldt, *read* "d'Armfelt."

Page 324, 3d line from top.—*For* "Gborg.," *read* "Gothenbourg."

Page 335, 6th line from top.—*For* "illusion," *read* "allusion."

Page 346, 16th line from top.—*For* "convaincu," *read* "convaincue."

Do., 12th line from foot.—*For* "la," *read* "ma."

Page 362, 15th line from top.—*For* "mandieroient," *read* "mendieroient."